KT-514-809

Whatever You Love

LOUISE DOUGHTY

ff

FABER & FABER

First published in 2010
by Faber and Faber Ltd
Bloomsbury House
74–77 Great Russell Street
London WC1B 3DA

This paperback edition first published in 2014

Typeset by Faber and Faber Limited
Printed in England by CPI Group (UK) Ltd, Croydon, CR0 4YY

All rights reserved
© Louise Doughty, 2010

The right of Louise Doughty to be identified as author of this work has
been asserted in accordance with Section 77 of the Copyright,
Designs and Patents Act 1988

*This book is sold subject to the condition that it shall not, by way of trade
or otherwise, be lent, resold, hired out or otherwise circulated without the publisher's
prior consent in any form of binding or cover other than that in which it is published
and without a similar condition including this condition being imposed
on the subsequent purchaser*

A CIP record for this book
is available from the British Library

ISBN 978-0-571-31344-0

FSC
www.fsc.org
MIX
Paper from
responsible sources
FSC® C013604

6 8 10 9 7

For Connie

You should remind yourself that what you love is mortal, that what you love is not your own. It is granted to you for the present while, and not irrevocably, nor for ever, but like a fig or a bunch of grapes in the appointed season; and if you long for it in the winter, you are a fool.

From *The Discourses of Epictetus*
(translated by Robin Hard, edited by Christopher Gill)

Contents

Prologue

Muscle has memory; the body knows things the mind will not admit. Two police officers were at my door – uniformed, arranged – yet even as the door swung open upon them, which was surely the moment that I knew, even then, my conscious self was seeking other explanations, turning round and around, like a rat in a cage. Muscle memory – not the same thing as instinct of course, but related: pianists know about this, and tap dancers, and anyone who has ever given birth. Even those who have done nothing more physical than tie their shoelaces know it. The body is quicker than the mind. The body can be trusted.

It has taken them longer than it should have done, to come to my house with the news. Betty was not carrying any form of identification. When the policewoman explains this she does so gently, neutrally, but I choose to hear criticism. I am sitting on my sofa, perched on the edge. The gas fire is on. On the carpet before me, a magazine from the previous weekend's newspapers lies open where I left it – I was reading it this morning, crouched before the fire. The more junior of the officers, a young man, thin and pale, is standing by the door. The woman in charge – older, blonde – has sat down next to me but her body is half turned to face me. I have invited them in. I have asked this news across my threshold.

I am trying to understand what they are telling me, the larger picture, but I seize upon a detail. They weren't carrying identification.

They. She was with her friend Willow. Willow and Betty.

'She's nine,' I say.

The policewoman is taking in my stare, drinking it like water – I see it in the way she stares back, assessing. She has been trained to meet my gaze, if circumstances warrant it. She will not falter. Her male colleague is the discreet one, looking at the floor. They are a team but I can pick whichever one I prefer to fasten upon. I have chosen her.

'She's only nine,' I repeat. Nine-year-olds do not carry credit cards or driving licences. My nine-year-old doesn't even have a mobile phone.

The policewoman mistakes my meaning. 'I'm very sorry,' she says.

At this point, Betty's younger brother Rees bursts into the room. He is clutching a stapler in his right hand. He flings himself at my lap, then thumps his forehead into it, a gesture born of fury and affection in equal measure and a wordless reference to the fact that I promised him an unspecified treat if he did some colouring in the kitchen while I spoke to the man and lady in the sitting room. I am overwhelmed with the feeling, distinct and self-conscious, that I love my son. I clutch at his shoulders, pulling him forward on to me, but clumsily. Sensing my desire outweighs his, he wriggles away then stands looking at me, waiting. The policewoman leans towards me, getting between me and Rees, and puts her hand out until it hovers an inch or two above my shoulder. Although she is not touching me, I find this intrusive.

'Mrs Needham, Laura, I'm sorry, but can you tell us how we can contact Betty's father?'

Our bodies often act of their own accord. They do it all the time. I should have failed my driving test, for instance – I stalled twice just trying to pull out of the test centre – but as we drove down Clarence Road, my hands gripping the steering wheel, the examiner said, 'When I tap this newspaper on the dashboard, I want you to perform an emergency stop. I want you to brake just as hard as you would do if a child ran out in front of the car.'

After he had brushed his hair back from his face he said, 'Thank you, Miss Dodgson. I will not be asking you to repeat that manoeuvre.'

Betty's father and I separated three years ago, when Betty was six and Rees still an infant. He and his partner Chloe live with their baby in the new development towards West Runton, the one they drained the estuary for. Controversial, that development, but the bungalows are bright and spacious, just right for people who are making a new start. I bought them a card when their baby was born. *May your new arrival bring you much joy* read the inscription, in flowing italics. *Love from Laura, Betty and Rees* I wrote beneath, in biro. I got Betty and Rees to draw pictures of their new baby brother and put them in with the card. When their father came to pick them up to visit the baby, I gave him a basket of toiletries I had bought for Chloe, from the Angel Shop on the esplanade. He took it with a look of surprise. The items in the basket were all white; white soap, white body lotion, a fluffy white flannel – with a broad white ribbon tied over the cellophane. He glanced down at the toiletries then back up at me, with a slow, appreciative look on his face.

I could not meet his gaze. 'Make sure you look after her now, won't you?' I said.

After he had left with Betty and Rees, I made myself a cup of coffee and sat at the kitchen table with it and a packet of biscuits, ripped open, staring out of the window. A salty coastal wind swept to and fro across my garden. The wind is like sandpaper round here. I stared and stared at nothing, at the bluster of the day. Twigs from the cherry tree outside our back door scraped and scratched, as if a neglected pet was demanding access. That tree should never have been planted so close to the house. Ten pounds, four ounces, thirty-two hours of labour followed by a ventouse delivery. I wondered if they did an episiotomy or let her tear. Episiotomies used to be routine with the ventouse but the tide has changed on that. I tore badly with Betty, so badly that with Rees I tore again, along the scar tissue. Unlike muscle, scar tissue cannot recall what it has done before. It is hard and stupid.

Neither my ex-husband nor his partner answers their phone. I imagine Chloe standing above the phone, the baby on one arm, seeing my number come up on the dial register and deciding not to pick it up. This happens. I hang up without leaving a message and call David's mobile but it goes straight to voicemail.

The policewoman's male colleague fetches my neighbour Julie to take care of Rees. Rees goes to nursery with Julie's young son Alfie and knows her well but as soon as she steps through the front door, he looks at me, then at the police officers and, as if noticing their uniforms for the first time, bursts into tears. Julie has to carry him kicking and screaming from our house. She does not look at me but as she leaves, I see that tears are streaming down her face too. I worry that she is upset about something and it is a terrible imposition to ask her to have Rees at this moment. Then I realise why she is crying. I realise it, but I still don't know it. My brain seems to be on some sort of loop. I am very, very calm.

I go to the kitchen and pick up my handbag from the table, which is still scattered with plastic plates of rice and peas – all Rees will eat right now – and a distressed heap of crumpled paper and gel pens, Betty's gel pens, her new pack in neon colours. Rees has been taking advantage of his big sister's absence in the hope of prompting a diplomatic incident when she returns. I turn the light off as I go back into the hall. I take my jacket from the coat rack at the bottom of the stairs. I am keen to be efficient about leaving the house. I want to get into their vehicle as swiftly as possible. I want to get to Betty.

I get into the back of the police car and clip my seatbelt, dutifully. I notice how clean it is inside – it is a car that does not habitually transport children – and part of my mind not only registers but appreciates this. It is only as we are turning out of our road that it occurs to me to lean forward and ask, 'What about Willow? How is Willow?'

'Willow is in the High Dependency Unit,' the policewoman says. 'She was thrown clear.'

'I'm going to be sick,' I say, and the policewoman glances in her rear mirror to make sure that nothing is behind us as she presses on the brake and brings the car to a swift, efficient halt. I pull on the interior handle but the child lock is on; of course, to stop people escaping. I feel a moment of dizzying panic but the young policeman unclips his seatbelt with one quick movement and, as soon as it is safe to do so, leaps out and opens the door for me. I make it to the gutter.

One thing I feared and it befell . . . My mouth convicts me. I am good. The Book of Job: I remembered it then, as I gagged and spat. The school common room: grey and white. Jenny Ozu.

It is a twenty-minute drive to the hospital, a red-brick, low-lying building. All the buildings round here are low-lying, as if the storm clouds that squat along this stretch of the coastline are too heavy to allow high-rise. The truth is, land is plentiful, although it often requires drainage to use. Not many people want to live here. We are thirty miles from the nearest decent-sized town and the drive is across flatlands of mud relieved only by the occasional onion field.

As we drive through town in the dark, rain begins to slant across the car – rain rarely falls vertically in this town. The policewoman must be new to the district because she goes down the esplanade when it is quicker to take the one-way system.

The shops on our left are shuttered and dark. The only light spills from Mr Yeung's, the chippy, where boys lounge in the window on high stools, heads lolling on the triangles they have made of their arms. On our right, beyond the railings, the beach melts into a wall of blackness, the waves a herd of sound. As we reach the end of the esplanade, a lone dog-walker makes his way along the pavement, bent into the wind. He looks like John Warren, a patient of mine in his late seventies who is partially blind and has calcification in both shoulders. I feel a flash of concern that he is out and about on his own in the dark.

The police car slows to turn into the main road. As it does, I glimpse a group of dark figures huddled together at the top the concrete steps that lead down to the beach. A couple of them turn as we pass and our headlights light their faces, pale and staring – migrant workers, Eastern European. The policewoman and her colleague exchange a glance as she turns the steering wheel. There's no cockle-picking round here but gangs are sometimes brought in for scrap-collecting. It's low tide, there's no immediate hazard, but it's a filthy night to be out and any beach is dangerous in the dark. The policewoman shakes her head.

We pull into the hospital car park, the place I come so often for work. Normally I drive around to the small courtyard at the back, where the Rehab & Therapies Unit is. The policewoman parks near the main entrance and her colleague jumps out quickly and opens my door. For a moment I think he will offer his hand to help me out but he stands back respectfully, looking down at the wet tarmac, face closed. As I rise out of the car, the wind whips my hair across my face. I clear it with one hand and walk firmly towards the entrance, my escorts falling in, one in front and one behind, as if I might make a break for it and run into the sea. I pray that no one I know will be on duty, for then my private bargain will unravel. Until I see her, there is hope. It is the only way I can put one foot in front of the other.

We enter through the white, low-ceilinged hallway of A & E. Instinctively, I glance around to see what injuries are waiting. There is only one group of people on the plastic chairs – an extended family, five or six women, three children. They all have thick dark hair and pale faces, like the migrant workers we saw on the esplanade. They probably come from the mobile-home park up on the cliff – another local controversy. In the midst of their group is a boy of seven or so clutching a wad of dressing to his forehead. It is soaked in blood and a line of blood stripes his cheek. As we sweep past, the group looks at us accusingly, as if we are jumping the queue. Behind the desk, the duty nurse is talking quietly to a doctor, indicating the group with a palm-upwards gesture of her hand.

We turn left through the swing doors and down a corridor that is painted creamy-white and hung with paintings by local artists, very bad ones, blue seascapes with cheery boats a-bobbing and gulls wheeling in the sky. The sea has never looked like that round here. Through another swing door, the pretence of cheeriness falls away to reveal dull brown walls that lead to the administrative offices. We are going a roundabout route to wherever Betty is.

I have never realised how long this corridor is. I feel as though I have been walking along it for days, noticing things I would never normally notice. We pass office doors, all closed, numbered, with nameplates of people I know, but the people are not here while Betty who should be at home *is* here, somewhere in this endless interior which is confusing and familiar as the landscape of a dream. That must be it. That would explain everything; the gulls in the paintings, the faces on the esplanade, the Book of Job. I am not here. I am asleep, twisting a damp duvet around my legs as I shift restlessly from side to side. Eventually, we reach a consulting room. The police-woman knocks lightly and then enters without waiting for a reply. The policeman gestures for me to follow in behind.

Sitting behind the desk is a doctor I do not know. I am grate-ful for that. He is an older man, nearing retirement I would say, with thin-rimmed glasses. He is writing a report. He closes the file as we enter and stands. 'Mrs Needham, please . . .' he indicates the chair in front of his desk. 'I'm very sorry,' he says, looking at the floor, clearly ill at ease with his task, mortified by it, in fact. He sits again, opens the file, glances at it, clears his throat. 'Right,' he says, then, in a tone of voice that makes it clear he is at the top of a list, begins, 'Er, multiple internal injuries . . .'

The room swings wildly. 'Oh!' I exclaim, bending forward in my chair. I close my eyes as I go down, so do not see his reac-tion. I take a deep breath and force myself to look up.

The doctor is staring. The policewoman steps forward and rests a protective hand on my shoulder, trying to steady me. I force myself to sit up straight. 'I want . . .' I say, gulping air so that my voice will be firm and clear . . . 'I want to see her.'

The doctor glances at the policewoman then rises from his desk. 'Of course, I'm sorry. I should – I'll go and see.'

He closes the door behind him. There is a long silence. I can hear the wind and rain outside. The policewoman says gently, 'Can I get you anything, Laura?' It is her way of apologising for the doctor's abruptness. I shake my head.

The doctor comes back into his office and closes the door behind him. His embarrassment is palpable; it has rendered him speechless. He looks at the policewoman and nods. She leans towards me. 'We can go and see her now.'

I rise from my chair, and have the sensation that I keep on rising, up and up above what is happening to me, soar-ing through the air, high above the hospital. Even as we turn to leave the office, as I step forward, all bodily feeling has left me and it is as if I am floating above myself. I cannot feel the linoleum beneath my feet yet I have the sensation it is spongy. The metal door handle is not cold and hard as it should be, but soft, air. As we walk down the corridor, I have the distinct impression that my new weightlessness extends to my hair and that it must be floating around my head – how else to explain the exposure of my scalp?

Despite all this, I must still be corporeal – I am putting one foot in front of another and, after turning no more than two corners, find myself standing outside a room. The police officers are standing either side of me and the woman officer is explaining something. I can see her lips moving, on the periphery of my vision. She is telling me that I must not move the sheet. I will be able to see Betty's face, but I cannot move the sheet. Her voice booms and fades. I catch a whole sentence. 'You can wait until another relative arrives.' I shake my head fiercely. She opens the door.

Betty, my Betty, is lying on her back on the high bed. Her arms are beneath the covers, which are folded neatly across her chest and pulled up high. Her eyes are closed. Someone has combed her hair. It lies neatly on the pillow, her long fine hair. Her face is composed, the only mark on it a long graze on the forehead, which has been cleaned of grit and dirt. She doesn't look asleep though, no, not that. Sleep softens and rounds her face – when she sleeps in at home and I have to wake her up, I always think, *my baby*, but now there is no softening or rounding. The permanence of this repose has caught her face precisely. Her features hold every day of her nine-year-old life; every experience, every hope or irritation. She is utterly herself.

I approach the bed. My chest is heaving. I realise the policewoman is holding on to me, in readiness for my collapse. 'Laura . . . is this your daughter, Betty Needham?'

I nod, and the nod releases what has been waiting for hours behind the dam of my face – a tidal wave of tears. The tipping point has come. My mind and my body work in concert at last. I reach out to touch her. The policewoman does not prevent me. I curl my hand so I can use the backs of my fingers to stroke her temple, the way I always do when she is most hurt or upset. 'Betty . . . Betty . . .' I say, and I sob and sob as I stroke her temple, oh so softly, and my knees give way and the police-woman is holding me up and the sound of my crying fills the room, the air, the world beyond.

They let me stay. I am grateful for that. They bring a chair – the other people who have entered the room without me notic-ing – one of the grey plastic ones from the waiting room, and they put it by Betty's bed so that I can sit by her and rest my hand gently on the covers while I wait for her father to arrive. They even leave me alone for a few minutes. A nursing auxil-iary comes in with a cup of tea and, avoiding my gaze, places it soundlessly on the cabinet next to me.

I am so thankful to have these few moments. When David arrives, that will be the beginning of all that must come next: Rees, our friends and relatives, the school. The rest of my life will have to start, then. For a moment, I attempt to peer over the edge of the cliff into that life, the life to come, but it makes me dizzy – literally, small spots appear before my eyes. To compensate, to right myself, I run through a brief, alternative narrative for what has happened to me in the last hour. The police came to my house to take me to the hospi-tal. When I got here, Betty was lying white-faced on the crisp sheets hooked up to a drip. The consultant explained the se-riousness of her injuries without euphemism. It was up to me to translate for her into terms that she could understand, so I told her she probably wouldn't be able to take her tap dance exam in the autumn. 'I'm sorry, darling,' I said, 'but it's going to have to wait until next year.' She has a way of bulging her face when she is indignant, distorting it, making her beautiful brown eyes monstrous. '*A whole year!*' Now, she is asleep. The consultant has told me to go home and rest but I am staying here, just in case.

I wonder how long I could keep this going, if it is possible to live with this alternative narrative for the rest of my life. I know – dear God, already I know – that this alternative is only mine as long as I am alone. Already, I am in love with alone.

I rest, breathe in the simple fact that it is just me and Betty, here in this room. My thoughts are full of her but I can think of nothing to say that I haven't said a million times, so I rest my hand on her and say, 'Darling . . . darling . . .' a few times. I watch her face and try and imprint the image of it on to my mind so that it will be there, just as sharp as it is now, forever; the scattering of freckles down her long nose – her heavy eyebrows and wide forehead. She has a grown-up face for a nine-year-old. It is already possible to see the adult in her. The chicken-pox scar just beneath where my fingers are stroking her temple – the curve of her lips. She has a lot of natural colour in her lips. It flatters her pale, freckled skin. She burns badly in the sun, as badly as any redhead. We have to be careful with her.

I don't want this small space of time to end, ever. I think of all the pictures of her I have in my head – the last time I saw her as she ran into school, chatting to her friends; and earlier this morning, before we left the house, brushing her long hair in front of the mirror in the hallway until it rippled in the milky light from the frosted glass panels on our front door. We were late, of course, but she would never leave the house without brushing her hair. Adolescent vanity had come to Betty early; the mood swings had started too. When she had finished brushing her hair, she stayed in front of the mirror to button her new corduroy jacket. We had bought it in a sale that weekend and she insisted on wearing it even though it wasn't lined and she would freeze at playtime.

'Mum, do you think the sleeves are a bit long?'

My darling. If unconsciousness of any sort could come to me now, I would be perfected, complete.

A small eternity, the door opens; David is standing in the doorway, tall and straight, still in his working suit, grey hair combed neatly back. He looks at me and his face is blank with horror, eyes staring wide. We fix on each other's gazes, locking in, conjoined by the paradox of shock and disbelief. Then his gaze shifts to the bed. He claps a hand over his mouth but it is too late. He cannot stop the sound escaping.

PART 1

Before

1

Muscle memory. My school friend Jenny Ozu was trapped inside Bach's Minuet no. 2 in G major because of it. She was doing a public recital at the Town Hall, although not much of the public showed up: it was a Tuesday lunchtime in the Easter holidays. Her audience consisted of eleven people, I counted, scattered over a dozen rows of straight-backed wooden chairs, including Jenny's mother and me.

Jenny sat at the piano, marooned on a wide stage that was framed in its turn by sagging velvet curtains. The Town Hall was little used and the air heavy with dust. She began her first piece, the minuet. (The programme, designed and printed by her mother, declared in proud italics *Jenny Plays Bach!*). She played the first line and a half beautifully. As she approached the repeat, I dug my fingernails into the palm of my hand. 'I'm really worried about the repeat,' she had told me. 'I just know I'm going to go straight on.' She had practised it again and again. When the moment came, she sailed effortlessly back to the beginning. I smiled at her, even though she was concentrating on the music. Then, she approached the same point, the point where she should continue with the piece but instead, she sailed gracefully backwards, again, to the start. I felt my face flush for her and glanced around. Surely no one but I and her mother, sitting at the front, frowning no doubt, would notice. Three times instead of two – it wasn't the end of the world.

When Jenny came to the same place in the music again . . . again, she sailed backwards. After her fifth repeat of the same two lines of minuet, she stopped, lifted her hands from the piano keys, and burst into tears.

Later, she told me, 'I'd practised the repeat so hard, over and over, my fingers wouldn't do anything else. I just had to stop completely. It was the only way I was ever going to get out.'

We were gloomy adolescents, that was what bonded Jenny and me. Her father was Japanese and absent. Mine was dead. We made it our business to be intellectually superior to the other thirteen-year-old girls. We made suicide pacts and walked around carrying library books with titles such as *Teach Yourself Swahili*. We lay on her bed and ate KitKats and said we were Nihilists. I went through a phase of copying out verses from the Book of Job. I pinned them to the front of my cupboard in the common room, so that the other girls could see. It pleased me to excite their bafflement.

> One thing I feared, and it befell,
> and what I dreaded came to me.
> No peace had I, nor calm, nor rest;
> but torment came.
>> *The Book of Job*, 3:25

The things that impress you when you are twelve, thirteen, fourteen: they form in your bones. I have forgotten vast swathes of my schooling but one picture has remained, as clear as day: the grey and white of our form common room, Jenny Ozu weeping in a corner because her mother slapped her again that morning, and me sitting at a desk copying out verses from the Book of Job in black felt tip, furious in my desire to discomfort our happier contemporaries. My mother was a widow who had just been diagnosed with Parkinson's disease. I was an only child. Jenny and I were obsessed with unfairness – it bonded us more tightly than any shared hobby could ever have done.

I may be righteous but my mouth convicts me;
Innocent, yet it makes me seem corrupt.
I am good.
I do not know myself.
The Book of Job, 9:20

By the age of fifteen I was adept at changing my mother's in-continence pads. 'Right, Mum, let's give you a little wipe, shall we? Here, what do you call a deer with no eyes . . . ?' My other friends at school apart from Jenny – my so-called friends, the ones who allowed me to hang around with them because I made them look cool and attractive – were making homemade skin treatments out of yoghurt and discussing barrier methods of contraception. I was learning that it was a good idea for my mother to skip the protein in her midday meal because it could interfere with the operation of the dopamines. She was already having problems vocalising, although she could still move her lips to mouth, 'No-eye deer.'

The district nurse visited once a week. I despised her even more than the social worker, who wore pop-socks but at least didn't keep calling me darling. The district nurse was as plump as the social worker was skinny. She wore tight jumpers and had breasts that began a foot lower on her body than they should have done. I saw her as a portent, a ribbed-sweater ex-ample of what I might become if I didn't lay off cheesecake and steer well clear of the caring professions. Her constant praise drove me demented. 'My,' she would say, watching me tip and count my mother's medication into her pill box. 'I've got stu-dent nurses ten years older than you who aren't this organised. You're going to be a proper little nurse, my darling.'

She wasn't the only one who assumed I was going to be a nurse. Our neighbours, the Coultons, dropped by every now and then. Mr Coulton would tramp through our house in his unlaced, cement-covered boots and go out back to mow our small, square lawn. It took him longer to find the electric socket in the kitchen than it did to do the mowing. They had twin boys, aged ten. Whenever it snowed, the boys appeared at our front door with shovels. 'Mam said to clear your path,' one of them would announce sullenly.

I knew I was expected to be grateful, although I couldn't care less whether our path was covered in snow – it would melt of its own accord soon enough – and as far as I was concerned, the garden could become a wilderness.

'I expect you're going to be a nurse, then,' Mrs Coulton pronounced firmly one day as she left our house. 'Such a good girl. So brave.'

In my GCSE year, I had a meeting with the school's careers adviser. She knew nothing about my mother but, to my enormous indignation, came to the same conclusion. 'You like the arts but still, that's good, you also enjoy biology . . .' she said, glancing through the form I had filled in.

'I like doing the diagrams. The plants. And ventricles,' I replied, sensing what was coming. 'I'm good at the heart. Left and right ventricle. But it's just because I'm good at drawing. I might be an artist, later, maybe.'

'Have you thought about nursing?' she said, rubbing the side of her nose with one finger.

I wanted to bite her. 'If I was going to consider that sort of profession,' I replied haughtily, 'I would want to – specialise.' I racked my brain for a speciality, one that involved a long word. 'Physiotherapy,' I said. I meant to say psychiatry but physiotherapy had more syllables.

The careers adviser made a small sound in the back of her throat, halfway between a cough and a bark. She was wearing a pen-on-a-string round her neck and it jumped every time she scoffed. 'Physiotherapy isn't just massage, you know, Lorna. It's highly academic nowadays. It's as hard to get a place as medicine, even harder some people say, and very difficult to get a position afterwards, but we're always going to need good nurses, Lisa, aren't we?' She beamed at me.

You're not even a proper teacher! I wanted to shout, *Who the hell do you think you are?* I smiled back.

A nurse? Didn't these people realise I was an intellectual? What, precisely, did they think it was about my current situation that was going to make me want to do it for the rest of my life? I got As in my science GCSEs and Bs in nearly all my arts subjects. My only dropped grade was a U in Geography. I was proud of it, determined to be brilliant or fail completely, like a firework. A nurse? Didn't they think that I might be getting enough of wearing thin rubber gloves as a schoolgirl? *T. S. Eliot*, I would say to myself, whenever I glimpsed one of the Coultons passing our bay window. *Will no one rid me of this troublesome prelate? Photosynthesis. The Great Reform Act of 1832.* My particles of knowledge were like the ingredients of a witch's brew, magic that would keep me safe from the Coultons and the health visitors and the dread weight of what my mother's illness was turning me into: a good girl, a little angel, someone of patience and understanding who effaced her own needs so effectively that she became a mere outline, helping others.

In an attempt to be bad, I tried to take up smoking, standing in the garden one night after I had put my mother to bed, but I puffed too many Silk Cut in a row and had to lie down on the damp grass and was nearly sick. I bought a can of Special Brew from the off-licence at the end of the promenade one day after school because I had seen a homeless man drinking it in the shelter on the beach and so assumed it was as bad as you could get. I went and sat on the pebbles but it was cold and windy and the beer tasted of detergent. Being bad was no fun, I concluded. I would have to stick to being brainy.

This was where Jenny Ozu came in. She was the only girl in my class less cool than myself. Nowadays, I suppose we would be Goths or Emos and revel in our oddness but popular culture reached our deserted stretch of coastline in diluted form, in those days – we were just odd. She got straight As, without even a token U. I pretended I didn't mind. I did a mix of arts and sciences at A level partly so that I could take Biology with her. I was fascinated by the straightness of her fringe. If we had had more imagination, we might have become what the rest of our GCSE form assumed we were, teenage lesbians, but sex was never a feature of our discussions and I didn't share my beer or cigarette experiments with her either – no, for Jenny and me it was pure brainache all the way through adolescence.

We split up dramatically halfway through the sixth form. I fell in with a crowd of girls led by a skinny tomboy called Phoebe, who claimed she had tried skunk once and lost her virginity to the local swimming instructor. 'Why do you hang out with that geeky chinky girl?' Phoebe asked me one day, in front of her three friends.

'She's Japanese, or her dad is . . .' I said, but without aggression.

Phoebe shrugged. 'Are you lesbians?'

I should have walloped her, or at least stuck up for my friend, but instead I shrugged.

'Cool!' said Phoebe. 'I've always thought it must be much more fun to be a lesbian. Men are so . . .' she looked around in the air for the necessary adjective. The other three girls watched her, hanging on her words. So, to my shame, did I. Phoebe had an auburn ponytail and cheekbones and a level of insouciance that made her glow. She seemed to have leap-frogged adolescence altogether. 'They're so . . .' then she burst into a fit of giggles. 'Mind you . . .' We all laughed like drains.

My friendship with Jenny was over after that but I didn't have the courage to tell her. Instead, I told myself that it was okay, that the bad things that had happened to me justified my own bad behaviour. I saw her around town occasionally, out on her own, or with her mother. If she smiled at me, I nodded and kept walking. I had had enough of being geeky. I wanted to be snide and happy, like Phoebe and her friends. I wanted to be normal.

Despite my lack of interest in boyfriends, my mother was obsessed with them. I was fourteen when she was diagnosed and a young fourteen at that: flat-chested, brown-haired and bookish, and with no idea how to pluck my eyebrows. Boys featured in my life in much the same way that creatures from a distant and disintegrating planet might feature, as something I really ought to be studying through a telescope to gain some idea of how to treaty with them when they came to visit. I was not convinced the visit would prove friendly.

Sometimes, her obsession took a morose turn. 'I want to see you settled, Duck,' she would say as she loaded sugar into her tea, by means of a teaspoon that began heaped but thanks to the tremble in her hands was level by the time it reached her mug, 'before I'm cold in my grave.'

In those days I watched the trembles carefully. Her consultant was gradually increasing her intake of Sinemet and even though I knew it could be years before the long-term side effects kicked in, the increased dosage made me anxious. 'I reckon I can hang on that long,' she would often add. Nothing the doctors said could convince her that her life expectancy was normal. As her only child and carer, it had been explained to me very carefully by the social worker, a tweedy woman who wore not only pop-socks but skirts that stopped above the top of them – my scorn for her knew no bounds. My mother would live as long as she would have done before her diagnosis, but the efficacy of the dopamine drugs would wear off in between five and ten years' time. When the mental disintegration came, it would be as a side effect of those drugs rather than a symptom of her disease. Sooner or later, I would have to choose between a trembling, slow-moving mother who could hardly swallow but was mentally alert and manageable or a more physically able mother who might become aggressive. Most families, the social worker told me, chose the former.

It became a kind of joke between me and my mother, her desire to see me 'settled'. At the time, I felt mostly amused or irritated by it, often both – it was only when I became a mother myself that the true poignancy of her desire came home to me. I was the only child of a widow with a degenerative illness and she was terrified that when I could no longer cope and she went into a home, I would be left alone. Throughout my teens, as her Parkinson's progressed, she came to regard it as her job to give me all the advice I might miss out on if she waited until I was sexually active. 'Never trust a man who doesn't look you in the eye,' it would be one week. The following week would come, 'If a man stares at you too keenly, he's not to be trusted, mark my words.'

My mother was forty-five when I was born, my father well into his fifties. I think it's safe to say I came as something of a surprise. My father was the maintenance manager at the local reprographics company. He died of a heart attack when I was eight months old. My mother went from being half of a middle-aged, childless couple to being a single parent within the space of a year. Given the shock of that transition, she did a brilliant job. Whenever I looked at photos of my dead father, my mother would say, 'He doted on you, did your dad, oh my yes, you were the light of his life.'

I loved my mum. She was old enough to be my grandmother but we were great friends. Her advice about romance, when it came, was full of vague generalities and devoid of any reference to the physical realities of relationships – there was little she told me that could not have been lifted directly from a dating manual, circa 1956. Once, as we knelt next to each other in our tiny square garden, digging up carrots, she said to me thoughtfully, as if it had been preying on her mind, 'If you ever go to a cocktail party, Laura, and you walk in and there's another girl in the same frock, it's important not to act embarrassed. Just look at her and shout merrily, snap!'

That one got repeated in the corridor at school, to uproarious laughter. Cocktail parties? Frocks? What planet was my mother living on?

Occasionally, I spied a certain sagacity in her words. One such comment I remember clearly because it resurfaced in the early days of my relationship with David. 'Duck . . .' she said to me solemnly, as we ate chicken and mushroom pie with peas and gravy for supper. 'Duck, there's only one way to make sure a boy's family likes you, and that's to make sure they didn't like the girlfriend that came before you.' It was ten years before the truth of that became apparent to me.

This is what I remember most clearly about the early days of David: the way he looked at me after we made love. He liked to lie on his back after sex, one arm behind his head. I would lie on top of him and rest my chin on his chest. He would stare at me, his gaze both thoughtful and possessive. I would tip my head back as I stared at him in return, moving it a little from side to side to enjoy the brush of my hair across my bare shoulders. Sometimes, he would massage my scalp, rubbing his fingertips hard against it. The light through my half-closed curtains gave the room a greenish glow, as if we were underwater. We could stare at each other endlessly like that, hardly talking, just gazing, as if we had never looked at each other properly before, as if we were trying to work out precisely who it was we had made love to.

Weekend afternoons were our favourite time – whole great rested hours together, our working weeks forgotten, white sky and winter weather outside and us, heedless of the cold and the rain and the people going past in the street outside my flat, heedless of the whole existence of other people's lives. It was always he who had to say, eventually, 'Fancy a coffee?' or 'We should go out and eat.' Left to me, we would have slipped into the night like that, careless of all other bodily needs, in the subtle grip of that lethargy. I had no sense that our time together, naked and sated, could ever end – or that something so easy, so natural, was granted to me only for the present while, mortal.

2

There is a look that a certain sort of man gives a woman before he has had sex with her but never after. I wonder where they learn this look, those men, whether it is something they are born with, or acquired behaviour. I wonder how cynical it is, if they even know they are doing it – my guess, from my limited experience, is that they do. David knew he was doing it, although I don't believe it was cynical: it was more an instinctive reaction to a woman he found attractive, that intent, expressionless stare.

It was in a pub, our first meeting. I was there with a group of other physiotherapy students one of whom, called Carole, was weeping copiously because her boyfriend hadn't shown up and she was sure he was seeing someone else. She left mid-evening, and the boyfriend came in not long after, with two friends. The boyfriend was David.

I saw him as soon as he came in the door – tall, dressed in a heavy coat that bulked out a neat frame. His hair was dark and needed washing. One of the other girls I was with knew who he was and nudged me saying, 'Look, that's him, Carole's boyfriend. He's such a jerk,' but I was already looking.

While he was at the bar, we discussed him. He was public property, after all. Carole's tears were the sauce with which he had been served and we had a right – no, an obligation – to pass judgement.

'Not bad . . .' I said, sipping my pint of lager top.

The others disagreed.

'Too confident,' said Abbie.

'I can't bear men like that, Carole should dump him,'

declared Rosita.

David finished buying a round for himself and his mates and only then did he look around the pub and see us, sitting in the corner. Abbie waved frantically. David and his two friends sauntered over, so laid-back they were almost visibly bending at the knees. As they neared our table, Abbie thrust her chest out and said in a sing-song voice, 'She's gone, you know. You've left it *too late*. She's *furious*.'

David shrugged, and pulled up a stool, then folded himself down on to it, opposite me. He nodded. I nodded back. We were not of an age where either of us would do anything so uncool as introduce ourselves. Abbie flopped back on the bench seat. 'Bloody hell . . .' she muttered, apropos of nothing.

We spent the rest of the evening around the small wooden table. The pint glasses piled up: the girls bought each other rounds and the boys bought their own. There was little in the way of shared conversation – the table stood between us like a demarcation line. That was the way relationships with the opposite sex were in those days; careful displays of mutual indifference punctuated by infrequent, clumsy sex. We talked about sex all the time amongst our peer groups, of course, but when any of us actually did it, we took care to reassure the person concerned, our friends and ourselves, that it was nothing personal.

The barman called time and a moment later strode over to our table and reached behind my head for the bank of light switches on the wall above me, flicking on a whole row with a single swooping gesture of his hand. Repulsed by the sudden fluorescence, we all started, like vampires at an unexpected dawn. Vanity amongst us girls was socially acceptable, so the three of us scrambled to our feet, dragging coats up our arms, winding scarves around our necks, flicking our hair, while the boys scooped up their pints with affected casualness. The lighting laid bare the grubbiness of the table we were sitting at

– the empty crisp packets half-folded in the ashtray, the sticky circles on the table's shiny surface. When I eased myself out from behind the table, I could feel that the carpet beneath my thin shoes was soggy. I was already thinking of the essay I had to finish by Monday, on anterior and posterior tibials. I wanted to get back to the house I shared with Abbie and two other students. I wanted a cup of tea and my lumpen single bed.

I was the first outside. David followed close behind. 'You'd better give me your number, then,' he said, as if we were concluding a previous conversation. Close to me, his voice low, I detected a Welsh lilt. It made him sound older than the boys I knew, more experienced.

I stopped and looked at him. Up until that moment, neither of us had given any indication that we were interested in one another. He stared back at me, his gaze both purposeful and blank, and in one deliberate, hot-eyed moment did the work of a whole evening's worth of flirting. It was a bold gesture and I knew it for what it was. I also knew it was quite beyond most other boys our age. I was impressed.

I did what I was supposed to do. I returned the stare for a couple of seconds, acknowledged it, then looked to one side with a hint of embarrassment, as if I was flattered but caught off-balance, intrigued but a little nervous. I glanced at the ground, which made my hair tumble in front of my face. As I looked up again, I had to push my hair back with one hand and play with it a bit to get it to stay behind my ear. When I eventually looked at David, he was smiling at me. I smiled back. *God you're cheap, Laura,* I thought.

He stuck his hand into the inside pocket of his bulky coat and pulled out a biro. I took it from him, then took hold of the hand, twisted the palm upwards and wrote my number on the fleshy part of his thumb. He winced melodramatically. While I was engaged in this, the others piled out behind us. They gathered around, watching, blowing white clouds of breath into the cold. When I had finished, Abbie grabbed my elbow and pulled me away. 'What was that about?' she hissed.

I shrugged as we strolled off, arms linked.

'Hey! Don't you want my number?' David called after me brazenly.

The other girls were close either side of me, hustling me off. I turned. Walking backwards, I called out to him, grinning, 'Well, you'll call if you want to, won't you?' He was staring after me, still smiling.

Abbie pulled me back round again. 'Carole will bloody kill you.'

'Not if you don't tell her,' I said. 'And anyway, he doesn't belong to Carole, does he?'

'I can't believe you were flirting with David!'

I hadn't even asked his name. That's how little interest I had succeeded in showing during the evening. Oh, I was pleased with myself.

David. I lay on my poorly sprung bed that night, wide awake, with the orange streetlight glimmering through the thin brown curtains and the shouts of the Saturday drunks ringing softly in the streets around our house. So it was David. I thought of how I had risen from the table that evening, in the cold glare of the fluorescent light, while he was still seated on the stool opposite me. I had to push past his shoulder to get by – my hip had grazed his shoulder. He had not leaned away to make room for me to pass. He had sat completely still. And I had pushed against him, slowly and deliberately. My body had asked his body a question. David. He had my number but I didn't have his. All I could do was wait.

He never called and I didn't see him again for over two years. I heard news of him from time to time, and whenever I heard his name in conversation, I felt that small folding motion in my stomach and had to be careful not to ask questions or react.

David had made it up with Carole. David and Carole had split up. A group of engineering students, him amongst them, had nearly got expelled from the university because of some prank involving a concrete mixer. One of them had hot-wired it and they had set it going then been unable to brake as it headed towards the riverbank. They had to jump for their lives. Two local cops were standing on the bridge watching as they waded ashore.

I had two boyfriends during my final year of study but I was going through the motions. Neither of them measured up to the one with the stare – or rather, neither of them measured up to my daydreams of him.

After I graduated, I stayed on at the Royal Infirmary to do my probationary year. Most of my fellow students went off to more glamorous cities but I needed to be able to visit Mum. She was in a nursing home on the outskirts of our home town, thirty miles away – I couldn't afford to be further from her than that. She could still walk with a delta frame, just, and her physio was getting her to do four hundred yards twice a day. Her larynx was going, though, and I was trying to persuade her to use audio feedback. I went twice a week, three times when I could. The home was good. 'Be nice to yourself,' the reception-ist always said to me, as I left, smiling brightly, my wave brisk and my eyes glittering.

It was at a house party – a twenty-fifth birthday for a friend of a friend. I only went because I was feeling miserable about Mum and forcing myself to do things I didn't want to do: the TENS machine principal of pain relief. During childbirth, we give women a small machine with two adhesive pads and sug-gest they electrocute themselves at the base of the spine during each contraction, on the basis that it will take their minds off the excruciating pain in their abdomens. I tried it with Betty. It didn't work for me. David said I might as well have got him to kick me on the shins. As my mother's health had deteriorated, I made myself go out to the sort of merry social occasions I disliked more and more often.

I arrived early. There were only half a dozen other people there, none of whom I knew. Half an hour, I thought, then I'm off. Then I saw him. Yes, it was definitely him.

The sitting room was over-lit. There was nowhere to hide while I observed him. I busied myself with extracting a glass of wine from one of those boxes with a plastic spout and a button that invites you, prophetically, to *Depress Here*. I talked animatedly to the other people that I didn't know in the hope that he would recognise me if I stood there long and conspicuously enough. Covertly, I managed to observe that he was with a short blonde woman. He had to stoop to hear her when she spoke.

If there had been enough other people there, I might have spent the whole evening circling him but the party didn't seem likely to fill up and I knew I couldn't hang around for long with no one else to talk to, so, emboldened by awkwardness, I went over and stood in front of him. He looked at me expectantly, with no flicker of recognition. The short blonde woman stared at me. I leaned towards him and said, 'Sorry, aren't you a friend of Carole's?'

'Carole . . .' he said, turning from his companion, who responded by turning away from him with a degree of ostentation and beginning an animated conversation with someone behind her.

He pursed his lips and furrowed his brows. 'Now . . . oh God . . .' he groaned rolling his eyes. 'Carole. That Carole.'

I exhaled, laughingly, as if I knew the whole story.

'Carole,' he said, shaking his head, 'she was mad, wasn't she?' His accent was slightly more pronounced than I remembered. Later, he confessed that he instinctively accentuated it when he met people for the first time. It was a useful conversation point when he was chatting up women and a way of testing men. There was nothing made his hackles rise more than an Englishman taking the mickey out of his accent.

'Er, yes.'

'And you were her friend?'

'For a bit, yes.' I took a gamble. 'I used to hear all about you.'

He groaned again. 'Well, that's blown my chances of ever shagging you.'

At this point, Shorty chose to re-appear at his elbow. She placed her hand lightly on his forearm and smiled at me.

I lifted my wine glass, 'Well . . .'

As I walked back to the drinks table, David followed. 'I remember you . . .' he said. 'Abbie.'

I shook my head and reached for a bottle on the table. 'Keep trying.'

He screwed up his face. 'God, now I really have no chance.'

I turned to survey the room and spoke to him out of the corner of my mouth. 'Try a different tack.'

He was surveying the room as well, as if we were spies trying not to acknowledge each other too obviously. Shorty had her back to us but the two women she was talking to in the corner were staring at me.

'Will you marry me?' he said.

'That's certainly different,' I acknowledged, dipping my glass in his direction.

I am sure that at that stage he still didn't remember our first meeting in the pub – although later he claimed he did – not even when he turned his back on the women glaring at us from the corner, looked down at me where I was half-perched on the edge of the table, and gave me that slow, deliberate stare.

I looked to one side. I should have waited for him to speak, but I was both too nervous and too sure of myself. 'Are you still in engineering?' I asked.

It was too ordinary a question. Immediately, I lost him. 'I'm working at a pen factory on the coast,' he replied, his voice flat, routine. He could have been talking to anyone.

'Hennett's? I grew up near there,' I said quickly.

'My family all live near Eastley. Well actually, they are Eastley. I've got a big family. Half of Aberystwyth lives in Eastley now.'

'I grew up behind the Recreation Ground, the new estate, lots of pebbledash, the one with . . .' I was gabbling. Despite our discovery that we had grown up in neighbouring towns, I sensed that his attention was elsewhere. He glanced around the room. Suddenly, it was full of people. The party had begun.

'I'd better . . .' he said, raising his glass and nodding towards the other side of the crowded room, where his short girlfriend was invisible behind the sudden influx of partygoers. I could think of no excuse to detain him. Never mind, I thought. Give it half an hour, then get your coat on and go up to him and ask for his number, suggest a coffee or something, just casually. That way, if he makes you feel like a prannet you can get out straight away.

I went to the kitchen. I gave it half an hour, then I got my coat on – green wool, with a belt – and returned to the sitting room. Someone had dimmed the lights. I pushed through the people, 'Sorry… sorry…' When I couldn't find him, I pushed through them again. 'Sorry…' The sitting room was crowded but small. There was no doubt. He had gone.

Two years later, I was fully qualified but discovering that my school careers' adviser had been right about one thing: posts as newly qualified physios were hard to come by. In the end, I got a job in a small unit at the local hospital of my home town. I didn't really want to move back home but my radius of opportunity was limited while Mum was still in the care home. I had a dim sense that some time in the future I would move back to my university town, which had things like nightclubs and cinemas, and resume the life of a normal single person. In the meantime, rent in my old town was cheap. I got a whole bed-sitting flat to myself five minutes from the esplanade for what I was paying for a room in a shared house when I was a student.

It was autumn – the town was unexpectedly golden, that year. It had been a good summer and holiday trade was up. There were optimistic reports in the local newspaper amidst talk of building a pier. Most seaside towns lament their tacky tourist image. We aspired to it. I was thinking of how I should make the effort to get out more. My life post-Mum was distant, indistinct, and I was vaguely aware that I was using it as an excuse. I had a nice bunch of friends at the clinic and we went out drinking once in a while. I still saw a man I thought of as my university boyfriend, Nick, who came over every other weekend but was due to move up north soon to take up a teaching post. My life was comfortably suspended between that of a student and that of the woman I imagined I would be in some misty future elsewhere, but only if the future was the one who took the initiative. I wasn't unhappy, just apathetic.

I was writing up some notes in my office when there was a light tap at the door. It was Mary, one of our occupational therapists. 'Can you take my four o'clock?' she said. 'The school have just called.' She already had her mac on. She was only halfway in the door and drumming her fingers on the edge of it, impatient to be off. Mary annoyed me – we were constantly making allowances for her childcare crises. Later, of course, I changed my tune on that issue, but that afternoon, I lingered long enough over my answer to give her a moment's doubt over whether I had been the right person to choose. 'I was really hoping to finish this lot . . .' I waved my hand vaguely over the papers on my desk, half of which were completed already. In truth, I wasn't busy that day. When Mary tapped on my door, I had been thinking about whether or not I should join a dance class of some sort to keep fit. Flamenco, perhaps. I had been picturing my hand movements and wondering how long it took to get good enough to wear a frilly dress and those severe eyebrows. The Town Hall did Ceroc every Tuesday but I fancied something a bit more dramatic. With flamenco, it wouldn't matter that I didn't have a partner, presumably. I could concentrate on clapping.

'Jamie's off,' said Mary, although she was too proud to allow a pleading note to creep into her voice, like most of us would have done, in her position.

I sighed, shrugged. 'All right then, tell your four o'clock where I am.'

'Thanks,' she said, stepping into the office and handing me the folder which she had ready in the other hand.

While she retreated, I pushed my papers to one side and laid the folder down. I opened it and glanced at the registration form: David Needham.

There was another light tap. 'Come in,' I said.

I had the impression that he stooped slightly as he entered, although of course he wasn't taller than the door frame – it was more a gesture of politeness, as if he knew he'd been fobbed off on me and was apologising for how much of him there was to fob.

I glanced up and thought immediately, oh, it's *him*, but again, he showed no sign of recognising me. Why should he? It was our third meeting in four years. He moved towards the chair in front of my desk but I gestured towards my examination table, which had a fresh sheet of paper on it. I looked down at his file as I said, 'Would you remove your shirt for me, please?'

He sat on the edge of the examination table and removed his shirt slowly while I watched. When he had taken it off, he stood up, took a step towards the chair in front of my desk and tossed the shirt over the back of it, then went back to the examination table and sat on the edge of it again, all without looking in my direction. His nipples were dark brown, and taut in the cool of my office. He had a thick mass of chest hair that tapered towards his belly button. He sat up very straight, holding his stomach in. I had noticed over my years of examining patients that men did that every bit as much as women. 'Is that how you sit when you're at your desk?' I asked, allowing a note of scepticism in my voice.

'Well, I work at a drawing board,' he said, a little defensively, meeting my gaze. 'It's difficult not to hunch.'

I looked down at his records and asked him some questions, then we went through the usual routine; stand in front of me, hands on hips, bend forward and back, then from side to side . . . My women patients usually respond well to this, understanding what I need and wanting to be helpful, whereas men are embarrassed by it, unused as they are to being observed. David, however, did not look embarrassed. He met my gaze steadily – it was hard not to take this as a challenge.

'Would you mind lying on your front while I examine you?' I gestured towards the bed. I stayed seated while he lay down, then said, 'Actually, I think it's better if we do this on the chair. Sorry. Would you mind?' He raised his head. I indicated the chair. 'Sorry,' I said again.

He sat up. 'Should I put my shirt back on?' There was a hint of irritation in his voice.

I paused. 'Not just yet.'

As he walked to the chair, I rose from behind my desk. 'Do you do much sport?'

'Football sometimes,' he said. 'Walking, does that count?'

'Depends how fast you walk. I think it would be a good idea to tape your back.'

'Tape it?'

'Sit up straight, shoulders here.'

I positioned myself behind the chair, rested my hands lightly on his shoulders and pulled them backwards, so he was in the correct posture. 'We aren't designed to sit, I'm sure the occupational therapist has told you. We're designed to lie down, stand and squat, that's it. Sitting isn't natural and if you slump like you do... I've checked your neck and your shoulder girdle; now I want to take a look at your joints. Would you raise your arms please?'

I get sleepy in the afternoons if my office is warm so I always keep it a little too cold for patients. He had goose pimples on his upper arms. His biceps were taut – he must have weight-trained at some stage.

'How's my posture generally?'

'Terrible, but that's common with tall people. I'm going to check your soft tissue.'

He had a lot of fine dark hairs across his shoulders and back. They were quite curly, which surprised me because the hair on his head was almost straight. There was a substantial scattering of white amongst the black: a premonition, as it turned out. He was to go grey not long after Betty was born. 'Okay, you can put your shirt back on now.'

He looked at me as I went back behind my desk and picked up my biro. 'I thought you were going to tape my back.'

I looked back at him as he picked up his shirt from the back of the chair and pushed his arms into the sleeves, shrugging it on to his shoulders. 'You're very hairy,' I said.

'Thank you,' he replied with a smile.

I smiled back. 'It wasn't a compliment, Mr Needham, it was an observation. Before I can tape you, I need you to go home and shave. I can tape your shoulder blades in place and it will improve your posture, but it's sticky tape. When you take it off, it will be like ripping a plaster off.'

He pulled a face. 'How much of this tape do you put on?'

I stood up again, slowly this time, and walked around the desk that stood between us. He stared at me, not yet the hot-eyed stare but something that was moving towards it, something that was observing me. I walked toward him. He was silent. I stood behind his chair, and paused for a moment. Then I lifted my hands and placed them lightly on his shoulders – very lightly. He had stopped buttoning his shirt mid-way and was quite still. It was an office shirt, a blue one, short-sleeved, the optimistic remnant of a summer wardrobe. Even though I had already touched his naked torso, there was something about the firmness of his shoulders through his clothing that was almost unbearably arousing. I loved his shoulders, not too broad, but sinewy. For a man who claimed not to exercise there wasn't an ounce of fat on him. I rested my hands there for a minute, then let them dribble down his shoulder blades, fingers splayed, as if they were two cascades of water. 'I place two strips here, going from top to bottom of your shoulders, like bra straps . . .' I paused. He didn't move or speak. I wanted him to turn around in his chair, put his arms tight around my waist and bury his face in my stomach – no, more, I wanted him to push me back on to the examination table and raise my skirt. My God, I thought, I'm sexually harassing a patient. 'Then I take another piece, and get you to sit upright, in a good posture, and I place it horizontally across here.' I drew a line from one imaginary strap to the other with the tip of my finger.

'Will this involve my nipples at all?' he asked quietly.

Phew, I thought. Now – technically speaking – he is sexually harassing me.

'Your nipples are quite safe,' I said quietly. I paused, removed my hands from his back, then walked back behind my desk.

He watched me but didn't speak. I sat and made a note on his file, acutely aware of how intently he was looking at me, and aware that neither of us was attempting a wisecrack of any sort. It was stalemate. In the formal scheme of our relationship – patient and physiotherapist – I was in the position of power, but it was as if we were now balanced precariously on either end of a see-saw, each of us waiting for the other to shift their weight. I sensed it was up to me to indicate whether or not I would welcome a further advance on his part.

I closed his file. 'I sometimes shave patients myself,' I said. 'It's quite difficult to reach your own back and you're very hairy. Do you have anyone at home who could do it for you?'

He pulled a face, lifted his hands to show me his palms were empty, then let them drop. 'No one.'

'Neither do I,' I said quickly, drawing breath immediately afterwards. Strictly speaking, that was not a piece of information that he needed.

His smile seemed to take about five minutes and stretch from one wall of my office to the other. His teeth were neat and white.

I was twirling the biro between my fingers as we looked at each other. All at once, it slipped my grasp and somersaulted across the desk. I made a clumsy attempt to grab at it.

'Do you often drop your biro?' he asked, still smiling.

'How's the pen factory?' I said.

'Great,' he said. 'I've been promoted. I get free pens. I'll get you some if you like. You obviously lose them quite a lot.'

'Why didn't you call?' I asked. 'Is that a euphemism?'

'The pens? Absolutely. Why did you run off?' he replied. 'You're always running off.'

'I didn't,' I said, hunting self-consciously for the biro amongst my paperwork.

'You did,' he said, 'but if you shave my back I'll forgive you. Let's do it at your place. Maybe we should go now.'

'My place is a mess.'

'I'll help you tidy up.'

I sat back in my seat and looked at him. How had this happened?

We looked at each other then he said, his voice thoughtful and soft, almost as if he was talking to himself, 'You're so slender. I'd probably snap you like a twig.'

His smile died – he stared at me, that unmistakable, brown-eyed stare. I felt my lips part, almost imperceptibly. I looked away. I smiled at the wall, then looked back and, yes, of course, he was smiling too and I felt dizzy with lust, wildly happy and very confused. 'Your front teeth are slightly longer than your canines,' I said. 'Has anyone ever told you that?'

'Is that good or bad?'

I finally located the biro, which had managed to slip between two sheets of paper. I made another note, closed his file, then looked at him and said something I had wanted to say to him ever since we first met that time in a pub, all those years ago. 'My name is Laura.'

3

We had sex that evening, up against a tree in the park. I had never done it on a first date before. I had never had sex like that on any sort of date – the boys I had gone out with previously were nothing like David. Physiotherapists tend to attract men who want mothering – and nothing could have been further from David Needham's mind.

After we had finished the professional part of our encounter, in my consulting room that afternoon, David looked at his watch and said, 'What time can you get out of here?'

'Five o'clock,' I replied.

'I'll wait in Reception,' he said, rose from his chair and left. Most men would have suggested it, rather than stating it. Most men would have waited outside the building, or arranged to meet me somewhere else entirely. He knew what he wanted. He didn't care what anyone thought.

At two minutes past five, we got into my car, parked behind the hospital. I felt a vague unease, based entirely on social propriety, that I might somehow lose face if we went straight back to my flat. 'I'm going to take you to my local,' I said, as I started the engine. 'Does great chips. That's if you're sure you don't have to go back to work?' I glanced behind me, began to reverse the car slowly.

'I rang my office and told them I was in a lot of discomfort and wouldn't be coming back today,' he replied, taking my hand from the steering wheel and placing it on his groin, so that I could feel his erection through his trousers. 'Which is absolutely true.'

I braked. It was still light outside. I glanced around the car park to make sure that none of my colleagues were within sight, then leaned over and kissed him on mouth. His lips parted immediately. My tongue grazed the hard-wet enamel of his teeth for a fraction of a second before I pulled back, squeezed his erection lightly, then withdrew my hand and returned my attention to reversing the car.

'*Fuck . . .*' he whispered under his breath, sitting back in his seat. I was grinning hugely, unable to believe my own daring. At that point, it was a toss-up which I was enjoying more – his blatant lust or the sheer surprise of my own. I have never behaved like this before, I thought delightedly, as I drove us to the pub.

We got mildly drunk together on a great deal more than alcohol. We clutched each other's thighs beneath the table. We kissed, in open view of the other drinkers. We fed each other chips. Halfway through the evening, his mobile phone rang repeatedly – he didn't answer but I could hear it in his pocket.

'Do you need to get that?' I said, on the third ring. He shook his head. When it rang a fourth time, he extracted the phone and, without looking at it, turned it off, then smiled at me. 'Let's go,' he said, softly, reaching out his hand, then placing it gently on the side of my head, just touching my hair. After all his hard flirting, his directness, the tenderness of the gesture made me melt.

I was over the limit so we left my car parked in the street and walked back to my flat. It was his idea to take a short cut through the park. The angle was difficult. He had to hold up one of my legs with his forearm hooked beneath my knee and bend his own knees, then guide himself in. Even though it was only autumn, the temperature had plummeted during the evening. My coat and dress were hitched up around my waist. I was wearing opaque black tights. He tore a hole in them. Later, I found pieces of bark inside my knickers. I was shivering with cold and the fear of discovery by passing youths or dog-walk-ers, so much that I couldn't come. He withdrew just in time and, with a deft hand gesture, came over his trousers. He kissed me ferociously and said he was sending me the dry-cleaning bill. The whole encounter was clumsy and only partially satis-fying and drove me lunatic with desire when I thought about it afterwards.

The early days of David were delightful and feverish and, also, a kind of hell. I thought about him incessantly. I thought about him so much I felt nauseous sometimes, drunk with it. I would think of him even while I was talking to him, even while we debated, in a desultory fashion, whether or not to see a film or just get something to eat. I wanted him even while I was having him: having him wasn't enough. My desire for him was so raw I was reduced to masturbating in the shower. I took to doodling his initials on bits of paper at work. If no paper was available, I wrote them on my hand. I thought about his haunches – an unprofessional word for an unprofessional as-sessment of that part of his body; part thigh-bone, part but-tock, part muscle where it tensed against me. The word took on a sickening allure: *haunches*. Most people think it's buttocks that do the thrusting, the gluteal muscles. In fact, it's the piri-formis, two small muscles deep inside the buttocks that join the hips to the legs. Male lecturers at university always took great pleasure in demonstrating the action of the piriformis muscles in front of female students. *Haunches*, though, a col-lective noun, and one that had appropriately animal implica-tions – there were two of them, the haunches, and two hands, two eyes – the eyes, the stare, the stare he gave when he held my head between his two large hands, immovable. Round and round they went, my thoughts of him. I wore out my images of him and then had to see him again to get a fresh set, only to find the old ones coming back again the minute we were apart, tumbling together and breaking apart like the shards of colour in a kaleidoscope. I would stop, in the middle of writing a report on one of my elderly patients, my pen lifted, momentarily confused that I was there, at my desk, writing a report, and not with him. My colleagues kept asking me if anything was wrong.

It was hard not to pester him – I knew enough of him and men in general to realise that would send him running for the hills. So instead I was left, day after day, with my fantasies and my longings and the sick little feeling I felt inside, all the time, at the memory of the way he held my head still while he kissed me. I never once chased him. I waited for him to call me, and when he did, I always experienced a small shock at the casualness of his tone. 'Hey you, how are you?' he would say. Was it possible he didn't realise how much I had been thinking of him? And I would respond, equally casual, 'Fine, how are you?' and be doubly shocked at myself. He's just a man, I would say to myself, while we exchanged news. He gets up in the morning, he showers and shaves and eats breakfast, and the rest of it. There are a million other men like him in the world. It's ludicrous to make him into something special: what do you know of him except he has a nice line in banter and fucks like an express train? So what?

He liked to put his hands in my hair when we made love, to hold my head still so that he could stare into my eyes. 'Give yourself to me,' he said once, fiercely, and I stared up at him baffled – we were having sex, what did he think I was doing? He hated it if he thought I was holding anything back.

I hated him sometimes, too – he drove me crazy, sometimes; often. I hated the way he would end a phone call abruptly if it occurred to him there was something else he should be doing. 'Listen, I'll call you later,' he would say, almost mid-sentence, then hang up. If he was busy, his definition of 'later' could stretch to several days. I tried it on him once. He got cross. He didn't like to hear about ex-boyfriends of mine. That made him cross too. He changed the subject irritably and was grumpy for a good hour or two – but he would have died before he admitted he was possessive. Once, in the early days, I caught him with my mobile phone in his hand, punching buttons with his thumb.

'What are you doing?' I asked.

'Checking what ringtones you've got,' he replied. 'You've had that one for ages.' Just before he turned away, I saw that he was flicking through my call log. I should have been worried or offended – if any of my previous boyfriends had done it, I would have gone berserk – but instead, and this bothered me, I was pleased, flattered.

He had very good table manners – for a large man, his movements were surprisingly small and neat. He had a strange grace. I never saw him drop anything, or trip over, whereas I did both all the time. He had no physical tics or mannerisms that I could discern and teased me mercilessly when I flicked my hair. He only moved if there was a purpose to the movement, yet beneath his apparent stillness was a sense of coiled energy. He asked questions all the time. I never saw him bored.

He was only half Welsh, on his mother's side, but in terms of his personal mythology it loomed far larger than half. He had grown up in a small coastal town not far from Aberystwyth but his family moved to Eastley when he was thirteen, where he promptly got into fights with English boys as soon as he opened his mouth. His accent was slight but became more pronounced when he was angry or felt threatened. He followed Welsh football matches, although he was indifferent to rugby. He teased me about being posh because of my English accent, which annoyed me because there had been a lot more spare cash floating around his childhood than mine.

When his mind was elsewhere, it was pointless trying to get

his attention. 'I'm task-orientated,' he said loftily, when I complained to him. We were in bed at the time. I groaned out loud and put a pillow over my face. 'What?' he said. 'What?'

Just before he had an orgasm, he would swear profusely, which I found amusing, although I was careful never to tell him that.

'There's only one way to make sure a boy's family likes you,' my mother had told me when I was still a gawky adolescent, 'and that's to make sure they didn't like the girlfriend that came before you.' Her face was becoming expressionless by then, the muscles increasingly immobile, speech slurred. She stared a lot. She rarely blinked. I had to remember how her face moved when she used to speak and add a layer of animation over her demeanour, along with volume to her words, a smile.

I was invited to meet David's family at a large gathering to celebrate the seventieth birthday of a favourite aunt, Lorraine. David had one sibling but an inordinate number of aunts and uncles and cousins who had formed an established Welsh enclave in Eastley long before his family arrived. It was winter, we had arrived after dark, sleet was falling softly. The world looked good but felt bitter. We had been on the doorstep in the cold, ringing the bell repeatedly, for some minutes, huddled together beneath the yellow light above the porch. Music was thumping from the bay window of the sitting room at the front of the house but the curtains were closed. David said if there was no answer in a minute he was going to bang on the window even though it would mean trampling a flowerbed.

At that point, Aunt Lorraine flung the door open saying, 'Yes, yes, all right . . .' Seeing it was us, she stood back to make a careful appraisal. She nodded once, leaned forward and hissed, 'You'll do very nicely,' before grabbing my arm and pulling me inside.

Then she turned to David, still on the doorstep, and declared, 'But you can piss off, boy!' and slammed the door in his face. I saw his expression just before the door closed and guessed that this was a joke played many times before and one he found excruciating. I, on the other hand, had had a large gin and tonic on an empty stomach in the pub before we came and thought it rather funny – mad, but funny.

Lorraine's hallway was decked with foil streamers. She was a hefty woman in beige, her face alight with a beamy smile. She cackled affectedly and pushed at my arm. I heard merry laughter from above and looked up to see that an uncle was descending the stairs, zipping his flies and ho-ho-ho-ing like Father Christmas. Lorraine linked her arm with mine and, leaving David on the doorstep, pulled me towards the sitting room, which bulged with people, noise and cigarette smoke. She flung the door wide and pushed me into a large number of coloured balloons and curious faces. The furniture and decor were lost behind the faces and balloons. 'Here she is!' Lorraine shouted above the music.

Before I could speak, another aunt was upon me. 'Ooh, let's take a look at you, girl, we've all been waiting.' I felt her fingers plucking at my coat sleeve. 'Well, you're a big improvement on the last one, I must say.' She leaned in close to me. Her breath smelt of gherkins. 'Wore a lot of synthetic fibres, did the last one.'

David was at my elbow. He didn't look amused. 'Leave her alone until she's got her coat off,' he grumbled.

Someone thrust a drink into my hand. 'Try this punch. It's disgusting.'

David removed it from my hand and said in my ear. 'Kitchen. Now.'

In the kitchen, he turned to me and said drily, 'God, they get more like a bad sitcom every time but hey, you're a hit and you haven't even opened your mouth yet.' He pulled at the fridge door, which resisted, relented. He took out a bottle of wine.

'What was wrong with the last one?' I asked, equally drily, sliding my coat off my shoulders, looking around for somewhere to hang it, then dropping it over the back of a kitchen chair. We had been going out for three months – I had just started counting in months rather than weeks. I longed to stop being sardonic with him. Why were we still wisecracking in private – in public, yes, but between ourselves? When could I stop pretending I felt less than I did? When would the signal come from him and how would I recognise it?

He rolled his eyes. 'She was an accountant. She had a voice like this . . .' He pinched his nostrils together and made a nasal sound.

'Stuck-up little cow,' said Lorraine as she blustered into the kitchen carrying a blue, oval-shaped platter, empty but for a few wisps of flaky pastry. 'We were terrified our David was going to marry her.' She pronounced his name the Welsh way, Dav-*eed*. She dumped the platter in the sink, on top of what was there already, and picked up another, full platter from the counter top, whisking off some cling film to reveal a neat arrangement of tiny withered samosas with cherry tomatoes dotted between. 'Thank God she got wise to him before that.' She handed it to me. 'You know what they say about Welshmen, don't you, girl? They make wonderful fathers cos they're such children themselves, but terrible husbands mind.' She turned away, then said over her shoulder, 'Be a love and take that through for me. I've still got the spring rolls in the oven. They'll be hot, anyway, even if that lot isn't.'

I understood this was a test and did as I was bid, pulling a face at David as I passed him with the platter in my hands.

As we left the house, three hours later, David slung his arm around my waist and pulled me in so close he made me squirm, digging his fingertips into me. 'You were great!' he murmured, and bit my ear. I was a bit drunk, a bit tired, and wondered if this was it, the signal – I had met his family and I had passed. I wasn't a stuck-up cow and I didn't wear too many synthetic fibres. Now we were a couple in public, so to speak, could we be one in private too? I wasn't afraid of eccentricity. Having always considered myself something of an oddball, I had found it easy to take his large, voluble family in my stride. Previous girlfriends from nice, nuclear families had found them all somewhat intimidating, I later gathered, had been put off by the smoking and shouting and occasional outbursts of anti-English sentiment. Those family gatherings were always on the edge of chaos. I had known from the first moment I had met David that he was chronically impulsive, giving of himself and self-centred in equal measure, and used to being indulged – now I had seen him in the context of his extended family, it made perfect sense.

Later, I came to love them, the aunts and uncles – even his parents who were probably the most restrained of the lot, and his sister who was four years older than him and married with three children and rarely spoke except to be even more sardonic than her brother. A whole family; and they swallowed me whole.

We had walked only a few hundred yards from Lorraine's house when David stopped suddenly in the middle of the icy pavement, turned to me, and looked at me as if he had just realised his pocket had been picked and suspected me of being the culprit. I looked back at him, thinking he was about to tell me he had left something behind at the house, or that his lower back had gone again.

He shook his head a little, then strode off down the road, leaving me to trot after him in the cold. He always walked at a ferocious pace. I caught up with him and pushed my arm through his – he had his hands shoved deep into his pockets. I peered round and up at his face, questioningly, but he ignored me and was silent the rest of the way home. When we got back to my tiny, two-room flat he wouldn't take his coat off. He sat slumped in an armchair while I made us both tea in the kitchenette, glancing at him from time to time as I tried to work out what was wrong. When I handed him the mug, he took it without comment and drank it in silence. I sat down in the opposite chair with my own mug and did the same, waiting for him to explain. I was expecting him to stay the night – he usually did – but all at once, he rose from the armchair, took his mug into the kitchenette and emptied the remaining contents into the sink. He rinsed it and turned it upside-down on the drainer. He came over to where I sat, stooped and kissed the top of my head – very tenderly, as you would do a child – then left.

Up until then we had spoken most days, but after that, I didn't hear from him for a fortnight.

My mother hated me going for walks on the cliffs. 'Cliffs crumble,' she said, and I whooped at her and said it sounded like a pop singer who sang novelty songs: Cliff Crumble. 'You may laugh,' she said, wagging her head, 'but the people who were in that cottage didn't think it was so funny, did they?' She was referring to an event that took place in 1953. A chunk fell off one of the cliffs and half of the cottage that was sitting on the chunk went with it. A photograph appeared in the newspapers afterwards and it still shows up on the cover of local history pamphlets in the library: a black and white shot – often given a sepia wash in the pamphlets – showing a wonky cottage with a wall missing and the sitting room open to the elements: a standard lamp, a sofa, flowered wallpaper. 'The people who were in that cottage didn't laugh.' In actual fact, the owners had had plenty of warning of the danger and were nowhere near at the time but this remark was typical of my mother who saw danger everywhere. One morning, she had looked up from her breakfast cereal to see her husband slumped on the kitchen table, dead from a heart attack at the age of fifty-six. One minute, she had been eating Weetabix – or whatever it was my mother had for breakfast – while I was asleep in my pram and my milk bottles sterilising in a bucket of diluted chemicals – and then the next, she was a widow. Cliffs crumble. Cars crash. Tree branches give way and stair carpets turn maliciously shiny beneath small, hurrying feet. It was amazing she let me out of the front door.

Later, when she was ill and I was her carer, she had no choice. Once a week, when the district nurse was there or when a neighbour popped in, I would pull on my old pair of trainers, the ones with the broken laces, and head up to the cliffs.

Cliffs crumble. David and I went up to the cliffs a lot in the early days of our relationship. Our first encounter, against the tree in the park, turned out to be a portent. He liked outdoor sex – he liked it a lot. Outdoors had never been my thing, particularly, but I was so crazed about him I probably would have done it on a bench in the High Street if he'd asked me.

Our clifftop walks answered both our needs. I would stride along and let the cold wind numb my face, and think of the sense of freedom I felt when I went there as an adolescent and marvel that here I was now, a grown-up, feeling freedom in an opposite kind of joy, trapped by my glorious obsession with David, loving my imprisonment. And half an hour or so into our walk, when we were high above the town with open fields on our left and the great grey heft of the English Channel to our right, David would hustle me behind a rock or fence and I would laugh and protest until the moment when I fell silent with the seriousness of it, rendered mute by the intensity of his desire and loving his desire so much my own hardly counted. Truly there was nothing better: the moments when this man that I wanted so badly wanted me even more badly in return.

*

He didn't ring me for a fortnight and during that fortnight I came to the conclusion, quite naturally, that I had been dumped. I resisted ringing him myself more out of pride than judgement. I couldn't believe that he didn't even have the courage to call me and tell me he had finished with me – I was furious and, in my fury, certain that my mourning for him was as good as done. When he eventually rang, I would be able to be suitably cool.

It was a Saturday morning. I knew it was him calling as soon as my mobile vibrated in the pocket of my jeans. There was no one else who would ring me on a Saturday morning. I contemplated screening his call even as I slipped the phone out of my pocket and raised it to my ear. 'Dodgson, hey Dodgson, it's me . . .' He liked to call me by my surname, a legacy of the boys' grammar school he had attended, where, after he had stood up to the boys who tried to punch him for his accent, he had thrived. He liked to use my initials too. LD. Disbelievingly, I heard myself say, 'Hi . . .' in a seductive, luxurious tone, as if I was languishing on my sofa dressed in a negligee and furry mules, twisting a string of pearls between my fingers.

'Fancy a walk on the cliffs, Dodgson?' I glanced outside the window, where a wild wind shook at the fragile panes of glass. I had just come back from a trip to the newsagents and was planning a cup of coffee and three biscuits with the weekend newspaper and the gas fire on maximum. I was still wearing my hooded fleece and parka. 'Sure,' I said. 'Yeah, okay.'

We met at the end of the esplanade where the cliffs took a rash swoop upwards, away from town, at an incline sharp enough to discourage both the very young and very old – on a day like this we would have the cliffs to ourselves. David was there first. He was wearing his big old suede jacket and a beanie hat. The middle button on the jacket was dangling by a thread, about to fall. It had been like that for as long as I had known him. He looked pale and handsome, a little tired – there were slight bags beneath his eyes. We stared at each other as we approached and I had time to appreciate, consciously and openly, what I loved about him, this man – the opacity of him, a mercurial mixture of pride and insecurity, a capacity for hiding things twinned with a terror of not being found. Here he was, this man, and that was all he was, and his life had collided with mine when we could so easily have never met, and I knew then that I loved him because of his faults, not in spite of them, and that I would no more change an ounce of him than sew that middle button back on his coat. It came to me that he had been involved with someone else when he and I met – I remembered those phone calls in the pub – and that he had not been open with me, and that he had discarded her, perhaps only recently, and that a similar fate would probably be mine, and that I didn't care: I felt the swoop and fall of all this and knew I was in bigger trouble than I had ever been in my life.

He smiled as I neared him. My stomach folded. All the reproaches I had been saving up for the last fortnight seemed childish and petulant. He held out his hand as I drew close and I extended mine. He took my hand firmly in his and pulled me after him as we turned to walk up the steep incline. We took wide strides, panting, layered in clothing and beaten by the wind. When I opened my mouth, the cold air snatched the breath from it. The sky above was hard white.

At the top of the incline, the walk was open to the elements. There was no fence between the path and the cliff and occasionally a tourist took a tumble from it; sometimes accidentally, sometimes not. Our coastal stretch was not picturesque but we were widely acknowledged as the best place for miles to come and top yourself. As David and I climbed higher, we reached the part of the walk where the cliff sloped up in crazed, jutting plates – the scrubby grass went right up to the edge, as if a hill had decided to stop mid-air. Further on, the walk levelled out and you could see over the edge but the early, irregular parts of the cliff were particularly hazardous because of the overhang. To our left was farmland. Sheep were grazing on the sloping field that led down to the river, the chill wind ruffling their dirty-white wool coats. To our right, the world swooped upwards and ended with improbable suddenness in sky.

David was striding hard. He had such long legs our gaits were out of step. I stumbled on the uneven grass. I let his hand drop and moved away from him a little, not meaning anything in particular, just making myself more comfortable to walk. He stopped and looked at me. I stopped too. He appeared to be about to speak, then changed his mind and continued walking. I followed, a little behind.

He said something to me, but the wind caught his words and I didn't hear properly, something about my kitchen.

'What?' I said, raising my voice.

He turned to me. The expression on his face was irritable. 'I said, you know, girl, I think it's just a bit peculiar that you're so keen on washing up but you never wipe the surfaces.'

'What?' I laughed.

He leaned forward and grabbed me by the arms, bending me backwards. 'Think it's funny, do you?' he said, mock-menacing.

Mock-menacing was his habitual manner before sex. It was foreplay, and a shared joke. When I wanted sex I behaved mock-defiantly, in a way I knew would provoke it.

'You and whose army?' I shouted above the wind, derisively.

'That's it!' he yelled. 'You're the bane of my life, you're going over!' He slung one arm beneath me and wrenched me off-balance.

This, too, was a joke he had pulled several times on our walks together, grabbing me and dragging me towards the cliff edge. David had inherited his Aunt Lorraine's love of robust physical comedy. Pretending he was going to throw me off the cliff was a prank he never tired of. He was also fond of pointing at a button on my jacket, mid-conversation, then flicking my nose with his finger when I looked down. This always made me smile, no matter how often he did it. When I got wise to the pointing-at-the-button trick, he would invent new ways of getting me to look down; telling me I had a mark on my shirt, asking me about my brooch. It delighted him when I fell for it.

Before, on the clifftop, I had always shrieked in alarm quickly enough to make him stop: but that day, something was different. Perhaps I had heard the joke once too often, or I was simply in a provocative mood after his neglect because instead of shrieking for mercy I yelled into the wind, 'I'll take you over with me!' I wanted to push him, to see how far he would go, to unsettle him after his fortnight of silence.

He pulled me right up to the cliff's edge, where it sloped sharply upwards and there was a dangerous overhang. Even then, I let him do it, thinking still that it was the old joke, that it meant nothing – but as we reached the edge and the first tickle of real alarm fluttered in my stomach, he did something he had never done before. With one swift movement of his arms and shoulders, he spun me round, so that instead of holding me face to face, he was grasping me from behind, both arms wrapped round me at chest height and holding my arms pinioned to my side. He bent forward, so that I had to bend forward too – and I could see right over the edge, to where the waves heaved and chopped against the rocky shore and the brown foam frothed beneath us. There were great, jagged lumps of concrete dumped among the rocks at this part of the coast, deposited years ago to protect the bottom of the cliffs from erosion. They were as big as cars, their corners and edges pointing menacingly upwards. If you went over at this point, you wouldn't stand a chance. Your skull would split as easily as an eggshell.

I let out a cry of fear, real fear, out into the freezing wind and air, and shrieked his name – I was dangling, completely off-balance, as helpless as a puppet, with only his weight behind me as counterbalance. I couldn't believe how reckless he was being. Beneath us, the waves leapt and broke apart over the concrete blocks, grey beneath but slimy with algae. The sea smelt acrid. Gulls shrieked and dived above us.

'Scared?' he yelled into my ear. 'Are you scared? You should be, LD!'

'David! David!' I hollered. 'Oh my God, we'll go over!' He didn't know the cliffs as well as I did. He was misjudging the overhang. For the first time since I had known him, it came to me that there was a touch of real lunacy in him – a lack of caution that could not be explained by impetuosity, a small link or wire missing in his brain in the place where most people tempered their impulses with the knowledge of the effect those impulses had on others.

Then, just at the point when I was departing from him in my head, baulking at my own collusion with his behaviour, he straightened and pulled back from the edge. 'We are, we are . . .' he said. He wasn't yelling any more. He still had his arms wrapped tight around me from behind. His face was buried in my hair. When he spoke, his voice was broken. I heard his words through my hair. 'We're going over. I've decided. Okay, okay?'

He pulled me back, away from the cliff edge, and turned me to him, then held me out at arm's length. I was shuddering from the cold, from fear, from disbelief. There was a moment when we stared at each other – him still holding me away from him. I gazed back, a question in my look. He gave the smallest of nods. I burst into tears.

He drew his head back, laughed at me, suddenly the old David again. He pushed me away from him, then grabbed me again and gave me a small shake. 'It's not supposed to make you *cry*, LD, it's supposed to make you *happy*!'

If the overhang had given way that moment and dropped us both into the sea, I think my last thought would have been that it was worth it.

My mother got her wish. She lived to see me settled. She was wheelchair-bound by then and unable to speak. She sat at the top table, next to me. One of the nurses from the home came with her to look after her, a young black guy called Ken who mashed her salmon with a fork and chatted to her in a strong Glaswegian accent while he spooned it down her. He was a patronising boy but sweet enough. He had God, big time, and took my mother very seriously.

After the speeches, one of David's uncles stepped forward with a clarinet and played a passable version of 'Stranger on the Shore'. David took my hand and pulled me on to the dance floor, a square of parquet tiling around which the tables were arranged, in a room at the back of the Milton Hotel; white tablecloths, heavy chintz curtains, the doorways and light-fittings festooned with broad ribbons tied in bows. Like most rooms in most hotels, it was overheated. The air was heavy with the scent of Aunt Lorraine's musky perfume, mixed with a hint of the cigars David's father and a friend had been smoking outside on the patio just before the speeches began. All day, I had been waiting to feel disappointed, waiting for a sense of anti-climax, but instead, all I felt as David pulled me towards him was an enormous and satisfied feeling of exhaustion. I allowed myself to be pulled in, folding into him and laying my head on his shoulder. He wrapped his hand around mine and held it against his chest, then bent and kissed my head. 'I love you, Laura,' he whispered: no sarcasm, no wit – a statement of fact, private and simple. The aunts and uncles slowly joined the dance around us and the wheezing clarinettist wheezed tunefully on. I closed my eyes, and let David lead me in a slow shuffle. Ken the nurse was pushing my mother in a gentle orbit around us. David held me close against his chest, as if nothing in the world would ever hurt me again. I couldn't believe he was mine at last.

PART 2

After

PART 2

4

Three days after my daughter has gone away; my house is full of people. I find I am thinking of Ranmali incessantly and praying she will not come to the house. Ranmali was the last person to see Betty alive.

Ranmali and her husband have run the newsagents on Fulton Avenue for as long as I can remember. It is the nearest shop to school and stocks milk and bread along with sweets and newspapers, so most of us local mothers see Ranmali several times a week. If we aren't dashing in at 3.25 p.m. to grab a necessity or two, we are ambling in at 3.40 p.m., distractedly attempting to calm our offspring as they shove and bump each other beside the El Dorado of the ice-cream cabinet. Ranmali is tiny, with a smile wide enough to plump her cheeks. 'Good afternoon,' she always says formally, with a nod, and although I know her name I cannot remember when I learned it and am sure she does not know mine. I am simply one of the herd of mothers who pass through, minds elsewhere. Lots of shops round here have signs in the window, *no more than two schoolchildren at any one time*, or *no unaccompanied children*. Ranmali seems to welcome the noisy gangs that descend on her every weekday afternoon – to me they seem more alarming than a crowd of drunks after closing time. She must know that the older boys lift stuff, from time to time. Maybe she thinks that is the price she has to pay, an occupational hazard. Maybe she likes children – she doesn't seem to have any of her own. Her smile never falters.

Her husband is a different matter. While Ranmali serves behind the counter, he comes out from the back room to stand

and watch us all, arms folded, grim-faced. I have said hello to Ranmali for many years but I still haven't a clue what her husband is called. We are all a little afraid of him.

It is not Ranmali's fault that her shop is immediately after the sharp corner where Fulton Road bends irrationally and becomes an avenue. It is not her fault that a driver came around the corner at that particular moment but all the same, I cannot bear to see her. She was there. Perhaps she cradled my daughter's head on her lap. Perhaps she fell on her knees in the road beside her, hands lifted palms upwards in the air. Maybe she stood by, for a moment or two, gazing down, then looked around wildly and screamed for her husband. Perhaps she stroked Betty's face. I have imagined the scene with a thousand different variations. Ranmali's presence is one of the few facts I have and therefore the only constant in my imaginings. My daughter, lying in the road: I should have been there, but Ranmali was there instead.

I know that the driver was a man. I know he has been questioned and that he was not drunk and that an investigation is under way. I do not want to know any more, for I know enough to know he is not human – he is no more animate than a bolt of lightning. He did not exist until his life collided with that of my daughter.

My house is full of people. I think about Ranmali. I think about her smiling face, transformed as she ran out of her shop after hearing the screech of brakes and a thump. Perhaps she was looking out of her window at the time. Perhaps she saw Willow being flung on to the grass verge and cannot now get the image out of her head. I think of Ranmali crying in her flat above the shop, unable to cook for her husband, rocking in a chair. I wonder if their shop is still open for business, if the other mothers fall quiet as they enter. Toni has told me people have been laying flowers on the pavement outside. I am not sure how I feel about this but think I am, in some oblique way, affronted. Toni has said she will take me to see the flowers whenever I feel ready.

Toni, Antonia Saunders, is the blonde policewoman who broke the news to me. After she took me home that night, she sat at my kitchen table with a cup of tea and explained that I would be appointed a family liaison officer who would guide me through the procedures that followed.

I looked at her. 'I want you,' I said.

Gently, she explained to me that it was usual for the family liaison officer to be someone different from the person who brought the news to a family's door. 'I'm not FLO-trained,' she added.

The acronym reminded me of my professional life – the NHS, an organisation that would collapse in a puddle of tax-payers' pennies were it not for acronyms. 'This *FLO-training*,' I said, 'how long is it?'

She gave a small, tight smile. 'Six days,' she said softly.

'I want you,' I repeated.

'I'll speak to my Inspector,' she said. 'We're a small unit out here.' I wasn't sure whether she meant that they were short-staffed as a result, or whether she was close enough to her Inspector to get what she wanted.

I didn't tell her the real reason why I wanted her: it wasn't in spite of the fact that she had brought the news to my door, it was because of it. She and the young male officer together formed the bridge I had just crossed, from my old life with Betty in it to the new, unimaginable one without her. Bridges can be crossed both ways.

My house is full of people but Toni is the only person I can bear. I am neurotically attached to her. She has given me her mobile phone number, along with an explanation that it will be turned off when she is off-shift, but she is around a lot anyway. I find her vastly preferable to the people who know and care for me, who have filled my house. David is here all day but leaves at night to go back to Chloe and the baby. He plays with Rees a lot. Rees understands only that Betty is not around and that lots of people have come to be with him so he won't be lonely. There is a lot of food in the kitchen, so as far as he is concerned, the atmosphere is festive. He is enjoying the attention.

Julie from across the road has taken charge of my kitchen, which is the hub of activity in a busy house. When friends and neighbours come with food in plastic tubs or Pyrex dishes – which they do a lot – she labels it and puts it in the fridge. Mrs Cracknell, a widow from the end of the road, sits at the kitchen table dressed in the sort of dark brown dress my mother would have called a frock, wringing a hanky in her lap. Julie gives her tasks from time to time out of kindness – making hot drinks usually. We all drink hot drink after hot drink: tea, coffee, herbal infusions. Some of them, I don't even recognise the taste. I drink whatever I am given – the hotter the better as I am frozen to the core – but I cannot eat a thing. Between them, Julie and Mrs Cracknell run a well-organised outfit, dealing with the physical needs of our many visitors. I might feel a vague sense of gratitude were it not for my low-level but persistent anger that anyone is in the house at all. These people are here because Betty is gone. I want them gone and Betty back.

My role in all this activity is simply to exist, to breathe and to carry on breathing. That is all that is expected from me as I move from room to room. If I go up the stairs, for instance, and meet someone such as Aunt Lorraine descending, she flattens herself against the wall and allows me to pass without comment. When David's father comes into the hallway from the kitchen and sees me standing there alone, in front of the mirror, he stops, then turns and goes back into the kitchen, even though he has his coat on and is clearly attempting to leave the house, as if I am an empress whose frown holds mortal sway, someone to be skirted with great care. Once in a while my son, wearying of the attentions of others, approaches me and clambers on my lap, or comes and stands next to me and hugs my legs. When he does this, I am aware of the other people in the room watching surreptitiously, holding their breath almost, as if I am made of glass and Rees's fleeting but ardent affection might shatter me. At such times, I want to scream at them all to *fuck off*. But there is no energy for screaming. There is no energy for anything except the motions of the day; sit in a chair in one room, sit in a chair in the other; drink the hot drink I am given and ignore the food on a plate before me.

At night, there are fewer people but there are always several who stay over. The Empress must not be left alone. I sleep in Betty's bed now, as I have done since the night I came back from the hospital, her duvet with the overblown purple flowers on it tucked tight around me and her impressively various zoo of soft toys lined across the foot of the bed. My bed, which I cannot bear to lie on, is available for guests. Aunt Lorraine uses it sometimes. Often, someone sleeps downstairs as well, sometimes David's sister Ceri, sometimes Julie or another neighbour. The spare duvet is rolled up each morning and stuffed behind the sofa. Someone has brought round extra pillows. I lie awake at night, staring at the plastic glow-in-the-dark stars on Betty's ceiling, imagining that I am her. During the day, I want nothing but sleep.

Apart from the regular visitors, there are people who come only once, and those are the people I hate most of all. They come for their own reasons, all needing affirmation from me, wanting to touch the hem of my garment. Sally, Willow's mother, is one of them. She is in the kitchen when I descend mid-morning, three days after what has happened. I stand in the doorway and stare at her. She comes to me and holds out her arms. I stay stock still while she puts those arms – her fat, hot arms – around me.

I realise something is expected of me, so I say, 'How is Willow?'

Sally steps back from me and has the nerve to look coy. 'She's still on the special ward, the one where they . . .'

'The HDU,' I say.

'Yes, the High Dependency Unit, they just want to make sure.'

I look at Sally's round, owlish face, with her big blue eyes all wide and open, stretched alarmingly with the effort of not saying anything inappropriate.

Still alive then, is what I want to say, *on the HDU all strapped up with drips and whatnot and next to the nurses' desk where they can keep a close eye, but still alive.* They don't allow parents to sleep on put-you-ups in the HDU. They have to keep the spaces next to the beds clear in case they need to bring in a crash team unexpectedly, so the parents with the most ill children get the least sleep, but still it's better than having your child in intensive care. I can picture my Betty in the HDU. I can picture how annoyed I would get having to sleep in a chair beside her bed and be woken up every few minutes by the nurses' chatter at the desk, how I would plead for her discharge, not realising how lucky I am, how much worse it could have been.

I look at Sally oozing sympathy and think, I've never liked you. We were only friends because our daughters were friends, and now everyone will think I avoid you because my daughter has been taken away and yours hasn't but actually it's because I never liked you in the first place and it's a relief not to have to pretend I do. I turn away, stiffly, and Sally gazes at me as I turn, her face open and distressed, and if I had the energy I would punch her with a closed fist.

Then comes the horror of Betty's funeral. It comes in a series of pictures: Aunt Lorraine and Julie dressing me in my bedroom, like a doll, buttoning my blue jacket and slipping on the kitten-heeled shoes I have only ever worn for job interviews – they have silver bows on the front, so even though they are black, I think of them as my silver shoes. Then, the town is passing by on the drive to the crematorium, the world unnaturally hushed from the inside of our sleek, sealed car. There is a single cloud in the sky. A boy cycles along a pavement sitting upright, with his arms crossed. All is quiet as we drive yet at the same time it is obvious that for others, outside the car, normal life is continuing. Two women walk down the street. They cross the road when we pull up at the lights. Other people drive past in other cars: talking, laughing, as if nothing is wrong. Then we are inside the crematorium and the next picture is the procession of the coffin. Why white? Why not blue, or purple – colours that she liked? I hate the white. I can't understand why everyone seems to require so little of me. David stands next to me, his brother-in-law on the other side, like bodyguards. David's sister holds her own children and cries. Chloe has come with the baby and is two rows behind, weeping audibly, in bits. David's parents are in the row between me and Chloe, alongside Aunt Lorraine, who is holding Rees on her lap. I want him on my lap but he seems all right where he is. Tears run down my cheeks throughout but I do not sob, I do not give way. It is an event that has nothing to do with my daughter. It is an intoned series of references to someone who is in a white box with gilt handles and who lived life to the full, apparently. I have grasped that Betty has gone but it is as if she has been vaporised. This ceremony is hell, but a hell for no reason, unconnected with the girl I loved and what has happened to her. It is just something to be got through so that I can get back to thinking about Betty. When I pray, and I do, I pray merely for this appalling charade to be over.

We emerge from the crematorium to bright sunshine. It was raining when we went in but now a glow lights the wet tarmac of the car park. We have been ushered out of the side door. On the other side of the car park, near the front, strangers are getting out of their cars in preparation for the cremation that follows hard on the heels of Betty's. They are hurrying, slamming car doors, straightening ties, already late. Our crowd – and it is a large crowd – stand around for a minute, blinking in the sun. Rees has come to me and taken my hand. A flock of gulls wheels high above us, sudden and shrieking. The racket punctures the mild sky and our collective mood. Everyone looks around.

'What do we do now?' I am not addressing the question to anyone in particular but David and Robert are still either side of me. David says, 'We're going back,' and for one brief, ludicrous moment I think he means back in time. Several of our party turn and walk slowly towards their cars.

All at once I feel unwilling to leave. Shallow as the ceremony was, it was one more loosening thread of the ties that bound me to Betty, one more unravelling. The end of it marks another small step that takes me further away from my girl and toward my life without her. I look up at the clear, open sky, then around, and the bright sun and iridescent puddles con me into a moment of euphoria, as if the worst is over. It is a cruel trick, for within a moment or two, as I stand there small and helpless, it clouds over again. I begin to shiver. Without speaking, David and I turn to follow the others back towards the cars. Our sleek vehicle awaits, and a man in a uniform who will open the door without looking at us.

As we walk towards the car, I see a group of women, all dressed in black, standing at the edge of the car park, on the far side. I assume they are here for the next cremation but they are not heading into the building. They are staring at us. There are four of them, two middle-aged, one elderly, one young. The older one is short and fat, the others tall and hefty – black-haired, pale. The younger one is clutching a bunch of small white flowers. When they notice me staring back, the younger whispers to the others and, in unison, they cast their gazes down. David has taken me by the arm and is guiding me into the car. I crane my head to look at them but for as long as it takes me to be helped into the back seat and buckled in, to have my seatbelt fastened and for the car to be started and driven away slowly – for that whole time, the women stay with their heads bowed, motionless. It is only as we pull down the drive towards the tall, wrought-iron gates that one of the middle-aged ones raises her head and watches our departure, her face expressionless.

5

After Betty's funeral, people begin, gradually, to leave me in peace. Aunt Lorraine stops sleeping over but still rings me every day and leaves a cheery message, almost always referring to how cold it is outside. David rings daily too, asking after Rees. David's mother rings less often and after a fortnight I say, 'Gillian, it's good of you to keep calling but I'm okay, really.' Julie still comes round every morning to take Rees to his nursery class, along with her own son. Officially, we shared the nursery run before but as I worked and she didn't, she would often call and say, 'Look, I'll take them, I'm going to the shops anyway.' She was always helping me out in her quiet, undemanding way, so it doesn't seem so unusual or offensive for her to be doing so now. She likes doing the nursery run, she says. Gets her out of the house. I know I will have to steal myself to face the nursery some time but I can't, not yet. The staff sent a card. 'How *is* she?' they will be asking Julie.

My boss at work, Jan H, sends notes about twice a week. Jan Harrison was called Jan H when she first arrived in order to distinguish her from another Jan, Jan Bennett, who already worked in our unit. Jan B left eighteen months ago but we are so used to the new Jan being Jan H that it has stuck. Janaitch. My GP has signed me off work with reactive depression to bereavement but that was just a formality – Jan H would have let me do whatever I wanted. She sends me little messages on office notepaper, from time to time, assuring me they are all doing fine without me, keeping me in touch. The notes are often light-hearted or inconsequential but in a way that never seems facile. She seems to have the knack of knowing what to say. *Just to let you know we are still thinking of you*, the last one read. *It's boring without you, hon. Last week was horribly busy. We had some relief but, mentioning no names, it isn't reliable. We are still getting referrals from the Upton Centre.* I like the fact that she is keeping me informed, treating me like a human being to whom something dreadful has happened rather than a creature from another planet. It is clear from the notes that she expects no reply.

I add the notes to the collection of cards above the fire-place. Most of the cards are white: white again – the colour of grief. They are usually decorated in some discreet manner, with small bunches of flowers or beams of heavenly light, stars in silver, embossed doves. I hate those designs. The personal notes are often clumsy, sometimes painfully so, but preferable all the same.

Amongst the cards and notes is another sort of note, one that does not belong there. It is on a folded piece of A4 paper, printed in a familiar typeface and, as usual, unsigned. *I am sorry for you*, it reads, and a small part of me admires its simplicity. I don't know why I have placed it amongst the consolation cards and letters but I think my impulse is generous. I am choosing to interpret it as an apology and by placing it on the mantelpiece am making a conciliatory gesture and also, perhaps, a transformative one, as if its proximity to the notes and cards from well-wishers will render it well-meant.

The days blend. Outside my home, the world continues to turn. I see it turn, from time to time, on the rare occasions that I look out of a front window. People leave their houses and get into their cars. Birds swoop. The postman cycles past in his bulky jacket. Observing these small turnings brings me a measure of calm, initially, but that feeling ebbs and flows and sometimes it seems that the rest of the world has returned to its ordinary life with insulting haste. Rees is my main problem, my darling Rees. As long as I have him, I cannot give up or be alone and still, more than anything else, I ache to be alone. What I find so hard is his normality – I know that this is only because his mind cannot absorb the permanence of what has happened, not yet anyway. I know that at some stage there will be tantrums, attention-seeking behaviour, and I am impatient for them to happen, impatient for acknowledgement. Until he understands what has befallen us, then how can I? I am trapped in routine with him. I have to discuss what cereal he wants for breakfast, or why he doesn't like his grey sweatshirt any more. Holding these sorts of conversations with him, I feel quite mad.

His nursery mornings are a blessed relief from the strain of being normal for him. Julie comes to collect him. He charges out, shrieking. Julie grimaces and says softly, 'See you later.' The door closes behind them. I give a sigh so deep that by the end it has become a groan. I rest my forehead against the frosted glass panel and close my eyes, waiting for the sound of Julie's car engine to fade, waiting for the silence that will follow. Only when it is completely quiet outside, beyond the door, do I turn and make my way slowly back to my kitchen, where I sit down at the table.

Sometimes, I am still there three hours later, when I am startled back to life by the sound of Rees crashing up our garden path, slamming himself against the front door: if it wasn't for Rees.

In the afternoons, I play with Rees or let him watch television. When he is back home, I feel able to take phone calls more than in the mornings because his presence gives me an excuse to be distracted. His noise in the background protects me from a proper conversation. David rings me then. I tell him what pictures Rees has brought home from nursery and what he had for lunch. In return, David gives me news from the outside world and I find myself thinking it is odd that he is out in it, until I remember that he has Chloe and the baby to think of. He'll be back at work soon, I know it.

'Did you hear about the trouble up at the cliff?' he asks me, one afternoon. I have no idea what he is talking about. 'Some local lads went up and broke all the windows. That policewoman came round.' He means Toni. 'I said if it happened again I would write to the *Post*. It might help.' I don't know why he is telling me this. I think, he will say almost anything to avoid talking about our daughter. It will be the state of the economy next, or European agricultural policy. I don't want to be unkind to him – everyone is entitled to do suffering their own way – so I nod, even though he can't see me nodding, and let his words and odd choice of subject matter wash over me while I hold the phone to my ear and gaze out of the kitchen window. After a while, I say to him, 'Do you want to speak to Rees?'

Rees can babble on to his father for an age. Sometimes I leave him to it and go upstairs, to Betty's room, and get under her duvet and pull it up over my shoulder, facing the wall. Rees comes in later, still holding the phone even though his father has rung off, and says, 'Can I watch TV now, Mum?'

One afternoon, I fall asleep up there and by the time he shakes my shoulder, it is dark outside. '*Mummy*,' he says, his voice full of upset, as if he is repeating himself, 'Mummy, *stop* sleeping in Betty's bed. It's *hers*.'

'Oh, sorry, darling . . .' I say, blinking in half-light from the landing. 'Sorry, what time is it?' I lift my watch to my face. It takes me a moment or two to focus. It is nearly 6 p.m.

I prop myself up on one elbow. 'Gosh Rees, you've been watching TV for ages. Time to brush teeth soon. It'll be bed-time soon, you know.'

His face crumples. When he speaks, I can tell by the high-pitched tone of his voice that he is trying not to cry. 'But what about tea-time? We haven't had *tea*-time.'

Rees and I begin to venture out. One afternoon, I decide to brave the playground. I haven't taken him there since what happened to Betty. We used to go almost every day before. I have been dreading meeting other mothers – going anywhere near the school is out of the question. They held a special memorial assembly for Betty, apparently. David went and read out a message from both of us – I told him to say whatever he thought was appropriate. The small part of me that is not quite dead knows I must attempt some semblance of normality for Rees, Rees who does not yet understand that Betty is never coming back.

So, we go to the playground. It's a poxy little playground, a tiny square of tarmac on the edge of our part of town, before the cliff path, where the clouds swoop low across the patch of waste ground that is awaiting redevelopment but has been left empty because of some quirk of the planning laws which no one understands. I approach it slowly, checking it is empty. It almost always is. We push through the creaky iron gate and Rees runs off to his favourite object, the climbing frame. I walk over to the damp bench and sit down. It isn't particularly cold but I keep my hands in my coat pockets. I like being huddled. Before what happened, I used to feel bleak if there wasn't another parent in the playground when we got here; bleak, lonely, bored. Where are all the other mums? I used to think: chatting somewhere in a warm kitchen, cradling cups of coffee in their hands, wondering whether or not to allow themselves that third biscuit. I always felt left out, if there was no one else around. Now, I would have carried on walking past if there was anyone else here, despite the inevitable tantrum from Rees.

Rees is swinging from the monkey bars. Not long ago, I would have called out, 'Careful, Rees.' What happened to Betty has released me from that anxiety and released Rees from my unwelcome and over-protective solicitude. What's the worst

74

thing that can happen to him if he falls off the monkey bars, a broken arm?

Sitting huddled on the bench, my arms pulled tight against my body even though I am not cold, I realise that I am in a strange, dreaming state, almost euphoria – floating. It has happened, I think to myself, calmly. The worst thing in the world has happened. My Betty has been taken away from me. I glance at Rees, unconcerned. How lucky he is. What are the chances, statistically speaking, of a woman losing both her children in tragic accidents? Minuscule, they must be. Betty's accident will keep Rees safe. Nothing will ever happen to him. I will never have to say, 'Careful, Rees,' again.

I close my eyes and tip my face to the sky, feeling the cool air. How perfect to be here, out of the house, Rees distracted, able to think of nothing but Betty: all the hours I spent here with her, holding her on the see-saw when she was a baby, fighting to keep her out of the sand pit because it smelt as though the foxes had been pissing in it again. And then, when she was older, forcing her to come along because Rees needed to let off steam on the way home after we had picked her up from school. She would sit on the swing, even though the chains had been shortened by the council to discourage older children like her. She would swing gently to and fro, grumpily, while Rees whooped and hollered with the other toddlers. 'Have you got anything to eat, Mum?' she would ask eventually.

I open my eyes again. The playground is full of Bettys – Betty at a different age on every piece of equipment. I am surrounded by her.

Rees is hanging from the monkey bars of the climbing frame with one hand and bicycling his legs in the air to reach the ladder at the end. I watch him, unconcerned. Next to him, Betty hooks her legs over the halfway-up bar and drops upside down, letting her arms droop, her long hair brushing the ground. She must have loved me so much, to give me this gift

– to sacrifice herself so that I don't need to be frightened any more. She was like that. She was the child who would write me little notes when she and Rees went to stay with their father. *Dear Mummy, I hope you won't be sad this weekend because I love you far far far far more than I love Daddy and Chloe. I know Rees was rude to you this morning but I think that was because he was worried and actually he really looks up to you. I hope you like watching your film. Please don't forget to feed the sea monkeys. PLEASE. from Betty xoxoxoxoxoxoxoxoxoxoxoxoxox*

Sitting on the bench, half-watching Rees, lost in my thoughts of Betty, I am content.

Then, a disaster: Gerry Mason comes down the path, pushing her one-year-old in a buggy and talking to her daughter, Maeve, who must be about four, I think – not quite old enough for Reception in any case.

I wait for Gerry to notice me, sitting on my bench enjoying my huddle. I stare at her until she does. She glances up and almost physically starts – clumsy of her. She hesitates, but Maeve has already crashed through the playground gate and Gerry's hand is raised to stop it swinging back against the buggy. She can hardly back out now. I continue to stare at her, unrelenting, and she drops her gaze. She pushes the buggy through the gate and glances round. She sees Rees on the climbing frame and grimaces at him – Maeve has already run off to the sand pit. Uncomfortable beneath my rock-like stare, she drops to her feet in front of the buggy and busies herself with unclipping the infant, who is perfectly happy where he is. I wonder where she will sit. There is only one bench. It is a tiny playground, after all – hardly worth it, really. She must be steeling herself, as she unclips the child. She will have to come over to me. She must be running phrases through her head.

I rise from the bench and walk over to the climbing frame. I lift Rees down and whisper to him, 'Let's go and buy some cake. You can choose what flavour.' He looks at me, astonished, then says, 'Lemon?' I nod. He allows me to put him on the ground. I take his hand.

We pass Gerry on our way to the gate. We are six feet away from her as we draw level and I let go of Rees's hand to take a step towards her, where she is still crouched in front of the buggy, still busy with the straps. I bend slightly towards her. As she looks up, she forces an uncertain smile. In return I hiss, 'It's not fucking catching, you know.' Then I turn and take Rees's hand and smile down at him. He smiles back. Hand in hand, still smiling at each other, we leave the playground.

It is the morning after the playground incident that Toni comes round. I am sitting at the bottom of my stairs, facing the door. I have been there for about half an hour, holding Betty's favourite scarf. She should have been wearing it that day, but she decided at the last minute that it didn't really go with her new corduroy jacket. It is one of those chunky, factory-produced, fake hand-knitted things, very long, with tassels at the end, in lots of different blues and greens – mermaid colours, Betty used to say. My mermaid scarf, she called it. Once, when she caught Rees tying it to the top banister, she was so furious I thought she was going to push him down the stairs. She had worn it incessantly that winter, and although I didn't like it particularly, it had now acquired the same talismanic power as all of her possessions.

I finger the scarf for a long time. Then I put it over my face and weep into it. I enter one of the recurrent moments I have been having, a moment of simple pain. Most of the time, the knowledge of Betty's absence is a complicated pain, a pain ad-mixture of anger and confusion and disbelief: but every now and then, there is a moment like this – pain as unalloyed as a sliver of glass, a moment when I cannot believe that I do not die of it as surely as I would die if someone thrust a very thin knife through my chest and out the other side. I always think

77

the same thing in these moments, a pure thought, a row of monosyllables undiluted by doubt. *It's my fault you're dead.*

It passes. The pure moments always pass – a thought enters my head or the phone rings or Rees crashes at me. Increasingly, I feel hurt by the passing of such moments. I want them back.

I am still sitting at the bottom of my stairs, the scarf now wrapped around my neck, when I sense the change of light in the hallway. I look up. A dark shape stands on the step outside, beyond the frosted glass. If I had been in another part of the house I would have ignored the light tap on the door but because I am looking at it, I recognise the shape as Toni.

She is in plainclothes, a brown leather jacket and loose black trousers. Her choppy fair hair is disarranged, as if she has been shaking her hands through it. She looks directly at me, in that straightforward way she has, which always makes me wonder if she got the job because of it or whether she has just been very well-trained. 'Hi,' she says, as she steps in. 'I've come for a cuppa.' If you saw Toni in a shop, you would never guess she was a police officer.

We walk down the hallway to the kitchen. Unlike most of the others – including Julie – Toni is unembarrassed by silence and does not attempt conversation for the sake of it. She sits at my table on a wooden chair and watches me while I fill the kettle, click it on, lift the teapot and two mugs down from their shelf. From the corner of my eye I can see her looking me over, taking in the scarf, my general demeanour.

'Are you sleeping at all?' she asks gently.

I shake my head. 'Not at night, anyway.'

'Eating anything?'

I pull a face.

I fill the teapot and bring it over to the table with the mugs. I sit down, and then remember milk and sugar and rise immediately to get them. I put the milk on the table in its carton – the sugar is caster sugar, for cake-making, still in its bag. It's the first sugar that comes to hand. As I sit again, Toni rises from her chair and fetches herself a teaspoon.

She pours for both of us. As she does so, she says, 'Laura I've got something I have to tell you. It's not good. It's awful, in fact.'

I stare at her. I had assumed this was one of her regular visits – she has come round weekly to update me on what they are doing to a degree I have found kindly but pointless – I have not, for instance, felt the need to know how long the car that killed my daughter was impounded for. For a moment, I think that perhaps Gerry reported me after my behaviour in the playground yesterday. But no, it can't be that. I didn't hit her, after all. I just wanted to. It comes to me that she must have some bad news about Betty – but what news could be worse than the news she brought to my door a few short and terrifyingly long weeks ago? Is she going to tell me that I have cremated the wrong child?

'It's Willow,' Toni says. She looks directly at me. I have been steeling myself to call Sally and make an arrangement to go round and visit Willow at home, putting it off by telling myself that Willow might find it distressing. 'She'd had quite a few problems since going home, the leg wasn't healing as well as they thought and they were considering surgery. It had been broken in so many places and was very swollen, so when she said it was still hurting they didn't realise.' My heart constricts. I stare and stare at Toni. She has the same expression on her face that she had when she told me about Betty. I realise what she is about to say before she says it but I have the same sensation that I had before, of the conscious part of my mind baulking at the knowledge. 'They readmitted her to the HDU two days ago because they were a bit concerned,' Toni continues. 'It was the temperature she was running that told them, apparently, well you know more about these things than I do. Her leg was still very swollen and the break wasn't healing well.

They took her over to the Royal Infirmary, to the paediatric intensive care unit there, but she died twelve hours after being admitted. Septicaemia, you know how quick that can be, but it should have been picked up. There'll be an enquiry.'

I lift Betty's scarf and bury my face in it. Dear God. The pain feels as intense as one of the pure moments, but still not pure. I can hardly bear it, yet hardly feel it. I could not begin to explain my feelings to myself.

'God. Sally . . .' I say, helplessly.

'Sally and Stephen were with her when she died,' said Toni. 'They had that at least.'

'Does David know?'

Toni nods. 'I phoned him before I came over here, in case he wanted to tell you himself. I think he would have liked to but things are a bit difficult for him at the moment so I offered.' *Coward*, I think, briefly. Toni continues, 'The funeral will probably be Friday. They're making arrangements today.'

I search my feelings, struggling to discover what there is inside me that is authentic. Can I honestly say that there is not some tiny part of me that is relieved I will not have to have the talk with Willow I have been dreading, about exactly what happened that day? Am I, perhaps, relieved that I am not alone any more, even though Sally is one of the last people I would wish to be not-alone with; relieved (and this is it, I think, most of all) that, for a short time at least, I will not be the focus of attention, that I can be a bit part in someone else's tragedy. How dreadful, that I should feel any of these slivers of relief, even momentarily. I feel sick. A girl has died.

'Things are going to be a bit difficult in town for a while,' Toni is saying, thoughtfully. 'We've had to set up something called a Gold Group. It's what we do when there's, well, what you might call a bit of tension in a community. I can talk you through it if you like, what we're doing, and the investigation, where we are up to.'

I nod, then rise. I don't want to talk through it, any of it. Betty is dead, now Willow. 'It's all right. You don't have to stay.'

That night, I cannot sleep. Normally I manage to doze for an hour or two before waking but that night unconsciousness eludes me entirely. I lie in Betty's bed, thinking of Sally and Stephen, the newness and rawness of their grief, how they are almost certainly awake too, wandering around their house and staring at each other from time to time, disbelievingly.

I lie like that for a long time, with my hands behind my head, waiting for the moment when I feel like turning on my side in the foetal position, closing my body up, in preparation for it to be deserted by my thoughts. The moment doesn't come. Around 2 a.m., I rise, look in on Rees who is breathing softly, and go downstairs in my dressing gown, clutching it around me, shivering. The house is dark and strange, as it always is at this time of the night. I make myself a large mug of camomile tea and sit at the kitchen table with the photo albums – David was always very good at that. He took hundreds of pictures of the children and in the old days always got an extra set of prints and sent copies of the best one to the aunties and a far-flung cousin somewhere in the Middle East, so far-flung I had never even met him. As a result, we always ended up with two copies of the less-good photos – the blurry ones where Betty or Rees turned their head or loomed at the lens; the ones where they are cross-looking or have their eyes closed. David would never throw anything away. There were half-full albums and yellow envelopes of prints all over the house. It drove me mad. Thank God for the advent of digital. Since he and I split up, the children were hardly photographed by me – on special occasions of course, birthdays and Christmases. But somewhere, there would be all the photos that David would be taking of them with Chloe and the baby, photos that didn't include me.

The last photo will be one of those, somewhere on David's

computer. I have lots of the early ones, the ones in the packets, that catch her as a toddler dressed in appalling cardigans given to her by the aunties; chubby arms, chubby chins. Who would have thought she would turn into such a straight, slender girl?

I sit at the kitchen table, nursing my tea. Here is my girl at six months, in a red rugby shirt, grinning at someone out of the picture. Here she is aged four, her hair in a severe pageboy style, her stomach still protruding plumply from a vest. She is waving garden shears at the lens but I can't identify the garden behind her – certainly not ours. It has flowers in it.

And here she is more recently, in a selection of prints that David took at her ninth birthday party – he gave me the CD as well as prints of the six best shots. I took her and three friends bowling and David joined us halfway through. Rees was allowed one friend. We all went for pizza afterwards. The photo I am holding is a large, glossy print of Betty with Willow and Priya and Elinor, her three best friends. The bowling alley – a hideously dark and noisy place – is in the background. They are all shouting at the lens, eyes wide, slightly mad with the noise and chaos of it. Betty and Willow are clutching each other in one of those wild, loving hugs that girls of that age indulge in, when they still believe that they will live together when they are grown-up. Willow wanted to be a vet. Betty was going to be a detective. They were going to solve mysterious animal disappearances together. Betty's hair is untidy. Willow is grinning and holding a hand up, pointing at her own face. She is showing off her new glasses, of which she was inordinately proud. They are beautiful, and drunk on the joy of the party and their passionately mutual friendship: the past was something they had yet to acquire and the future was pizza and ice cream down the road, ten minutes away. Their lives were no more than the glorious, abundant present. They had four months to live.

*

Julie drives me over to Sally's house on Friday. I have sent a message via David that I don't feel able to come to the crematorium so soon after Betty's funeral but that I would like to come to the house – a message comes back, that is fine. Julie takes the boys to nursery as usual, drives to the crematorium, then comes back to get me.

'How did it go?' I say, as I climb into the passenger seat and fasten my seatbelt.

She shakes her head. Her face looks drawn. For the first time, I wonder about the cost of all this tragedy to her and people like her in our lives, people who take it upon themselves to carry on as normal, who feel guilty for being too upset, but whose lives are also diminished, thrown awry by what has happened. We do not speak for the rest of the drive. We park the car in the street that neighbours Sally's – her road is full. As she locks her car door, Julie says, 'I'll get the boys at the usual time and take Rees back to ours. You stay as long as you want.'

I brace myself as we mount the stone steps up to Sally's front door but it is opened by a relative I do not know, a middle-aged man who says, as if by rote, 'Thank you for coming.' To my relief, there is no acknowledgement of my special status. Once we are inside, a teenage girl takes our coats over her arm. Her understanding of what is happening is unsophisticated. She gives us a bright smile before turning sharply and trotting up the stairs, to put the coats in a bedroom. Sally's house is a mirror image of our house, the same Victorian terrace but the other way around and much smarter, coloured glass everywhere and stripped floors, endless framed photos of her children over every wall. From the hallway, I can see down into the kitchen, which they had extended the year before. It is full of light, people. Above the kitchen door, there is an A4 size photo of Willow on a hillside, her hair wind-whipped, wearing a bright smile. It has been printed out on white copy paper and sellotaped clumsily in place. Julie and I stand in the hallway for a minute, and I see that there are framed photos of Willow lined in rows on a shelf beneath the mirror. At that point, Sally herself emerges from the sitting room to our left and says, 'Come in you two, it's cold out here in the hall. Come and get a drink.' The woman who dealt with my tragedy in such a heavy-handed fashion seems bizarrely determined, outwardly at least, to make light work of her own. I stare at her as she turns to the kitchen. I wonder if her doctor has given her drugs.

David and Chloe are at the far end of the kitchen. David sees me and pushes through the other people to get to me – Chloe, of course, stays where she is. David embraces me warmly, as if we are the only two people who understand what is really going on here, which of course we are. 'I'm so glad you could come,' he whispers. It occurs to me that although David and I have spoken every day since the accident, we have not seen much of each other. It hasn't seemed odd before but now, in the comfort of his brief embrace, it does.

Somebody shoves past behind me, bumping my shoulder. David glares past me and for a minute I think he is about to speak sharply – I half-turn but he pulls me back gently with his hand on my upper arm. I lean in to him. He smells of David. 'I feel so strange,' I say to him.

'I know,' he says softly, still very close to me, speaking into my hair, 'so do I.'

Julie comes to find me after half an hour and says she has to leave to collect the boys. While she and I are talking, David excuses himself and goes to speak to Chloe. I have had enough already. It is my first social event since the accident and just standing and talking has exhausted me. I want to leave with Julie but I haven't spoken to anyone but David so far and feel I ought to stay. David returns to us and hands me a small glass of sherry.

84

Julie slips away. I sip the sherry and regret it immediately. Even a small sip makes me dizzy. David holds a plate of sandwiches up to me. I pick one up and eat the corner, then stand holding it, not wanting to put it back on his plate. 'God, Laura,' he says quietly, 'I'm worried sick about how thin you are.'

'I'm okay,' I say.

'No, you're not,' he replies.

I would like to spend the whole occasion with David but am determined to be brave. I must not be selfish about what has happened to Willow. I must acknowledge who we are mourning here. I go back out into the hall and into the sitting room where groups of older relatives are seated. A woman who is standing by the mantelpiece comes over to me and says, 'Laura?'

I nod.

'I'm Willow's godmother, Vivie,' the woman says. 'We met last Easter. It was good of you to come when you've got so much on your plate.' We both grimace at the euphemism, and it comes to me where I have met her before. She was at an Easter-egg hunt one of the other mothers had arranged in the park, a year or two ago. She brought a giant thermos flask of coffee and half a dozen plastic mugs. She told me about why she had never had any children of her own, something to do with being adopted.

We stand in the middle of the sitting room, talking politely, for a while. I think to myself, how well I am doing. I allow myself the tiniest blush of pride at my own ability to talk normally, to transcend the part of me that still wants to scream at the inanity of anything but my own loss. Perhaps this is what the loss of Willow is doing for me, offering me a perspective. How appalling that I should be benefiting, even a tiny amount, from someone else's misery. Vivie the godmother talks on, quietly, unobtrusively. I nod.

Towards the end of our conversation, something odd

happens. I am standing talking to Vivie. We have not moved from our positions. I feel a scrape and a sharp pain against my shin. I turn and see a small woman with brown curly hair standing close behind me, scowling. Behind her is an armchair. I guess that she was sitting in her armchair and, in standing, has somehow scraped her pointed heel along my shin, although I can't quite work out how, or why. I look at her with a surprised, half-smile, waiting for her to say, 'I'm sorry,' but she simply glares at me, then turns away.

I watch the small woman leave the room, then say to Vivie, 'Who was that?' She shrugs.

Not long after that, I realise that I am desperate to go back home – I should have got a lift with Julie. I say goodbye to Vivie and leave the sitting room, wondering if I could sneak out, without saying goodbye to anyone. I would be forgiven, after all. I have done my bit. I hesitate, glancing down into the kitchen, which is still full of people. I can't face going back in there.

Upstairs, in the master bedroom, I am unable to find my coat. There is a heap of them on the main bed but, pushing through them, I do not see mine. I go into the small bedroom next door, where there is a group of teenage girls lounging around, on the bed, on huge cushions on the floor. It looks as though they have all been crying. Willow was the youngest of four children. I see her older sister, Beeny, by the window. She stares at me, eye make-up smudgy, then says dully, 'Hello.'

'Hello Beeny,' I say. 'Do you know where the rest of the coats are? I've got to go.' She turns her face back to the window.

As I come down the stairs, Ranmali and her husband are at the front door, in their coats, about to leave. It is the first time I have seen them close enough to speak to since the accident – they came to the crematorium for Betty's funeral but not back to the house. Although I have been dreading seeing Ranmali for weeks, I suddenly feel relieved that we have encountered each other and wish I knew her well enough to embrace her. There is a conversation she and I must have, some time, and although I am not yet ready for it, I am pleased to see her.

She is buttoning her woollen coat. She turns and looks up at me as I descend. She stares for a moment, then her eyes fill with tears. I am not alarmed by this because I know her polite, precise English will not stretch to platitudes. Her husband is standing next to her, already buttoned tight, ready to go. He has pulled a hat over his neatly oiled hair, but is staring up at me from beneath its brim. His expression is not warm or sympathetic, like his wife's. It is like the expression he adopts when too many schoolchildren are crowding into his shop.

As I reach the bottom of the stairs, he steps forward. His wife puts out a hand and rests it on his arm. He glances at her briefly, then looks back at me.

I stop where I am. I think, he wants to say something but can't. I realise that in all these years I have never heard him speak.

He bows his head briefly and then says, so quietly I can hardly hear. 'I am sorry, Mrs Needham.'

I nod in return, a curt acknowledgement of his condolence, and half-turn to go towards the sitting room to continue the hunt for my coat, but he takes another step towards me and I realise there is more he wants to say.

He leans forward, as if he does not want anyone else to hear. 'My wife is mistaken,' he says.

I look at him. His face is expressionless. His mouth scarcely moves as he talks. 'She makes a mistake.'

I am forced to bend my head closer to hear him. There are deep lines on his face, grey grooves that betray his age, but his teeth are small and neat. 'The car, my wife thinks, but I believe she does not want to know, it was not normal. It came too fast.

That driver was too fast. He should be punished.'

I stare at him. I have a feeling that he wants to elaborate but that the shock on my face has silenced him.

'I am sorry,' he repeats, and turns away.

I look past him at Ranmali. The tears still stand in her eyes, brimming so fulsomely it seems odd they do not fall. She glances at her husband, then at me. Then she shakes her head. I am not sure whether she means that her husband is wrong, a little deranged even, and I should take no notice of what he is saying, or whether she is simply expressing the wrongness of everything, of the whole situation. She turns and opens the door behind her, then speaks to her husband sharply in another language. He does not look at me again as he leaves.

My hand is still resting on the swirl of wood at the end of the banister. I swing backwards and sit down on the bottom of the stairs. I put my head in my hands, unable to process this information. I was doing so well, this morning. I was managing to think about Willow, rather than the fact that Betty is absent. Betty would have wanted to say goodbye to her best friend. Why isn't Betty here? I realise the small progress I have made by coming here was illusory. It has taken a huge effort of will for me to come but I have felt as though, for the first time since the accident, I have managed to take a brief holiday from my own grief – only possible because of the fresher grief of others. But Ranmali's husband has reminded me that my own tragedy is waiting for me, as soon as I collect my thoughts. It has been displaced as temporarily as the coat I cannot locate. I will be shrugging it over my shoulders again before I step outside.

He should be punished. I don't even know his name.

I hear a shuffle from the sitting room. The door opens and the hallway is filled with murmuring voices. I sense a general movement from within, people preparing to leave. I rise from the stair. Sally's mother, Willow's grandmother, comes out first and as she sees me she gives a small start. I know she is about to say something and I can't cope with any more so to forestall her I say, 'Mrs James. I'm going to go now.' I feel old, as old as the cliffs. And tired. I'm so very, very tired.

Mrs James looks around her. 'Is David going to drive you home? Or have you got your car?' She is one of these women who believes it is her job to look after everyone, I think, even in the midst of her own tragedy.

'No, I'm going to walk.' I can see her looking down the hallway, looking for someone to summon to take me home. 'I need some air.' My voice is a little louder than it needs to be.

She looks back at me. 'Of course you do,' she says, softening. All at once, to my surprise, we move together and embrace. We stand like that for a minute in the hallway, the walls around us aflame with pictures of her dead granddaughter, and for a moment, just a moment, I experience a little comfort. Then I pull back. 'My coat . . .' I say weakly. 'It went upstairs,' as if it has escaped from me like a recalcitrant child.

'I'll get it for you, dear.'

'It's the . . .'

'Yes, I know. I saw you when you came in.'

I step back and she climbs the stairs slowly, a little arthritically, gripping the banister. The feeling of exhaustion has not left me and although I do not want a lift from anyone, let alone David and Chloe, walking home is the last thing I feel like doing. My legs are lead. I give a harsh exhalation of breath at the thought that Mrs James, in all her age and grief, is the more nimble of the two of us as she mounts the stairs to go and find my coat.

Mrs James is gone a long time. People keep going past and looking at me, then looking away. By the time she descends the stairs, I am desperate to leave and retrospectively sincere in my desire for fresh air. Mrs James is frowning slightly as she comes down, my coat over her arm – a distinctive dark purple, with a ruff, the smartest item and most expensive item in my wardrobe.

'Very odd, dear,' says Mrs James, as she holds it out to me. 'The big girls must have been playing with it. It was in the top bathroom. There's something on it.'

She extends her hand and I take the coat without looking at it. 'I'm sure it's fine. Will you tell Sally, you know.'

'Yes, don't worry, I'll tell her.'

I slip out of the front door, the coat still in my hand. Mrs James closes the door softly behind me. It is only as I pull the coat on and button it, that I see what she means. There is a long strip of fluid right the way down the front, bleach or some other corrosive cleaning fluid, which has burnt through the top layer of the material. The coat is ruined. I shake my head, and lift my face to the rain. It feels cold, good. I cannot piece together all the separate elements of this strange morning and decide that, of course, it must be me – I am the strange one, standing in the rain.

6

A few days after Willow's funeral, Toni comes round again. It isn't one of Rees's nursery mornings so he is in the sitting room where he has pulled all the cushions off the sofa and chairs and piled them high in a wobbly tower. He says he is making a helicopter. Toni and I leave him to it and walk through to the kitchen but she declines the ritual of tea and says, 'Would you mind if we went into the garden so I can smoke a cigarette?' I am flattered by this, presuming she is not supposed to smoke on duty and that asking if she can in my garden is a sign she likes and trusts me. I want to be liked by her, I am not sure why. I want her to like me more than all the other bereaved relatives she has dealt with. I feel competitive towards them.

'Not as long as you give me one,' I say. Toni responds with a straight-mouthed expression.

'It was good you made it, Sally's house,' she says, as we sit on the low wall at the back of my garden. 'I'm sure it wasn't easy but I'm sure Sally and Stephen appreciated it.'

'Are you their liaison officer too?' I ask.

Toni nods, and I feel a pang. I don't like the idea of her sitting in Sally's immaculate kitchen, empathising. Still, at least she'll be getting a decent cup of coffee there. From here, I can see through to the sitting room, where Rees is jumping on and off the bare frame of the sofa with both hands raised high above his head, attempting flight. Toni hands me a cigarette, then bends to offer me a light – her lighter is a flamethrower but the cold breeze extinguishes it repeatedly and after three attempts I say, 'Light yours first and I'll light mine off it.' When I have done this, I exhale and say, 'How do you know I was there?' then burst into a fit of coughing because I have had to inhale so hard.

'David told me. Are you all right?'

I cough until I am purple. 'No, I'm fine. I used to smoke when I was a student but I haven't for years. David hated it. I started again after we split up, to annoy him mostly, but then I realised it was a bit of a pointless gesture, so I gave up again.'

'Do you want a pat on the back?'

I shake my head. 'Do you and David talk about me a lot?'

'Of course. You know what men are like. It's more acceptable for them to talk about someone else than themselves, or worry about other things, as if, I don't know. You know the way some men are, problem-solving.'

'I'm the problem.'

'You know what I mean.'

'Task-orientated.'

'That's another way of putting it.'

'I used to think, sometimes, this sounds a bit odd, but sometimes, when we were still together, I used to tell David he should have been a cop. He was always concentrating on things, drove me crazy.' I cough again. 'It was great when he concentrated on me, though, intense, you know. He would have made a good police officer.'

We both smile briefly at this suggestion, are quiet for a moment. The sky above us is blanket white. On the bare trees, one or two tiny buds are beginning to form. They seem premature. 'Such as?' I ask, aware that my tone is a little sardonic.

'Such as what?'

'What other things?'

'Well, you know. He's been very composed in public, very good with the press, trying to calm things down. He went up before the television cameras last week, which I thought was brave of him but he said he would if it would help with the problems we are having in town. I'm just a bit concerned.

Outwardly he seems to be doing well but you know it's often the ones who are doing well at first who completely collapse later on. The ones who go under quickly, well the ones who seem worst hit – I suppose . . .' she dries, briefly, 'well, maybe that's a more natural reaction.'

My cigarette burns slowly on its own while I stare at her. 'The ones that go under quickly like me,' I say.

'Yes, like you,' she admits, looking at the cigarette between her fingers then taking a long drag. 'I didn't mean to imply you're doing anything wrong. Quite the reverse in fact.'

'Television cameras?' I have not turned on the television since Betty went away, or opened a newspaper.

'Laura . . .' her voice is still gentle but I think I detect a hint of exasperation. 'It went national, not any more, but for a bit it was. Last week it was just local telly.'

This explains something I have wondered about. 'So is that part of your job too?'

She nods, then adds, 'Did you look at any of those folders I gave you?'

I roll my eyes. 'I work for the NHS, remember. We have a leaflet for every occasion. We have a leaflet on how to deal with your feelings if the water fountain isn't working and the number for the support group for people who've been annoyed by water fountains.'

'I know a lot of the way things are put sounds patronising.'

'Look, there isn't a single inane phrase I haven't heard from you or anyone that I haven't used myself. People die on me at work too or I have to tell people they'll never be able to do something. I'm not made of glass.'

A small silence follows. I wonder if she can translate my burst of antagonism, whether she understands how important it is for her to realise that I am a fellow professional, how unbearable I would find it if she treated me like a victim. It isn't that I want her to be my friend – I know that is not what she is here for – but I want her to accord me a friend's equal status, emotionally, intellectually. At the same time, I can feel something small and childlike inside me, something that wants me to cave in to my need of her. I want to know what she says about me to her colleagues.

'Are they all like me?' I am trying to lighten the tone.

She pulls a so-so face.

'Better or worse?' I prod.

'Every bereaved relative is different, that's the first thing they teach us,' she responds firmly. 'Whenever you go and knock on someone's door, you never know what's behind it.'

It is unfair of me to want her to treat me like an equal. If I was her equal, she wouldn't be here. I try to give her what she wants. 'It's like I've been in a swimming pool, treading water, just managing to keep afloat. And now I look around for the first time and see that the water I've been swimming in is milk, or purple, or full of frogs. So many weird things have started happening.'

She is looking at me. 'What do you mean?'

I tell her about how strange I found Willow's wake, how everything about it seemed detached, surreal, even the conversation with Ranmali's husband, which should have horrified me but bewildered me. I tell her how it was difficult to walk home, how with each step, I felt as if the ground beneath my feet was spongy and could dissolve at any moment. And now. Television cameras? Nobody from the press has come near me but for some reason they are bothering David.

Toni sighs and stubs her cigarette out on my garden wall. I have the feeling she is going to say something she has been preparing for a while, something she has been holding on to until the appropriate moment. 'We interviewed Ranmali and her husband separately. Their accounts differ slightly. It's a matter of interpretation but it's important. What charges we bring could depend on it.' I know that the driver of the car was initially arrested on suspicion of causing death by dangerous driving, a category-A offence and very serious. The car was impounded and they took his clothes. The drink and drugs tests they did on him were negative. He was released on police bail. They are appealing for other witnesses – and without them, it is possible that the charges against him could be downgraded to causing death by careless driving, a less serious offence. Careless is less bad than dangerous, in the eyes of the law, despite the fact that the outcome for my daughter was exactly the same.

'Have you been lying to me?' I say.

She shakes her head. 'When you are grief-stricken and depressed it's easy to get paranoid but, take it from me, it doesn't help. No one's lying to you, but we haven't pressed information on you when you don't seem ready for it, that's all. It's all there, when you're ready.' She has never been quite this firm with me before. 'Are you sleeping at all?'

'You always ask that. Stupid question.'

'Not really. It will come back eventually you know, sleep, and appetite.'

'I don't want them back.'

'I know. I know you don't.'

I throw down my cigarette. 'Please God don't tell me you're coming round here to make sure I'm going to get normal again. Go and see Saint Bloody Sally if you want normal. She does the grief thing much more *normally* I'm sure.'

'I don't.'

'When I'm awake, in the night I mean, not the daytime. It's the best time. It's the only time I am alone.' Toni is looking at me. The sky is still white, a great, aching arc of white. I am as raw as a newborn baby, I think, and it is not a sentimental image. I am thinking of how red babies are when they are first born, beneath the white smear of vernix, like a thing that has been skinned. 'I mean, I know I'm alone all day long, well, as much as I can be. I don't mean that. It's the only time I'm really alone, when everyone else is asleep. It's the only time I don't feel watched.'

'Who do you think is watching you?'

'Everyone,' I say, and it is only as I say it that I realise how true it feels. 'They watch me all the time. When I'm walking down the street, in the shops. I don't want to go to the school ever again. There'll be hundreds of them, and even on an empty street you never know when someone might look out of their window or drive past in the car. Everybody thinks they know me. The other mothers are the worst. They all think they know what I'm going through, just because they have all imagined it, just because they love their own kids. I saw a woman in the playground and I thought, she's glad it's happened to mine. She thinks it makes it less likely it will happen to hers.'

Even though Toni is looking at me, I don't mind her looking. Her looking doesn't feel like watching. She is being paid to be with me. She has a good excuse. There is another silence then she says, 'You do know that there isn't anything they could be doing that would be right. You'd feel insulted whatever they did.'

'I hate them,' I say.

'I know.'

'Maybe I always hated them. Maybe I only thought I liked them because we were in this club together, the parents' club. Sally, I haven't got a thing in common with her. She's one of these wholesome types. She's into dolphins, inner wisdom, and those stupid names she's given her children. She's always trying to get me to help at school, sit on all the committees she sits on or run clubs. When I had trouble feeding Rees, she offered to come and sit with me while I tried. I can't stand her. Now everyone is going to think we should be joined at the hip. They'll be expecting us to go around together. She's doing it the right way, I bet, being all dignified and letting people make her feel better and tell her that Willow will always be with her and would want her to be happy. She won't. Betty has gone away forever and now so has Willow. They haven't made the world a better place. They haven't enriched all our lives with their love and innocence. They're just *gone*.'

Toni's voice becomes very gentle, which I take as a sign of admonishment. 'Don't you think you might be guilty of judging her in the same way you think people are judging you?'

'I'm just sick of being watched, the whole time. That's why being awake at night is so good. The dark. Knowing they are all asleep. Knowing that just for a few hours they have stopped watching me.'

There is another long silence. 'Laura, I'm sorry, but have you had any thoughts about hurting yourself? You do understand why I need to ask that, don't you?'

Of course she needs to ask – stubborn, selfish Laura, made even more stubborn and selfish by her grief, has refused all offers of counselling. I haven't even read the leaflets and the brochures the bereavement counsellor gave me after our one short and from her point of view entirely unsatisfactory chat at the hospital. Poor Toni. She landed a double shift when they gave her me.

'Is duty of care in your remit too?' I ask. 'Poor you.'

She smiles. 'No, it isn't, strictly speaking. I'm just asking.'

I look down. The cigarette I tossed so carelessly lies in the scrubby winter grass, the tip still aglow. I step on it. 'Who was the pathologist? Who signed off on Betty?'

She pauses. 'David Bradley.'

'I know him.'

Through the window, we can see Rees standing alone in the sitting room, looking around. He has bored of his helicopter made of cushions and is wondering where I am. He will come running out any minute, a demand on his lips. He usually says, 'I'm hungry,' when he means, 'I want attention,' but the very

97

act of making the demand convinces him it is hunger he feels and he is furious when attention is all he gets. These small episodes of fury have not increased in frequency since Betty went away, but they are more intense. I sense I am about to pay for my sneaky fag in the garden.

I stand up. Toni stands too. 'You want me to come with you?' she asks.

I shake my head. 'I know him,' I repeat. 'You think it's a good idea?'

She nods. She knows what I mean. For the first time, I am thinking about stepping outside the darkly enveloping fact of Betty's absence to examine the detail of it. 'One step at a time, but the information is all there when you need it. I can talk to you any time, about all the other stuff.'

I'm not interested in the other stuff. I don't want to hear what a Gold Group is or why, for some reason, strangers seem so intent on owning what has happened to me, to my girl.

'There's something else I would like you to think about doing . . .' I glance at her as we walk back into the house. 'I just think,' she continues, 'well, I know you and David are separated and you obviously won't be supporting each other in the same way you would if you were still married but, all the same.'

'You think it's odd we're not spending more time together, talking about Betty.'

She nods.

'Well,' I said drily, 'if you knew the full story of our break-up you might not think it was all that peculiar.'

'I understand it was a bit acrimonious.'

'That's something of an understatement.'

'Can't you two find a time when you can talk together, at all, just the two of you, you know, share what's going on? I'm asking for his sake as much as yours.'

I scoff out loud as we step inside. Through the kitchen, Rees comes towards us head down, torpedo-like. 'I doubt Chloe would allow that.' Rees charges into me and clutches at my legs, begins to howl.

Toni gives me her characteristic grimace. 'I'll get back to you on that.'

David Bradley is one of those men who could play himself in a television drama. On casual acquaintance, he seems two-dimensional; a quiet, clever stalwart, a vertebrae in the backbone of the NHS – thinning hair, small, hunched shoulders. I used to wonder about people like him, both men and women. My professional life was built around them, those restrained souls who seem to have wiped the slate of their personality clean in order to be good at what they do. Do they seethe, beneath, I used to think? Are they full of things? What are their secret lives? No one would ever have accused me of being secretive, before. Chatty when I was in a good mood, obviously glum when I was not. If people asked me how I was, I told them. Sometimes, they got whole stories. But Bradley, and people like him: the secret ones, the tidy men and women – I used to wonder.

Bradley deals with death as he would any other professional colleague. When he is asked a question, he gives an answer and he never patronises the grief-stricken. One of my patients was a woman who suffered nerve damage in one leg after an epidural that went wrong during the birth of her second child. Two years later, her husband committed suicide by closing the garage door and leaving the engine running in their Volvo estate. The pathologist was Bradley. I took the woman to see him. She couldn't believe that her husband would be so selfish as to kill himself, leaving her a disabled widow with two small children. They didn't have any money worries – with my help, she had got a good settlement out of our local NHS Trust. It became clear to me as we spoke with Bradley that she was hoping her husband's death was accidental, that he might have forgotten to turn the engine off. (Before stuffing his coat beneath the garage door, reclining the driver's seat and lying down . . .?) He hadn't left a note. It was clearly an impulse suicide.

I think a lesser man than Bradley might have told the widow what she wanted to hear. He might have made himself feel better by offering her ambiguities designed to let her invent her own story. Bradley did nothing of the sort. He took her through the report line by line and gave her the cold facts, as they had been discovered, entirely free of interpretation. Later, an open verdict would be recorded at the inquest, but not once did Bradley say anything that the widow could interpret as permission to delude herself. He paid her that compliment. He left the rest of her life in her own hands. In his position, I am not sure I could have been that strong, that principled – I have always wanted to be liked too much. David Bradley is my man; he will tell me what I need to know.

I drive down the esplanade; it is a harsh, grey day. Few people are out and the shops are doing poor trade. Suddenly, a plastic bag swoops down from the high periphery of my vision and lands on my car windscreen with a slap and flutter. Startled, I flip on the windscreen wipers, which whisk the bag to and fro before throwing it back up into the air. I slow right down to catch my breath and see as I glance to my left that Mr Yeung the chippy has boarded up his window and hung a 'closed' sign on his door. Odd, I think, how one shop closing can make a whole row of retail outlets look derelict. It seems so quiet downtown. A lone dog lopes across the road in front of me, the last animal alive in a post-apocalyptic landscape. I shake my head. This trip is taking all my nerve. I cannot allow myself to be unsettled by a plastic bag.

Bradley's office is at the far end of Southside Road, almost out of town, in a cluster of municipal buildings of the sort that members of the public don't usually need to visit. The buildings themselves are ugly brick cubes huddled close together just off the main road, exposed to the wind that whips smartly down from the rise. A sea view – that rectangle so greatly beloved of all those who don't live near the sea, who don't have to look out of their windows and see the endless crash of it, day after day – such a view is Bradley's. He is expecting me. As I sit down, we exchange the briefest of preliminary remarks. Glancing at his desk, I see that his report lies on it, ready for me. He pushes it towards me. 'Take a look,' he says, 'then ask me anything you want to know.'

It is in a pale green plastic folder. Betty's full name and date of birth are written in a neat, sloping hand on a sticker in the top right-hand corner. I reach for it and pull it on to my lap, opening the cover quickly. I can't allow myself to hesitate; it's all here, the bleeding, the lung and chest trauma – cause of death was multiple internal injuries. It is easier to read than I had expected. The terminology renders me professional. I scan it once, then read it slowly and properly from the top. While I do, Bradley waits, half turned away from me in his revolving chair, attendant but detached.

'Why was this break so bad?' I ask. 'The left femur.' I still have my head down, reading. Betty's left leg was broken in two places. It is not the kind of thing I was planning on asking him about. The break to the femur did not kill Betty, after all. It was the internal bleeding that did that.

Bradley pauses. This is uncharacteristic of him and makes me look up. His face is still expressionless. 'The vehicle had bull bars.'

We stare at each other and all at once I understand his pause. He has stepped outside the remit of our discussion and is giving me a detail that I do not need to know. The car had bull bars. That means it was a four-wheel drive. I shouldn't be surprised, but I am. I realise that, until now, I have had no physical image of the vehicle that killed my daughter. Had I been asked to conjure one, I would have thought of something old, second-hand, driven by a youth or a man in his twenties, perhaps – someone a little careless but still within the speed limit. How fast he was driving is now in doubt. What he will be charged with is also, now, in doubt.

I am realising something. It is coming over me in a wave, like one of those dramatic climaxes in a disaster movie when the scene goes into slow motion so you can observe the expression on the actor's face as he or she leaps from the path of danger; a rush of water, a wall of flame, a falling building. Up until now, the fact of Betty's death has obscured the manner of it.

The driver of the car that killed my daughter was not some callow youth in a beaten-up, second-hand rust bucket. The driver was a man who could spend tens of thousands of pounds on a gleaming four-by-four with bull bars. This driver, this faceless, mythical creature whom I have refused to admit into my thinking is no longer some shadowy thing, a grey ghost who came and took my Betty. He is taking shape, acquiring substance with each new detail that I learn about him.

I don't know whether Bradley can guess at what is forming in my head but he adds, 'It is unproven that he was driving at excessive speed, Laura.'

'I know,' I say shortly. All at once, I am suspicious. 'Why do you say that?'

Bradley sighs.

'He had convictions, didn't he? He had previous.' I am fishing.

Bradley removes his glasses and looks at them as if they don't belong to him. He glances to one side, out of his window, puts his glasses back on and looks back at me. 'Laura,' he says, 'I'm sorry but I'm speaking to you in an official capacity.' He intends this as obfuscation rather than confirmation but I know it to be both.

I drive back along the esplanade. I would like to park and go for a walk on the beach but Julie will be bringing Rees home soon. I have to get back. As I drive slowly, glancing from time to time at the choppy grey water, I fail to notice that the lights at the pedestrian crossing are flashing. A group of teenage lads, the sort that hang out at the chip shop, are already striding across the road. I brake suddenly. The car slides forward to a halt, then stalls. All at once, they are surrounding the car, two of them gesturing and shouting obscenities, the others looking on with sullen, dead expressions on their faces. One of the two who is shouting, the tallest of all of them, leans across and bangs his fist down hard on the bonnet of my car. His face looms and leers through the windscreen, a long white face beneath a brown cap, acne scattered in an arc across his cheek, eyes blaring. He calls me a stupid cunt. I'm inclined to agree. He takes a long time to move away from my window and by the time he does, I am breathing so hard that it is a moment or two before I am able to restart the car. I drive home slowly, my heart thumping in my chest.

Once I am inside my own door, the adrenalin from the incident drains away and my legs shake. I wish I had one of Toni's cigarettes. I know that after the expense of energy this morning, a darkness will descend upon me this afternoon as sure as night following day. It was like this after my trip to the playground, and Willow's wake. Anything other than being at home on my own costs me so much, depletes me, leaves me entirely in the grip of what I have been gripped by ever since my daughter was killed. *Was killed.* Was killed by somebody. Didn't just die. Didn't dissolve into thin air in a puff of smoke. She was a whole human being, a life, my life, and somebody came along in a car and killed her.

Then I see it, on the mat, a small white envelope. I pick it up, recognising the type and shape of it, the fact that my name is not written anywhere. I open the blank envelope and unfold the sheet of A4 paper. Typed on it, in the usual typeface, is one sentence – like the last one, just one sentence, again – she is quite succinct these days.

I hear you've gone quite mad.

That night, I wake after an hour or two of sleep, the way I do most nights. I lie on my back on Betty's bed for a long while, then turn on her bedside light, a rotating starfish, and pick up my watch from her bedside table. It is 2.34.

The rotating starfish throws orange triangles around the room. They wheel slowly, passing over the opposite wall, across the ceiling, down the other wall. The hypnotic effect is deliberate – we've had that light since Betty was a baby. Baby Betty would lie in her cot and kick herself to sleep while the orange triangles whirled around her. We used to watch her from the doorway sometimes, peering round, spying on her. Kick kick kick, her little legs would go. Kick kick kick. Then, all at once, she would go still, as if someone had flicked the off switch, a still form in the gloom beneath a slowly turning myriad of orange.

After another long while, I push back the duvet and go to the bathroom. I lift my nightie and pee in the dark. I don't wash my hands. I pad down the stairs, my arms wrapped around myself against the chill of an unheated house. When I reach the bottom of the stairs, I go to the coat rack and lift down my coat, my heavy woollen one, old but comforting. On the same peg is Betty's woollen scarf, her mermaid scarf. I wrap it round my neck. I look about for shoes.

Outside, the air is crisp, cool as water, clear and soft. Night air, I think, better than coffee or any other stimulant. I feel more awake than I have done for weeks as I walk briskly down the street, my arms still folded across my chest, my nightie dangling beneath my coat. I don't have any socks on and my walking boots – the first pair of footwear that came to hand – rub briskly on my feet, which has the same effect as the bracing air: it makes me feel euphoric.

The streetlights on our road are sparse and dim. They give off a soft, white glow, so soft that they hardly seem to be on and I wonder if there is some vast switch somewhere in the Town Hall that dims all the lights at this hour. Every house is dark. I think how interesting it is to be able to see the lining of people's curtains in a way you can't usually when the houses are lit from the inside. As I turn the corner on to the main road, I see a single window alight, a small square one at the top of the detached house on the corner. Someone is up and using the bathroom – I don't know the occupants of that house but feel briefly affronted that I don't have the night to myself.

The main road is deserted. It takes me ten minutes to walk its length and in that time only one car passes, at speed, someone hurrying to be home. I cross the road just before the roundabout and marvel at how easy it is. I am used to negotiating my right to be in a road, whether I am on foot or driving a car, used to feeling that my occupation of any given space must be carefully managed and only then with the permission of others. It is exciting to feel I own this night, emboldening. Why haven't I done this more often?

It used to take us twenty minutes to walk to Betty's school – longer if Rees insisted on getting out of his pushchair, as he often did. It was always a relief to reach Fulton Avenue, the penultimate road. *Nearly there. We'll make it just before the bell.* If we were on the left-hand side – the side opposite Ranmali's shop – then I would sometimes bid Betty goodbye and let her run on alone from there.

I am on the left-hand side now. I am standing on the pavement. I have my back to Ranmali's shop and am facing the playing fields, the gates of which are padlocked with a heavy chain. Tied along the railings are bunches of rotting flowers, heads shrivelled until they are unidentifiable, hanging at diagonals. Some are wrapped in cellophane and these have degraded more quickly than the others, brown slime inside. Some of them have notes attached. I step towards them and try to read one but rain has washed away the writing which is no more than a few slanting, pale-blue lines. At the bottom of the railings are more flowers, also rotting, including a couple of more recent ones where the blooms are still identifiable: there is one with pink chrysanthemums. Next to it is a row of three cuddly toys, two teddy bears and one soft duck. The duck has been splashed by mud from passing cars and lies on its side, fur matted. One of the teddies is blue. It is wearing a yellow T-shirt and a yellow hat.

I turn my back on the rotting flowers and the blue teddy. To my right is the way back home along the main road and to my left, the sharp corner where Fulton Avenue becomes Fulton Road, the road that Betty's school is on. I close my eyes. The cold air washes over my face. In my head, I see a large black car with bull bars come swinging round the corner, Willow being flung sideways on to the verge, Betty flying straight up into the air. I hear the brakes, the thump.

When I open my eyes, I am on my knees in the middle of the road. A light rain is falling. I can feel the rough tarmac and tiny stones against my bare legs. I am making a screeching sound. A yellow rectangle of light snaps on in the flat above Ranmali's shop. A curtain moves. The screeching sound continues. A small figure rushes towards me. Ranmali bends to lift me up from the road and my fists swing at her. I think I manage to hit her but the blows are so wild and she is so small and soft I have the sensation that I am beating the air as much as her. I can hear her husband shouting. Hands grab at me. I continue to flail at the black air and screech. A car approaches, slowly it seems to me, the blue light on top spinning elegantly, with all the gentle grace of the starfish light that I have left swirling on Betty's bedside table. It makes an interesting pattern on the sheet of corrugated iron that Ranmali and her husband have nailed across what used to be the window of their shop. A second or so later, a van pulls up behind it. As the men in uniforms approach, I suck in air to scream again. They are moving slowly and carefully, it seems to me, as I thrash around on the ground. Slowly and carefully, one of them kneels next to me, then lies down and takes me in a bear hug, a parody of a love embrace, holding me firmly against him and talking to me softly all the while. Ranmali and her husband have melted into the dark. The other policeman is standing waiting, looking down at me and his colleague. He is holding a small, thin canister in his hand, which I later identify as CS spray. His colleague clutches me tight, my face against the shiny yellow bulk of his high-visibility jacket, and continues to talk to me, over and over, his voice low and soft, 'Easy now, it's okay now, easy . . .' He has a deep voice, coaxing, but I carry on howling and thrashing – lost to myself and fighting them because they want to bring me back, kicking and struggling all the way down the long, dark tunnel into which I am so ready to fall.

7

I am of average height and slender build but it still takes two police officers to get me into the back of the van – once we are in, one of them pins me down on the floor of the van, lying on my side, while the other places his hand underneath my head, to cushion it. When we get to the emergency admissions room of the psychiatric unit, they help the orderly hold me down while the duty doctor gives me 10 mg of Diazepam – I check it on the notes the next day because I am interested in how fast it works and how quickly it wears off, after about five hours – 10 mg is quite a large dose, 5 mg would be more normal.

The next day, I am tired but coherent and the first thing I say to the psychiatrist who interviews me that morning is that I won't take drugs. Why don't I try a course of Venlafaxine? asks the psychiatrist, a young Asian woman with a wary air, clearly uneasy about dealing with another professional. Later, I hazard a guess that she has discussed my stubbornness with other staff members on the unit because that afternoon, when I am back on the ward, a nurse comes and sits next to me and says, 'You know, there's nothing shameful about admitting you need a bit of help, now and then. Think about what you would say to yourself if you were one of your patients.' When I don't reply, she rises from her stool with a sigh and mutters resentfully, turning to go, 'If you were diabetic you'd take insulin, wouldn't you?' They think I am refusing because I am wallowing in grief or just proud or some vastly annoying combination of the two. Perhaps they think I am doing it to spoil their day, to make them feel less successful. I don't bother telling them that when you have watched your mother disintegrate after many years of dopamine you develop a passionate hatred of long-term medication. Besides, I have a new resolution. Everyone thinks that after many weeks of coping, I have finally imploded but I know the reverse to be true.

Eventually, they send in David.

I am sitting in the day room when he arrives. As soon as he comes through the door, I announce that they have agreed to discharge me. I have been brought in on an emergency section but am now a voluntary patient. They have suggested I stay but reluctantly conceded I may leave.

David looks like he is in pain. He draws up a straight-backed plastic chair and sits down next to me. I am seated on a high, orthopaedic armchair, designed to allow infirm people to lower themselves and rise again. It feels throne-like. The day room smells perceptibly of cigarette smoke even though nobody is allowed to smoke in here. In the far corner, an elderly man sits in a chair similar to mine, talking to himself. Most of the time his words are no more than a mumble but every now and then he hollers a phrase that makes it clear he is having an argument with a long-dead wife.

Every time I see David I think he looks older – but if that were true he would look ancient. Perhaps it is simply that, between times, I forget how old we both are now and it is a shock to be reminded. I look at him and feel empty of emotion – no, not empty, but my feeling for him is no more than a background note, a slight, dull, pointless aggression. I would rather talk to Toni than him, any day. He rests a hand on the arm of my upholstered chair. 'Look, I know you really want to go home. I know you must be desperate to see Rees.'

At the sound of Rees's name, I feel a stab of pain. 'How is Rees?' I say. I don't want him to see me in the ward. It would frighten him.

David pulls a face that indicates, *okay, sort of*. Rees will not be traumatised by his stay with his father. He has done it often

109

enough before. At least he will have regular meals, distractions.

David grimaces. I know you so well, I think, and I know you are building up to something.

'Laura,' he says. 'You left the door open.'

I look at his hand on the arm of my chair. I think, he has put it there as a substitute for putting it on my arm. He is gripping the chair tightly. He looks at the floor. In the far corner, the old man shouts, 'Jezebel! Harlot! Cunt!' An auxiliary wanders in with a watering can and tops up the water in the vase of fading tulips on the windowsill.

'When you left the house in the night,' David continues, 'you left the front door open. Anyone could have walked in. *Rees* was asleep upstairs, Laura. He stayed asleep and the police came and got me so I was there when he woke up in the morning but what if he'd woken up? Laura . . .'

It comes again, the stab of pain at the mere thought of Rees, of my inexcusable desertion of him, not just that night but ever since Betty was taken from me. Something inside me folds inwards and I feel a dark, maternal panic – I close my eyes briefly and squash the feeling down. I cannot allow myself to love Rees, to even think of Rees, I cannot, or the separation from him will be unbearable. I give a deep sigh. I look at my hands and pick at some rough skin around my right thumb-nail. *But nobody did walk in*, I want to say to David. *Rees didn't wake up. Rees is fine. He's fine with you and Chloe.*

David draws breath and says, 'I want you to let Rees stay with us for a bit, just for a bit, Laura. I can take him to nursery on the way to work and Julie has said she doesn't mind having him after like she does now. Chloe is happy to do the other afternoons. She's got her mum around a lot to help anyway. If you don't like that then I'll do short days for a bit. I can ask for whatever I like at the moment.'

So that was what he was anxious about. 'Of course,' I say, turning my face away. 'Of course you can keep Rees for a bit.'

I don't need to be looking at him to feel his relief. It radiates from him, like body heat.

'What about you?' he says, tenderly, and lifts his hand from the arm of the chair and places it on mine. 'I'm so worried about you. We all are.'

We? Which 'we' is this, then? He doesn't sound all that desperate to me. He sounds relieved. He has got what he came for, custody of Rees. 'Well, Toni seems to be keeping a pretty close eye on me.'

He presses his lips together. 'She's good, isn't she? I didn't know they did that.'

'Liaison, it's called.'

'Even so.'

'Well, there probably isn't much call for it round here.'

David shakes his head and speaks with what seems to me to be unwarranted bitterness. 'Christ, I don't know how you can say that with everything that's been going on.'

You've got what you want. You can leave now, I think as I rise, but what I say is, 'Better go and clear out my locker.' The old man in the corner is quiet now, staring toward the window. His lips are moving methodically but they make no sound.

Back home, I toss my handbag and a plastic bag of clothing on to the bottom of the stairs and run up to change and shower. David offered to drive me back but I had to wait to be seen before I could be discharged and in the end he had to leave, so I got a minicab home.

I have been alone a lot recently but this is the first time I have not had to think of and prepare myself for Rees's imminent return. I realise what a weight it has been, having to perform for him. As I pass his bedroom door on the way to my room, still wet and wrapped in a towel, I feel a pang of guilt as I glimpse a collection of trucks lined up neatly on his bedroom floor. Rees likes to have all his trucks ready to be driven at any moment. He drives each one in turn, methodically, pushing it around the room before returning it to its place. I have overheard him talking to them, explaining why they have to take it in turns. Will he be missing me? Will he be confused? Not yet, I think; it's only been two days, and anyway, he is robust. If I have learned anything since Betty went away, it is how robust Rees is. I will make it up to him, one day, I think vaguely. If I have the opportunity to miss him, maybe I will be capable of doing that sooner. As I dress in fresh clothes, I try to analyse my briskness. Am I really so indifferent to how my son is managing without me? No, it is simply that I know that at the moment David and Chloe can look after him better than I can, and I have plans.

I clatter down the stairs. I toss the plastic bag towards the kitchen and check my handbag for keys, purse, mobile phone. I lift the car key from its hook by the mirror. I slam the door shut behind me as I go.

I park in the car park at the back of the High Street and stay in the car for a moment. I can feel my energy, my courage, begin to fade. I need coffee before I go in – I get one to take away from Gregg's on the High Street and then walk slowly back through the car park and into the atrium of the modern building that houses the council offices, sipping the coffee through the tiny hole in the lid which makes it burning hot and plastic-tasting. The library is on the second floor of the council offices and I take the stainless-steel lift, just as I used to when I had Rees in his buggy. The lift doors open directly opposite the glass doors into the library and I will be able to see immediately who is behind the Enquiries desk.

I know one of the librarians quite well. Naomi has children at Betty's school and works in the library part-time. Her youngest was in the same year group as Betty but a different class. I have avoided other parents from the school successfully up until now. I can't go in if Naomi is working today – this way, if I see her, I can press a button quickly and stay in the lift.

The lift doors open. There is a young woman I don't know behind the desk. I step out of the lift, clutching my Styrofoam cup. The coffee is not allowed inside, of course, so it gives me a good excuse to hover in the hallway while I finish it, glancing through the wide swing doors. No sign of Naomi behind the Loans and Returns desk either. Good. The coast is clear.

There is no bin, so when I have drained my cup I squash it and stuff it into my coat pocket. As I push through the swing doors, a man in an electric wheelchair approaches so I hold the door for him. 'Do you want me to call the lift?' I say as he passes through.

'I can manage,' he snaps in reply.

I stride past the Enquiries desk. To the right of it is the children's books section. I have spent many an hour there over the past few years. The section I want is at the back, just past the encyclopaedias.

The library doesn't keep back copies of the national newspapers but it keeps copies of all three of the local papers – the broadsheet for the whole region, its trashier, tabloid rival, and a free paper for the town which has some news on pages one and three but is mostly advertisements for local shops and restaurants. Only the broadsheet is available online but even if they all were I would still have wanted to come and see the hard copies. It is layout I want, photos, column inches and size of headings. What has happened to Betty has ended my world but the world has not ended; the world is still going to school or work, eating, sleeping, watching television. I want to know what the end of my world means to the rest of the world. I am ready for that now.

The newspapers are filed the old-fashioned way, in wide wooden drawers, in reverse date order, the most recent edition on top. I move swiftly, knowing that if I stop to think about it I will lose the ability to do it. I pull open the drawer for the broadsheet. The most recently filed paper is last week's – this week's will be lying on a table somewhere. The headline is about plans to build a new secondary school on the edge of town. I lift the papers one by one, turning back the clock. Working this way, the first glimpse I see of my girl – and it makes the breath catch in my throat – is a small headline in the bottom right-hand corner of the front page: *Council probes road safety.* I know it is a follow-up story about Betty and Willow because in the first sentence I catch sight of the phrase *double tragedy.*

I work backwards and as I do, the girls spread and populate the front pages. They gain importance. I carry on past *Second Victim Dies.* Willow is resurrected. I pass over, *Hit and Run: Man Arrested* – I will come back to that one later – until I reach the day when the news broke. There is my daughter. It is a large school photo, not the most recent one. They must have got it from David. My eyes swim and my vision blurs.

It takes me a moment or two, then I lift the papers, one by one again. I extract the relevant half dozen and lay them on top of the drawer unit. Then I turn to the drawers for the other papers.

When I have selected the ones I need, I peer carefully around the unit. There are chairs grouped around a set of tables in the open area in the centre of the library but that is far too public an arena. I could go and ask for a key to one of the three carrels by the windows but that would be drawing attention to myself. In the end, I sit down on the floor, out of sight, behind the units.

I read methodically, and I discover that a nine-year-old girl was killed instantly on Fulton Avenue on 18 February at 4.35 p.m. She had left school late after her Capoeira club and was on her way to a tap dance lesson at the Methodist Church Hall on Holly Road, where her mother was waiting for her. It was the first occasion she had been allowed to walk round on her own.

Her friend, who was crossing the road with her at the time, was injured and is being cared for in hospital but is expected to make a full recovery. The driver of the vehicle stopped after the accident but then drove off. He later attended the local police station where he was arrested. Police are appealing for any witnesses to the incident.

It is only after Willow's death that the local papers gave free reign to an angle they must have considered from day one. The driver was a recent immigrant to the town, aged fifty-four. He lived in the caravan park on the clifftop that sprang up five years ago to house the migrants who work mostly on the industrial estate beyond Eastley: there is a pet-food processing plant there that takes local fish waste, a sofa factory, a packaging centre, enough businesses to replace the industrial agriculture that used to make our town viable. I can't remember whether the businesses came first or the migrant workers. There has been some bad publicity about enmity between different groups of workers, the Koreans versus the Eastern Europeans, I seem to remember. One report refers to a statement from the Upton Centre.

The tabloid appears twice a week and the free sheet is every weekday. Their coverage is so brief it is barely literate but I get more of a day-by-day account from them. Two days after Willow died in the District General, a group of youths went up to the caravan park on the cliff and threw bricks through the windows of one of the mobile homes. An altercation between the youths and a group of men ensued. Several men are helping police with enquiries. The following night, in the small hours, someone threw a metal bin through the window of Mr Yeung, the chippy.

Mr Yeung the chippy has been on the esplanade for as long as I can remember. The family who run it now are Korean but they are the third owners in recent years, nothing to do with Mr Yeung, whoever he was, who opened the chippy decades ago. On the same night, another bin was thrown at Ranmali's shop. The window was damaged but did not smash. That explains the corrugated iron.

Now I understand Toni's solicitousness. Now I understand how the rest of the world is viewing what has happened to my girl through its own particular prism. The reports make the attacks sound co-ordinated but I doubt it. I have seen the lads who hang around, the same bunch you get in every town, too old to be taught anything, too young to learn. It was probably the same ones who punched the bonnet of my car.

I am avoiding what I don't want to see but eventually am forced to face it. I turn a page, innocently enough. It is an edition of the broadsheet that appeared three weeks after Betty was taken away from me. There, relegated to page two, is the same photograph of my girl, wearing the same strained expression she always adopted for school photos. And next to it, right next to it, is him, the man who killed my daughter. Underneath, the caption reads. *Hit and run: girls to blame.* He has a heavy-set face, large-browed – the photograph is black and white and his eyes are strangely pale and bleached-looking. He is dressed in a jacket over a thick jumper. He has a slight smile. His name is Aleksandar Ahmetaj; I think of him immediately as Mr A. He was driving a black Toyota land cruiser, with bull bars.

I close my eyes. What I cannot bear is that the photographs are equal size.

As I leave the building, I scrabble in my handbag for my mobile phone. When my fingers locate it, they close around it and turn it over a couple of times, confirming its shape. I lift the phone out and turn it on. It plays me a merry tune as I cross the car park. I am so impatient, I don't even unlock my car and get into it. Instead, I sit on the low wall at the back of the library and flick through the contacts list on my phone. I dial Jan H.

I am expecting her voicemail but she picks up the phone herself.

'Jan,' I say, 'it's Laura.'

The briefest of pauses, then, 'Hello,' she says warmly. 'How are you?'

Of course. Poor Jan. This is the first time I have spoken to her in person since what happened. It must sound odd to her that my voice is so bright, so normal. 'It's okay,' I say quickly, 'it's not, I mean, I'm ringing for a favour, a practical favour. Thank you for the card. All of them. I'm sorry I haven't – well, I know you won't mind about that, I'm okay. How's everything going?'

'Well it's going,' she gives a false little laugh. 'Fucking awful, if you want the truth.' Her voice becomes low, simple. 'We miss you, hon.'

'I know,' I say, looking down at the toes of my boots, then up at the sky, 'I miss you too.' It comes to me that that is true. I do miss my workmates, and I don't mean I am just missing them because they were part of the life I had before Betty went away. They were, are, a good bunch, a gang. Work was the one thing that sustained me through David and Chloe. My husband and his shiny new love: to Jan H and Maurice and Andrew and Sunita they were nothing more than a cliché, a sick little soap opera, something I must be consoled about in the same way I would be consoled over a nasty bout of flu. My husband's infidelity, so all-consuming, so painful to me, was no more than a story to my team, fit for mockery, derision: but what perspective can they offer me now? The routine tragedy of my marriage could be tumble-dried by gossip, emerging clean and shrunken, but the loss of Betty cannot be reduced without insult. They will know that as surely as do I. It is why I have been avoiding them, why I avoid everybody.

'Listen, I've been thinking about coming back . . .' This is not true, but under the circumstances, I don't feel guilty. Jan H would not blame me for the lie.

'Really?' I hear the frown in her voice. 'It feels soon.' I can picture her at her desk, windmilling a biro between her fingers, a habit we shared.

'I know, I know it is, I'm not sure at all, actually. I've just been thinking about it, I was just wondering, how would you feel if I came by one day, after hours? I know it sounds a bit strange. I just want to come and see how I feel about the unit. I don't really want to come when people are around . . .'

'You mean visit, visit the building?'

'Yes, when it's empty, just to see how it's going to feel, like a rehearsal.'

'Of course, don't be daft. When do you want to come?'

I feign vagueness. 'Don't know really, soon, so's I can think about it over the weekend. Later on, tonight?'

'Tonight?' Her voice is startled. 'Tonight's not good to be honest, hon. Team B are having a late meeting, I mean, you'll be bumping into people. You know what Team B are like.'

The Rehabilitation and Therapies Unit is behind the main hospital building. Most of our offices close at 5 p.m.

'What about tomorrow?'

She makes a dry sound, 'Tomorrow's fine, Friday night, you'll have the place to yourself. Might be a bit bleak though.'

'What time do you finish?'

'God, if I'm not out of here by six I'll cut my throat.'

'Can I meet you at six, at the front? Would you mind leaving me with the keys, I can bring them round to you later, if you like? And would you mind not mentioning this to anyone? It just feels a bit weird.'

'You can leave them at the porter's lodge, if you like. Laura, are you sure this is the best way of doing it? There's an awful lot of people here would like to give you a big hug when you step back in the door.'

About this, I am able to be completely honest. 'I know. I just need to brace myself a bit before I go for that one.'

'Fair enough.'

As I unlock my car, I think that I now have an insight into my own power, the way in which my distress gives me leverage over others, how their solicitude bends them to me.

On my way back home, I drive down the esplanade. I want to see if Mr Yeung's have repaired their window – they have, and appear to be open for business again. A moment later, I see there is a parking space on a meter on the beach side of the road. I have a sudden desire for cold air. Swerving the car inexpertly, I pull in to the space, and then spend forever manoeuvring to and fro. I need to walk to process what I know, as if the mechanical process of moving my leg muscles will allow me to think about the information I have and project forward, towards the information I do not yet have, to try and link the two. The beach became my chosen venue for walks after David filled me in on a few choice details about him and Chloe. I don't go up to the cliffs any more.

I lock the car and walk down the steps, stumbling slightly on the shingle. There is a little tea-coloured sunshine. It gives the beach an apricot glow, softening the wet pebbles, making the slowly rushing waves appear benign. It is busy for that time of day: dog walkers, the unemployed, retired people – everyone seems to have seized the chance to convince themselves that winter's grip is loosening. I stride and stagger across the rough shore, hardly looking at the sea, all the way to the far end of the esplanade. At that end, the beach slopes sharply – to go back up to pavement level, you have to climb a tall flight of steep stone steps with an iron handrail. I pause for a moment, wondering whether to go back along the beach or climb upwards. I am cold. I walk over to the stone stairs.

Halfway up the stairs, I pause to fumble in my pocket for a tissue, the same pocket into which I crumpled my coffee cup at the library. As I extract the tissue, shreds of polystyrene escape from the pocket and the wind snatches them up. They look like snow. I watch the shreds swoop upwards once, loopily, then tumble to the beach. Beyond them, close to the water's edge, is a family of four; two parents, a young boy and a baby. The baby is in his father's arms and the young boy is lifting stones up to show the baby, as if he wants the baby to take one and throw it into the sea. The mother is laughing. The father takes the stone from the young boy and hands the baby to the mother, then reaches back with his arm, way back, and throws as hard as a professional cricketer. The young boy jumps with glee, mouth open, then stumbles on the pebbles and lands on his backside. The mother and father bend simultaneously to help him up. The young boy is my son, Rees, playing on the beach, happy with his family.

When I get home, I make myself more coffee, even though I am still hollow and speedy from the last one. Coffee has been my staple diet for the last few weeks – I have a piece of bread occasionally. If I am feeling really strong, I will attempt a Cup-a-Soup. The loss of appetite seems so insignificant to me I find it odd that people keep asking me about it. I am not avoiding food. It just doesn't register. I make myself a piece of toast with marmalade now, for instance, then leave it on the plate on the kitchen countertop, not deliberately, it just doesn't seem important. As I am about to leave the kitchen with my coffee, I remember the toast, return to the counter-top, take a single bite and lose interest before I have even swallowed. I leave the rest on the plate, knowing it will still be there, cold and congealed, when I come back down later.

I take my coffee up to the bedroom. Our computer, a cheap old PC, is on a small desk in the corner. The kids' stuff always took up so much room downstairs that our bedroom was the only place for the computer to go. I have not turned it on since

Betty went away and in truth I didn't even use it much before, using my work email address and Internet access for most things. I open Google, then type in Betty's name.

The news stories from the nationals do not tell me anything new – they are more in-depth and sensitive elaborations of what has appeared in the locals. A couple of pieces investigate the local unrest angle. There is a long article in one broadsheet that uses the accident as a peg to hang a whole piece about cultural clashes between different migrant groups who have settled in coastal towns. Before I lost Betty, I might have been interested in such a debate but now I find it offensive. These articles are missing the point. The point is Betty. Eventually, I find the picture of him, my Mr A, the same one that the local papers used. I print it out.

Outside, the light begins to fade. The sky deepens swiftly from white to grey to grey tinged with purple ... indigo, black. The day closes. A winter's evening descends as surely as rain. I do not draw the curtains, or turn on the light, and soon the room is lit only by the square glow from the computer screen. I might be any office worker, unable to leave until a task is finished, or a student hard at work on an essay – I can remember the days of that absorption, the shrinking of the world to an individual task, the way the world flips open again when you draw away and turn on a light.

I reach down to the printer, pick up the sheet of A4 paper with the printed photo of the man who killed my daughter, one movement, down and up – foolish: the caffeine has drained from my system and there is nothing in its place. The movement makes me dizzy. *I hear you've gone quite mad.* Malevolence outside my window, in the dark, I feel it pressing in upon me. Betty is gone. Rees is absent. I picture him as I saw him on the beach, missing his step and plumping down on the pebbles, David and Chloe bending simultaneously to help him up, laughing. The white square of light from the computer screen on the table is just enough for me to be able to regard Mr A. He is staring out of the photo at me, with that half-smile; boxer's nose, large earlobes. This is no callow boy, dumbstruck by the horror of what he has done. This is a man.

I stare at the photo. I try to read his gaze, each fold on his face, the slight frown. He arrived here four years ago. Last year, he was prosecuted under labour welfare laws. On the beach, once David and Chloe had lifted Rees from his sitting position on the pebbles, Chloe brushed down his trousers with her hand, still laughing, her corkscrew curls falling in front of her face. I study the photo in the same way that a spy might study the face of a counterpart in a rival organisation. I am calm as I make this promise: I am going to find out what you love, then whatever it is, I am going to track it down and I am going to take it away from you.

PART 3

Before

8

David got to hold her first. Sheena the midwife checked her over, pronounced her a sparkling ten on the Agpar scale, swaddled her and handed her to her father. I was on my back on the high bed; dazed and disbelieving. Sheena and the trainee midwife were seated on stools at the foot of the bed. The delivery room was high-ceilinged, echoey. I heard Sheena say quietly, 'Now, I don't really like putting stitches here because there's a lot of nerve endings but I think we better had.' I'm not going to like this much, I thought, and I didn't.

'In all directions then, is it?' I called down to them, when I could speak again.

'I'm afraid so, but don't you worry, we're going to sort you out now.' Sheena lifted her head and beamed at me. 'You're going to be just fine now.' Sheena and I worked together for three years before I had my daughter and she delivered half the babies born in this town during that period. She walked on water as far as I was concerned.

I turned my head to watch David who was sitting in the chair next to my bed, holding *her*, our girl, smiling down at her while they worked on me. His face glowed as though lit by a campside fire. It took a lot to render David speechless but he was silent now, lips pressed together, gaze locked so firmly it would have taken a crowbar to shift it.

I had had 50 mg of Pethidine but was learning the hard way that that didn't help much when it came to stitching torn muscle – another pain stung through me, so sharp and hot I could not locate its starting point, knew only that it finished somewhere deep inside. I gasped out loud but David did not lift his gaze from his daughter. I didn't mind. She was too swaddled for me to see her but watching David's face as he stared and stared at his new baby girl was almost as good, as though his face was a reflective pool. Eventually, I was allowed to raise myself. Sheena sent the trainee midwife out to make me tea and toast and then leaned forward and took Betty from David's reluctant grasp. 'Let's give Mum a turn, shall we?' she said firmly. She handed Betty to me. At last. I lifted my T-shirt, the one I later discarded because it was bloodstained, loosened the swaddling a little and placed my new baby girl at my breast. She stared up at me with midnight-blue eyes and latched on. There was still a little blood on her forehead. Sheena, watching, gave a broad smile. 'Sure, you're not going to have any problems with that little person.'

Sheena was right. We never did. It was as though Betty had spent her time in the womb flicking idly through textbooks on what was expected of a newborn baby. She fed every four hours. She smiled right on cue, at six weeks. She held her head up nicely at three months. David and I were the smuggest parents on the planet, which, considering how smug all parents of newborn babies are, is saying something. We had only two topics of conversation, in those early months. The first was the utter superiority of our baby to all other babies ever born, and the second was the utter superiority of our parenting to that of all other parents. In the post-natal classes, I would listen with a small smile to the tales of other mothers – how their babies were awake all night, how they just wouldn't latch on, how the antibiotics they had taken for mastitis had given the babies thrush. When I got home, I would relate every detail of these conversations to David and we would sit together over dinner and unpick each one of their complaints, shaking our heads. Why did other parents make such a meal of it? What was their problem?

Betty was eighteen months old when I got the phone call from the home. I had been expecting it for so long that I didn't expect it any more and when it happened I experienced a strange sense of vertigo, similar to the one I felt when David dangled me over the clifftop: a weak, hollow sensation. 'I'm very sorry,' said the doctor who made the call. 'I've got some very bad news.' My mother had been frail for years. It was a chest infection got her in the end.

My mother was not part of my daily routine – she had never been able to bathe my baby daughter with me, or babysit. I missed her absence more than her presence. I missed the mother who died in her sleep after many years in a nursing home but also the mother I would have had had her illness not taken a grip when I was so young. In that sense, my mourning had a level of self-indulgence quite startling in its purity. I had been called brave so often during her illness that I handled her death with a degree of cowardice to which I felt quite entitled, as if I had been storing up self-pity all those years, only liberated to indulge it when my mum was no longer there as a living example of how much worse her situation was than mine. I mourned the person I would have been had I been raised by a healthy mother.

Three weeks after my mother's funeral, David came into the bedroom one evening, where I was sitting up in bed reading a book called *A Good Innings* – Sunita at work had lent me her battered paperback copy. Her father had died of motor neurone disease. As long as you got past the chapter on learning to rebirth yourself, she said, it had some interesting things to say. I had just read the line, 'It can be hurtful to realise that others around you regard grief for an elderly parent as excessive or self-indulgent.'

David was standing by the bed, working both shoulders

backwards. 'I think I'm going to have to get health and safety to look at my chair again,' he said. He had tried any number of different designs of chair in front of his desk at work, nothing helped. It was David that needed redesigning, his tall, poorly constructed frame.

I glanced up at him, over the yellow oval of light that fell on the book from the reading lamp clipped to the headboard behind me. My reading glasses were perched on the end of my nose, so I looked at him over them, a level look. Seeing he had my attention, he took a step towards me and turned around. 'It's here,' he said, 'lower than before, right down here.' He prodded at his lower back, then arched backwards, wincing.

'Take a Nurofen,' I said, and returned to my book.

Then there was Betty and all the glorious shapes of Betty; Betty who clambered into our bed each morning and huddled down between us for all of thirty seconds before she decided it was time to stand up and use my pillow – over which my hair was still strewn – as a trampoline; Betty who would wear nothing but her purple dungarees with the appliquéd dog on the bib front. Dog trousers, she called them. She would have slept in them if we let her. If I put them through the wash, she would howl as if she was being tortured. After she had started school, I came across a video cassette of her at eighteen months and went to the trouble of extricating the old video and TV from the pile of junk in the box room in order to watch it. She was lumbering in her tiny fashion around the sitting room of Aunt Lorraine's house, at some large gathering with adults seated on sofas, bashing people's knees with an inflatable hammer. Although the adults in the scene were off-camera, it was clear from the shrieks of laughter on the tape that we all considered this to be exceptionally clever and amusing behaviour. Every now and then, Betty turned to the camera and waved the hammer gleefully. It took me a few minutes to work out what was bothering me about the scene. It was only when she pointed a finger at the camera, then at something the camera couldn't see, turned back and said, 'Shoosh!' that I worked it out. She wasn't talking. Why wasn't she talking? I thought, momentarily baffled. Ah, of course, she was only eighteen months old. She couldn't talk. How strange that there should have ever been a time when she couldn't talk, when even 'dog trousers' was a distant and unimaginable accomplishment. This was something that always amazed me. Each successive Betty erased the Betty that preceded her – yet they were all still inside her, like a Russian doll, or one of those paper strings of figures you make by folding a sheet many times and cutting it, then unfolding it again.

Lorraine's house was the usual venue for these get-togethers. It was a large, red-brick semi, vaguely Edwardian, on the very edge of Eastley, the next town along the coast from ours. I felt warmly towards it, remembering that I had been a hit on my very first visit there – as a result I was close to Lorraine in a way I wasn't to David's reserved mother. David's mother and father were quiet, pleasant people who gave me the distinct impression that I wasn't quite good enough for their beloved only son – nearly, but not quite. Lorraine, on the other hand, was easy to please. She liked people who laughed at her jokes and helped her carry dishes from room to room. It wasn't much to ask and I joined in with alacrity. I thought of her as my ally.

If anyone knew in advance which way my marriage was likely to go, it would have been Lorraine. We were washing up in her kitchen one Sunday afternoon – or rather I was washing up while she loaded the dishwasher. David's sister Ceri was in and out taking orders for tea or coffee from the half-dozen relatives in the sitting room. 'What's the chance of that brother of yours mowing my lawn while he's here?' Lorraine said to her. 'Or are the boys glued to the armchairs for the rest of the day now?'

'Not much,' Ceri replied coolly. 'Uncle Richard is showing him the paint stripper.'

'Oh hell . . .' muttered Lorraine. Uncle Richard, her husband, had a merry laugh and angina. Lawn-mowing and DIY were both out, but that didn't stop him purchasing labour-saving devices as if he was opening a museum dedicated to them. David was always required to admire the new labour-saving device when we visited, on account of how he designed such things himself. He probably would rather have been mowing the lawn.

A little female solidarity was called for. 'I can't get him to do even ours,' I said to Lorraine as Ceri bustled out of the room again. 'The weekends are always so busy and he's never back from work before half past eight these days.' In fact, I didn't mind that he often worked late and missed Betty's bedtime. It was easier to put her to bed alone than to have her over-excited by David's return just as we were on the final page of *No Roses for Harry*.

Lorraine did not respond immediately, but continued loading the dishwasher. 'Off down the boozer with the boys, is it?'

There was something about the way she said it, a dryness in her tone I had not heard before, that made me pause in what I was doing, my hands still in the foaming suds – she used a different brand of washing-up liquid from mine and I had put too much in. It was frothing up over the sides and on to the countertop.

'No, no . . . well, not that often I don't think . . .' David went to the pub after work sometimes but recently he had been too busy, I thought. I realised I didn't know which it was: the office or the pub. He didn't volunteer the information and I didn't ask. I never asked David questions, after all, it was always the other way around. This was pre-Chloe, when as far as I knew,

David and I were happy together and my life with Betty was absorbing enough for me not to question that.

I still didn't know any different, there in Lorraine's kitchen, but what came to me then was an awareness that I didn't know any different – knowledge that my ignorance existed.

Aunt Lorraine lifted the door of the dishwasher awkwardly – her bulk made her stiff when she bent. She twiddled with the dial, pushed two buttons with jabs of her plump forefinger and the dishwasher made a *je-jung* sound as it bounced and ground into life. She picked up a tea towel from the countertop and wiped her hands. Still without looking at me, she said thoughtfully, 'Well, there's a price to pay with a boy like our David, I suppose.' She looked at the door, towards where her sitting room was full of her husband and her relatives. Her expression was clouded. 'I should know that as well as anyone . . .' she muttered.

I didn't know what she was talking about. A price? What price was I paying for having David? What price had she paid for Uncle Richard? It seemed an odd way to refer to a relationship – was there always a price to be paid? If so, I wasn't aware that I was paying one.

We finished clearing up, then took coffee for ourselves and went into the sitting room where Uncle Richard was playing a board game with the older of Ceri's two boys – the youngest boy was upstairs with Betty. Everyone else was sitting on chairs around the room. The paint stripper sat, admired and then discarded, amongst half-finished wine-glasses on the dining table. 'They are playing weddings,' David informed me, referring to our daughter and her cousin, and pulled a face. I sat down on the arm of the sofa and leaned towards him, reaching out a hand to smooth down his hair where it was sticking up and crinkled, towards the back of his head. He moved his head away. I had only meant to be affectionate but the sharpness of his movement suggested irritation, as if he thought I was trying to infantilise him.

The door from the hallway opened; in walked Betty. She had an old net curtain round her shoulders and was using one hand to clutch it in place. In the other, she held a sink plunger, thrust before her like a ceremonial mace. On her head, she was wearing a yellow T-shirt that she had helped herself to from Lorraine's laundry basket and which I knew to be in lieu of a gold crown – in Betty's mind, the line between brides and princesses was blurry. Both got to dress up and be worshipped and that was fine by her.

We broke into spontaneous applause. All the adults gave their own, particular sort of exhalation – vocalised in my case, a long 'Aaah . . .', a sigh from Aunt Lorraine, a grin from David, an explosive chuckle from Uncle Richard, who reached out to grab her, destabilising the yellow T-shirt. Whatever the different quality of those reactions, they all meant the same thing to Betty as she pushed herself free of Uncle Richard, replaced the T-shirt on her head and stood in the middle of the room, clutching the rubber plunger and beaming round at us all. *All I have to do is walk into a room*, she was saying to herself. *That's all I have to do.*

I leaned over and kissed the top of David's head and this time he did not move away but reached out a hand and squeezed my knee in acknowledgement of our shared pride. In that respect, nothing had changed. We were still the smuggest parents in the world.

When Rees was born, it was payback time. It began with the trouble I had feeding him. He wouldn't latch on if his life depended on it – which it would have done were it not for the joys of formula milk. I developed mastitis and had to take antibiotics. Oh, and he screamed all night. It was only then I realised what a mistake I had made in having our easy baby first. 'God,' I said to David one evening, 'I had coffee at Sally's house this morning.'

'Mmm . . .' he murmured, wiping down the hob, while I sat on a high kitchen stool, a wide-awake little Rees in my arms. I launched into my tale with some enthusiasm. This sort of story was what filled my day at that point in our lives.

'I was trying to feed him, you wouldn't believe how smug that woman is . . .' The youngest of Sally's four children, Willow, had just gone up to Reception with Betty and Sally was incredibly broody. She had watched me trying to feed Rees at her kitchen table and made one suggestion after another. By the time she said, 'Have you tried lying flat on your back with him across your shoulder?' I had been ready to scream. The harder I had tried to get Rees to latch on, the more frantic he had become. I was sweating profusely – Sally's kitchen was overheated, I had just had a hot drink and both breasts were full, the pads in my nursing bra sodden with warm milk. In the end, Sally had almost snatched Rees from me and walked around her kitchen with him on her shoulder while I removed my zip-up fleece, took deep breaths and tried to calm down. Rees, meanwhile, had become more and more hysterical. By the time Sally handed him back – unwillingly, for it was admitting defeat – he was beetroot-coloured.

'Honestly,' I burbled to David, as he stood with his back to me, attending to a boiled-over, dried-hard crust of something on the hob, 'someone should explain to that woman that childrearing doesn't have to be a competitive sport. It's only because she's got nothing else going on in her life, that's why she's so obsessed with being helpful. And then, when I did finally get him latched on, she tried telling me that . . .'

I told this story to David in the same way I told him all my stories about my day with Rees, with an air of cheery desperation to which he never responded. I was trying to re-conjure his fascination with Betty when she was a newborn, our shared joy at that time. But by then, Chloe was on the scene.

Chloe arrived in our lives before Rees was born, before he was even conceived, when Betty was four years old. David had just been promoted and was Chief Designer. He didn't design pens – their designs were set in stone – he designed the machines that made the pens, the cutters and pressers and enamellers. As far as I could work out, being Chief Designer meant he did less designing, rather than more. It meant he got dragged into endless managerial meetings with the men who decided how many other men and women lost their jobs because of his improved designs for the machines. David was a draughtsman at heart. What he liked was spending hours over huge wooden boards with lots of very sharp pencils resting in a line in the groove across the top. When he got promoted, he spent more time with the men in suits and less time with the sharpened pencils. Chloe was his replacement, hired from a rival firm.

I knew. I know everybody says that with hindsight but I did, I had a premonition. David came home from work two weeks after his promotion and said, almost as soon as he was in the door, 'The new me started today.'

He was standing in the hallway, flipping off his shoes. I had come from the kitchen to greet him, as I still did in those days. Betty usually flung herself at his legs but a favourite cartoon was on television and she was settled in front of it.

'Oh, yes?' I said, and even then, even before I knew his replacement was female, I felt something in my stomach.

He passed me, on the way into the kitchen. 'She's called Chloe,' he said, over his shoulder.

I followed him. He went straight to the bread bin and tossed back the lid.

'I've made chicken,' I said. 'What's she like?'

He paused for a fraction too long. 'Okay, nice. Her CV is amazing. I'm dying to talk to her.'

I walked past him, to fill the kettle. While my back was turned, he added, 'Might take her to lunch tomorrow.'

I could have written the rest of the story there and then, that very evening.

9

My suspicions began as quickly as the affair but it was six months before I confronted him. It says something for David's wilful guilelessness that, throughout that period, he continued to have his phone bill itemised. I can still recall the sickening sense of trespass I felt, the dread, as I extracted those bills from the cardboard file he kept on a shelf in the box room – your spouse's personal paperwork: pornography for the distraught. The rhyme we were taught in General Science, I remembered it then, as I stopped halfway through the bills to close the door on to the landing, even though I was alone in the house at the time. *Little Johnny took a sip/But now he'll sip no more/For what he thought was H2O/Was H2SO4.* How many lies can you tell in six months? At a conservative estimate of one a day, that's nearly two hundred lies, each one a droplet: *drop, drop, drop.*

I rang the number that appeared with suspicious frequency on the bills, in such a shuddering fury that I didn't take the precaution of withholding my own mobile number before I dialled. Why should I? I had nothing to hide. The phone went straight to voicemail. *You've called Chloe Carter's mobile phone. Please leave a message after the tone.* Somehow, even knowing her full name was painful. She was not a phantom Chloe. She was Chloe Carter. Examining the bills, one after the other, I knew that what I had suspected was true – David and Chloe's affair had begun very soon after that first lunch. There was no extended period of flirtation or wary skirting of each other, I was certain of that. That wasn't David's style. I recognised the pattern of calls; the short ones when he broke off hastily for some reason – he was forever ringing when he was on his way from one meeting to another – I remembered how frustrating I had found that, in the early days. Then, the long ones: fifty-six minutes was the longest. How easy it is to spend fifty-six minutes talking in the early days of a relationship. It goes by in a flash. You have talked of nothing at all.

And so, late that night: an ambush. The setting was our bedroom, with its mushroom-coloured walls and the satin cushions I insisted on, which David always hated. (In revenge, he hung a tasteless watercolour above our bed.) The protagonists: David and I, with a bit part for our daughter. The scene opens with the heroine, myself, waving a mobile phone bill in her husband's face. Cue an aria of denial.

Exhaustion adds a special edge to a couple's shared hysteria. His admission, when it finally came, was defiant, but after a further hour of tears and bellowing, Betty staggered in from her bedroom in her blue spotted pyjamas, hair awry with static from her pillow, demanding tearfully that we tell her why we were doing 'that shouting'. She wanted me. I was a limp, sodden rag. David carried her back to bed and I can only presume her softness as he settled her was what finally undid him. Without meaning to, she and I had played the nice and nasty policemen in David's interrogation. When he came back into our bedroom, I looked up at him. I knew my face was dissolved in misery, never a good look. I didn't care. I was devoid of pride. 'Is it over?' I asked brokenly, choking on the threat implicit in my words. 'Are you going to stop seeing her now? Is it over?'

It was half past three in the morning. We had been arguing for nearly four hours. His shoulders drooped. 'Yes,' he said, and covered his face with both hands. 'It is, it is. It's over, okay, I'll tell her, it's over.'

If I had asked him at that moment if the moon was made of

blue cheese, he would have sworn on bended knee that it was, that it always had been and always would be, until the end of time.

David was always sincere; that was what made him so hard to resent. He would think a thought or feel a feeling and out it would tumble from his mouth, like jelly beans from one of those bar-top sweet dispensers, tumbling in coloured curves, unpackaged and immediate. 'She just seems so vulnerable, somehow,' he said to me once when, out of sheer masochism, I demanded he explain what had attracted him to Chloe. 'Sort of vulnerable but brave, a bit like you were, I suppose, coping with your mum and never having had a dad, and she's like that although it's a very different situation, sort of fragile but just incredibly clever at the same time.' It was like being lacerated with a broken bottle. 'She's incredibly good at design, much more intuitive than I was. She should be earning twice what she is.' I saw that he had completely forgotten who he was talking to, chatting to me as if I was a mate, as if I expected – let alone wanted – honest answers to my questions. 'She's had a really tough time actually, dreadful family. It's amazing she's got such a good sense of humour.'

Another time, when I was ranting about her perfidy, he rounded on me and said, in a tone of voice quite chilling in its calm and logic, 'Look, if you met Chloe in a pub or something, you'd like her, honestly, you two have lots more in common than you'd think.'

'We're both fucking you, you mean.'

'Apart from that,' he replied with a patient sigh. 'You even . . .' he was going to say something he thought the better of – unusual for David to stop himself, so it must have been quite spectacular in its tactlessness. 'You both lost your dads when you were young.' Chloe was half Irish. When David had told me this, my heart had sunk. I could picture their sneering conversations about English-English people all too easily. Chloe's father had died when she was a toddler, although her mother lived locally and there were various siblings around up north. In the previous weeks and months, I had prised far more information out of David than was good for me. I even knew she was allergic to tomatoes. I was glaring at him.

'We even what?'

'You both like going for walks on the cliffs . . .' he concluded, a little lamely, and turned away, point made.

Not after that, I didn't.

At that stage, I had no idea why he was so determined, in the face of my justifiable disdain, to win me round to the idea of Chloe being a nice person. At that stage, I still thought of her as a storm to be weathered rather than climate change.

For a few months he and Chloe stopped having sex, I think, although I am sure there were still many strained lunchtimes at work when they met and clutched hands beneath the pub table. It was probably this period that did for me, in retrospect – I should have turned a blind eye, let it burn itself out. Instead, I made myself into an obstacle, something as devoid of personality as a concrete paving slab.

He moved out for a while, to a one-room flat above a pub in Eastley, so that he could 'think about what's best for all of us', but Betty's bewilderment and misery were so obvious that after four months he came back. His return filled me with optimism. I began to think the worst was over. At that stage, I still believed I held the advantage, that it was only a matter of time.

The first phone call came one morning. David was at work, Betty at nursery. I was on my knees before the open door of the freezer. I had removed the drawers and was chipping at the furry lining of ice inside the cabinet with a blunt knife, a job I found satisfying out of all proportion to its actual worth. The phone was on the floor beside me. I had just extracted a slab of ice and was holding it, ready to lob it up into the sink. I put the knife down and answered the phone. I should have put down the ice. 'Hello?' I said. 'Hello . . . ? Hello . . . ?' There was a brimming silence. 'Who is this?' Meanwhile, my other hand grew wet and numb as the slab of ice defrosted on my palm. I hung up, put the phone back on the floor, lobbed the ice, continued with my task. I dismissed it, that first time, trying to pretend I didn't know it was the start of something.

The phone calls came in fits and flurries after that: sometimes several a day, sometimes nothing for a week. When I had withheld numbers barred from the landline, they started coming through on my mobile. I couldn't bar withheld numbers from that as David's office and Betty's nursery numbers were both automatically withheld via their respective switchboards.

The rows I had with David about these calls were the most bitter of all and marked the final unravelling of our relationship. David swore blind it wasn't Chloe. 'She says she isn't doing it and she wouldn't lie about something like that,' brow furrowed, expression all earnest. 'She isn't like that. She's very honest and actually a really nice person.' I was incandescent. I didn't need him to tell me what she was like. I knew what she was like – she was a woman who had an affair with a married man who had a small child. That was what she was *like*. As the situation deteriorated between David and me, he even accused me of imagining the calls, or making them up.

I knew what she was doing. It was a cheap trick, designed to make me look hysterical and paranoid in David's eyes, and in that, wholly effective. She was prowling round my home, scratching at the door. She was telling me, *you may have got him back for now but I know where he is and I haven't given up.* It was then – and only then, I swear – that I began to hate her.

The letters were later, I think – yes, they came later.

*

Then I pulled my trump card – well, in truth, it was not so much my trump card as the last card in my pack, my final bid to keep my family intact. During a brief period of reconciliation with David, one Friday night when we were both drunk and feeling uncharacteristically sentimental, I managed to fall pregnant with Rees.

Rees bought me another year. I knew David was seeing Chloe during my pregnancy but I kept up the pretence that I didn't. Perhaps I thought that if I tried long enough and hard enough to turn us into a happy couple with their second child on the way, I would somehow be able to do it all on my own. For a while after Rees was born, David tried – the fact that Rees was such a difficult baby bought me more time than I would have otherwise had. David was not so callous that he was going to walk out on me during those early months, when the only way we stayed on our feet was to take it in turns to do the night shift.

He was never a louse. Had he been more of a louse, our marriage might have survived – I might have been able to turn a blind eye but no, he didn't sleep with women unless he told himself he was in love with them, I knew that. He loved her. He loved her all the more because he couldn't have her. He couldn't have her because of me. The logic of it all was so simple, so ordinary, it made me weep.

'Each unhappy family is unhappy on its own. Happy ones are all alike. Or something like that.'

'What?'

'I think it's Russian, *War and Peace*. Maybe it's Jane Austen.'

'God, Jane, you're so pretentious.'

Jane looked unhappy.

I was in a queue at the supermarket when I overheard this conversation. Jane, a woman I did not know, was ahead of me in the queue, with a friend who was holding a baby. There was some hiatus at the front, a customer disputing the till receipt, something about it saying on the sticker it was two for four pounds, not £2.69 each. The people immediately behind the unhappy customer were sighing, glancing at each other, but I wasn't in any particular hurry that day and anyway I was intent on listening to the two women in front of me. The one holding the baby must have been Jane's close friend, or maybe older sister, as she was criticising her intently. 'You always do that ...' she was saying irritably, joggling the baby up and down.

'Always do what?' Jane responded wearily.

'You know. Books.'

'Well I like him, what am I supposed to say?'

'I know that. That's bloody obvious. I just think you've got to get to know him, that's all. All that glowing and beaming. It's no good, you're in cloud cuckoo land.'

'You've just forgotten.'

This enraged big sister. She leaned in towards Jane, across their shared trolley. 'I haven't forgotten any of it, all right? I'm just being realistic. I know what that's like, all of it, all that snuggling up on the sofa in front of the TV. I did it, all right? I'm not that old. It's like that for everyone. Lasts about, what, maximum three months?'

The queue began to move. Jane, clearly offended, made no reply, and pushed their trolley an inch or two further forward. She turned to one side and I saw that her eyes were wide with the effort of not appearing too angry – or perhaps she was trying not to cry.

Tolstoy. *All happy families are alike but each unhappy family* ... How did I know that? I had never read any Tolstoy. Then it came to me. I remembered the quote from a pub quiz I had done a few years back. I wanted to lean forward and tell them but suspected I would get a mouthful from big sister. She didn't look like the kind of woman you messed with in the supermarket queue.

Out in the car park, loading my bags, I had just heaved the last one into the boot when – *three months*, common as muck, according to that woman, all that lovey-dovey stuff. Not realistic. Not what you should base a life's decision on. Three months was how long David and I had been going out with each other when we had that scene on the cliff. Maybe that was it. Maybe that explained everything. I slammed the boot lid down, then stopped, resting on my knuckles, head down, breathing. I thought of how he had dangled me over the edge that day, how beneath the playfulness of the gesture there was a real, confused kind of anger. I had felt it and thought it the resistance of a man who did not want to face the truth of his feelings – he loved me, it was frightening him. When he held me over the cliff and made me look down at the chopping waves beneath, I thought he was showing me, and himself, what our lives would be without each other, the bleakness awaiting us if we did not seize this moment. How wrong I was. He was angry with himself for making the wrong decision, even as he was making it – and angry with me for making him do it.

This was the worst of Chloe. She made me re-write my whole relationship with David, re-interpret the smallest of actions and gestures, even ones that occurred long before she came into our lives. When he held me over the cliff and made me look down at the waves, I thought, there in the supermarket car park, he wasn't showing me our lives apart, he was showing me our lives together. He was showing me what was coming, the cold brown water awaiting me when I was no longer his precious love object, when he would be ready to let me go, drop me over the edge.

Now I knew what Aunt Lorraine had meant: the price I had paid. David was a man who liked a gesture. He thrived on drama. He was the sort of man you should have an affair with but never marry – but even those sorts of men have to marry someone and David had married me, precisely at the

143

stage when we should have split up. Then, along came Betty, and we had the passion and the newness of a baby. But once that was gone, and we were just a couple with a child like any other couple . . .

The re-interpretation didn't stop there.

David had taken the kids to the playground while I was shopping. When they all got back, I was sitting at the kitchen table. Bags of shopping were heaped on the table, and the floor. It was a winter's afternoon, grey outside and gloomy in our low-ceilinged kitchen but I hadn't turned the lights on, although the central heating was blazing and the frozen vegetables in one of the supermarket bags were starting to defrost, the bag already sitting in a puddle of water. A two-litre carton of milk had destabilised another bag and yoghurt and butter from the same bag was spilling out, as if the groceries had decided to creep out in their own, hesitant fashion and observe their new environment. I was sitting at the table in the half-light, sobbing copiously. David was first into the room, holding Rees who was sleeping on his shoulder and didn't see me. Betty was in the hallway, kicking off her shoes. As he came in, David flicked on the light, saw me, took one look at my face, flicked the light back off and turned to the hall. 'OK,' I heard him call merrily to Betty, 'I said TV if you were good and you've been very, very good!'

After he had got the children settled in the sitting room, he came back into the kitchen, where I was still sitting in the gloom. He put the light back on but didn't look at me. He filled the kettle and flicked it on, then began picking up the shopping bags from the floor and putting them on the counter top. I watched him, stared at him, a piece of crumpled kitchen roll twisted between my fingers. I blew my nose. He lifted the bags up two at a time. When he had finished, he opened a cupboard door and began to unload the shopping.

He did it methodically, as he always did, starting with the tins, and then putting the fresh stuff, eggs, cheese, fish, in a neat pile next to the fridge. He paused over a packet of gnocchi. I thought, he's trying to work out whether' it came from the refrigerated cabinet or not.

'Did you fuck Abbie?'

He stopped, put down the gnocchi, said softly without looking at me, 'What now, Laura?'

I half rose, my legs trembling, and repeated in a loud voice, 'I said, did you fuck Abbie? What do you mean *what now*?'

'So,' he said, opening the cupboard door next to the one he had just filled and putting the packet of gnocchi in it. 'Who is Abbie? Some friend of yours I've never met? The girl in the café I supposedly looked at about three years ago?'

'Abbie! You remember Abbie! Large breasts, just your type. Carole's friend.'

He had continued unloading the shopping but now he stopped and turned to me. When he spoke, it was in a tone of quiet desperation. 'You're asking me to remember some girl who knew some girl that I had some insignificant relationship with at university a decade ago?'

'It wasn't insignificant to Carole!'

He turned and closed the kitchen door, even though the television was blaring loud enough for the kids not to hear us. He wheeled round. 'Are you out of your mind?'

I spoke with icy fury, enunciating each syllable in a descending register. 'Did. You. Fuck. Abbie. Simple question. Yes or no?'

'Of course I fucked bloody Abbie!' he exploded. 'Half the sodding engineering school fucked bloody Abbie! Happy now?' He opened the fridge door then slammed it shut again.

'While you were going out with Carole?'

He crashed his fists against his forehead and made an *aargh!* sound. His eyes were clenched tight shut.

'Just another simple question, darling,' I spat across the

kitchen table. 'Or do they all blend into one? Were you still going out with Carole when you fucked Abbie, or is it that hard to remember?' He turned to go, grabbing at the door handle.

I was shaking with triumph. 'That's right! Go on!' I shouted after him. Then I turned and picked up a small jar of Mayonnaise Light from one of the bags on the table and hurled it. The kitchen door closed behind him as the jar of mayonnaise reached it and sailed straight through the glass panel without a millisecond's pause in its trajectory.

Later, on my hands and knees, I cleared up the broken glass and mayonnaise with a dustpan and brush. David was putting the kids to bed upstairs. 'Silly Mummy threw something for a joke! Look what she's done!' I knelt on the wooden floor, sweeping carefully. The jar had broken apart in large shards so there were two types of glass mixed in with the cream-coloured slime. Even that seemed symbolic. Which glass was I – the thick, jagged pieces of the jar, or the small, brittle shards from the panel in my kitchen door – and which was *she*? We were unmistakably incompatible, yet bound up together by the same oleaginous mess. *Fuck*, I thought, exhaustedly, I am tormented by metaphors. They have infested my home like the nits Betty brought back from nursery – just when you think you've got rid of the little bastards, you find another one. Why does mayonnaise go translucent when it gets warm? Am I the only one who finds that sinister?

I started to laugh, there on my hands and knees, at the stupidity of my own behaviour and the predictability of its result. At that point, David descended the stairs, slowly. I sat back on my heels and looked up at him, smiling wanly, as if I expected that he too would appreciate the idiocy of what was happening to us. He looked down at me without expression. I was tired, contrite, and seeing the funny side: he was just tired.

*

Then there was Betty, Betty and her uncomplicated love. No matter how much re-writing I did of my relationship with David, Betty could not be re-written. She was her own story. Chloe couldn't lay a finger on her.

My life as David's wife was only a fraction of my life. My life as Betty's mother, her and me together, that was the fabric, the meat of it. We had sailed into an ocean I remembered; Chinese boxes made of paper, rainbow writing, a strict moral conservatism accompanied by a belief that the police were there to arrest naughty children as well as bad grown-ups. One afternoon, we were walking to the shops, me pushing Rees in his buggy and Betty walking alongside, we passed a constable who nodded at us. I smiled back. When we were safely out of earshot, Betty glanced backwards, looked down at her infant brother and pronounced, 'He looks ashamed.'

I was so surprised I stopped and looked down at Rees, who was sitting gazing around with the same impenetrable thoughtfulness as always. I carried on walking, glancing at Betty. She had a self-satisfied expression on her face, and I realised that she was pleased with herself for using the word, for applying it. It didn't matter whether it was appropriate or not. She had come across it, in a book or during a lesson, been told its application to wrongdoing, and was now trying it out for size, seeing how it felt when she had said it.

Another time, she pronounced, as she and I were waiting for Rees to wake from a Sunday afternoon nap at home, 'Mummy, if we lost Rees, we would weep and weep and weep.'

I was so startled I burst out, 'Oh, don't say that!' but she didn't respond, just carried on whatever colouring task she was engaged in at the time. She wasn't talking about the possibility of anything really happening to Rees, she was just experimenting. She knew the word 'cry'. Now she was trying 'weep'. Real loss was no more than a concept but words were like extra fingers that she grew each day. They had to be wriggled about to see how they worked.

At the bottom of the stairs one morning, before school, she stopped me in the action of buttoning her coat so that she could fling her arms around my neck, pull me down towards her at an awkward angle and whisper passionately in my ear, 'I love you *too much*.'

'I love you too much too,' I replied, holding her, cosy and complacent. Even when I was at my lowest depths over David, especially then, there was comfort in her physical form, in the compact, clinging shape of her; what a package of a person she was. This was what I loved, more than anything, and this could never be taken away from me. So what if I had only succeeded in borrowing David from himself? He had left me with this, and there would be years and years of this, these embraces.

Rees was fourteen months old, a fat toddler, bumping and beaming everywhere he went like a tiny comedian of the old school, when David came to me one evening as I was sitting watching television. Our daughter, our solemn little Betty, was in year one at school. She and Willow were already best friends. There was a girl called Ariana who was giving them some bother, trying to get between them. We had just had the hall painted, to brighten it up. We wanted to replace the cheap frosted glass in the door but couldn't afford it.

The children were asleep upstairs. They had gone down without fuss, for once. I had a casserole in the oven. I had un-corked a bottle of wine. It was a Friday night, our favourite night of the week in years gone by. I was waiting for David to get changed before I served up dinner.

He came into the sitting room, sat down beside me on the sofa, and took one of my hands between his. He looked down at our entwined hands and said, 'I know things have been really difficult for you, the last couple of years, I do. I know you think that I've been completely selfish but really, I really do know that it's been very hard for you too.' I turned to him, smiling, and felt a rush of love for him. That hurt me afterwards, that, for a second or two, I believed it was affection rather than guilt that made him take my hand between his two so tenderly. I thought that he was going to go on to tell me how sorry he was for all the pain he had caused. Perhaps he was about to suggest that we go away for a weekend together, just the two of us, that he had spoken to his sister who had occasionally offered to have the children overnight. Is there any limit to the self-delusion human beings are capable of? It is like a desert that stretches as far as the eye can see.

I stroked his hair – it was always a bit dry and fluffy unless he combed it properly. There was still plenty of it, though prematurely grey. In the mornings, it was the sort of hair that could be described as a shock. It suited him, though, a touch of the mad professor, even in his business suit. He had changed into jeans and pulled an old brown T-shirt over his head, rumpling his hair on the way, so I reached out a hand and, gently, with the backs of my fingers, stroked his hair back from his face and said, 'I know, love. I know you know. I know you never meant to hurt me.' Let's not call it naivety. Let's call it idiocy. What else could have made me use a line straight from a Country and Western song? Blind, stupid and blind – but above all, stupid.

His head was still bowed. I bowed mine slightly, in an effort to get him to look me in the face. 'Hey,' I said gently. 'It's okay. I've made Moroccan lamb.' It was an idiotic remark. I think something inside me was beginning to realise the seriousness of this preamble and was trying to keep the conversation on the domestic, the mundane. I have always used food as code, as signal to those I love. I'm good at it. They get the message. I had the sound on the television down low until I was sure the children were asleep. Dimly, in the background, the studio audience for the quiz show I had been watching broke into thunderous applause.

I rose slightly, to go to the kitchen and pour us both a glass of red wine, but he kept my hand firmly in his, so that I would remain seated.

There was a moment's silence, then the knowledge of what he was about to say came crashing down upon me, as hard and wide as a ceiling collapse during an earthquake, like our whole house coming down, for indeed it was. I pulled my hand out from his – forcibly as he resisted – rose from the sofa and began to back away from him. He looked up at me, his face open and his gaze pouring pity.

I do believe that at that moment I went, temporarily, quite mad; mad with the humiliation of it, mad with the knowledge that after years of battling and with the children as my unknowing foot soldiers, I had still lost.

It was never going to be a civilised separation. I don't do civilised. What followed was ugly – had someone described it to me before, I would not have believed how ugly it could get.

10

The first anonymous letter came two months after David had left the family home, as the lawyers put it, and set up house with Chloe. *Dear Laura* – the intimacy of that opening. It made me wonder about the word *dear*. You are dear to me. Oh my dear. Dearie dearie me. Its use seemed far more sinister than a simple *Laura* would have done. *Dear Laura, I wonder just what you think you are gaining by all this . . .*

David and I were not on speaking terms, at that point. We communicated by email and text only, using the minimum amount of words that allowed us to make arrangements for him to see the children. He knew there was no point in getting smart with me on that score, although that didn't stop him trying, in his angrier moments.

The letter arrived on a Tuesday morning. Betty was at school, Rees at nursery – he had just started three mornings a week as I was due to go back to work on a part-time basis soon. After I had dropped him off that morning, staying for a few minutes to make sure he was settled, I had gone to the supermarket then waited at the shoe repairers, so by the time I got back, it was almost time to go and pick him up. As I came in the house, three plastic bags on each arm, I kicked the door closed behind me and picked up the post, noting the plain white envelope with my name handwritten on the front. It was my first name only, no address or stamp, so it must have been hand delivered. The only other item was a note in a brown envelope from the health centre, about Rees's inoculations.

I dropped both items of post in the plastic bag that contained the shoes I had just had re-heeled and went down into the kitchen. I put the bags on the table. I turned the kettle on. I unclipped my hair clip because a section of hair at the front had fallen out and was annoying me, then went and stood in front of the fan oven, which had a glass panel that doubled as a mirror for the purposes of inserting clips in one's hair. I re-clipped. While I performed these self-consciously mundane actions, the letter in the handwritten white envelope was glowering away in the bag, like the grey-hot embers from a coal fire. I knew in the same way I knew when Chloe started work at David's office, when I answered that first phone call: there are things we know in our brains and things we know in our bones. I've learnt to trust the bones.

Eventually, the bones sat down at the kitchen table and pulled the bag containing my newly heeled shoes and my post towards me, delicately, as if it was a box of chocolates I had been saving as a treat. First of all, I pulled out the paper bag containing my shoes and took them out – they were the smart court shoes I only ever wore for job interviews, the ones with the kitten heels and little silver bows. My silver shoes: I'll never wear those shoes again, I had thought as I handed them over to the man behind the counter. I was going through a phase of smartening up my clothes in the sad, brave way that people do after their spouse has left them. Half a dozen saggy or bobbled jumpers had gone down to Oxfam. My silver shoes, the ones I never wore, had been reheeled.

I put the shoes on the table to prove to myself that I didn't believe in bad luck. After that, I took out the envelope from the plastic bag and held it in my hand for a moment or two, turning it over as if I expected answers on the other side and pulling a face when the other side revealed nothing. I examined my hand-written name, which gave away only that the author had neat, sloping writing. The envelope was the self-adhesive sort and firmly sealed. The letter inside it was typed.

Dear Laura,

I wonder just what you think you are gaining by all this? Do you imagine you are ever going to get your husband back! Let me tell you, you aren't. He's left you for good and why? Do you ever ask yourself that? If you loved him as much as you like to pretend then why can't you just let him go and be happy with someone who really cares for him?

I feel sorry for you. It must be difficult being such a bitter person especially when you have those two children to care for but do you ever think about them in all this? What must it be like for them! They have a right to see their father and you might think you are getting back at your husband but actually you are hurting them!

He has left you for good so it's time you got used to it, don't you think? Otherwise you and the children will suffer in the end. I know this is hard but I'm only telling you the truth that your husband is not prepared to say to your face because he is a bit of a coward (who can blame him) but he should just say it to you maybe it would be better that way. Perhaps when you read this you might think about that. If you weren't like this in the first place maybe he wouldn't have left.

Yours truly,
A Friend

I couldn't quite believe it, so I read it again and, once I was over the initial shock, gave an open-mouthed exhalation, small but vehement, of amazed satisfaction. It was the babbling quality of the letter that gratified me so much, the way that almost every sentence pretended reason while oozing spite of the most uncontrolled kind. I read it for a third time. *A Friend*? Who did she think she was kidding? *I feel sorry for you*? That was playground-level insult. And what about the veiled threat in *you and the children will suffer*, not to mention the disloyalty to David? *He is a bit of a coward.* And this was a woman who David had told me, more than once, was an exceptionally gifted graphic designer. The mad tone might be deliberate, of course, to make identification difficult. I could already picture David holding the letter and saying, 'Chloe would never have written this. She isn't like that.' If so, then she was less mad than she seemed but more manipulative than I had given her credit for. My God, I thought, she *really* hates me. I went to the fridge and cracked open a beer, even though I never drink during the day and Rees needed picking up from nursery in twenty minutes – it was a symbolic beer. *She hates me.* I felt a wild desire to celebrate. I had got under her skin in a way I had never imagined. Here was I, thinking she was all happy and triumphant with my husband, and all along she had been obsessing dementedly about me every bit as much as I had been about her. I should have realised when the phone calls started. I had thought of them as something meant to get at me, rather than a symptom of her own distress – but this letter was unmistakably distressed in its bitterness and incoherence. I nearly punched the air.

I think what surprised me most was that she didn't sign it. *A Friend.* From everything David had told me, I wouldn't have said that anonymity was Chloe's style, but his refusal to believe me over the phone calls had already proved he was hardly a reliable character witness where Chloe was concerned. If she was as calm and pleasant a person as he liked to make out – in comparison with his fruitcake of a wife – then I would have expected a letter from her to consist of a long, carefully assembled collection of phrases in which she laid out, point by point, why I was being so unreasonable. What I got was barely coherent.

A Friend. Was that sarcasm, or melodrama?

Perhaps, and only perhaps, that was the point at which I started to get over David.

*

Dear Laura. The next letter was signed, but only with an initial. Like the first, it was hand delivered, but this time I was in the house when it arrived. It was around the same time of day, a week later. Chloe must have guessed I was at home as my car was parked outside and it was such a gloomy day I still had the hallway light on. I could have been looking out of the front window as she tripped up the steps to my front door but, as it happened, I was upstairs in Betty's bedroom, pulling clothes she never wore from mangled tangles in her chest of drawers. I heard the letterbox. It makes a clatter.

I had been in all morning, so I had already picked up my post. As I came down the stairs, I saw the white envelope immediately. It was the sole item on the mat but for two pizza parlour leaflets which had arrived earlier. I picked the envelope up, turned it over again, looked at my name written in the same neat hand on the front, then went straight to the sitting room window. I looked up and down the street but it was empty. There was no fading sound of a car engine and we live in a quiet side street. She must have come on foot. It crossed my mind that I had a fifty per cent chance of guessing which direction she had come in and could probably catch her if I ran but instead I walked slowly back out to the hallway, and sat down on the bottom of the stairs. This second letter didn't have the shock value of the first but it was disturbing to think that only minutes earlier, this woman that I had never met, the architect of all my recent misery, had been at my front door.

Dear Laura,

I suppose you are feeling a bit better in yourself now you have made your husband hand over almost every penny of his salary. I suppose you think that you deserve that big house all to yourself. Well all I can say is enjoy your consolation prize. You might think he still cares a bit for you because he is being so kind and considerate but that's just because he is a soft sort

of person who will always take the path of least resistance.
And because he has those poor children to think of. Anyway,
soon enough you are going to be realising he is gone for good,
you will have to do that very soon. I am not saying this to be
unpleasant only because it's the truth and someone has to tell
you don't they?

Yours truly,
E

This letter left me feeling less triumphant than the first. It worried me that the mad tone was so exactly replicated, for that suggested it was genuine. Unpalatable as it was, I could not rule out the possibility that this woman would, one day, be a part of my children's lives. Why 'E'? So far, I had refused to let Betty and Rees meet Chloe but if David didn't come to his senses, then they would. I had comforted myself with what Sunita and Maurice at work had told me. 'Look, love,' Maurice had said, over a drink in the pub one evening. Maurice enjoyed being the only man in our office. There was nothing he loved more than dispensing male wisdom to us women and we played up to it no end. 'Thing is,' he said, sipping his cider and slowly folding a beer mat between his plump fingers, 'there's no chance this new bird of his is going to go the distance.' Sunita had nodded, 'He's right, you know,' she said, nodding at Maurice, nodding at me. 'The affair that breaks up a marriage never survives, you know, all that guilt and tension, not exactly a good starting point, is it? Sooner or later he'll dump her and go off with something completely different.'

At this point in the conversation, there had been a silence during which Maurice and Sunita exchanged looks and silently acknowledged that I might not find this an entirely comforting thought.

I agreed with them though, which was lamentably arrogant

on my part. I just couldn't believe that David would stay with a woman knowing his association with her had caused me so much pain. I had already written the narrative of their relationship in my head, successfully removing my own desires from the picture and concentrating on the story of them. He would dump her for someone else, I had decided, after a long period of arguing about his guilt and regret over the break-up of our marriage. By then, it would be too late for me and him, of course. When he asked if we could try again – and he would do that before he had actually left Chloe – I would explain very gently that I simply didn't love him any more. He would be devastated.

I had even fantasised about how gracious I would be to Chloe's replacement, one day, about how we might get to bitch about Chloe together. 'God, Chloe was a nightmare,' this unknown woman would say to me, several years in the future. 'She was so manipulative. I can't believe David left you for her. He must have been mad.'

But – and I couldn't accept that it was any more than a 'but' – if that didn't happen, or didn't happen soon enough, then at some point, I would have to tackle David about these letters. I would have to lay out the ground rules for Chloe's association with my children.

I was so intrigued and baffled by 'E', that I missed the implications of the penultimate sentence.

David and I remained on non-speaking terms for several weeks more. When he came to collect the children, I would stand at the front door and watch them trip down the steps and run down the path to him. He stayed at the gate. Then one Sunday, inevitably enough, came the occasion when Rees, still young enough to be clingy, refused to go with him, running back and throwing his arms around my legs. As he tried to clamber up them, monkey-like, I bent and picked him up and looked at

David, who was holding Betty by the hand and standing wait-ing. I began to say, 'It's okay, Rees can stay,' when I saw the look on Betty's face. Her lower lip was in a precarious downward curve. If they both refused to go with him, I knew I would be held to blame.

David kept his face expressionless as I walked down the steps to the path, holding Rees on my shoulder. When I got close to him, I said, 'So what have you got planned this afternoon?'

David was smart enough to take his cue. 'Aunt Lorraine has said they can help her make chocolate pudding. And Uncle Richard has got a new DVD. It's about dinosaurs.'

I looked down at Betty. 'That sounds good, doesn't it?' I said brightly. She nodded.

Rees allowed himself to be prised from me, still whimpering but without hysteria.

David mouthed, 'Thanks,' as he turned away.

When the children got home from their Sundays with their father, I always quizzed them carefully about what they had done. He had promised me they would not meet Chloe with-out my permission, so he couldn't take them back to his place, wherever that was. When it was too cold for the beach or the playground, that meant either trips further afield in the car or visits to Aunt Lorraine's house, which had become a sort of no-man's-land or neutral territory between us.

'So, did you help Aunt Lorraine make chocolate pudding?' I asked Betty casually, as I washed her hair in the bath that evening.

'I did the stirring!' piped up Rees, who was sitting on a soggy bathmat, wrapped in a towel, making spaceship noises while he wiggled his fingers.

'No, you didn't!' spat Betty. 'I did the stirring, you just helped!'

Before Rees could open his mouth to scream abuse at his

sister, I jumped in with, 'I'm sure you *both* helped Aunty Lorraine lots and lots.'

'So did the lady!' Rees said.

I was combing conditioner through Betty's long hair. The comb snagged on a tangle. 'Ow! Mum, you're *hurting*!'

'Sorry darling, sorry . . .' I concentrated on the combing for a few minutes. Betty had fallen suspiciously silent. 'Which lady?' I asked eventually.

'Daddy's friend,' Rees confirmed helpfully.

'She came later,' Betty said quickly. I was not sure whether her nervousness was because she had been urged to deceit by David or whether she was simply picking up on my mood.

'Her name's Eddy,' said Rees, pulling his towel over his head and rolling around the floor.

'Eddy's a boy's name,' said Betty, in a tone of voice that made it clear she had only just restrained herself from adding the word, stupid. 'Her name is Ee-dy!'

As soon as the children were asleep, I sent David a text. *Who the fuck is Eedy?*

His reply must have been carefully composed, maybe shown to Chloe before he sent it, as it took half an hour to come through. *Edie is nickname for Chloe. Battery went flat and Richard couldn't find leads so she came. Lorraine invited her in. Wasn't planned. Sorry.*

I did not trust myself to compose a measured reply, so for once in my life, I had the good sense not to respond.

Edie. E. I wondered if he called her by her surname as well, or her initials. I wondered if he played that trick on her, the one where you make someone look down by pointing at something on their top or jumper, just so you can flick their nose with your finger as they drop their gaze.

A week later, David rang. I listened in silence while he gave a full and detailed explanation for why he had had to call Chloe to help him jumpstart the car that Sunday, why Lorraine had invited Chloe in, and how he thought it was probably for the best that the children met Chloe unexpectedly and quickly like that without turning it into a big drama. He told me he was sorry that he hadn't been able to consult me first and it honestly wasn't planned and I would just have to take his word for that. Then he altered his tone and told me, with insulting gentleness, that he and Chloe were going to have a baby.

11

The next morning, as soon as I had dropped the kids off, I went up to the cliffs. I had an idea that it would be good to go to the spot where David had threatened to throw me over the edge to acknowledge that my marriage was over. I am not sure why I thought this was a good idea – maybe for the same reason that physicians performed blood-letting in the eighteenth century. Maybe I thought that if I caused myself some extra emotion I would feel drained afterwards – not better, perhaps, but too exhausted to care.

Everything is reversible except a child. A child will always be there, I thought, no matter what.

I did everything that I knew would cause me most pain. I walked slowly, taking long strides, up to the point where David had grabbed me with that strange mixture of passion and aggression, nearly ten years before. As I walked up the slope, I pictured me and him walking together, hand in hand, about to spend the rest of our lives together. I pictured the way he turned on me, perhaps not even knowing himself what he was about to do. I rubbed at my upper arms as I walked, feeling the grasp of his hands on them, the firmness of his grip, remembering my sudden knowledge that this was more than his usual messing around. I remembered the unexpected venom and passion in his gaze. Inevitably enough, I wandered up towards the edge of the overhang. Ten years on and still it had not dropped into the sea. Time it did, really, I thought.

As I walked slowly towards the edge, I was already picturing myself staring over it, at the huge chunks of jagged concrete below and the brown shingle and the grey and white of the

English Channel. I began to shiver violently and it was more than just the cold. I was contemplating how easy it would be. I was thinking about looking over in the same way I had done that day but without David's arms to hold me. I was imagining tipping forward, slowly at first, letting my centre of gravity pull me, arms outstretched in a simile of flight. I was wondering if falling like that stole the breath from your body, whether maybe you were already unconscious when you smacked against the ground, or whether your mind screamed all the way down at the irreversibility of your decision. One moment of bravery, that was all it would take. After that, you would have no choice.

I would like to say that as I approached the overhang, I was indeed contemplating throwing myself off, just standing on the edge and tipping, maybe without even looking down. I would like to say I felt the pull of gravity, the magnetic force of the concrete blocks below. The truth was, I didn't even get close to the edge. Before I was near enough to look over, I pulled back, afraid and shivering, hating my cowardice, convinced that a life of post-David misery was what I was destined for, was nothing more than I deserved.

As I turned to go, I saw the encampment, a group of mobile homes, four or five of them in a neat row and the others grouped haphazardly around. The first few, the neatly arranged ones, had not attracted controversy – they had been placed there by the landowner who had registered them as holiday homes. The others had been added more hurriedly and local migrant workers moved into them at the landowner's request – some deal he had struck with the leaders of the group concerned. It had made the local newspapers due to planning concerns.

From where I was, I could see down into the patch of land in the middle of the haphazard grouping. Two cars were parked next to each other, both with their bonnets up, and men stood around regarding the cars, raising their arms occasionally. Beyond the mobile homes, there were four other cars, three of them second-hand saloons but the fourth a new-looking four-by-four. It stood out enough for me to wonder if it was a collective decision amongst the group to pool resources into one smart car that was the public face of the group, while the rest of their vehicles were half-broken, run down. As I watched, a woman descended from one of the mobile homes with a bundle in her arms and crossed the land, ignored by the men, before disappearing behind another of the homes. It was a brief glimpse of other lives, different from my own, a reminder of how narrow my own concerns had become. I chided myself as I strode back down the hill.

All I've proved is that suicide isn't an option, I thought, walking back to the car park, and I think I knew that already. I had left my car unlocked but no one had come near it. There was no one else around at that time on a Monday morning.

I went shopping. I bought myself underwear in the tacky new womenswear shop that had opened up when the betting shop closed down and while I was paying for it got into a long conversation with the assistant about how well maroon contrasted with pale skin. Afterwards, I ordered a coffee with amaretto syrup in a large white mug at the only decent Italian café on the esplanade and sat conspicuously in the window for the rest of the morning, reading the newspapers.

There was one moment, though. It came around three weeks later and was completely unexpected. Julie was babysitting for me. There was a meeting at the school about the new numeracy and literacy programmes. I didn't normally go to that sort of thing – Betty was doing fine and Rees wasn't anywhere near that stage yet – but I was going through a phase of making myself go out. I had been hoping that some of the other mothers that I liked would be there and that there would be a move to the pub afterwards. As it was, nobody I liked had shown up, not even Sally, and everyone else had sloped off home immediately.

It was around 8.30 p.m., already dark. A deep mist had descended upon the town, as it often did on damp winter evenings. I had left the car at home in case there was any chance of a drink and as Julie wasn't expecting me back immediately, I turned left at the roundabout and walked into town. I couldn't go to a pub on my own and there was nowhere else to go, bar the chippy, so I descended the stone steps at the end of the esplanade and went for a walk on the pebble beach in the dark, not feeling particularly glum or contemplative, just because I had the freedom to do it when most evenings I was trapped at home.

No one else was around. The mist was heavy and the sea lost behind the mist. I walked into it, down to the water's edge, then stopped still to listen.

I felt it then. I felt its pull, in the deep quiet of the enveloping fog and the constancy of the waves. The gravity of the clifftop had not done it, but the chill mist, the invitation in the gentle shushing sound of the water, they spoke to me in a way that the drama of vertigo had not. Perhaps you are not a coward, after all, they seemed to whisper, perhaps you just needed to be asked nicely. *How easy it would be,* I thought to myself. *Remove your shoes, remove your coat – you don't need to strip completely. Or you could keep everything on and weight your pockets with pebbles if you want to make it quicker. You've never been a strong swimmer and the water is very cold. If you just keep going as far as you can, you'll never make it back, even if fear gets the better of you. Just a few determined strokes and you'll be too far out before you know it.* The waves shushed-and-fell, oh so gently, shushed-and-fell, against the shingle. Nothing was visible beyond the mist – out there was chill water and more mist. Its density was an illusion. If I walked into it, it would part to reveal itself and more of itself, its apparent solidity always just beyond my reach. *The water is freezing. You'll be numb before you know it.*

I would like to say it was thoughts of my two children that kept me from walking into that mist – it was, in a way, but not in a way that reflects well upon me. I thought of Chloe's pregnancy and how pleased Betty and Rees would be when they found out they were going to have a baby brother or sister. Then I thought of how, if I died, they would be raised as part of a brand-new family, whole and logical, of how Rees, not much more than an infant himself, would regard Chloe unquestioningly as his mother. I thought of him saying to a friend, when he was grown, 'My real mother died when I was just a toddler, so I don't really remember her.' It wouldn't matter if he got on with his step-mother or not. She would still be the dominant figure in his life, for good or ill. If I did what I wanted to do, that misty night, Chloe would have it all, everything I had ever loved or cared for. It wasn't love of my children that kept me safe that night, it was hatred of her.

Strange, the way the little things get to you, the way they slide in like acupuncture needles and like acupuncture needles have disproportionate effects. Some months after I found out Chloe was pregnant but before Harry was born, Aunt Lorraine rang me one evening to ask what Rees wanted for his birthday. We had an earnest discussion about just how many Hot Wheels cars a three-year-old needed. He was desperate for more plastic track so that he could make a loop-the-loop for the Hot Wheels cars to whizz around and had also put in a formal request for a hamster. I was a little concerned the two requests might be connected.

'More cars,' I said to Aunt Lorraine. 'Utility vehicles, you know, fire engines and tow trucks and police cars.'

'Has he got an ambulance?'

I thought about it. 'I think he's got three.'

'Well at least they don't get lost all the time, not like all those tiny doll things Betty liked.' It wasn't the dolls themselves that got lost, it was the tiny rubber clothes; the tiny pink bikinis and stretchy orange mini-skirts and tiny-tiny turquoise rubber boots. All the mass-produced dolls that Betty loved came with outfits only suitable for lapdancing but they seemed domesticated souls at heart. There were tiny dogs as well, and tiny dishwashers. 'That yucca you brought round for me for my birthday's still going strong, you know. I've still got the ribbon round it.'

I had not seen Aunt Lorraine on her last birthday – it had occurred during the period when David and I were not even on speaking terms. I had remembered the date and bought a card for her but was paralysed by indecision over what to write in it. I had no idea how much his family knew about what had happened between me and David. I could have written simply *love, Laura*, but my name, standing alone, was still such a strange concept. *Love, Laura, Betty and Rees*? Equally odd. I hadn't yet accepted we were a trio, that a whole corner of our lives was irrevocably gone. In desperation, I signed the card, *Laura & co*, put it in its envelope and sealed it, then tore it in two and put it in the paper-recycling tub.

So I hadn't sent Aunt Lorraine a birthday card and I had felt bad about it because it was always me that did the cards and presents for David's family, of course, and I thought well she won't get anything from us then, and she might wonder why.

But, clearly, David *had* remembered Aunt Lorraine's birthday. And so had someone else, someone Aunt Lorraine was, in a momentary lapse of concentration, confusing with me. David hated plants. He would never dream of buying a plant for anybody, let alone putting a ribbon round it.

There were only two people in the world that I still trusted to love me: my children.

When Chloe and I eventually met, it was, of course, a huge anti-climax. David engineered it with his usual efficiency, making sure it was in a public place and that we were diluted by the children. He sprung it on me one Saturday morning, ringing me at home and saying that he wanted to take Betty and Rees to the new rollerblade park that had opened up at the leisure centre in Lower Banton. (It was a disappointment, I later learned. The rink was tiny, they played hard rock at unspeakable volume and there was nothing to eat except junk and fizzy drinks from vending machines.) I told him I had already promised Betty we would go to Wellingtons, the discount clothing store in the High Street, to try on new trainers. He agreed she needed the new trainers, then added, oh so casually, 'Well, why don't you do that first and then we'll meet you at the beach café and take the kids off from there?' We. Us. Him and Chloe and the tadpole of unknown gestation she was carrying inside her.

Unlike many beach cafés, ours was actually on the beach, in the lee of the esplanade wall. You could only meet at it rather than in it as it was no more than a sheltered kiosk with a couple of firmly anchored windbreaks either side of four or five cheap tables. The fare was unpleasant – sugared drinks in cartons and white-bread sandwiches with processed cheese – it wouldn't have lasted two minutes on the High Street but the kiosk's location gave it a spurious charm. It's surprising what tastes good after a walk on a cold, windy beach, as long as you have no desire to linger over it. David had chosen the venue for the handover with great care. We would all be feeling cold and brisk and businesslike.

The kids and I were there first – I made sure of that. I bought them each a hot chocolate made from a machine, the froth on top induced by some sort of chemical reaction between hot water, sugar and the additives in the powder. I had a black coffee. The three of us sat huddled at a green metal table, cuddling our drinks. Rees and Betty were moany because it was getting near lunchtime. The sky overhead looked as chemical as our drinks, a swirl of greys and yellows, high and motionless.

After five minutes, I saw David and Chloe approach, walking carefully alongside each other with their hands shoved in their pockets, like a couple who usually hold hands but have decided not to on this occasion. David saw us and raised a hand. At his gesture, Chloe looked up from where she was stepping carefully across the shingle and as she spotted me, she stumbled. She was small, shorter than me and tiny next to David. She was wearing a purple duffel coat over jeans and a purple and brown hat in a tea-cosy shape. She dropped her gaze as soon as she saw us, allowing me to watch her approach in exactly the way I had anticipated. I was surprised. I had expected something a little more glamorous. I felt both relieved and insulted. I stared, hoping she would lift her gaze again and see me watching her but she did not.

'That's her, Mum,' said Betty, and I was bolstered by the disdain in her voice.

'Daddy! Daddy! Daddy!' called out Rees.

'Now you will remember what I said, about being polite?' I said to them both, leaning in towards them. Betty pulled a face. I put my mouth close to her hair and whispered, 'I love you, darling.' She smiled at me.

As Chloe and David approached, they would have seen the three of us leaning conspiratorially together.

Rees hopped down from his chair, making the table rock. The Styrofoam cups containing our drinks wavered dangerously and some of Betty's lukewarm chocolate slopped on to the table. '*Rees . . .*' she hissed, furiously.

'Hey, you!' cried David, sweeping him up.

Chloe crunched to a halt on the gravel, standing before us. 'Hi, I'm Chloe,' she said brightly, looking at me, keeping her hands in her pockets.

'Hi,' I said back, equally brightly. Betty looked to one side.

David went up to the kiosk to get him and Chloe a coffee. Chloe sat down on the metal chair next to me. Up close, I saw that she was, in fact, incredibly pretty, fawn-like, with a delicately boned little face and wide pale eyes. In her loose coat it was impossible to tell how pregnant she was but her features had none of the puffiness some women acquire in the later stages. Her skin had a pink glow and her eyes were bright. Her woollen hat was pulled down over her ears giving her a goofy, quirky quality, but I could see that underneath it she had hair the colour of a brown envelope, in corkscrew curls. Her earrings were small silver teardrops. I had the feeling she had dressed down.

I was only able to glance rather than stare, but even that was enough to see what David might have seen in her when they first met – beauty and fragility combined with a ready, brave little smile. No wonder he believed her incapable of malicious phone calls or hate mail. Regarding her like this, so normal, so cheerful, it was hard to believe it myself. I was profoundly disappointed. I had hoped to see that she was wrong for David and to be able to feel that their relationship, baby or no baby, would be a disaster – but they fitted, I could see that. I could see that here was a woman who would bring out his protective and possessive side.

I had always thought of myself and David as right together, but now I saw there was a sliding scale about these things. Maybe he and I had always been like two pieces from one of those ridiculously difficult jigsaw puzzles where the picture consists of nothing but autumn leaves. You keep selecting pieces that look as if they must match but when you try and jam them together you find they are slightly unaligned. They used to have those jigsaws in the nursing home where my mother had lived for the last few years of her life. I always thought they were made so difficult in order to take an elderly person long enough to die, and perhaps give them an incentive to do so.

There was no queue at the kiosk and David returned almost immediately. As Chloe wrapped her hands round her milky coffee, I saw that her nails were manicured and painted with translucent, pearly varnish. *The hands of someone who doesn't have kids,* I thought. *Yet.*

'It's not very windy at least,' I suggested.

Eagerly, they both agreed.

We managed ten minutes or so of careful conversation. Rees sat on David's lap throughout. Betty refused to join in, in any way, swinging dangerously on her chair and shooting me sidelong glances that said, *why are you making me do this?* She was wearing a pink puffa jacket and jeans – jeans were the thing, these days, rather than the dresses and tights she had loved so much less than a year ago. Pink was still in, just about, although other mothers had already warned me that any day now she would extract every single pink item from her wardrobe and declare that pink was for babies. Every time she turned her head to me, her long fine hair whipped across her face. I had wanted her to have a ponytail that morning but she had refused. She didn't acknowledge Chloe at all, which was uncharacteristically rude of her.

After a while, David checked his watch, rather clumsily I thought, and said, 'Well, we'd better get going. It's going to take us forty minutes.'

'What are your plans?' Chloe said to me.

I looked at her blankly. Plans? Then I realised, oh yes, I've got the afternoon to myself. I had not thought beyond this en-counter. A variety of responses occurred to me. *Well, as you*

170

pair of lying toads are taking off with my children maybe I'll just walk into the sea and drown myself – or, perhaps – *I have a toy boy who works at the chippy. I thought I might go and fuck him for a couple of hours.*

I looked down the beach. Two elderly couples were wandering in the distance, a few dog walkers were out. A dog would come in handy at moments like these, I thought.

'Go for a walk, probably,' I said, lamely. 'Get some exercise.'

We all rose from our chairs. As we did, a sudden gust blew up and our near-empty Styrofoam cups somersaulted off the table, scattering a few drops of liquid from each in their varying shades of brown. Chloe gave an awkward little laugh and grabbed at hers, then turned and ran a few steps down the beach in pursuit of mine.

While her back was turned, David gave me a steady, grateful look. I wondered if he had expected a scene.

I was wrapping a scarf around a protesting Rees as Chloe returned to us. As soon as I had finished, tucking the ends into his jacket, he pulled it out and unwound it again. 'He won't wear a hat,' I said.

'Do they have to have helmets for rollerblading?' Chloe asked David.

He shrugged.

'Well, I'm not wearing one,' mumbled Betty.

'You'd better give them something to eat as soon as you get there,' I said, carefully addressing this remark to David alone. 'Low blood sugar. You'd better make sure they eat first.'

'I'm sure there'll be something,' David said.

I bent and kissed my children. Betty leaned into me, no longer a sullen pre-teen but a shy, sad eight-year-old saying goodbye to her mother. 'I don't want to go,' she mumbled into the folds of my coat, a catch in her voice.

I felt a rush of guilt and protectiveness towards her. Here was I, thinking only of my own drama, and here was she, the most important thing in all this, along with her brother. 'It's okay,' I whispered gently, 'I'll be fine. You'll have a good time. And I'll be fine, I promise. Go on, now. Go on.'

'Bye, Mum. Love you,' she whispered.

'Love you too.'

I watched the four of them walk off down the beach together, Rees holding his father's hand, Betty slightly apart. I sat back down at the table for moment then decided I wasn't in the mood for sitting on my own. There would be plenty of opportunity to do that at the weekends from now on, after all. I rose again, turned my face to the wind, to the wide curve of the bay, and set off down the shingle. Black seaweed was strewn across my path as I walked down to the sea, a brown, foaming grumble. The crunch of my boots on the pebbles was loud in my ears.

Not long after her ninth birthday, Betty and I were alone together at the kitchen table, one Sunday morning. Rees was out at football practice. It was just me and my girl. It was autumn and the kitchen was full of weak, pale sun, honey light. Betty was writing a story for her literacy homework and had been bent over it for some time. Her teacher was a Mrs Cavanagh, a strict woman. Betty liked her. She liked pleasing authority figures.

I was sitting at the table reading clothing brochures from which I never purchased anything but whose contents had to be browsed before they could be discarded, just to confirm that I would never want to buy anything from them. Somehow, I had got myself on a mailing list for women in late middle-age and I seemed to receive an inordinate amount of catalogues advertising trousers with elasticated waistbands. I liked looking through them because they made me feel better about myself. The models they used were slim young girls but with the hairstyles and make-up of much older women. Although they were smiling they looked tense, as if they were gazing around thinking, how did I get here? I've wandered into the wrong photoshoot. And *what* am I wearing? *Ugh.*

I was gazing at a particularly hideous blouse and cardigan ensemble when Betty said, without raising her head. 'Mu – um . . .'

I looked at her. 'Yes . . .?'

She stopped what she was doing and gazed up towards a ceiling corner, frowning as if she had just spotted a cobweb. It was a pose she adopted whenever she had a big question to ask.

I braced myself. *Why did Dad not love you any more?* I had had a lot of those sorts of questions recently. *How does the seed get inside the mummy's tummy?* We had already done that one. *Willow says she's got a bird's nest inside her and that we all have to have one or otherwise we can't be ladies.* That one had taken a bit of deciphering. I only worked it out after I asked Sally, who had explained periods to Willow by drawing a woman's torso and saying that the woman's tummy was getting ready to grow a baby all the time and that it was building a nest for it, just like a bird, except the nest was made of fluid to hold the baby safely, like a cushion. Once a month, the mummy's tummy realised that there wasn't a baby coming just yet, so it let the fluid drop out and started building a new one. I thought it was rather a good analogy, actually, a lot more coherent than what my mother had said to me. 'The womb is sad it hasn't got a baby and it weeps!' Willow, however, had passed on a slightly less coherent version to her classmates, and they all thought that growing up meant growing twigs and branches inside. Betty had wanted to know if it would hurt.

She had always been of a philosophical bent, Betty. One of her first sentences to me at the age of two or three was, 'I can't see my eyes.' Her tone at the time was both thoughtful and declarative. It wasn't a question.

So when she said, 'Mu – um . . .' in that meandering fashion, I was expecting something similar. *What's the universe made of?* or *Where was I before I was born?*

Instead, she asked, solemnly, 'If an octopus was stung by a jellyfish, would it be all right?'

Betty, you were only nine. You weren't my ally or my angel or my friend. You were a child. It was my job to keep you safe. I failed.

12

In the habitual trajectory of these things, that point – my meeting Chloe and realising she wasn't a monster – that would have been the point at which I got a life, or at least a haircut. I would start going to the pub with friends, join the dance class that my involvement with David had prevented, all those years ago. After a few months, I would meet a man in a similar situation to my own, recently parted from his wife and still shaky. He would be living in a flat in town and the first time I cooked him a proper dinner at my house he would become moist-eyed and talk at length about how difficult he found the separation from his children. Later, I would take him upstairs, creeping on the creaky wooden staircase, to show him my two asleep in their beds, and he would smile at them from the doorways of their bedrooms, and say of Betty, 'She looks like you.' As we turned to go back downstairs, he would stop me on the landing and embrace me, hesitantly, kissing me on the mouth in a small, gentle way that would feel like being nibbled. The sex that followed – not that night, but some weeks later – would be satisfactory rather than spectacular. We would become great friends. After a few months, we would begin to talk, tentatively, about whether we should move in together and then maybe have a baby so we would end up with two of mine and two of his and one together. Those around us would breathe a collective sigh of relief.

I could see the rationale in this scenario – I could admire the neatness of it, which was why I would rather burn in hell than participate in it. But I could also see how there was more mileage to be had from magnanimity than victimhood.

As an experiment, I tried being cheerful to Chloe the next time I met her, on their doorstep when I went to pick up the kids.

'Hi, how are you?' was all I said, when she opened the door. I was slightly surprised it was her and not David answering, which was what allowed me to be brusque and polite with her. I wondered if David had persuaded her to answer the door, or if she had insisted on it.

She gave me a hesitant glance and I saw that she was used to the idea that I was something to be afraid of, pitied. She was trying to work out what lay behind my friendly tone. 'Fine,' she replied, glancing behind her to see if the kids were coming.

At the far end of the corridor, David was kneeling in front of Rees, buttoning his coat. He was talking to him softly in their own little patois, his English heavily accented and the odd word of Welsh. Rees loved it. He could *boyo* with the best of them. Then he looked round and saw me. 'Mum!' He broke free from his father who, turning to me, raised his hand in greeting. Rees and Betty both pounded past Chloe without a word to her and flung themselves at me.

'What do you say to Chloe?' I asked as I embraced them. I looked at her. She gave a thin, disconcerted smile.

Three days later, I received another letter. This one came in a cheap yellow envelope of the sort you have left over from packets of notelets and cards bought in stationers that sell balloons and outsized teddy bears. There was nothing written on the envelope itself, not even my initials, and that angered me because the children were both at home when it arrived and one of them could easily have picked it up and opened it. It looked like the sort of thing one of their friends would send. Fortunately, they were playing together in Rees's room, some loud game that involved shouting at each other. I think they were pretending to be head teachers.

The envelope was only partially glued down, which gave the impression it had been sealed in haste. Inside was a folded piece of lined paper, roughly torn from a notepad. This was the first handwritten one. I unfolded it. It contained only three words, written in neat, sloping capitals: *BULLY FOR YOU.*

There was the pounding of feet above me. I slipped the envelope and piece of notepaper into my cardigan pocket.

'Mummy, what's that?' asked eagle-eyed Betty as she reached the bottom of the stairs.

I turned to her, my lips dry of explanation, but was saved by Rees jumping the last three steps and shouting, 'Charge!' as he thumped into Betty's back. By the time I had calmed the row that ensued, Betty had forgotten her glimpse of yellow.

For the rest of that afternoon, I kept the note in my cardigan pocket, glowering away in there. It gave a slight rustling noise as I moved around the kitchen, making tea. I forgot it during the meal, then my fingers encountered it when I pushed my hand absently into the pocket in search of a tissue.

After I had put the children to bed, I went downstairs, sat at my kitchen table, pulled the note out of my pocket and looked at it. *BULLY FOR YOU.* What did that mean? Bully for me, why? Because I had seemed visibly recovered from the hysteric she had thought me to be? Because I had consented to her and David having the children back to their bungalow? Had I asked to be congratulated on either of these developments? Had I asked for her opinion at all?

This letter made me a little frightened. It had been written and delivered in haste at a time when she must have known the children would be home from school. That seemed to me like an act of temper, an escalation. It was only a matter of time before David asked me to let the children stay overnight with him and Chloe. I had to sort this out.

I thought about it long and hard that evening, as I cleared up the teatime mess and the kids' toys, as I settled in front of the television with a mug of tea in the same way that I did most evenings. I thought about it that night, when I lay awake in the small hours. It was a cold night and I had put an extra blanket on top of my duvet. After lying awake for half an hour or so, I decided to get up, use the loo, check the children.

Betty was breathing with her usual sweet heaviness. She always slept with her long limbs flung wide and splayed about her in improbable contortions. She tossed and turned a lot as well, her friends told me. When they had sleepovers, none of them would share a bed with her. Human origami, I called her. I smiled down at her as she lay, spread all over the bed in a tangle of hair and limbs. I extracted her duvet from beneath her legs and pulled it up gently, over her shoulder. She murmured and turned. I could imagine how Chloe would be making a great play of liking Rees; easy, open Rees, younger, and a boy, but what about my girl? How would Chloe feel about her? Everybody said Betty looked like me but then people always say that about mothers and daughters. Chloe would be making an effort towards her at the very least. David was as fiercely protective of Betty as any father. Chloe would surely know that in a straight choice, David would pick Betty over her any time. That alone made Betty a threat.

I felt uneasy for Betty as I looked down at her – I didn't think Chloe capable of harming her but I felt as if some of her malevolence towards me could somehow spill over on to my daughter, as if yellow slime were creeping underneath the door of Betty's bedroom. What should I do? If I raised it with David, would he even believe me? He hadn't believed me over the phone calls. I hadn't shown him the letters. If he accused me of sending myself hate mail then I would never forgive him and whatever tentative moves we had made towards a working rapprochement in the children's interests would be thrown into violent reverse. How could I trust him, or be civil to Chloe, with this going on? How could I not trust him, or not be civil to Chloe, when my children's long-term welfare was at stake?

I bent and kissed Betty's soft head. I went to the bathroom. As I washed my hands, I looked in the mirrored door of my bathroom cabinet. The bathroom lighting did not flatter my skin. I could not rely on David as an intermediary, I decided. He was not capable or trustworthy when it came to handling Chloe.

The opportunity came a fortnight later. I had agreed to let David pick the kids up and take them back to the bungalow. 'We are going to do arts and crafts together,' he said proudly, as he loaded them into his car. I sensed a new resolution in his voice, a determination to prove to me that his access to the children would be beneficial to them as well as to himself. I had planned an exciting afternoon clearing out the under-the-stairs cupboard. *Bully for you*, I murmured to myself as the car pulled away from the kerb, Betty and Rees waving frantically from the back seat. Bully for both of you.

I had agreed to pick the children up at 5 p.m. The new housing estate that David and Chloe lived on was at the end of a long, curving road on the cliff side of town. It was one of those strange estates where the houses are very open at the front, no fences between the neat squares of garden, no way to get from your own wavy-glassed front door to the car in the tarmac drive without being seen by at least half a dozen neighbours. Such openness implies an idealised view of family life, I suppose, wifey waving hubby off to work each morning while kids smile from a window, happiness in full public view. Maybe that's why people buy those houses, because they realise there will have to be less screaming at each other. Not for me: give me my narrow terrace and the tall scrubby hedge in front of it and thick walls between me and the neighbours. Let me do my screaming in peace and privacy.

I parked on the immaculate kerb outside their house and looked at their immaculate tarmacadam drive, and lost my nerve. I had been planning on saying I wanted a word with Chloe in private but how to manage that without prompting questions from David? Maybe I should write a few threatening letters of my own.

David answered the door. 'Hi,' he said distractedly, running a hand through his hair, which had a lot of something sticky in it.

'Busy afternoon?' I said, nodding at his head.

'Oh, yes,' he said, as his fingers met a gluey tangle. He tugged at it and winced. 'They've been making something.' He looked at his fingers and frowned. 'Want to come in?'

I shook my head. 'Better get them back.' Rees had recently joined some miniature football league for boys like him who were too small for the school clubs: nine o' clock on a Sunday morning.

David turned back into the bungalow and there were sounds of commotion from inside, beyond the hallway, where I could just glimpse a brightly lit white kitchen. I stayed waiting by the open door, although it would have made more sense to step inside and close it behind me. Eventually, the children emerged followed by Chloe, who chased them smilingly down the hallway towards me. They had their coats and shoes on already and were both clutching droopy drawings on large pieces of black sugar paper. Rough paper and crayon, I thought, a non-parent's idea of what children like – arts and crafts are a lot more sophisticated these days. I had an unwelcome image of Chloe in a stationer's shop, buying old-fashioned wax crayons because she thought my children would like them – and a packet of notelets with yellow envelopes.

Chloe and I had exchanged a neutral nod, the children and I had already turned to walk back down the path, when Betty suddenly shrieked, 'My angel!' and darted back inside the house.

'Betty!' I called after her.

Rees paused for a minute, then ran after his sister.

They scooted past Chloe, back down the hallway and into the kitchen. I could hear Betty shouting at her father, 'Where is it? Where is it?' and David replying, 'Where's what?'

'My *angel!*'

Chloe and I were left on her doorstep. She gave me a half-smile and a shrug, and I saw that this might be my only chance. 'Chloe,' I said, quietly, tonelessly. 'I think it should stop.'

She stared at me. I stared back. I wanted her to see that I was not looking for a fight, that I was giving her this chance, privately, to admit what she had done, apologise maybe, or at the very least say it wasn't going to happen again.

She could not hold my gaze. 'What . . . ?' she said, glancing anxiously back into the house, clearly hoping David or one of the children would come to her rescue. She was dressed in trousers and a clingy polo neck sweater that revealed the neat bump of her pregnancy. The tight curls of her hair bounced as she moved her head. Her hallway felt overheated to me, in my coat and hat and scarf.

I knew that if I was too abrupt or indignant, I would lose. My strength lay in my rationality in the face of her behaviour. 'I can understand the phone calls,' I said calmly, in a low voice. 'David probably does too. I haven't told him about the hate mail but if I get another one then I'm going to have to show them to him.' I paused for effect. 'My other alternative is to go to the police.' She stared at me, her expression wide, her face effortfully still. 'You know, I am sorry to say this, but you're lucky I haven't been to the police already. It is a criminal offence. I'm not going to make a big deal out of it but I want it to stop, whatever you think of me. I'm the mother of David's children and that's not going to change.'

She closed her eyes and exhaled slowly. 'Oh God . . .' she said.

When she opened her eyes again, she could not meet my gaze. There was still commotion from the kitchen behind her but we didn't have long.

Despite myself, I felt a rush of sympathy for her. I remembered how difficult my pregnancies were, emotionally that is, how skewed life seemed. She had been as obsessed with me as I had been with her, and here was the simple truth: I would one day move on to a new life, if not a relationship with the suitable divorcee I was destined for then some other sort of love perhaps – whichever it was, it would be a life and a love in which she and David would play no part. But I would always be a part of their lives. She and David would never escape me. Had that dawned on her yet? Did that explain the letters?

'Chloe, it's time to stop,' I said, still speaking gently but with a slightly more insistent tone.

At that moment, Rees came charging out of the house and crashed against my legs. 'I HATE PURPLE!' he shouted. I took a wild guess that whatever Betty's angel was made of, it was purple coloured. David was in the kitchen doorway, kneeling down and talking to Betty who was on her way out, consoling her over something. We had seconds. I stared at Chloe hard.

Her cheeks were flushed, her eyes wet. She raised a hand and placed it instinctively on the small rise of her abdomen. I guessed her to be around five months. She bit her lip and looked into the middle distance behind me. 'It will stop,' she said, so quietly I could hardly hear her, then slightly louder, 'It will.' She looked directly at me and nodded once. There was resolution, rather than regret, in her gaze.

'Good,' I said, again careful to keep my tone neutral.

As I walked down the immaculate tarmac driveway, I swung Rees up into my arms. Betty was bouncing beside me waving her angel – a toilet roll painted purple – in the air.

'Baked potatoes!' I said cheerily. I had put them in the oven

182

before I left home. Betty loved nothing more than golden pools of melted butter, a puddle of mayonnaise and the droop of warm grated cheese.

'Yum!' said Betty.

'I hate potatoes,' Rees contributed, happily. He loved them too.

At the gate, I turned to wave goodbye to David and Chloe but they had already gone back inside their bungalow, closing the door behind them.

And stop it did.

Later, I wondered which of those two threats it was that had worked – to show the letters to David, or to go to the police. Perhaps it was the combined effect. There was no doubt in my mind that it was threat rather than guilt that had made Chloe stop. It must have been the police, I thought. Chloe would not have been frightened of me showing the letters to David – if she had been, she would have stuck to phone calls, something I could not prove. She must have felt sure that even if I showed him the notes, she could convince him she was not responsible. He thought me paranoid, after all, no doubt a thought he had shared with his new love. The police, though, would have been obliged to take a more even-handed approach. Malicious communication. I looked it up. It's a criminal offence. At the very least, they would have had to look into it.

The police did look into Chloe, in the end, and me too, but in a way that neither she nor I could ever have anticipated. Each one of us leads our ordinary lives, full of such ordinary things: we shop, we eat, we argue about which film to see. We worry about when we will find time to fix the droopy hem on our favourite skirt or whether we should clean out the fridge. We try olive spread instead of butter, for a bit. We sleep. We make love. We fill our lives to the top of the cup, with routine so brimming that routine is the whole fabric of life, its meat and material. And we never know that waiting for us, there on the horizon, is the big thing, the thing our routines obscure – until it is upon us, that is, like an ocean liner looming huge and sudden through the mist – the thing that will create us. Only when it happens do we realise it was always there, that all our choices were leading up to – *this*.

13

This was my problem with Sally: I did not like her and knew I never would but it was impossible, for a variety of reasons, to actively dislike her, which left me in a strange, insincere limbo. She was the mother of my daughter's best friend, so we were thrown together more than was comfortable for either of us – her friendship towards me often seems as effortful as mine to her. This, on its own, would not have been enough to prevent me disliking her as, in common with most parents, I had hypocrisy down to a fine art. My problem was that although she was an unspeakably irritating woman who sincerely believed she knew the best for everybody all the time, there was a large streak of kindness in her that was hard to overlook. Three months after David left, when I was at my lowest ebb, she turned up after school one day to collect Willow and when I opened the front door, I saw she was carrying four plastic bags of groceries. Seeing me glance down at them, she said, 'Just got a few things for you,' and marched past me, straight into my kitchen.

'The girls are upstairs,' I said, following. 'Shall I put the kettle on?'

'Have you got any lemon and ginger?' she asked, plonking the bags heftily on my counter top and opening my fridge.

'I'm not sure,' I said, opening a cupboard door, knowing full well that we hadn't. I turned to look at her. She was filling my fridge with the items she had bought.

'The quails' eggs were on offer,' she said without looking at me, 'so you'll have to eat those in the next couple of days. I looked for some of that special salt but I don't know what it's called. It's sort of brown salt. Do you know what it's called?'

I thought that perhaps she had gone ever so slightly mad but with Sally it was always hard to tell. 'No, is it special?'

'I think so.'

There was organic chocolate, a vegetarian moussaka, a single steak in a plastic tray, a packet of Greek-style yoghurts in different flavours, some mixed olives, some salami . . . When she had finished, she turned with a small smile and said, 'I saw a bottle of Baileys but then I thought, no alcohol. I know you like a drink or three, my dear, but it's not really a good idea right now, is it? There. Do you recycle your plastic bags?'

It was all I could do to recycle newspapers, and then only intermittently. 'Yes, sure,' I said. 'It's a bit full, let me.' I took the bags from her and jammed them in the gap between the toaster and the wall, then returned to my tea and coffee selection.

'Mint will do,' she said, 'or fennel.' As I poured the water into the cups, she sat down at my table and added, 'I just thought you might need things buying for you, if you know what I mean. Just things, really, little treats. I thought maybe nobody's buying anything for you at the moment.'

I didn't know what to say to her. I don't like moussaka and would probably end up giving the chocolate to the kids, although at least one of the yoghurts would be gone before Sally got home that evening and the olives and salami would go down very nicely with a glass of wine in front of whatever delights that evening's telly viewing had to offer. I sat down opposite her with a bemused smile and just at the point when I was going to thank her with genuine warmth, she said, 'You know, you could really cheer this kitchen up a bit if you painted the units and changed the handles. Yellow. Why don't you try yellow? You can get paint that sticks to those surfaces although you'd have to wash the grease off first. It's quite reasonable. You'd have a new kitchen in no time.' I remembered why David and I had always disliked her and laughed about her behind her back: perfect plump Sally and her perfect plump husband and her oddly named and strangely perfect kids. Her kitchen had just been completed: glass portholes in bare brick and slate tiles on the floor and the faint scent of vanilla hanging around even when she wasn't baking.

Willow and Betty ambled into the room as if they were bored with each other, nine-year-olds practising to be teenagers. Willow went over to her mother and Sally slung one of her hefty arms around her daughter's waist and pulled her towards her. '*This* one is starting to say she wants to walk round to dance class on her own on Tuesdays.' She beamed at me proudly, then took a sip of her tea.

'Betty,' I said, as my daughter opened the fridge and peered into it. 'Did Willow leave her fleece in your room? It's cold outside.'

The discussion about whether the girls should be allowed to walk round to their dance class on their own rambled on throughout that winter, with Sally and me agreeing a united front. We might allow the girls to do it when the weather got a bit better. They stayed at school an extra hour for Capoeira club on Tuesdays so it was often dusk by the time they emerged. When we had reached agreement in principle, there then followed a period of protracted negotiation about which route they were to take home. If they took the shorter route, leaving school and going down Fulton Road and Fulton Avenue, then they had three roads to cross in total, only one of which had a zebra crossing at the right place. There was a longer route that involved only one road, with traffic lights. '*Mu-um.* I'm not a *baby.*'

Sally was insistent that the longer route was best. I disagreed with her on principle. 'Fewer roads, maybe, but more paedophiles,' I muttered, as we discussed it in the school playground one afternoon.

'What?' she replied, startled, pushing her thick hair back behind her ear. Sally was not the sort of woman who thought you should joke about something like that. Her eyes glittered.

'Only joking,' I muttered, feebly, but she had already turned away.

A fortnight later, we decided we would let them do it. They could walk round to the Methodist Church Hall on their own as long as they went the long way round and crossed the road at the traffic lights.

Rees had a new obsession at that time, a spindly girl from nursery called Rebecca. Rebecca wore pebble-thick glasses and said her *r*s like *w*s: 'Shall we play horses now Wees?' I couldn't quite see it myself. Speccy Beccy did a ballet class immediately before Betty and Willow's tap class, so I had agreed with her mother Miriam that I would pick Rebecca and Rees up from nursery, give them snacks at our place, then walk them round to the Methodist Church Hall. I had told Sally I was happy to walk Willow back after their tap dance class had finished but she turned up at the Church Hall anyway, clutching the home-made drawstring dance-kit bag which Willow had left behind that morning. She had a smaller child in tow that I didn't know, a neighbour's daughter who was trying out Rebecca's class. I suspected she had engineered this as an excuse to be waiting at the Church Hall when her daughter turned up.

There was no one point at which I started to worry. It happened more gradually than that. It grew, in the same way that the sky darkens at dusk. Capoeira club finished at 4.30 p.m. and it was a ten-minute walk round to the Church Hall for an adult but the girls would have to collect their belongings from school and then they would chat and amble – I wasn't expecting them before 4.50 p.m. Their class started at 5 p.m. I had braced myself for the possibility that they would be late but that was okay, it was their first time making their own way.

They would learn.

When it got to 5 p.m., and then passed 5 p.m., I became aware of a slight feeling of unease inside, like indigestion. I did not even identify it as present in myself until I looked at Sally. The little ones had finished their ballet class at the same time as the big ones' tap dance started and they had already tumbled out of the hall and into the changing room. Sally was kneeling and fumbling to undo her neighbour's daughter's blue wrap cardigan. At the same moment I glanced over at her, she looked up at me, and we saw our formless thoughts reflected in each other's brief, inarticulate gaze. Even then, we did not acknowledge to each other, even by our expressions, that anything might be wrong. She looked away first, turning back to the child she was dealing with, who seemed unhappy. I had been doing some colouring with Rees and he had been so demanding about it that I had left Rebecca to get changed back into her clothes on her own. She was kneeling in front of me with her ballet bag, folding her leotard neatly, unperturbed by my inattention. Sally finished getting her charge back into her own clothes and only then approached me and said, lightly, 'Getting on a bit. They'll miss the warm-up. Should I walk round?'

I didn't want to concede that was necessary. 'They came out really late last week.' It was true. After last week's Capoeira club, I was standing outside the school gates in the rain for twenty minutes. First the club had finished late, they said, when they finally came running, cheeks flushed, and then Willow couldn't find her coat.

Sally nodded although I could see she didn't agree. 'Oh well, let's give it a bit, then.' She turned and went back to her neighbour's child and started helping her put her dance things back into her bag. The child had a trembling lower lip and I guessed it had been Sally's idea to bring her round and that the child herself – and maybe the neighbour too – was less than enthusiastic. By way of contrast, my charge Rebecca appeared to have an unnatural amount of self-possession. Once her bag was packed, she pulled on her coat and shoes without being asked and then sat primly on an upright chair, waiting for me to be ready to leave. Meanwhile, Rees bored of his colouring efforts and, while I picked up the felt tips, decided to race up and down the changing room like a tiny hippo, scattering ballerinas left right and centre. The other mothers were shooting can't-you-control-him glances my way. Somebody would be in tears soon.

Sally finished gathering and comforting her neighbour's child and then came over to me and said, 'Why don't I just see if they're coming down the road?' It wasn't phrased as a question. Before I could reason with her, she turned to the neighbour's child and said, 'I'm just going to see if Willow and her friend are on their way. Stay here with Rees's mum and Rees and Rebecca.'

Now I had three of them to keep an eye on. At that point, Rebecca's mum sent me a text. *Meeting running over, can u take R back to yours? V. sorry. Miriam.* I liked Miriam. She was a mess like me. I texted back. *No probs.* I couldn't remember whether Miriam knew I was due to stay late at the Hall anyway, to wait until the end of Betty's class. They'll all need feeding as soon as we get back, I thought, I'll cook them all rice and peas, that's quick, and easy. I texted Miriam again. *No hurry. Stuck here anyway so pick R up from mine whenever. Will feed her.* She texted me back. *Thnx!!!!*

At that point, Rees attempted a cartwheel down the crowded room. As a gymnastic manoeuvre, it was an abject failure but he managed to take out a couple of tutus in the process who turned on him with the ferocity of pit-bull terriers. He made an 'Aargh!' sound and hurled himself backwards on to the squishy sofa pushed up against one wall, which destabilised a carton of juice left precariously on the arm. The juice tumbled. Another girl stepped backwards on to it. The carton exploded and mango and coconut spurted everywhere in a tropical spray. I glanced around to see which mother was stupid enough to leave a carton of juice balanced like that and then saw that Sally's neighbour's child was standing next to me and sobbing softly. I didn't even know her name. My phone began to ring. I scrabbled in my handbag.

'Hi, it's me, look, I've walked all the way to school . . .' Sally's voice had a breathy quality. I realised that because she was worried, that had allowed me to remain casual. We had chosen opposite corners.

'Why don't you go to the office?'

'There's no one around. I'm sure the clubs are out.'

'Why don't you go and check?' I refused to panic until there was good reason to. Betty and Willow were probably sitting outside the school office, waiting. They had probably forgotten they were supposed to walk round on their own. One of them would be feeling poorly or have lost something. One of them had sprained an ankle. Sue, the school secretary, had said to them, *just wait there. If one of the mums isn't here soon I'll call them.* Then some other task had distracted her and she had forgotten to ring, forgotten the two nine-year-olds sitting plaintively on the plastic chairs outside her office. School secretaries are supposed to be models of efficiency but Sue was a bit scatter-brained.

'All right,' Sally said. 'Call me if they show up.' As if I wouldn't bother.

My first feelings of nausea began when Sally returned to the Methodist Church Hall. She had retraced her steps all the way back instead of calling me again. This was a bad sign. 'There's no sign of them,' she said loudly, staring at me hard. Her fear was making her aggressive. 'I went to the office. Clubs finished on time. I walked all the way around.'

'Which way did you go?' I ask.

'The long way,' she said, 'the way we told them to come. We

both told them, didn't we? I went that way there and back.'

I thought of the long way, tracing the route in my head, the streets that ran off it, the friends' houses they would have passed. They would have gone past Jason Wellington's house. Jason was a boy in their class with attention deficit disorder who exerted a huge fascination for the girls because of his loudness and charm. 'Jason's got a new rabbit,' I said, triumphantly, and Sally looked at me as if I was mad. Without bothering to explain, I phoned Jason's mum. No, Betty and Willow weren't there.

By that point, other mothers in the changing room had overheard our conversation and dropped their own. Our anxiety was contagious. Two of them offered us their mobile phones despite the fact that Sally and I both had phones clearly visible in our hands. Another mother said she knew a boy who went to Capoeira, a Year Five boy, not one we knew. She offered to ring the boy's mum and see if he was back yet. We already knew that the club had finished on time but Sally and I both fell upon this extra source of knowledge, which suddenly seemed hugely significant. The phone call was made. The mum didn't know. Her son was going to a friend's house after Capoeira but she said she would call the friend's mother. After a few minutes, she called back to say that her son was picked up by the friend's mother as expected. I was annoyed. What use was *that* information? I realised that what had seemed like an avenue worth exploring was a dead end, a pointless distraction.

The room was buzzing with useless information by then. All the other mothers wanted in on the act, both ones we knew and total strangers. Other phone calls were being made, a network of enquiry spreading out with us at its centre. News dribbled back to us along those lines of enquiry but none of it was the right news. I didn't care about knowing anything but the one thing I needed to know. *Where is my daughter?* Why were all the other mothers clouding my head with the bits of knowledge they had acquired – Ferhal goes to chess club which finished at the same time as Capoeira, Shelly goes to play centre on Tuesdays, it has started to rain – all this information was getting in the way.

I had to get out of the changing room. I stood up. 'I'll go and look again,' I said to Sally. Rees flung himself at my legs. Rebecca was still sitting, calm and unconcerned, on the upright chair, swinging her legs gently. The neighbour's child was still sobbing, ignored. 'Which streets did you go down?' I said to Sally.

'I went the long way,' Sally repeated, openly cross with me now. 'I said. The way we said.'

Oh God… My sensations of nausea were almost overwhelming now. My stomach was full of air. 'They must have gone the other way,' I said weakly, trying to ignore the fact that if they had, they would have arrived long ago. Suddenly, the short way had to take ten times as long as the long way. My brain baulked at any other explanation. Short, long, the words had become elastic, almost meaningless. 'I'll go that way, I'll check.'

Sally said firmly, 'No, listen, right. This is what we're going to do. I am going to go again with the car so I can drive round. I'll do all the side streets. You take the three little ones back to your house. I've got the car. The traffic was terrible on the main road, backed up, but once I'm off it, it will be fine.'

'But wouldn't it be better if . . .'

'No.'

It made sense. She had the car. I was on foot. She could drive around, cover more territory. I could take the three small ones home with me – Rees, Rebecca, and the crying child whose name I still didn't know – and give them tea. She would find Willow and Betty and give them the biggest telling-off of their lives. I had never observed Sally angry but had a feeling it could be fearsome. Then she would bring Betty home and pick up the neighbour's crying child and take it away and Miriam would come for Rebecca and I would press a drink on her and tell her the whole story and she would say *Oh my God*, then leave with Rebecca and, at last, normality would be restored in my life. I would put my children to bed and pour myself another drink. It is going to happen like that, I said to myself. Everything is going to be okay.

It was gone half past five by then and the tap class would be finishing soon. I wanted to leave the Church Hall before the other girls came tumbling out and ran up to me and said, 'Where's Betty? Where's Willow? Why weren't they here?' Wherever the girls were, they would know that they were not just late but disastrously late. Three quarters of an hour late: nothing, in grown-up terms – for a child, a lifetime. They are not disobedient girls. The phrase 'out of character' sprang to mind and I pushed it down. It was a phrase I had heard on television, at press conferences. I was not ready for it.

I realised that my growing panic was exacerbated by the fact that Sally had become calmer, the breathy quality gone from her voice. 'I'll give Susie my number so she can call me if they show up. Then I'll drive around,' she said. She was rising to the occasion, whereas I was falling from it, as if from a great height. I nodded and nodded and nodded. I didn't want to go home with the other three. I wanted to drive around the streets with Sally looking for my daughter but I knew that if I insisted on accompanying her, or waiting here, then that would be counter to what was sensible when there was a minor hold-up like this. It would be admitting that something was seriously wrong. I was clinging on to normality by the fingertips. I was trying to follow the script.

'I'll call Katie's mum and tell her you've got her,' Sally added. 'I can pick her up from yours and drop her off when I bring Betty back.'

Katie. So that was the little squit's name. 'Come on,' I said cheerily to the younger three. 'Rees, Rebecca, Katie. Get your coats on.' Rebecca shot me a look of contempt as she rose from her upright chair.

I ignored the concerned glances of the other mums as I ushered the three small ones out of the door. It was a twelve-minute walk to our house. All the way, I talked to tearful Katie, quickly and calmly, with that forceful tone of voice that adults use to children when they are demanding an answer. 'I'm going to make rice and peas for you all when we get back. It's Rees's favourite. Do you like rice and peas?'

'No . . .' she sobbed.

'Never mind,' I said. 'I'll make plenty because Rees's big sister will be home soon. Have you got a big sister?'

'No . . .'

'I have,' said Rebecca, laconically. 'I've got two of them.'

Rees adored being in charge. I told him he could take the girls up to my room and show them a game on the computer. He led the way authoritatively, stomping on the stairs. I put my phone on the counter top next to the hob while I cooked rice and peas, so that I could snatch it up in a millisecond when Sally called. The routine of making food was calming, though. I made an inordinate amount, enough to feed everyone back at the Methodist Church Hall.

Miriam arrived while the children were sitting forking rice into their mouths. Even snivelling little Katie was eating. I was eating my own half-portion from a cereal bowl, standing up and watching them while I leant against the counter-top. I often ate kiddie-food with the kids and I had thought to myself as I served, *to not-eat would be an admission that something is wrong. Eat.*

Miriam had texted me to say she was on her way. When I heard her knock, I ran to the front door even though I knew it was only her, pulling it open, ready to fall upon her – but she almost fell on me. 'Oh my God,' she burst out, tumbling in.

'You won't believe the afternoon I've had I had to threaten to report my boss he's a bloody psycho, Rebecca Rebecca, Becky darling we have to go *right now*, I'm in such trouble . . .' She rushed past me down the hall.

'Don't you want . . .' I followed.

'I'd love to, I'm so sorry, you've been such a star, I've got to snatch this one up and get going,' she replied with a sigh. I felt a swoop of despair. I was relying on Miriam to stay with me, so that I could tell her, impressing myself with my own calm, about this afternoon's little hiatus. I had let her in the house without comment. I couldn't suddenly announce that, yes, I was fine apart from the small fact that my daughter was missing. I wanted to grab her by the lapels and shout into her face, 'Betty is missing!' but I didn't say anything. As we descended into the kitchen, I watched myself with a measure of disbelief, behaving as if nothing was wrong. From wanting her to stay, I suddenly needed her to leave as soon as possible.

'Oh, hello, Katie!' declared Miriam. Rebecca jumped off her chair, rice and peas abandoned, and called out 'Mummy!' She leapt into her mother's arms. I felt weak and sick.

'Get your shoes on *right* now, darling, okay? I didn't know you knew the Wiltons,' Miriam was gesturing at Katie but talking to me.

'I don't,' I replied, breathing deeply. 'Oh God, Katie, I hope Sally has rung your mum. She'll be wondering where you are.'

Katie looked down at her plate.

'I can take her back if you like, she's on my way, won't take a moment,' said Miriam, having picked up on the fact that whatever was going on was an emergency arrangement of some sort.

'Oh yes, thank you,' I said. 'I don't even have her number.'

Katie hopped off her chair, ran to Miriam and stood very close to her. Miriam pulled an amused face at me and began ushering Katie and Rebecca towards the door.

Rees, unconcerned, continued eating his rice and peas.

After I had closed the door behind them, I leaned my head against the glass. Why didn't I stop Miriam leaving? Why didn't I say, 'Please, I don't know where my daughter is, please *please* stay with me.' I drew breath and walked back down the hallway.

'Can I watch television?' asked Rees, who knew exactly what the answer would be.

'No, you've already had computer.'

'Can I have an ice lolly?'

'Yes.'

'Can I have the last raspberry one?'

'Yes.'

I picked up Katie's plate in a sincere but misguided attempt to continue behaving normally. Before I could turn away from the table with it, my arm began to shake. I put the plate back down and leant with my knuckles resting on the plastic tablecloth, breathing. Then my legs began to shake too. I sat down. Rees was at the freezer cabinet, with his back to me. I thought, *be normal again before he turns.* As he turned, I fixed a smile on my face and said, 'Bath time soon, straight after that ice lolly, okay?'

'Can I do some drawing?'

'We'll see.'

I looked behind me, at the kitchen clock. It was gone six. *Why hasn't Sally rung me? What possible explanation can there be for her not ringing me, even if it is just to update me, to tell me there is no news?* I would give it another five minutes. Five minutes precisely. I would call her and if she didn't answer her phone then, that was it, I was slinging Rees in the car and going out to find Betty myself. What was I doing, stuck at home, waiting? What was wrong with me?

Four minutes later, there was a firm knock at my door. My body froze and clenched. I rose swiftly, leaving Rees colouring at the kitchen table amongst the half-finished plates of food, the discarded lolly stick in a plastic bowl by his side . . . I can still see that table – the plates, the scattering of neon gel pens that I should not have let Rees use, the lolly stick at a diagonal in the plastic bowl, stained raspberry-coloured halfway up its length.

I was expecting to see the wavery bulk of Sally through the glass, the lower heads of Betty and Willow either side of her. I was welling up with anger and relief, already, prematurely ready to shed tears of fury and gratitude. My feet continued to walk down my hallway even as I saw it wasn't an adult with two children on the other side of the glass. Those feet walked towards the door as my eyes and my brain registered two adult forms beyond the glass, two dark uniforms. My hand, my automatic hand, reached out to grasp the interior door handle, to open the door, the swinging door, the door that swings open again and again in my memory – the door that will never again close properly in my head. Muscle memory, instinct, call it what you will: I knew, of course I knew. My body was recalling disaster, dredging up the physical sensations of it even as my mind closed itself against that knowledge, turning round and around, like a rat in a cage. The door swung open. Two police officers – there were two police officers on my doorstep, one man, one woman. I stayed standing upright but I began to fall. The officers' faces were open wide. They both looked at me, their gazes huge. When the woman officer spoke, I saw her lips move but I heard her voice inside my head rather than through my ears, reverberating.

'Mrs Needham?'

PART 4

After

PART 1

A NOTE

14

Friday evening; it is dark and wet by the time I leave my house: embracing dark, a bitter wind – my natural habitat. I think of the cliffs, out there on the edge of town, waiting in the night, and of how I used to go up there as an adolescent and stand near the edge and holler my rage at life's unfairness into the huge maw of the sea – an adolescent may be excused their love of melodrama but it is less seemly in an adult. How would I have felt at fifteen if I had known how many times I would be back, raging again and again? I think about the cliffs as I get into my car: the black waves jumping and clashing. As I drive down my road, I pass various neighbours all hurrying in the opposite direction, heads bowed against the bitter, freezing rain. Everybody wants to be at home on a night like this.

It is the first time I have driven to the hospital since the night I visited Betty there. I take the one-way system, unable to retrace the route of that evening. At the hospital, I drive around to the small courtyard at the back, behind our unit. The courtyard is a source of much grumbling on the part of female staff as it is ill-lit and we often leave work after dark in the winter. I park the car in the corner, under the trees, where it is pitch black. I grip the steering wheel and breathe heavily. If I seem upset, there is a chance Jan H will insist on staying with me, which would be disastrous.

Five minutes late, I get out of the car and cross the courtyard. Rounding the corner of the building, I see that Jan is waiting for me at the door to our unit, a single-storey building with an ugly, pre-fab feeling, even though it's built of brick.

She is wearing her pale blue mac, belted tightly, and has her back to me, looking towards the main part of the hospital. She turns as I approach, immaculate hair swinging, handsome face creased with expectation.

'Sorry,' I say, hurrying up to her.

She throws her arms around me. I haven't seen her since the funeral, and then it was only a brief hand-clutch in my sitting room, surrounded by others. I have been so absorbed in the coming task that I have not prepared myself. We embrace for a long time.

I pull back and she hands me the keys. 'I left the light on in your office and the kitchen,' she says, wiping at her eyes with a gloved hand. 'You'd better turn them off when you lock up.'

I nod, wet-eyed. She doesn't need to tell me, it is just something to say. She grabs my forearm and gives it a little shake. 'Are you sure about this? It's such a filthy night, bad enough . . . it feels weird, leaving you here.'

'Go home and have a glass of wine with Don,' I say. I embrace her again but briefly, by way of dismissal. 'Have one for me too.'

'How's Rees?'

'He's fine. He's with David for a bit.'

'Okay, if you're sure.'

I dangle the keys from my finger. I raise my eyebrows. 'Is it the new one?' I mean the porter. There was a new, younger one arrived just before I stopped work. We had all discussed how he was a great improvement on the bad-tempered old one. 'Easy on the eye,' as Jan had put it.

Jan shakes her head. ''Fraid not.' She is already backing away towards the main building. 'Call me at home if you want, later? I've got to go to the shops but I'll be home in an hour.'

'I'll call you Monday, it's okay.' I turn sharply, while she is still looking at me. I want to appear confident, so there is no danger she will come back to check on me.

Jan has left the door unlocked. I step inside, into the darkness of the hallway, reflexively comforted by the cheap carpet, the fire extinguisher on the wall, the noticeboard with the poster advising the elderly to get a flu jab – my old life, my life before, the normality of it all. To my left is the Reception desk, where Maurice sits. Beyond the curve of his desk, still to the left, is the darkened corridor that leads to our consulting rooms. To the right is the square of plastic chairs where the patients wait and, beyond that, the kitchen. I go into the kitchen and look around. Everyone is very good about washing their own tea and coffee mugs, in our unit. Everything is put away but for a jar of decaffeinated instant coffee that has been left next to the microwave. I go over to the counter and pick it up, open a cupboard to put it away – am felled.

The coffee jars and boxes of teabags are kept on the lower shelf of the cupboard. On the shelf above are mugs. We each have our own and are a small enough unit to know whose is whose. Mine was painted for me by Betty, two years ago. It came from one of those paint-your-own mug kits – plain white enamel, on which she painted a signal – a flower, green stem and spiky leaves, yellow centre, red petals, round and full and out of proportion to the rest of it: a flower like no flower that has ever really existed, a child's sign to say, *I love you. I did this for you.*

I was right to come here alone, ulterior motive or no. How could I have forgotten the mug? I close the cupboard and walk carefully and purposefully to the kitchen door, where I flick off the light switch and stand for several minutes in the doorway, breathing. I must not let this distract me, I think. It must be fuel.

I walk swiftly back to the Reception area and sit down at Maurice's desk. For a moment, I sit and stare at his computer, turned off for the weekend, blank-faced, asleep. My face fills the screen, my scrawny, black-eyed face. Is that really what I look like, now, or is it a trick performed by the slight curve of the dark, the way it distorts my reflection? I switch the computer on at the side of the monitor and it gurgles at me, like a pet.

I open the Upton Centre file, where referrals are listed in alphabetical order of surname. I scan it quickly. I was right. Once I have found what I need, I print it out, then turn everything off and make sure nothing is left disturbed on Maurice's desk. He is a particularly immaculate and efficient receptionist and he must not know I have even been here.

Before I leave, I take a walk down the darkened corridor. I don't need to go to my office but I want to turn off the light that Jan left on. It is only a few steps but the strangeness of being there in the dark, after hours, seems to elongate the short walk along the thin carpet: thin, cheap, our block was built out of small change. The door to my office is made of some orangey plywood. The metal handle squeaks as I turn it, swings back to reveal my office, which is square and brightly lit by the fluorescent tube above the desk. The filing cabinet in the corner with the empty vase on top, the cork noticeboard behind the desk with out-of-date circulars pinned on it – all is untouched, free of dust, as if I was in here earlier today, leading my normal life. I wasn't a great one for personalising my work space – no photos of David or the kids. The only non-functional item is the birthday card my workmates gave me last summer, which is still pinned to the frame of the bottom right-hand corner of the noticeboard. Opposite my desk is the chair in which my patients sit and against the wall, the examination table with the cupboard above it. In the corner behind the desk are a paper shredder and the bin I use for recycling. It isn't the same office that David first visited me in, all those years ago – that was in the main building – but for all its functionality and anonymity, it might as well be. This was the unchanging context of my life, this blank, and despite all that has happened to me it is still here, waiting. Again, I feel the sensation that comes to me on the clifftops; time, folding and parting, folding and parting, like one of those paper puzzles the children make. *Say a number . . . say another number . . .* a random choice selects an animal for you to be or a task to perform, and it's that simple and accidental, the slippage between what we are and what we might have been.

Then there is the window, a perfect black mirror in which my reflection stands, facing me, nothing beyond it, nothing outside.

I flick the switch. The fluorescent tube makes a buzzing sound and dies. I am in darkness. I turn to walk back down the corridor, closing my office door behind me. The only light comes from the Reception area, and as I walk, I see a shadow flicker in that light, a grey shape moving quickly in the yellow glow, small and fleet, as if a creature has dived for cover at the far end of the corridor. I move swiftly down the thin carpet, the one that always makes enough static to raise my hair and give me a small electric shock when I earth the charge by touching something metal. The Reception area is empty. The shadow must have dived into the kitchen. I stride to the kitchen door and push it back. It swings. The kitchen is empty. 'Betty?' I say hopefully into the dark.

By the time I get home, I am shivering with the cold. I plug in the kettle. While it boils, I remember how once, after we were married but before we had children, I had a heavy cold that I called the flu in order to gain David's attention. It was hard to get David's attention when he was distracted, a little exaggeration was sometimes needed, something that played on his knee-jerk chivalry. David's reaction to any problem was to solve it. So when I told him I thought I had the flu, he made me a hot toddy. What did he put in? I tried to remember as the kettle boiled; lemon juice, honey – whisky. I drag a kitchen chair over to the cupboard above the fridge-freezer. Our few spirit bottles were always kept up here, to keep them safe from the children, 'To keep them safe from me,' David used to say, but neither of us were great drinkers. Student drinkers, David and I had been, beer and crisps in the pub, wine with our Friday dinner if we were feeling sophisticated. Our taste in alcohol never really graduated.

I fetch down the bottle of whisky, which is dusty even though it has been kept in a cupboard. I find a large white mug. There is no lemon in my fridge, of course – I haven't bought any fresh food in weeks – but somewhere at the back of the herbs and spices cupboard I know there is a green bottle of some yellow fluid full of e-numbers that claims to be a substitute.

Our kettle is slow. While I wait for it, I check the telephone. There is a message from Aunt Lorraine, trying to sound cheery but wondering why we haven't spoken for a while. I remember that my mobile, in my handbag, is switched off. When I turn it on, I find there are three missed calls from David. He only left a message on the last one, saying shortly, 'Hi, it's me. Can you call me? On the mobile.' There is background noise I can't identify.

This is unusual. After our bad patch, David insisted I call him at the house in the evenings rather than at work or on his mobile, an act of loyalty to Chloe, I suppose. If so, it was an act of loyalty Chloe herself didn't seem to appreciate. If she answered the phone at all, she would hand it straight to David, and even when David answered, I could feel her presence behind his words, the ghost of her in the pauses between his phrases. She couldn't leave us alone. It took me a while to find such behaviour gratifying and even when I did, any small sense of victory I might have felt was spoiled by the fact that David could still not see her for what she was. David might never believe what she was like, but I knew, and she knew I knew.

Why had it all started again, now, the letters, after Betty? Because she thought I was weak again? Didn't she realise that after losing Betty, there was nothing she could do to me, that I was strong as an ox?

I call David's mobile. He answers immediately. I can hear hubbub in the background.

'It's me. Where are you?' I say.

'Stag's Head,' he replies. 'I've sneaked out for a pint.' This is also new. 'How are you?'

'Fine,' I reply brightly. 'I thought there was something wrong with Rees.'

'Oh God no, sorry, he's asleep. He had a busy day so I gave him a bath and got him in early. Chloe's mum is over, so I made my excuses.' His tone is matey. 'Listen, I think we should have dinner. Soon. I don't think I handled it very well, when I saw you in the unit.'

Handled, I think. I am something that must be handled. There is a strange pause on the end of the line. Even though he is not speaking, I can hear that his voice has cracked. I don't know what to say, so I listen in silence. He is gulping.

I sit down on a kitchen chair, my hot toddy forgotten. I listen. After a while I say, gently, 'You okay?'

'No, I'm not,' he replies in a whisper, and then his voice goes completely. 'I miss her every day, Laura. I miss her so badly. I don't think . . .' he fades out again. I imagine him with his head down over an open newspaper, trying to hide his distress from anyone who might be seated nearby. When he speaks again, his voice is lowered but every bit as broken and wretched. 'I just want to talk about her, please, please. Please can we meet for dinner, just us, just nothing else?' And then he does it. He says my name, in that plain way of his. 'Laura . . .'

'Of course we can.' I realise I have been waiting for this, ever since Betty was taken away from us, that there is no one I want or need but David.

'When? When are you free?'

When am I not free? I want to say. What, or who, does he imagine restricts my movements? 'Well, I can come now if you like.' I sense a moment here, a door ajar. 'Or you can come over if you like.' It occurs to me as I say this – and it is a shocking, transgressive thought – that if he comes over, we might have sex.

I can hear him thinking it through. 'I don't think it would be a good idea if I came to the house.' I wonder if he has had the same thought.

'Because you would find it too difficult or because you'd have to explain to Chloe later?'

There is a pause. 'Both.'

'Okay, where?'

'There's a new tapas place, at the end of the road here. It was quiet when I came past.'

'I know I've seen it. Not exactly doing a roaring trade.'

His voice has reacquired its normal tone but I can hear effort beneath. 'God, I'm starving, actually.'

'Me too.'

This is untrue but we need this exchange to lighten the mood, to make this unexpected meeting possible. I look at my watch in the same spirit, an empty gesture. 'I can come now if you like, just give me a minute to have a cup of tea and put my coat on.' It is quarter to eight. If David put Rees to bed himself then he must have only just got to the pub – the Stag's Head is on his side of town, only a few minutes' drive from his housing estate. I wonder how long he will have before he has to explain to Chloe where he has been, that he has seen me: ridiculous under the circumstances, but gratifying too, his need for subterfuge.

*

He is waiting in the restaurant when I get there. The restaurant is nice, in the way that new restaurants always are: clean table-cloths and polished glasses, a suffusion of red in the decor and a glowing manager at hand to greet the handful of customers who have bothered to make it out on a night like this. It is on a long road of launderettes and takeaways on the new side of town that is all boxy housing estates and roundabouts. David is already seated, in an alcove in a far corner. He is facing the door, like a detective who needs to keep an eye on who comes in or out. As I approach, he looks at me and tries a smile. I realise I despise him; words can scarcely describe how much. I hand my coat to the manager who has followed me across the restaurant and is hovering in anticipation, then slide into my side of our cubicle. I look at David and feel calm, strong, reserved. I cannot believe this is a man I wept and pleaded for, a man who brought me to my knees. When he came to see me in the hospital I thought how little I felt for him but I've gone a step further. My new plan, I realise, is the first secret I have ever kept from him. I am learning something he could have told me years ago, how easy it is to despise someone you are deceiving.

He gives me a half-smile.

'So,' I say lightly, as he hands me a menu, 'Chloe's babysitting for us while we have dinner.'

'Chloe and her mother,' he corrects me.

'You order,' I say, handing him back the menu. I think: we are meeting because his own grief is inadequate. He needs to borrow a little of mine.

'What do you want to drink?' he asks. Perhaps Chloe is sick of his grief – however much she loves him, she must feel ex-cluded by our loss. Perhaps he has realised it would be a good idea to give her a night in watching television, laughing at something stupid, without having to deal with him and his inability to find stupidity amusing.

'Beer,' I say. Oh no, she won't be watching television. Her mum is there. I have the impression she and her mother are close and that David finds this difficult, although I can't recall how I might have learnt this. He was unused to having in-laws as a feature in a relationship, I suppose. He got an easy ride with me in that respect, if nothing else.

'Me too,' he says.

I am only guessing, but I resent being used as a substitute. If he is having difficulty with Chloe, or she with him, then they should sort it out between them.

The waiter approaches. David glances down the menu and rattles off an arbitrary list of tapas drawn at random from each section of the menu, concluding with, 'Two beers.'

The waiter sighs and rattles off his own list, a choice of seven or eight different sorts of bottled lager. David looks at me and I shrug. He chooses. After the waiter has gone, we sit in silence until he comes back with the bottles. It is a long silence and a grateful one. I feel us appreciating it, and each other, and I soften, just a little.

When the waiter puts the bottles of beer on the table, pouring first mine then David's, the moment is broken.

David asks about my brief stay in the psychiatric unit. 'Will there be any follow-up?'

I shrug. 'Not as far as I'm concerned.' We are not here to discuss me. It is just something he has to get out of the way.

I ask him a few desultory questions about work. He went back for two weeks and then realised it was too early, he said, and had to stay at home for a bit. Now he's doing short days. They've been very good. I tell him about the notes and cards from my team. I do not tell him I have spoken to Jan H or that I visited my office only an hour before. He has no right to know what I am up to. Our attempt to make ordinary conversation peters to an end and we return to silence. The only other people in the restaurant are a couple on the far side of the room. They are eating in silence too.

The waiter brings an oval-shaped metal plate of green beans, slimy with olive oil and scattered with pink cubes of ham. He places the plate on the table between us and turns away. David pushes the plate towards me.

I nod at them. 'Thought you said you were hungry.'

He shakes his head in reply.

'Do you remember when we had to take her to hospital?' he says.

'The UTI?'

'White as a sheet.'

When she was three, Betty went down with a urinary tract infection, one of those things little girls are prone to. The first we knew about it was when she had what's known as a rigor, one step down from a febrile convulsion. She was at home playing, one Saturday morning, when David carried her into the kitchen to show me. She was white as a sheet in his arms, goose-pimpled all over, mouth and eyes half open, trembling from head to foot. I took her temperature. 39.4, but no other cold or flu-like symptoms. I said, 'Get the car,' even though we both knew it was parked outside our house. At A & E, I carried her in and demanded they do a lumbar puncture straight away but the house doctor said, 'Let's try and get some bloods first.' David and I both held her down and she still kicked the doctor's glasses off his nose.

'She didn't like that doctor, did she?'

David smiles. 'Certainly didn't – mind you, neither did I.'

'He was young.'

'The nurses didn't like him either.'

'Yeah, they didn't.'

The arrival of tortilla dissolves this memory and David falls silent again. All at once, unbidden, I remember how, in the early days, when I knew he was coming to my flat at the end of the day, I would get undressed and into my silk kimono, with nothing underneath. It was a ludicrous garment, pink silk with huge, full-blown flowers in a deeper pink. It had a green sash that never stayed tied unless you pulled it into a tight bow. I liked to answer the door to him like that, like a housewife from a seventies porno video. I liked to pull him in, rough in his outside coat, reeking of the cold outside. Sometimes, he would push the kimono from my shoulders before we even said hello. We had sex on the communal stairs, once, me with the kimono tied tightly round around my waist with its party bow, him still in his huge coat, boots on his feet, mud on the carpet – the journey we have been on, from there to here.

Then, with a rush of bitterness, I remember that he has been on the same journey with Chloe. The early sex must have been even sweeter with her, tinged as it was with all the power of something forbidden. What was I, in the early days? A new girlfriend: but her, she was something he wasn't supposed to have. Then, as if that was not enough, he went on to have a baby with her too, a tiny human being to redeem their guilt. I imagine all the things I don't like to imagine – them staring together at their new child. I can picture it all too clearly. There is nothing he has done with me that he hasn't done with her, until now.

Why is he here, in this restaurant, sharing reminiscences and pretending to be my equal? He has her, and a new baby – and now he has Rees into the bargain.

I sit back and sigh. I have made an attempt to pick at the tortilla but what little appetite I had is gone. We are silent for a long while and while we are, the waiter brings dish after dish of tapas to sit beside the untouched green beans.

He is watching me, his eyes intent. 'Do you still hate me, after this?' he asks. He was always disturbingly good at guessing what I was thinking.

I look away, making a small, scornful sound at the back of my throat. 'God, even now, it's all about you, isn't it?'

'That's not what I meant.'

'What did you mean?' The tone in which I say this makes it clear I don't expect an answer and he doesn't attempt one. Instead, he picks up a fork and prods lightly at a thick chunk of chorizo. The fork springs back.

He tosses the fork down on to the tablecloth and says, in a harsh voice, 'Look, it's not as simple as you think, okay? It never was, but it particularly isn't now. Right?'

'What?'

'Me and Chloe. It was never the easy ride you thought.'

'I never said it was.' I can't believe we are having this conversation. I look away, then back at him, muttering, 'I don't bloody believe this . . .'

'That was why you kept calling us at four in the morning?'

It is an unfair hit. It was only a phase, those four-in-the-morning calls. I was beside myself. The kids were too, waking at all hours of the night, and sometimes I simply couldn't stand the thought of him and Chloe being asleep when I was not. I wanted to share it with them, some of what I had been dumped with. I'm not proud of it. I wasn't proud of it at the time. I knew it was only playing into their hands, cementing my position as their common enemy. I should have had more dignity but I couldn't help myself.

If he is going to hit below the belt, then so am I. 'Why are you raising all this now?' I say calmly. 'Don't you think it is a bit late? Something more important has happened.'

'I know,' he says, raising his hands. He pauses for a moment, then says, looking down at the table, 'Things are very difficult at home at the moment.'

'Of course.'

'No, I don't mean Betty. Even before Betty. Chloe, well, I've had to look after her a lot.'

Despite myself, I am intrigued. This is taking this evening's disloyalty to Chloe to a different level. He was always so proud of himself on that score. 'I don't talk about you to her and I don't talk about her to you,' he said to me once, smugly, as if that made it okay to be fucking us both at the same time.

He leans forward towards me and lowers his voice, even though no one else is nearby. 'About two months after Harry was born, she went into a real tailspin. At first I didn't take it too seriously.' *I bet you didn't.* 'I'd been there before, after all. I told her it was natural. I was expecting her to lift up, after a while, like you did. Harry was colicky, you know, first baby and all that. It was a difficult birth. She lost a lot of blood. They probably should have done a section. He fractured her coccyx on the way out. They didn't realise at first. She was in a lot of pain and we didn't know why for ages. And then he wouldn't feed. She was having a difficult time, I could see that. Anyway, maybe I didn't handle it well.'

The waiter materialises beside our table. It must be obvious to him that he is intruding – David sits back and neither of us looks at him – but he doesn't go away. After a meaningful pause, he says, 'Is everything all right?'

Glancing at the table, I see we have touched nothing. To get rid of him I say, 'Could I have another beer, please?'

'Of course. Sir?'

David shakes his head.

Once the waiter has gone, David leans forward again on his elbows. 'She went right down and she doesn't seem to have come back up.'

'Is she taking anything?' I ask.

David shook his head. 'She won't. She won't take anything. She keeps talking about restarting feeding but that's ludicrous. She won't listen. And then, about three months ago, she started rejecting Harry. At first it was just, you know, I would get home from work and he was howling and his nappy hadn't been changed all day. He was soaking wet, Laura, honestly, drenched through. Then I spoke to the neighbour. She told me that she can hear Harry screaming every time she walks past our house. She walks her dog all the time this neighbour. Every time, she heard him. I asked Chloe and she went berserk and said all sorts of things about the poor woman. You wouldn't believe the names she called her. It was after that she started getting secretive.'

He stops and puts his head in his hands.

I think of the time I told him about Chloe making those phone calls, and the vehemence with which he insisted she was incapable of such behaviour. I think of how I haven't even shown him the letters because of how convinced he had seemed of her innocence. I am biting my tongue. Do you believe me now? I want to say. Shall we pause for a moment to allow you to compose your apology?

He lifts his head. His face is wretched. 'She rang me up at work one day. Harry was about four months old. She said, you've got half an hour to get here, or I'm going to hurt the baby. Then she hung up.'

'God . . .'

'I got there as fast as I could. She was upstairs, under the duvet. Harry was in his cot, crying. The door to his room was closed. When I went in to her, she wouldn't get out of bed. She was fully clothed, but she wouldn't get up.'

'You have to *make* her get help, see a doctor, start the process at least, so she can get some medication.' The irony of this remark does not escape me.

'I know, Christ, Laura, I've thought of going much further than that. I had an appointment to see Dr Calder. I've been scared to go to work. It was all about to really kick off, when this happened.'

I see that the waiter has placed another bottle of beer on the table without either of us noticing. I grasp the neck of the bottle and push the segment of lime down with one finger. I don't know what I think or feel. For a few minutes, I have not thought about Betty, which makes me feel guilty, and confused. I am having to realign everything I have assumed about Chloe and their lives together. The truth is that despite the phone calls and the letters I have always assumed that they were happy. How could they not be – how dare they not be, when their life together had been bought at such cost? I wonder about that immaculate bungalow. Is it chaos behind the cupboard doors? Is that how she does it? I always thought her manipulativeness was reserved for me but now it appears I was no more than a symptom. It all fits, and although it is an unkind reaction I can't help feeling gratified – everything David is telling me fits with the phone calls and the letters and the way she has always tried to seem so sweet and innocent. He left our marriage thinking he was getting away from an unhinged, jealous wife and he was going to something worse. I am aware of just how tasteless this train of thought is, under the circumstances, so I do not voice it.

Wait a minute. I lean forward. 'Are you telling me that with all this going on, you've been happy to leave her looking after *Rees*? She has post-natal psychosis and she's looking after my child?' All at once, I feel murderous. I feel like driving round there right now and telling her that if she treats my son half as casually as she's treating her own baby, then I will rip her stupid, loony little head off.

David looks briefly horrified, then starts to back-pedal. 'No, no, she's been much better since, since we lost Betty, I mean she's really trying hard. I know it sounds dreadful the way I've put it but somehow, well it seems to have made her snap out of it a bit. She's done her best to be supportive, she's not an idiot. It's the long term I'm worried about though. I just feel it's all waiting in the wings. How long can she keep it up?'

But I know she is not okay. I know because I've had four anonymous letters since we lost Betty. Chloe feels threatened. 'I want Rees back.'

'You can, of course you can. Any time. I just wanted to give you some time.' He sits back but keeps his voice low. 'Anyway, I just needed to tell you. It's not as simple as me being comforted by my new partner and baby, that's all. She seems to have pulled herself together a bit but I know it's not going to last. I have to watch what I say. Can you imagine that? At a time like this, I have to be careful. God knows how I'll explain tonight. And it's sick that at a time like this I'll even have to do any explaining. You'd think she'd have some sense of bloody perspective.' I note the bitterness in his voice.

I am calculating fast. I don't know what to do. I want to tell David about the letters because I think that now, for the first time, he might believe me. But what if he challenges Chloe about them? My son is living in her house. I want to go there now and snatch Rees back. But if he stays with them for a little longer, even just a few more days, I can do what I have set out to do.

David must be able to read the worry on my face even though he doesn't understand the extent of it. 'Look, please don't worry about Rees, honestly, you don't think I would leave her with him for a second if I thought she wasn't up to it? She's much better with Rees than she is with Harry, that's how weird it is. She's always loved Rees, right from the start. They get on like a house on fire. That's why it's been so hard for me to understand why she hasn't bonded at all with Harry. I thought her own baby would, well, you know. Honestly, please, I really shouldn't have said anything. I've probably made it sound much worse than she is. She really has been a lot better, lately.' He is clearly sincere when he says this and I struggle to believe there is accuracy behind the sincerity. 'I would never have gone back to work for a minute if I thought she wasn't okay; I've got Harry to think of too, remember. And her mum is around a lot to help, although to be honest that's a mixed blessing.'

'Will you tell her you saw me tonight?'

He looks at the table. 'I'm not sure that's a good idea.'

'It's okay,' I say, 'don't tell her.'

He stays looking at the table for a long while and I know that his thoughts have moved away, far away, from Chloe and the state of his relationship with her, or me, or even the well-being of his two small sons. I stare at him and I know where he is. I am there too. He gives a deep sigh, then lifts his gaze to meet mine, and we stare at each other, just as we used to all those years ago when we first met but with so much else swimming in our gazes, sad, wide acres of it. Eventually, it is him who breaks the spell by looking down.

'Is it ever okay, for you?' I ask gently.

He looks at me and sees it is not a trick question, that I really want to know. He looks at the table, the spread of food. Am I imagining it or has the waiter brought more while we have been absorbed in our conversation? We can't have ordered all of this; it seems ludicrous. *Look, here is normal life, spread before you. You would have smiled at this, before. You would have wanted it. Look at how the rest of your lives are going to be, brimming with things you no longer desire.*

'For a few minutes, sometimes,' he says plainly. 'When I go in to pick up Harry in the morning, remember that bit, when you're half asleep? Sometimes I get all the way to the kitchen with him on my shoulder, and I put the bottle in the microwave. Sometimes I get that far before I remember, because I'm only half awake and thinking about what he needs. I never get as far as the actual feed, though. I remember before then. I think about it as I look at him, while I'm giving him the bottle. I just think about Betty while I'm looking at him. He looks like Betty, you know, really like her. I don't think I'm imagining it, I thought it before.'

I know the second I am awake. As soon as I register consciousness, the knowledge comes upon me, like a huge dark wave, so huge and dark it pins me to the bed. Even if Rees is calling me from the door of my room, sometimes, I cannot lift my head.

'Television,' I say. 'Now you have Rees, I've been watching television a bit, in the afternoons. I saw something the other day, one of those black and white things set in an office in New York. The Empire State Building. Women in hats, lots of wise-cracking. I went a whole hour.'

'Have you tried reading?'

'Can't do books, too serious. Magazines sometimes, something really shallow, the more shallow the better.'

'Good,' he says, and manages a half-smile. 'We need that, good.'

We both have one hand lying on the tablecloth. At the same time, we withdraw them. He looks down at the food, then back up at me and we stare at each other. The first meal we ever had together was a curry. Halfway through it, while we were talking, he tore off a small piece from the naan bread on his plate, dipped it in the dhal and then held it out to my lips. I paused mid-sentence and opened my mouth to him, quite naturally, without comment. Later in the meal, he found a particularly good piece of meat from the lamb bhuna we were sharing, stabbed it with his fork and held it up to me, again without comment. This time, we were more leisurely, more self-conscious about the gesture. I leant forward slightly, looking into his eyes. He placed the meat gently in my mouth, then withdrew the fork slowly as my lips closed upon it. As a seduction technique, it was highly effective – inside, down there, I was awash – but he did it later in our relationship too, long after he needed to seduce me. It wasn't all the time, just once in a while: a bite of bagel, an apple chunk, a crumbly piece of coffee and walnut cake on a plastic fork . . . If this tapas restaurant scene had been a meal from our old days, he would have lifted one of those green beans, dripping in oil, and offered it to me, and my mouth would have opened as easily as that of a bird.

We stare at each other. In a moment, the waiter will reappear. When he does, we will ask for the bill. When we have paid, we will leave the restaurant in silence, our dinner uneaten, our heads full of thoughts we have not uttered. Our hands will not have touched. He will not have fed me anything. Our daughter will walk between us as we leave, not with us, not here.

15

Mr A is fifty-four years old. He lives in the caravan development up on the cliff – the one there has been all the local controversy about. I know this because of my dealings with the Upton Centre. The Upton Centre is on the other side of Eastley, not far from the industrial estate. It was a Youth Centre when I was growing up, the sort of place that believed a ping-pong tournament every Thursday night would prevent the local teenagers from sniffing rags soaked in the petrol they had stolen from the nearby tyre factory. The industrial estate was a couple of miles inland – were it not for the armies of shrieking gulls that wheel in the harsh sky you could be in the flatlands of the Midlands. Burnt rubber, that area smelt of, I remember, a smell that hung in the air like a solid object and gave the whole district a post-disaster feel, as if it was some sort of radioactive zone that should be patrolled by men in white suits with breathing apparatus – an atmosphere of blank dereliction that was perfect for disaffected youth.

I went to the Youth Centre once for a disco, with Jenny Ozu. We wore huge scarves and drainpipe jeans and hairslides. When we got there, we spent the evening clinging to the wall and drinking flat Coke out of paper cups while gangs of boys jumped arrhythmically on the dance floor, arms flailing. Every now and then, one of the boys would wheel up to us and flash a flat half-bottle of vodka he had pulled from the pocket of his baggy trousers – not so much offering us some as threatening us with it, threatening us with the nameless consequences of the fact that he was drinking it. Eventually, inevitably, a fight broke out, and Jenny and I went back outside to where her mother was waiting for us in her car with the radio on and a pencil in her mouth as she worked her way through a puzzle book.

Places like the Upton Centre move with the times. Now it is an advice centre for local refugees and economic migrants. A one-stop shop, it calls itself. Most of the staff there have a week's training in refugee issues but think nothing of ringing us to demand a better service for their 'clients' when we have been treating them for years – in our office, we regarded referrals from the Upton Centre with suspicion. I once had one where the advice worker had sent over a report stating that 'her client' suffered from chronic back pain due to the 'psychological consequences of displacement'. When I questioned and examined her client, a shy Kosovan woman in her fifties called Marina, I thought she had a possible prolapsed disc and put her on Co-dydramol until I could sort out her referrals. Marina did suffer from the psychological consequences of displacement. She was also an insomniac desperately worried about the teenage children she had left behind in Priština, but she had a slipped disc.

Mr A comes from the same group, mostly ethnic Albanians from Kosovo but also some Bosnians I think. It is a group that has had a lot of dealings with the Upton Centre but mostly on the legal rather than the medical side, due to the fact that although some of their extended family unit are legal migrants, some are not. There have been health problems too, as there always are in socially deprived groups. One of the other women has been visiting our unit regularly, and this is how Mr A's name has come to be on our records. The referral, for chronic back pain, again, came through the GP. Mr A was named as next of kin, although it isn't clear what relationship, if any, he is to the woman. He is the leader of the group, it seems, so it may be no more than that.

The industrial estate at Eastley is my first port of call. I have to be careful because it isn't far from Hennett's, where David and Chloe work, although he isn't there much at the moment and Chloe is still officially on maternity leave. I drive past the Upton Centre, set back from the main road, then Hennett's, then reach the industrial estate, the working population of which is almost entirely migrants. The grey metal gates are standing open and there is no security or reception hut. I drive through, straight to the far end, passing the vast dark warehouses with their huge doors like open mouths and the squat brick buildings with flat roofs and no windows. Here is the underbelly of all our lives, the places where things are stored and shipped and put together. There are no shop names or hoardings here; no coloured signs, no invitations of any sort. There are no passers-by to entice in. You would only come here for a reason.

I park my car in the deserted overflow car park and as I climb out of it, the first thing I notice is the stink of fish waste from the cat food processing plant next to the car park, then as I walk past it, upwind, that strange burnt-tyre smell from my youth, the hot thick scent of things unwanted. There is a small roundabout in the middle of the industrial estate, planted with sagging tulips. There are even two benches, placed with their backs to each other, in the middle of the roundabout. I wonder if workers come out to sit there in the summer, with their backs to each other, staring at the warehouses. There is nowhere else to eat your sandwiches, that much is certain. I pull my coat around myself and tighten the belt as I walk. This was the sort of place where both my parents worked before they had me – my father's old factory was on a similar estate on the edge of our town, my mother was a secretary there, that's how they met. They were already both in their thirties by then and both of them still living with elderly parents. I can't imagine their courtship, having always suspected them of being the sort of people who never expected anyone, let alone each other. What little I have guessed at of their early lives made me fear the same fate, in the hard, determined way we always fear what we are destined for. It was my father's early death and mother's illness that licensed me to defy that fate, a thought that made me grateful and guilty and lonely. There is camaraderie in doing what you were meant for, after all, even if you hate the thing itself. I found myself in the pub with Maurice at the end of an evening, once, on a night when he became uncharacteristically morose. 'I don't know why it's always me that suggests coming the pub,' he said, sneerily, having had one pint of dry cider too many. 'It's not as if I've really got anything in common with you lot, you dedicated types. I never wanted to work for the NHS . . .' He took a long gulp from his pint, then added, 'I wanted to have my own hot-dog van, that's what I wanted.'

'Why didn't you?' I asked.

'It wouldn't have suited me,' he replied.

Not far past the roundabout with its drooping, bleached tulips and empty benches, I find what I am looking for. I cannot stop and stare at it – I have to keep walking, albeit slowly, as if I am on my way somewhere else. The roll-down door is open and the workers inside are clearly visible. They are all wearing coats and hats or headscarves – they are unprotected from the wind. In the middle of the warehouse are rows of trestle tables piled with open cardboard boxes. Nearest to the door, I can see a table covered in a heap of zips. There is a young woman sorting the zips according to size and colour – a pile of short green ones, a pile of long black ones, some brown ones of varying lengths. There is a large bin beneath the table and as I pass, the young woman is fiddling with a zip that is broken. After three attempts to shift it up and down, she bends slightly and tosses it into the bin. While she does this, she is smiling and chatting to the young woman next to her who has a table piled with squares of brown leather. A voice calls out and an older woman approaches the young woman with the zips and begins to remonstrate with her. The young woman stares back sulkily as the older one retrieves the broken zip and holds it up.

I keep walking but I am making a stupid mistake: I am staring. They are alerted to my presence in the way that people often are when you stare at them, even though they are looking away. They both turn towards me and in the same instant, the older woman and I recognise each other. I look away immediately and quicken my pace but feel her gaze on my back as I stride towards the main gates of the industrial estate. I only saw her for a moment, but I am sure she was one of the women who came to the crematorium on the day of Betty's funeral, and I am quite sure she knows who I am too.

When I reach the main gate, I have a problem. The road leads straight out on to the deserted highway which, after passing Hennett's and the Upton Centre and two other factories, heads back into Eastley. The industrial estate is fenced and there is no other route back to my car apart from the one that passes the warehouse and the roundabout. In the end, I walk aimlessly up the grass verge next to the road, for fifteen minutes or so, with lorries whooshing heavily past in a rush of exhaust fumes, making me sway in the downdraft. I reach a small lay-by where there is a seat made of concrete full of pebbles and sit down on it for a few minutes. It is freezing cold and my nose is running and I don't have a tissue. I squeeze my nose with my fingers. To my left, there is a thicket of brambly thorn bushes with shreds of tissue stuck to the lower branches. If I was truly desperate, I could extract a big enough shred to wipe my nose but I don't like to think what else those tissues have wiped. When I feel enough time has passed, I rise and walk slowly back to the main gates of the industrial estate. I make sure I am walking on the other side of the road as I approach the roundabout but my caution turns out to be unnecessary. The roll-down door has been lowered and padlocked. There is no one in sight. Nonetheless, I feel sure of one thing: this is where the women work but not the men. I won't find him here.

Driving back along the dual carriageway, I slow the car as I pass Hennett's. I wonder if David is there today, or whether he is at home with Chloe and the boys. 'The boys' . . . it has a cosy, easy feel: two boys. Hennett's has a neat pebble driveway and an open area with a smiling receptionist. Whichever receptionist was on duty whenever I visited David's office, they always seemed to be wearing an engagement ring, as if they all put the same one on as they sat down in the chair behind the desk, instead of a uniform. As I drive past, I imagine Chloe pulling into the neat pebble driveway on her first day at work there – she would have had a small hatchback, I guessed, immaculately clean, purple perhaps. I imagine her parking behind the building and then walking around to Reception in neat, swift movements, legs scissoring. I imagine her smiling brightly at the receptionist and saying, 'Hi, I'm Chloe. I'm starting work today. I'm here for David Needham.' Perhaps she would have extended her hand. Perhaps she exclaimed in admiration at the receptionist's engagement ring.

As I drive back through town, I hear my mobile phone ringing, in my handbag, which is on the passenger seat beside me. It rings twice, then stops. Then it starts again a second and then a third time, the same each time, two rings then nothing. On the fourth try it rings six times before going to voicemail and, a few moments later, there is the penetrating beep that tells me someone has left a message. I pull in and mount the grass verge just before the one-way system and, flicking on my hazard lights, pull my phone out of my bag. The call log tells me I have four missed calls from a withheld number. I wonder if it could be Toni – her cop phone always registers as withheld – but when I listen to the message on my voicemail, nobody speaks. It is a long stretch of nobody speaking that goes on for longer than I listen to it, which is several minutes. After a while, I end the call to voicemail and toss the phone on top of my bag, then pick it up and listen again, my hand over my other ear to impede the drone of passing traffic. It sounds as though somebody has accidentally called my number as they are walking along the street, the phone in their pocket. I can hear muffled footsteps and background noises, cars and conversations passing, an indistinct acoustic of public space. Then, just at the point where I am convinced that somebody has called me four times accidentally, I hear something I didn't hear the first time – a long sigh, a sigh that makes me feel cold. It is not a sad sigh but a malevolent one, a sigh of satisfaction. It is so close to the phone's microphone that I feel a sudden shock, as if someone has just tapped me on the shoulder in my own car. The phone is not in someone's pocket or handbag; it is in her, or his, hand, close to their mouth – the intimacy of it – a mouth near my face.

After the sigh, there comes more background noise, but I don't listen. I press the 'end call' button with a fierce jab of my thumb, then delete the message, then go to my call log and delete all the registers. I throw the phone back into my handbag and restart the car's engine. As I pull out into the road, a car comes round the corner behind me, too fast, and blares its horn in fury as it swings by, the arc of sound making a dying howl.

My free local paper, the weekly, is waiting for me on the mat when I get home. When there were other people in my house, immediately after the event, this paper always disappeared as soon as it was delivered – I realise now that people were protecting me from reports about Betty and Willow. There was a council meeting about parking regulations; Witchard's Factory Wardrobes was having a sale; secondary schools' admissions policy was under review. It is surprising what can seem insulting, just how much can be taken personally.

I unfold it and turn the pages rapidly, as I sink down at the kitchen table. The tensions in the town have not abated, it would seem. Last Wednesday, a young woman was followed out of the Chinese takeaway on Clifton Rise by three or four youths who began taunting her about her accent. When she told them to go away, one of the youths took her takeaway from her hand, removed the lid and pushed the hot food in her face and hair. A local councillor is quoted as saying that newcomers to the town must understand the strength of local feeling about unemployment. I wonder if the young woman was one of the young women I saw earlier that day in the warehouse, smilingly sorting through the zips or patches of leather, feeling safe amongst her friends and colleagues, until a strange woman passed by staring at her and reminded her there are always a thousand reasons to feel uncomfortable, to know you are not safe. I shake my head. I must not start to think all things are linked. I will go mad.

It is dark outside. I decide to give myself the evening off. I open a bottle of wine and go to the cupboard that houses the posh glasses we never used and find the most expensive glass in it, a large globe on an ultra-thin, twisted stem – the sort of glass that people hold up in restaurants and turn in the light to see the true colour of the wine. I put them both on the tray and then it occurs to me, like a light coming on, that I could have a smoke – in my own house, another transgressive thought. I seem to be having a lot of them recently. Rees is away. No one need ever know. I have two cigarettes in a packet of ten at the back of the drawer where I keep the old instruction leaflets to white goods I discarded years ago. Eventually, I find the packet, a little crushed, beneath the warranty for an electric sandwich toaster. The cigarettes in it are ancient and dry. Despite what I pretended to David, I was never a serious smoker, any more than I was a serious drinker. It was a just a rebellious gesture.

I put the bottle of wine and the expensive glass and cigarettes and hob-ring lighter on a tray, then walk through to the sitting room. I put the gas fire on full, turn on the television, then turn the sound up, drink my wine and smoke my fags, too quickly, one after the other, tapping the ash on to the tray, my feet up on the sofa even though my shoes are still on.

Some time later, I jump awake and, as I do, spill wine on myself. I have fallen asleep with the television blaring, the two cigarette stubs on the tray, my expensive wine glass clutched between my fingers and balanced on my chest. That is what has woken me, its tipping – luckily there was only a little left in it. I sit up, disorientated. The wine bottle is two-thirds empty. The room smells of the cigarettes – disgusting, I think. On the television, a group of people in a studio are crammed together on a lurid yellow sofa, shrieking like hyenas. I fumble for the remote control and flick the TV off. Suddenly, I am back in my house, in the semi-dark, alone, surrounded by everything that has happened. I want to sink back down but force myself to stand, unsteadily, and put down my wine glass on the tray, pick up the tray and turn towards the kitchen. The start of it awaits me there, the ritual, the slow but certain process of closing down the house for night-time, checking doors, turning off the lights, acknowledging to myself I am alone. I perform it. I make myself, although all I want is Betty's bed, the whisper of her duvet cover as I pull it over my shoulder, the hypnotic wheeling glow of the orange starfish light, my thoughts of her. I don't want to do anything but think of her.

Unusually for me, I sleep, and in the morning I am bleary and sluggish. I wander slowly downstairs in my dressing-gown. Coffee and two bites of toast fail to revive me. My home phone rings as I am halfway up the stairs, on my way to get dressed.

It stops by the time I get back downstairs but starts again a moment later.

'Laura, hi, it's Toni.'

I am in such a flat, distracted state, that it takes a moment or two to register. 'Toni,' I say.

'Are you okay. You sound sleepy. Did I wake you up?'

'No, no, I'm fine, just haven't been up long. Had a lie-in, for once.'

'Good.'

I smile to myself. Toni, my mother hen.

'Are you in for the next half-hour?' she asks.

'Yes, sure, I'm not even dressed yet.'

'Great, I'm going to pop round. Is it all right if I bring a colleague with me?'

'Yes, sure, I'll put some clothes on.'

'Well, you don't have to for us.'

I look at my watch. It is mid-morning already. 'Did you call me yesterday?' I ask. 'On the mobile, several times in a row, just missed calls?'

'No, I would always try your home phone first or leave a message.'

'Oh, okay.'

Toni looks around as she steps in the door.

'Rees is staying with David for a bit,' I say.

'Yes, I know,' says Toni.

I look at the colleague Toni has brought with her, a junior-miss version of Toni, younger but with the same direct look and choppy fair hair. Her eyes are twinkly and very round. She looks like one of those perky, efficient young women to whom nothing really bad has ever happened, although I try not to be judgemental. I should know, of all people, how deceptive appearances can be. 'Rees is my son,' I say.

'Hi, I'm Jane,' she says. 'How old is your son?'

'He's four,' I say.

Jane stops in my hallway and says, 'I like this mirror.'

'Thanks,' I say, smiling a little to myself as I turn to the kitchen. It is a perfectly ordinary mirror. I have got used to certain police-officer traits, thanks to Toni, chief of which is the way they observe things out loud all the time, in order to demonstrate how observant they are. Maybe it's a technique they are taught to relax relatives or victims and to unsettle suspects, one that becomes such an ingrained habit that they do it without realising. We are all the same to them, ultimately, the people they deal with – the civilians, the not-Us. I think of how the child lock was on in the car the night they drove me to hospital, how they walked behind and in front of me across the hospital car park, as though I could turn into a suspect at any time.

Toni is carrying a dull-blue cardboard folder and I guess immediately this means this visit is more formal than her previous ones. I decide not to bother with the offer of hot drinks and feel a reflexive if brief anxiety that the young officer, Jane, will think me rude. As we sit down, the three of us, Toni puts the folder on the table and launches into a prepared speech. 'Laura, you know that Mr Ahmetaj was initially arrested on suspicion of causing death by dangerous driving.' It occurs to me that Toni thinks I am getting better, getting strong enough, perhaps, for what she is about to tell me. Outside in the garden, from somewhere close by my back door, comes the wailing of a neighbour's cat.

Toni turns to Jane. 'We've kept Laura informed as much as possible. I've been popping round on a weekly basis.' She smiles at me. 'We've had a few cups of tea over the last few weeks, haven't we?' I smile back, but uneasily. 'Laura knows that causing death by dangerous driving is a Category A offence and she also knows that because of that, we have to gather evidence for such a serious charge. We've also talked a bit about the difficulty of prosecuting charges like that, the burden of proof and so on.' I don't like this Toni. I like the one who had a sneaky fag in my garden.

'The car was impounded, wasn't it?' asks Jane. The two of them are off on some sort of police officers' riff together, as if they are on a training exercise, which in some ways I suppose they are. There is an obvious hierarchy between them, a sense of deferral on Jane's part and guidance on Toni's. This annoys me. It reminds me I have a defined role as well. *Hello,* I want to say, *remember me? The name is Laura.*

'Yes, we took the clothes too, and the drink and drugs tests were negative.' Toni turns to me. 'Do you remember I explained that the driver was released on police bail while we gathered evidence?'

I nod.

'Well, that's what we've been doing. We've taken the statements from Ranmali and her husband, obviously we did that a while ago, and there were skid marks on the road. We've had the vehicle examined. But the problem we have is that there were no other witness statements. There was Willow, of course, but she was unwell for a while, and then we lost her. This is difficult, but, we've come to the conclusion that there is no firm evidence he was driving dangerously.' This is not a shock to me. Toni warned me weeks ago that the charges might be reduced to causing death by careless driving, a much less serious charge. 'He gave us a statement and under our new family charter, you have a right to see it. It's here.' I look down at the folder on the table. 'I can leave it here with you, if you like. I can read it to you, now if you like, or leave it with you, then you can call me later if you want to talk things through.'

They are both looking at me. Now I understand the formality, why she has brought a companion. I have rights. Maybe I am going to complain, or sue them in some way. Maybe I am going to hire a lawyer. *I am on my own,* I think. *This is the beginning of the end of their interest in me. They are cutting me loose.*

Toni is watching me. 'As a result of our investigations, the charges against him will be downgraded. Laura, I hope you understand, we're sorry but this was always a possibility and it's what often happens in a case of this type. A lot of people do get upset at this point, and I know it's hard for you to comprehend when you've lost someone you love but the truth is there's . . .'

I cut her off. 'What will he be charged with?'

'Failing to stop at the scene of an accident.'

'Which means, what?' Suddenly, I begin to hyperventilate, great deep gulping breaths. 'What? What will happen to him? What?'

'Probably a two hundred pound fine and points on his licence.'

Briefly, I am returned to the night she came to take me to the hospital to identify Betty's body, the sense of unreality I felt as I walked along the endlessly strange and compulsively familiar corridors – my gentle but abiding conviction that I was dreaming.

They are both looking at me. There is a long pause. They have said what they came to say. They are nice people and concerned for me. They want to leave me with the impression that they are there to serve me, help me and are trying to imply by their silence that they are at my disposal but I can feel their desire to leave as flat and solid as the table at which we are sitting. I know they will not go until I dismiss them, so after a while, I say, quietly, 'I would like you both to leave now, please. Thank you.'

They rise from their chairs, leaving the folder on the table. I remain seated. Toni lifts a hand, the same way she did that night, a gesture to indicate she would like to touch my shoulder but does not want to be presumptuous. She was expecting tears, I think, anger, maybe even hysteria – she would probably have preferred them to my unnatural calm. I can feel the strain in their quiet movements, their determination to be appropriate. At the kitchen door, Toni turns and says softly, 'I'll call you later, when you've had time to look at the statements.'

I still don't look at her, but I nod, very slightly. They leave me sitting there and let themselves out, to walk to their car in silence, to breathe sighs as they get in, to talk about me as they drive back to the police station, to get on with the rest of their job, their lives.

Mr A's statement is written in a scrawled but legible hand by whichever police officer took it down but it is in the first person, from Mr A's point of view. The reason he was driving down Fulton Road was that he had been to visit the school, Betty's school, my daughter's school. He had an appointment with the head teacher.

The school my nephew goes to is very bad. We heard the other school was a good school but they would not let my nephew go. They say he must wait. I know the school he means, St Michael's, a small, single-intake primary on the side of town nearest the clifftop rise. I've had some professional dealings there, with the special-needs co-ordinator. She has had to refer several children to us, or their GPs. It's an area of high economic deprivation and over a third of the children who go there are on the special-needs register, although technically it's a mainstream school. They have to suspend Year 6 children, eleven-year-olds, for smoking in the playground. There has been a lot of trouble between the children of the migrant workers and the children from the local estates. *My nephew was having problems there,* the statement continues, *some very bad boys. We went to the other school to see.* There is more about how bad St Michael's is. It was clearly a matter that had preoccupied Mr A. *This is the best town we live in but the school for my nephew is a big problem for us. We go to speak to the teachers many times, my cousin goes and says to the head teacher about how unhappy my nephew is in the bad school. The head teacher there is a woman who is not listening to what we are saying. We do not want to leave the town. We have business here now and apart from the school things are the best, so far. We do not understand why my nephew cannot go to another school as it is our only problem, our difficulty. So we make a meeting with the head of the other school, to see.* Mr A is not the only one to be confused by the vagaries of the schools' admission system. Betty's school is in a residential area of Edwardian semis. Even though it is double intake, the waiting list is long. We are twenty minutes' walk away and only got Betty in because her entry year had a freakily low level of siblings. *We spoke to the teacher there. We had to wait in the office.* The head teacher of Betty's school is a Mr Coe, a short gruff man much beloved by the children but disliked by most of the parents, including myself. He is red-faced and short-tempered and to me it is a mystery why the children like him – Betty always talked of him in tones of adoration. *Normally my cousin, a woman, would go but that day was late, so I go in the car with my nephew. I want him to see that my nephew is a good boy, works hard, always polite. We talk to the man. He is a nice man, reasonable, but he says he cannot help. As we come outside the school, my nephew runs. He kicks at a thing, you know, a triangle. He fell.*

As they were leaving the school, the nephew was playing with and tripped over a plastic traffic cone which someone had left in the middle of the pavement and hit his forehead on a low brick wall. His head was bleeding heavily as Mr A drove hurriedly down Fulton Road and around the corner. As he did, two girls ran out into the road. There was no time to avoid them. Neither he nor his nephew were wearing seatbelts. Mr A slowed the car and stopped as soon as he could safely. He didn't know what to do. He saw the woman run out from the shop in his rear-view mirror. His nephew was screaming and had blood on his face. He drove on. He didn't know what to do, so he took the nephew back to the camp, to his mother, and the women took him to hospital, then Mr A had a conversation with the other men. That was the way they always did it. When there was a problem, they would get together to discuss what was the best to do for everybody. Later, he came to the police station. At this point, the police officer has used official language. *Later I presented myself at the police station where I was arrested.* It has always seemed odd to me when that phrase gets used in the newspapers, that people should present themselves at police stations and meekly submit to arrest, offer themselves up on a platter. Arrest has always implied physical violence to me – a car chase, or a door being broken down, maybe a scuffle.

Now, I force myself to think, the moment is now. This is the moment that I know: the nephew, that is what he loves. It must be unusual for a man like him to get involved in education issues – that is considered women's work in nearly every culture after all – perhaps he went along because the head teacher of Betty's school was a man and he thought he should try to deal with him, man to man, not realising that schools' admissions is not within the head teacher's gift. It was more than that, though, I think. Even mediated by the help of an interpreter and the officer taking the notes, Mr A's affection for his nephew comes through. The nephew, this beloved nephew, the centre of all their lives, was the boy I saw in A & E that night as Toni and her colleague marched me through on the way to identify my daughter's body. As I strode past that child, wondering cursorily why he was there, I was unaware that his kicking at a traffic cone had lead directly to my daughter being taken away from me. I wonder at what point on Fulton Road the girls were as the boy kicked at that cone – halfway down, perhaps? I wonder at what point one of them said, 'Quick, look, I've got some money, let's go to the shop, quickly.' Maybe the other one said, 'We'll be late.'

It is him, the nephew, that is what he loves. Two hundred pounds and points on his licence. Willow was thrown clear. My daughter went straight up in the air. *I hear you've gone quite mad.*

I do not have long, I feel that in my bones. When the local paper reports that Mr A will only be prosecuted for failing to stop at the scene of an accident, those white spotty youths will be up that caravan park as soon as they have sunk a few pints of strong cider. I rise from the table.

Later, much later, after my arrest and all that followed, I will think of this moment. I will think of it over and over again. Did I know what I was going to do next? Was there premeditation? Was there any conscious thought process at work as I rose from my kitchen chair? I don't remember one. What I remember is a strange blank as I went to the knife block that sat next to the kitchen sink. Aunt Lorraine bought us the new knife set as a wedding present and there were jokes in the speeches about them. Everyone bought us kitchenware – we had the best-stocked kitchen on the south coast. Two weeks after I found out I was pregnant with Betty, when I came home after the six-week scan, I put the knife block with its expensive steel knives and their dimpled steel handles in a high cupboard. My embryo could hardly crawl from the womb to play with them but already, hormonal protectiveness was making me feel queasy at the sight of them. I do not remember when the knife block and its contents were reinstated in their place on the counter-top but there must have come a point where I became complacent, when I didn't believe in danger any more – when I thought I was doing my job rather well.

Smug, I think to myself, as I walk calmly to the sink. That

was what happened. You got smug.

There is a very long, very sharp knife, which I think must be for slicing meat, but it is too long to fit into my handbag and, anyway, would be unwieldy. The smallest, the one for slicing vegetables, is the easiest to hold but the blade is no more than ten or twelve centimetres. I don't think it's big enough. There is a serrated one, which is, so David once informed me authoritatively, a tomato knife. I choose the next one up, a smooth blade, easy enough to grasp, and it will fit in my handbag if I put it in at a diagonal. Back in the days when I still cooked, I used it to cut up frozen chicken fillets so that they would defrost more quickly.

That was what I was thinking about as I wrapped it in a tea towel: frozen chicken fillets. Perhaps part of my brain was still refusing to believe that Betty was gone. Perhaps the knife was to go and save her. Perhaps it was to protect myself, what was left of myself, because I was going to go near him, Mr A, enter his orbit. I cannot believe that I consciously thought myself capable of killing someone.

16

My first visit to the camp is unproductive. Topping the rise brings me into view of the rear side – most of the trailers face the other way, towards the mud track that cars can come down. I wonder what happened when the local youths arrived with bricks and stones. My guess is that they did it under cover of darkness; they wouldn't have got near otherwise.

The only way to get near the camp without being observed was on foot. Approaching in a car meant leaving the tarmac road and driving along a muddy track in plain view of the dozen mobile homes parked in haphazard positions on the boggy estuary flats. If you turned off before that, though, and parked in the car park before the clifftop path, it was possible to approach the camp from a different angle, walking obliquely away from it, as if toward the cliffs. There was a small rise that hid you from sight of the camp for most of the path, until you reached the highest point, where the ground slopes upwards, the point where David pretended to nearly throw me off. The camp couldn't see you until that point, and you couldn't see the camp. Even when it came into view, at the peak of the slope, my guess was that most who walked in that area chose not to notice it. Most people choose not to notice camps, after all – most drive past them on motorways or on flyovers, and process the caravans or trailers merely as vehicles. Most of us have set ideas about what homes are. Chloe and David's immaculate bungalow wasn't that much different from a trailer in shape, although much larger, of course, but for them, I am sure, the trailers would scarcely register. Chloe would have gone for a walk up on those cliffs and not even realised there were people down there on the estuary flats, even as she topped the rise and turned right to the clifftop path.

The estuary land was privately owned and there was an on-going battle with the local council about the owner not having planning permission for permanent dwellings. The battle – as far as I understood it – revolved around how permanent the dwellings and dwellers were. The Upton Centre had been help-ing the residents fight the case for not being moved on, on the basis of healthcare, schooling for their children. It had been dragging on for years.

I do not know what I am planning but I know I will be able to watch the camp unobserved if I carry on past the sloping part of the clifftop path until the small brick shelter beyond it. The brick shelter is open and has a bench, but it faces the sea, so I can only crouch down by the side of it – I can see the camp in the distance but if anyone looked this way I doubt they would be able to see me, just a small shape by the side of the shelter. On my first visit, I am there for two hours but the only people I see are a couple of men who leave a trailer and get into one of the cars and drive off down the track. I wait a long time, getting so cold and stiff I can hardly stand up after-wards. Next time, I think, I will come better prepared.

The following day is a Saturday and I visit twice, once in the morning and once in the afternoon, dressed more warmly this time. I am hoping that as it is the weekend, there will be more movement, but the industrial estate must stay open for shifts because by the time I get there, the camp seems largely deserted. Two young women go from trailer to trailer at one point, and at another, a group of children emerge from one and run off in the direction of the fields, but they are dressed in coats and hats and in a tight knot, their backs to me as they run off, so I can't be sure whether the nephew is among them. There are more walkers out and about at the weekends, and even though it is rainy and grey and not that many people pass, I don't like to stay for too long. On my second visit, I leave frustrated and deflated. I go home and drink a whole bottle of wine. Halfway through it, I send David a text saying *Sorry haven't rung to speak to Rees v tired will call tomorrow.* He doesn't reply.

It is my third visit, early Sunday morning, and the weather is still grey and damp. Out to sea, the waves mirror the sky, heavy and heaving; the tide is high, the clouds low, the rest of the world crushed between. I have bought a Thermos flask of coffee with me and one of Rees's plastic water bottles, into which I have poured a little whisky – the water bottle has dinosaurs on the side. Today I am determined to watch the camp for as long as it takes. Events will overtake me if I do not do something today.

The whisky is encouraging. I have had only a half piece of toast for breakfast, and two cups of tea, but the whisky is gone before I even unscrew the lid of the Thermos. Intermittently, my mobile phone makes a soft purring noise in my handbag, just audible above the wind. I ignore it.

I am there long enough to get stiff and cold despite the coffee and whisky – I guess it is around an hour. There is definitely a sense of more people around, down in the camp below. Some men come and go, in cars. The two young women come out and hang washing from a line between two trailers. Then, finally, I see them. I am sure it is them, the group who came to the crematorium, or some of them at least. They are leaving the camp and walking at a diagonal up towards the cliffs. If they carry on in a straight line, they will join the path several hundred yards ahead of where I am crouched beside the shelter. Perfect. I stand swiftly and go into the shelter, so that they will not see me as they mount the rise. As long as I stand just tucked inside the shelter's edge, but peering round, I will be able to see them as they join the path. I may have neglected to bring binoculars but I have taken the precaution of wearing a hat with a brim, pulled down low. I lean against the edge of the shelter watching, the cold wind in my face.

They must be walking slowly. I don't see them for a while and begin to fear that while I have been in the shelter, they might have changed their minds and headed back to the camp. Perhaps I have been spotted. Perhaps, in view of all that has gone on recently, they are being extra cautious. Then, finally, the group appears on the path. I watch for a moment, making sure they are several hundred yards ahead of me, with their backs to me, before I slip from the shelter and follow.

The oldest woman, short and plump, is in the lead. I can tell she is the oldest by the way she walks, a stiffness in her gait. A young woman and one of the middle-aged women are just behind. The fourth woman in the group – young by her way of walking – is further back and holding hands with the boy. The boy. I watch the boy as they walk – around eight years old, I think, short for his age but sturdy, with a rolling step that is already, somehow, adult. I stare at the boy as I walk – slowly; the group is slow and I don't want to risk catching up with them until I am sure. The middle-aged woman is tall and dressed in a brown coat and, even from behind, I am fairly certain she is the woman I saw both at the crematorium and the warehouse. She has an air of authority. The younger woman looks familiar from the back too but I don't think she was the one sorting zips – maybe she was with the group in the A & E department that night. It is the boy I am really interested in. So that is him, I think. It must be. That is the nephew, the precious nephew whose education Mr A was so concerned for, whose head injury made him panic and rush to hospital and leave the scene of a fatal accident. Fury and hatred swell in me, huge as a mountain. All children fall over in the street at some time or other. What was he panicking about? The nephew is alive, isn't he? There he is, healthy as anything, short for his age and sturdy, fully recovered from the bump on his head – his uncle dared to panic over that, a graze? While they were waiting in A & E for someone to give them a dressing, my Betty was lying on a bed having her face washed with a sponge and her hair combed by a nurse who was saying to her, *Let's make you look nice for Mummy, you poor little love.*

My heart is thumping. I am nauseous with it, short of breath even before I quicken my pace. There they wander, the little group, on my cliffs, and it is all coming together, all the things I have thought, always, all the unfairness of everything; my father's death, my mother's illness, David and losing him, Betty and Willow, everything that has ever happened to me has combined in me to produce this moment. I begin to run. The back of my neck prickles with sweat and my heart thumps quickly and cleanly inside me. I am approaching them with demonic swiftness, my feet noiseless in the wet grass. They do not hear me above the wind and the waves on the shingle. The boy has fallen behind. The boy. He is no more than a few metres in front of me. The air above is white. To our left, the grassy slope falls away towards the camp. To our right, the slope stops suddenly; air. Down below, the waves break against the concrete blocks and the rocks and the pebbles that surround them. I only realise what I am about to do in the split second before I do it.

I grab the boy from behind with both hands. My left hand fastens on his upper arm – my right clutches a fistful of his jacket. It is a cheap, padded jacket, its brown fabric synthetic and slippery in my hand. Also in my right hand is the knife, still wrapped in a tea towel. My grasp is clumsy but the left hand around his arm is like a clamp. As I grab him, he half-turns with a weak, astonished cry. Close up, his little-boy's skin is very pale and I can see downy dark hair on his upper lip. I revise his age upwards. He is tough-looking despite his size but I have the advantage of surprise and it is easy for me to pull him towards me roughly so that he has his back to me and I have my arms wrapped round his shoulders from behind. I wheel him round to face the cliff and we stumble towards it together. He cries out again, louder this time. He calls a name, almost lost on the wind but enough for the women to turn. They do so in unison; there is a chaos of movement as the women scramble towards me, wild-eyed with shock. I have a second only but it is no more than a few strides to the cliff edge. As I reach it, I hold the boy out in front of me but pulled to one side, towards the cliff – the gesture is unmistakable and, still a few metres away from me, the women freeze. There is a moment of breathlessness, a tableau. The oldest, the grandmother, has scarcely moved from her original position but is on her knees in the wet grass, her mouth open in a cry, one hand resting on the ground, the other stretched and lifted. One of the young ones has her by the shoulders. The youngest woman is nearest to me – she could reach me easily but one of the others has shouted at her to halt. The middle-aged woman is halfway between them and staring at me. She speaks to the young one, rapidly, staring at me all the time. The others have terrified, pleading expressions, but her face is hard. She continues to speak to the younger woman, who looks desperate, ready to spring upon me. When the younger does not respond, she snaps. The younger takes a single step backwards. The boy whimpers but does not struggle, although under normal circumstances, I would guess him to be stronger than I am. I think they have told him not to move. They have no idea what I am capable of. It is the only time in my life I have inspired real fear. I am flush with it, giant-sized.

They all wait, staring hard, the grandmother breathing in great heaves. They stare and, I think, they understand disaster when they see it.

I shout above the wind. My voice is high and hard. 'You think you know who I am!' I bellow. 'But you don't! You don't

244

know anything! Don't you understand?' I have no idea where the words are coming from. 'You think I couldn't do this!' I give the boy a small shake and as I do, the knife wrapped in its tea-towel slips from my grasp and both drop. I readjust my grip on the boy. The grandmother lets out a shriek. The younger one beside her drops to her knees and closes her eyes.

It is stalemate. I am still breathing wildly and the white air above me is whirling. The sound of the waves is deafening. I think we might all stay here forever. I feel as strong as a statue.

Then, from the grassy slope that stretches away behind the women, I hear a shout. The women turn. Running up from the camp, it is him.

The hard-faced woman bellows at him. She has her arm outstretched. She is shouting at him to go back. He cannot hear her above the wind and waves and continues running towards us. When he is close enough, she bellows again and he stops. Behind him, others have come out from the trailers and are watching.

The younger is still facing me. She holds out her arms. 'Please . . .' she says, haltingly, looking at the boy. *'Please, to me.'* The boy says something, her name perhaps. His voice is terrified. The young one looks at me, tries to smile, then beckons with both hands, as if the boy is reluctant to go to her and she is coaxing him.

I lift my chin, towards *him*, the man who killed my daughter, waiting down the slope, arms lifted, face a mask of fear and bewilderment.

The young woman does not understand, but the hard-faced one behind her is watching us. She speaks harshly, explaining, and the younger woman says, 'Okay, okay. He comes.' She looks at the boy, 'To me,' she nods several times.

I lift my chin again. The hard-faced one speaks and then begins to walk backwards. They have to help the grandmother, weeping helplessly, down the slope.

They walk down hurriedly, in a huddle. The boy's reedy voice calls out for them a couple of times but they do not turn.

As they approach him, Mr A, they speak briefly, then pass. He raises his hands in the air as he approaches me, as people do in cop movies, to show they are unarmed. When he is a few metres away from me he stops. I flick my head for him to come closer. As he does, the boy wriggles and I tighten my grasp on him. The man lifts a hand and gestures, patting the air, as if saying to both of us, easy, easy . . .

I stare at him for a moment. He is taller than I realised from his photographs, a bear of a man, but gone to fat, muscular arms and a fluid belly. His cheeks are peppered with short, grey stubble. His brows are heavy but the hair on his head thinning. His large dark eyes remind me a little of David's, expressive, able to be both kindly and harsh in quick succession, I would guess. There is a similar cast to their features as well, large noses – they could almost be cousins, except this one is so much more obviously out of shape. I feel the odd sense of readjustment I felt when I met Chloe for the first time – that strange mixture of thrill and shame and anticlimax we feel when we realise that someone we have hated is a person rather than a thing, corporeal and complex.

'Do you speak English?' I ask, and marvel at the normality of my voice.

He nods.

'Do you know who I am?'

He nods again.

'I want to talk to you,' I say.

He looks at me. His gaze flicks down to the boy, then back up to my face.

I glance back at the sea. 'I don't care if I die,' I say. 'Do you understand that?' The boy is limp in my grasp, like a sack of potatoes. I have almost forgotten that I am holding a child.

We stare at each other. The sea continues to crash – the gulls still scream. I feel, again, as though I could stay there forever. It begins to rain – gentle, spitting rain.

Then, slowly and stiffly, Mr A drops on to one knee. He bows his head. 'We pay,' he says. 'We pay for things. It is always fair. I understand. I think you understand.' He raises his arm towards his nephew. 'This boy. He does not pay. It is not him.'

I am shivering now, a combination of the cold and adrenalin and shock at my own actions, but despite the wildness of what I am doing I feel almost supernaturally calm and logical. He knows who I am, I think. When I went to the industrial estate, that woman recognised me from the crematorium. They all know who I am and why I am here. 'Look at me,' I say. He raises his head. We stare at each other, and I see something in his eyes. I do not know if that something is born of experience or simple fear but it is unmistakable. I see understanding of pain.

'I pay,' he says. 'You want me . . .' he gestures over the cliff, 'I go now. I do this now but you must let the boy go. You must leave alone.'

That won't do it, I think. That won't be enough. He understands but he doesn't understand. If it was as simple as wanting him dead, I would have waited for him in the lane, with my foot ready to slam on the accelerator. The knife would be in his fat belly by now. It would be too clean, too simple. It isn't like that. Nothing is ever like that.

'I will,' he says. 'I will . . .' he chokes on the words, suddenly, the emotion overwhelming him. He fights back the tears, trying to quell them with heavy breathing. I can see panic in his face. I can see him thinking, I was doing well, winning the argument, I must not lose control now.

My muscles are suddenly weak. I let go of the boy and drop to my knees in the wet grass. The rain is pouring down now. I don't care any more. I don't care about Betty or Rees or David or Chloe or anything. The boy breaks free from me and runs down the slope, past his uncle, shrieking, and Mr A, still on his knees, scrambles over to me. As I close my eyes I think, he is going to push me off the cliff with one hard shove and then it will be over. I feel glad.

He carries me down the grassy slope in the rain, almost at a run. People surround us, a huge hubbub. I open my eyes briefly and see the angry face of an adolescent boy, shouting – someone next to him is pulling at his shoulder, pulling him away – he turns and begins shouting at someone else. A girl of about ten is jumping-jumping, repeatedly, grinning and pulling my arm, trying to look at me. An elderly woman gives a toothless smile. Two other women stare, hard-faced, one raises her arms. Everyone is calling out instructions to each other. I close my eyes again. Someone pulls off my shoes. My hair is soaked. They are still shouting at each other. The rain pours down. I am turned sideways and lifted through the door of a trailer, non-too-gently, then lowered to a settee or bed. I open my eyes briefly again as two pairs of women's hands pull me into a sitting position. One of them puts my shoes on the floor and a woman lifts a small, painted glass of clear liquid to my lips. I cough and splutter, taste a flavoured after-burn at the back of my throat – heat, mostly, and a hint of fruit. The first one holds my head and the second tips the remainder of the drink into my mouth. Then they lay me back a little but still in a sitting position. One of the women turns and picks up a pile of coloured blankets from the arm of the settee and unfolds two of them over my lap. I close my eyes and let my head loll back. I can hear excited talk at the far end of the trailer, and movement, and guess that the men and the children are being ushered out. I feel a cool hand pushing the wet hair back from my face.

A few minutes later, I open my eyes to see that the trailer has emptied but for the two women near me – neither of them are the women I was following on the cliff; they are younger. One of them is holding a china cup and saucer. She holds it out. I sit up a little on one elbow and she extends the cup further. In the cup there is a tea bag floating in hot milk. I take a sip. It is loaded with sugar, which I normally don't have in tea, but it tastes good. The girls watch me in silence as I drink. I pause and look at them, and nod thank you, but they do not smile, just continue to gaze at me.

As I finish the tea, an older woman comes back into the trailer and shoos the young women away. She takes the cup from me. She is a plump woman – her dress is ill-fitting, but glancing down I see that she has finely turned ankles and smart shoes. Her hair is straight and drawn back in a ponytail but the few strands of white hair at the temples are curly. She nods at the settee. I nod in return, then lie down. She draws the blankets up to my shoulder. I do not close my eyes. I lie awake, keeping my mind blank.

Two other women enter, followed by a child. There is discussion in low voices. One of the new women opens a cupboard and takes out a clay jar of utensils. She leaves, comes back a few minutes later and takes out plates. After a while, I smell cooking outside, somewhere in the camp. During this time, the child who has come in, a small boy, stands halfway down the trailer, staring at me with his finger in his mouth. I try to smile at him but he remains solemn. Eventually, one of the women shoos him out. A few minutes later, she and the others leave. I am left alone for a long time. I do not move.

It is getting gloomy outside by the time someone comes back, the plump woman in the smart shoes. She is holding a plate of food. She approaches me and hands me the plate, white china with a scalloped edge. As with the cup and saucer, I have a feeling I have been given the best crockery. The food on the plate is a kind of stew made with dark beans or pulses in gravy with lumps of sausage. I am squeamish about sausage but eat it anyway, not wanting to cause offence. The beans are delicious, rich and meaty tasting. The whole time I eat, the woman stands in front of me, watching. I feel embarrassed. I wish she would sit down next to me, eat something herself.

As soon as I have finished, she holds out her hand for the plate. As I hand it over to her, I say, boldly and clearly, 'Thank you.'

For the first time, her expression reveals feeling. She gives a small, half-smile, then turns away. She takes the plate outside, closing the door gently behind her. I am alone again.

After a while, I push the blanket to one side and stretch. There is a small electric light in the ceiling but it gives off no more than a dim glow in the gathering dark. It comes to me that I am expected to leave. I slip shoes on to my feet, and stand. I fold the blanket neatly and place it over the arm of the couch. I am still wearing my own coat, and scarf. I have lost my hat.

A few paces away, there is a plywood door, ajar. I push at it gently to see it is the toilet cubicle, which is immaculate – so much so that I doubt whoever lives in this unit ever uses it. I need the loo but feel too shy, so, staying in the main part of the cabin, I lean in and turn on one of taps. I run cold water over my hands, then pass them over my face, around the back of my neck.

While I am doing this, the door to the mobile home opens suddenly and I jump. A young man sticks his head in, sees me and looks confused. Behind him, from outside, I hear voices shouting at him. He backs out.

I open the door and step down. It is now dark. A few metres away, I can see a table and a fire – the women are cooking outside, in the cold. It is windy and smoke from the fire billows erratically. A group of men are seated to my right, beneath a kind of awning, the sides of which suck in and out in the wind. As I step down, they stare at me without hostility. Mr A is not among them.

I don't know what to do. I want to speak to someone, to thank them for looking after me. I want to ask them if they think me mad, if I am mad. I want to go back inside the mobile home and sleep for the whole of the night. I want them to keep me hidden.

The men resume their conversation. The women are by the fire. No one approaches me. I turn and walk past them, back to the path and the upward and downward slope that leads towards the car park. As I walk, shoulders huddled against the wind, I pull my gloves out of my coat pocket and feel the hard, jangly shapes of my keys.

I have reached the bottom of the slope, when I hear footsteps and turn to see that a young man is right behind me – I had not heard him approach because of the noise of the wind. 'Sorry,' he says, heavily accented, raising both hands. He is a little out of breath. He must have run after me.

I take a step back and regard him. 'What do you want?' I ask. It comes out more hostile than I intend but he has surprised me.

He frowns. 'Man will come, my uncle.'

'Your uncle?'

He waves a hand in the direction of the town. I think he is telling me that Mr A is his uncle, and that he will come and see me – but how will he know where I live?

'Does he know where to come, where I live?' I ask.

The young man nods. 'Is it okay? We know. It is in the papers, the road. It is just the number I need to tell.'

'Thirty-eight,' I say. 'Yes, it is okay.'

The boy smiles, sweetly, he is good-looking and charmingly shy. 'Good, good.'

We nod at each other, then I turn.

The car park is sinister in the dark, my car the only vehicle. It appears huddled beneath the yellow glow of the single light source, a wall bulb set into the small, cubicle-shaped building that was once a public lavatory but is now boarded up. I hurry down the path, keys at the ready. Once inside, I lock the doors down and fumble to get the key in the ignition. Now I have been cast out from the shelter of the camp, I push a distance between it and myself, feel afraid again. I long to be home.

When I get home, I go around putting the lights on in every room. My house feels huge and empty. I draw all the curtains, make sure the heating is on max, then sit at my kitchen table with my head in my hands. The young man said he would come but he didn't say when.

I wait at my kitchen table for most of the evening, without any real sense of what I am waiting for. Outside it is dark and the wind throws rain against the black square of my kitchen window. From where I am sitting, I can see down the hallway to the frosted-glass panel of my front door. I am waiting for a shadow to appear in the panel. I have a recurring picture in my head – the two shapes on the night I learned that Betty was dead: Toni and her male colleague, the quiet young police-man who hardly spoke, myself walking down my hallway not knowing I was living the final seconds of my old life; two dark shapes through the glass; my front door swinging open upon them; the looks on their faces. To think of it is a kind of hell, a kind of purgatory, a kind of bliss . . . Two dark shapes through the glass, my movement towards them . . . the door swinging open, again and again . . .

There is a sharp tap on the glass panel. The glass is thin – the rap of his knuckles is light but still makes the whole panel shake. I am on my feet and moving towards the door. It is just one dark shape this time, bulky and indistinct. I think, after what I nearly did this afternoon, maybe he has come to kill me. It would make sense. They would have all had a discussion about what to do about me, by now. He wouldn't want to kill me near his own camp. He would do it here, in my house. It is dark outside. No one will see him come and go.

The door swings open, just as it did that night. Mr A is standing on a lower step – he has stepped down and away from the door. I wonder if he thinks me afraid of him – despite what I have just been imagining, I am not. He stares at me but slightly off-kilter, as if he is worried about being thought presumptuous. Without speaking, I step back to allow him in.

I turn and walk back down the hallway to the kitchen, hearing him close the door behind him and wipe his feet on the mat just inside the door. I fill the kettle and plug it in, the ritual. As I turn from the kettle, he steps into the kitchen and the bulk of him briefly fills the frame. He looks about himself, uncertainly, and I gesture towards the kitchen table. He sits. I wonder what my kitchen looks like to his eyes: solid, curiously empty of people, how ridiculous that I am living in a whole house on my own. I don't need him here to think that.

It occurs to me that offering tea is ludicrous and I open a cupboard and get out two small glasses, shot glasses with two stripes of red around the middle, an unwanted Christmas gift from many years ago and scarcely used. I don't look at him as I place the glasses on the table, take a bottle of whisky from the cupboard above the fridge. It is a high cupboard and I feel too self-conscious to fetch a chair. The whisky is at the front, just within reach, although I am forced to stand on tiptoe. As I do, I am aware of Mr A. watching me, the stretch and reach of my body. I pull the bottle down and turn, a little flushed, to place it on the table. The kettle finishes boiling and turns itself off with a hard click.

I sit at the kitchen table and, without asking Mr A whether he wants it or not, pour us both a large slug of whisky and put the bottle down between us. He stays motionless, watching me, trying to work out what to do. I pick up my glass and glance at him but make no gesture that could be interpreted as 'cheers'. Instead, I sip carefully and put the glass back down on the table, cradling it between my fingers. I am aware that, in some cultures, it is a grave insult to drink from a glass without acknowledging your company. I have done it deliberately, to remind him he is a supplicant here.

Carefully, he copies me.

After another long pause, another two sips each of whisky – he only drinks when I do – Mr A begins, haltingly, to tell me his story.

'I grew up in village . . .' he tells me, then pauses, as if trying to gather his strength. 'My father is boss at the local place, you know, the cucumbers in vinegar, they put in jars. I have many brothers. My uncles, they are farmers. My mother clever woman, she teaches how to dance. Life very good for us, very good. Big house. Then, when war comes, many leave but we all move to city but we come back. There is no food in city. The soldiers, not rebels, how is it?' He looks at me.

'Militia?' I suggest, coolly, 'Militiamen?'

'Yes, this is it, militia, they come and take brothers, and their children, the sons. They take all away. Two other brothers away fighting. They kill the men and boys with rifles but my mother, she is stabbed.'

He is expressionless as he tells me this, even makes a small stabbing gesture with his hand, as if he is telling an anecdote. I stay very still, opposite him, watching.

'My wife and children leave before the war. I do not know of them, I think my wife has other husband. The only left from my brothers is nephew. He is baby. He is not killed. He is left in forest, next to the dead ones. I find him, in the night, and that is how I see brothers' bodies. I go into the forest at night, even though I do not know if they have gone away yet. I went to find brothers and their sons. I look for many hours. Then I hear the baby crying and follow, the sound, the crying very weak. Baby is lying on the ground still wrapped in his cloths. It is youngest brother was baby's father. He is lying on ground

254

next to the baby. There is moon, by then, the sky, things in . . .' he is searching for the word *clouds*. I do not help him. 'They move, the things, so I see. My brother,' he points at his face, 'he has no eyes.'

At this point, he stops and looks at me. His gaze is large and watery but still expressionless. His voice has the same even tone throughout, even when he gets to the bit about the eyes. When he gestures with his fingers at his own eyes it is not for emphasis, simply to make sure I understand. How opaque we are made by our faces, I think. I look at his – heavy-set, pale and jowly, and realise that because it is almost motionless, because his lips hardly move as he speaks, many would assume that he is able to distance himself from the tale he is telling me. Before Betty was taken away from me, I might have assumed the same. Before my daughter was lost to me, I might have attributed his apparent stillness and control to a lack of feeling but now I know, to my cost, that appearing unfeeling is the price we sometimes pay for being able to speak at all. Mr A's words are careful and in their plain, hesitant way, articulate, but behind the words, I hear all sorts of things. I have been given that insight.

'I pick up baby and carry it back to village. The schoolmaster comes to my house when day comes and says they are still in the area and that if I stay, they come and shoot me and the baby. The women are all gone by then, no children, they all go on buses. There is no one to be for the baby except me. I go to the schoolmaster's house and his wife gives me bottle with water, and, and, and . . . sugar, sugar in it, for baby, and tells me we go now, go, go. They are very scared. First I want to leave baby there but they say no and then as I am walking down road I think no, is better this way. I have baby and baby has me, uncle. Is good this way. It takes two days to get to town. There are other towns but I thought they might be there. At first the baby cries all the time, then he sleeps, then he sleeps too much

I think. I think the baby will die. There is a farmer, my uncle knew, on the town. I go to the house, the farmer is gone but the wife is there. She is twins and she feeds baby, you know, like a mother. I think this saves life, otherwise, no good. She is good woman, very scared but good, so, we go to city . . .'

He slows to a halt, mid-sentence, and although he has given no indication of it I know that, quite suddenly, he is exhausted by his story. Neither of us speaks for a long time, as if we have to let his story rest between us, pause for breath. A memory of a school history lesson comes to my mind: a male teacher – we called him DtheR, I don't know why – was telling us about life in medieval England. He was talking about child mortality, about the Black Death, starvation, how any parent knew when they had a child that that child – or any other family member for that matter – could be snatched away at any moment. I remember I interrupted him and I remember what I said. I put my hand up and said, 'But, Mr Rogers . . .' That was his name, Rogers. 'Do you really think people were more unhappy then than they are now?' I meant it as a philosophical question but Mr Rogers exploded, 'Well, Laura yes I do. Yes, I think if you're starving and your third child has just died and another toe has just dropped off because of your leprosy, yup, I think you'd be pretty unhappy.' It was a disproportionate response. I could tell by the way the rest of the class rolled their eyes that I had them on my side. 'But,' I trilled, all wide-eyed, Little Miss Intellectual, 'Don't you think that happiness is relative to ex-pectation?' I can still recall Mr Roger's sigh, his look of despair. Oh Mr Rogers, if only you could see me now.

We sit there, Mr A and I, at my kitchen table. His shoulders are bowed, as if they sit heavily on his body. He makes a brief attempt to start again. 'We come here, after the war, it finishes . . . there is a lot of . . . it was my brother-in-law, the work. The nephew, he was a boy by then. School. Work.' He finishes.

There is another long silence between us and I realise that

Mr A has come to an end – not that his story is complete, it will never be complete, but that he has simply come to the end of his ability to speak. I have read enough Upton Centre reports to know the rest myself. And so, the chain of responsibility for my daughter's death that begins with Aleksander Ahmetaj – it goes back through the nephew, through the person who left a traffic cone on a pavement, through the unknown children at St Michael's who bullied the nephew for having a strange name and a strange accent, then further still, way back, ending with a militiaman who spared a boy baby after he had carved out his father's eyes. If I am looking for someone to blame, for where blame begins, should I find the militiaman who left a baby to cry in a forest? Why stop there? Who, or what, imbued that man with the small streak of mercy that stopped him killing a baby when he had already done so much worse?

For most of the time he has been speaking, Ahmetaj has been staring at the kitchen table or into his whisky glass, but now he lifts his head and looks at me. His eyes are hard eyes and the expression in them unfathomable but something in them gives me a glimpse of him as a younger man. I imagine him twenty years ago, before the belly grew on him, when his broad shoulders and large hands were proportionate with a young, strong frame. I imagine him in a vest, a farm worker or factory hand, confident, from a family that is well-respected in his village. He probably made a good marriage – I wonder what went wrong there. I would guess that his childhood and youth were probably, in many respects, a good deal happier than mine. I picture him in a suit, dancing on his wedding day, and all at once it comes to me, an obscene desire to fuck him. Something of the shock of this thought must show on my face for he is staring at me. I want to do the most inappropriate thing I can think of doing and I don't even know why – I want to fuck this man, right here on my kitchen table, hard and hurting. I want to obliterate everything else that has happened to us and everything between us and everything else that has gone on elsewhere, that has nothing to do with us.

It is a ridiculous thought. It flares and dies in an instant. I stand up. I am standing in front of him. I look down at him. He looks up, his gaze large and confused. I turn and walk to the kitchen door, then look back. He rises awkwardly from his chair.

I lead the way upstairs, to the main bedroom, the one I have not slept in since Betty went away. I am heading for the marital bed, the bed I shared with David. I go into the room without turning on the light, sit down on the bed and remove my shoes, then my socks. He stands in the doorway, staring at my bare feet, as if trying to face the implications of them, the knowledge of what I intend. He looks at my face and I stare back aggressively. I feel as powerful as I felt when I dangled the boy over the cliff edge. He sits down on the bed next to me and bends to unlace his shoes but I turn and push him back, so he is lying on his back, then straddle him. As I pull his shirt up, out of his trousers, his large belly, white and hairy, moves, there is motion in it; I avert my gaze and my fingers move quickly, so I will not lose my nerve. I pull his leather belt undone, unbutton his trousers, unzip his flies. He is wearing cheap white underwear, soft underpants like the sort I buy my son. His dick is straining in them. I take a guess that he has not had sex in a long time. I kneel up and remove my jeans and knickers swiftly, then extract his penis from his white underpants and, without further ado or even looking at him, straddle him again, guiding him in.

I have not had sex for a long time either – there has been nobody for me since David. David. I close my eyes and think of David. I liked to straddle David in this position sometimes, me on top, holding his arms above his head in a parody of domination that made us both smile, wordlessly. Sometimes, he pushed my arms behind my back and held my wrists together and we

258

laughed and bickered about who was in charge as we fucked – and then the moment, that moment, when the physical intensity of it would loosen his grasp and I would sink down on to his chest and he would push his hands in my hair and we would kiss long and deep and say each other's name and sometimes cry, and I think, as I fuck Ahmetaj with my eyes closed, of how it stayed that good with David right up until the end and how it bewildered me. David. My thoughts of David combine with the friction of my body against Ahmetaj's body, the slip and slide of skin, and my flesh remembers something. It remembers the easy and profound intimacy of sex with the man I loved, and I don't come exactly but I feel something, some basic response of muscle and blood. I sink down on Ahmetaj's chest, become still, and, not knowing what to do, he lifts his hands and lays them gently on my back.

As soon as his hands touch me, I pull away. He slides out of me. I hate the fact that I have let myself feel anything, which was not what I intended; I meant to have the advantage over him. Swiftly, so that I will not have time to think about it, I move down on him. He has lost his erection. His penis is small and pale and flaccid. He is not circumcised. As I go down on him, I smell hair and sweat and fat and know I must work quickly. I take him in my mouth and it feels sad and soft, like cod's roe. He raises his pelvis slightly in shock at the sensation, gives a small cry, goes from flaccid to orgasm so quickly that he seems to bypass the erect stage altogether. My mouth fills and I gag and swallow quickly, then pull away and get off the bed.

I leave the bedroom without looking at him, go to the bathroom, spit into the sink. I am naked from the waist down but still wearing the rest of my clothing. I pee, then brush my teeth. While I brush them, I look at myself in the bathroom mirror and feel detached enough to note that that is the first time I have fucked someone I haven't liked – how I had never understood before that it was possible, even easy, to do it for reasons that had little or nothing to do with the person you were doing it with, and how it feels as not-good afterwards as I always suspected but that a cold, hard part of me is able to detach myself enough to feel interested that I have tried the experiment. This is how men fuck, sometimes, I think, out of bitterness and need and a lust for control – all sorts of things that have so little to do with desire.

When I return to the darkened bedroom, he is asleep on his back, his mouth open, making a gentle snorting noise, short and intermittent, on each intake of breath. I pick up my knickers and jeans from where they lie discarded on the floor. I take them into the bathroom where I sit on the bidet and wash myself, front and back. I dry myself roughly with the hand towel and pull on my knickers and jeans.

I go downstairs, straight into the kitchen, where I pour myself a shot of whisky, down it in one. I pour myself another and, this time, raise the glass to myself. *Cheers, girl, bottoms up! Today you have discovered what you are, and are not, capable of.* I down it, then rush immediately to the sink, on the point of vomiting, but instead I gag and spit. The whisky stays down, a hot lump inside me, hard as a ball bearing. *My mouth corrupts me. I do not know myself. I am good.* No, I think, *my mouth convicts me*, that's it: *convicts*, not *corrupts*. Raising myself from the sink and wiping my mouth on a teacloth I think there, it's done, I've done it, and I can't ever take it back. When I had that meal with David, I felt triumphant at the thought that I had something I couldn't tell him about, my scheming to find Ahmetaj. Now I know that was nothing. Now I have something that he must never know as long as we live. I've fucked the man who killed our daughter and given myself a suit of armour against David – and with that realisation comes the knowledge that that was the whole point, to do something that David could never understand or forgive, to have something to hide from him and hold against him, and I know now that this

260

is how it will always be, that anything I ever do with another man will be a coded message to David.

After a few minutes, I hear Ahmetaj coming down the stairs. His look as he comes into the kitchen is that of a bewildered boy. He does not understand the rules of what we are doing, knows only that I am in charge. He comes over to me and, clumsily, attempts to put his arms around me but I push him away. I know he is desperate to leave now, as desperate as I am to see him go, but we are not quite finished yet. I nod at the kitchen table and he sits again. I sit down opposite him and refill both our glasses.

As I put down the bottle, I say, 'You said, you want to pay.'

He looks at me, confused. Hasn't he just paid, in a way he cannot comprehend? But no, he hasn't. That was just an extra, that mutually humiliating fuck. That was about David, not Betty.

'You want to pay,' I repeat.

One corner of his mouth lifts. 'You want me, over the cliff.' He speaks the words heavily but his expression has lightened a little, is almost sardonic.

Yes, yes, that is what I want. I want you as dead as my daughter is dead. I want you wiped off the face of the earth. I stare at him. *I wonder what you love,* I think. Your nephew? Possibly, but it might not have been love that made you save him, that night in the forest, it might have been simply need, a need to save yourself. How can I know? You may not even know yourself. Maybe the things that have happened to you have wiped all love from your life. Is there anything left to kill? What would I have been killing if I sent you over the cliff, in the dark? It comes to me that in all the maelstrom of hatred and madness since Betty went away, I have never seriously wanted or imagined him dead. I have wanted to hurt him, not kill him – there is only one person I have ever wanted to kill. I rise from my chair and leave the room, to go to the sitting room. When I return, he has not moved. I hold out what is in my hand, a small collection of envelopes, mostly white, one yellow. He looks at them but does not take them. I put them down on the kitchen table, between us, then lift my hand and almost touch his shoulder. I sit down and, as we regard each other, I say, 'Mr Ahmetaj.' He looks at me in surprise at the sound of his name. 'You have told me – your story. I want to tell you something too.' He nods, uncertainly, and I think of how he carried me in his arms from the clifftop down to the trailer when he could have shoved me over the edge. He is strong, and I am as bony as a baby bird these days. For some reason, I think how that is how my father might have carried me as a young child, if he had lived, and how people who grew up with fathers must sometimes envy their younger selves all that protection. At least I have no protected self to envy. Ahmetaj looks at me, waits for me to speak.

17

It is David who calls, a week later, just after midnight. I am in Betty's bed but awake, of course, lying on my back and staring at the ceiling. I hear the phone ringing downstairs and scramble from the bed. Midnight. I had thought I was fully awake but as I clump swiftly, clumsily down the stairs I realise I must have been dozing because what I am thinking is, *something must have happened to one of the children*. The phone stops before I get there but I stand over it, breathing heavily, waiting for it to ring again. When it does, I snatch it up.

'Laura,' David's voice is low and needy, thickened with distress.

'Darling, what is it?' I haven't called him *darling* for years, but I know from the way he says my name, and the late hour, that something – and a sickening thought occurs. 'Oh no, oh no, it's not Rees?'

'No, no, Rees is asleep. I've just given Harry a feed. I can't belong.' His voice is so choked I can hardly hear what he is saying. Belong? Then I realise what he said was *be long*. 'I'm sorry, there's other people here. It's difficult but I just need, I need to tell you. It's Chloe, Laura. She's disappeared.'

'What?'

'She's gone. We had an argument last week, a terrible one, that's why I've not been in touch, but I thought things were getting better, I thought things were improving. I was worried but I thought everything was fine. She went out for her walk. I've been encouraging it, the walking. They said it was good for her to get out as much as possible, gentle exercise. They found her car, in the car park.'

'David . . .'

'Her handbag was in her boot. It had everything in it. Purse, mobile. There were some books she said she was taking back to the library on the back seat.'

'What about the car keys?'

'No.'

'Then . . .' I stop myself. I was about to say, then she was planning on coming back to the car, probably. If she wasn't planning on coming back, wouldn't she have left the keys in the ignition or the boot? Isn't that what people do?

'Are the police there or do they have to wait twenty-four hours or something?'

'No, Toni's been earlier, she's not here now. Normally you have to wait but considering. They took a statement from me this evening but I've been with – I've only just had a chance to call you. I've just given Harry his feed. They've already talked to the doctor, Laura. What am I going to do?'

'I'll come over.'

'No,' his voice is sharp. 'No, don't, it wouldn't be a good idea. I'm sorry, I just really needed to talk to you. Oh God, Laura, I can't do this, not after Betty. I just can't. I know I should have been more sympathetic and listened to her more. I've always been frightened for her, Laura, right from the start. Why would she leave her car in the car park and not even take her phone or any money?' I can hear him struggling with himself. 'I begged her to take something, Laura, to get a prescription for something, anything, I begged her to do that or get help and I'm frantic but I'm angry, I'm so fucking, fucking angry.' His voice is harsh, the words running close and hard together. 'Me, Harry, Rees, for fuck's sake, doesn't she think we've been through enough? I'm sorry. You're the only one I can say this to. I don't want to sound callous but I'm just so *fucking* angry.' He puts his hand over the receiver and there is muffled talk in the background, then he comes back to me and says, 'Sorry, it's gone midnight. God, that has so little meaning. Were you asleep?'

'Who's there?'

'I'll feel terrible if you were asleep.'

'No, darling, of course not. Of course I wasn't asleep.'

There is a long silence on the end of the phone. When he speaks, his voice is calmer. 'I have to go.'

'I know, it's okay. I'm here. Call me.'

'I will. Bye.'

I put the phone down gently, very gently.

I leave the house at first light. Rees will be coming home soon, after this – I feel a surge of joy at the thought. I drive through town, along the wind-whipped esplanade. The shops are still shuttered and the streetlights still on, throwing half-orange patches of light around the grey dawn. The sea crashes ceaselessly, waves topped with white froth. A little freezing rain is falling, lightly. I drive to the car park at the bottom of the clifftop rise and pass it slowly but there are no cars in it at all and no sign of a police cordon or any evidence of investigation. I drive back into town and take the one-way system, out on the main road that leads to the caravan park.

I park in the tiny car park with the squat square building and walk up the grass rise. I don't know what I am going to do if they are still there but, in my heart of hearts, I know they won't be. Sure enough, I see, as soon as I reach the crest of the rise. The cars are gone, even the ones I thought were wrecks. The washing lines have been taken down. The caravans are securely locked, curtains drawn. All is neat and tidy. The whole group has gone. They have not waited for me, or the police, or the gangs of youths in town with the half-bricks and bottles. I think about the women. I think about the smiling one in the warehouse, the one who tossed the zip into the bin so casually, just doing her job, just getting on with it and chatting to her friend. I think of the plump grandmother on the cliff, her face carved with so much. I think about the sombre middle-aged one who stared at me at the crematorium with a look that suggested she could guess what I was really like. I don't think of Ahmetaj or the nephew or any of the men. I think of the sombre woman, of how she would have received the news of their departure, how she would have set about pulling clothes from a washing line with swift, efficient movements, folding them with one quick motion, her mind running swiftly through everything that must be done.

I do not linger. I do not know who else might turn up soon. All I can do now is go home and wait until it is time to call David.

It is Toni who brings Rees home. He is very excited to have a lift in a police car. He clings to me like a bush-baby for ten minutes and then snaps out of it, jumps down, runs around the house, from room to room shouting at things, the way he used to do whenever we came back from holiday.

I look at Toni. 'How is David?' I ask.

She looks back at me, with a gaze I cannot fathom. We are standing in the hallway and she gestures into the kitchen.

As we descend into the kitchen, she asks for a drink of water, then watches me while I fill a glass at the tap. When I have handed it to her, she takes a sip, then puts the glass down, says quietly, 'Laura, when was the last time you had any contact with Chloe?'

I look back and say, 'I don't know, the wake, I suppose. I saw her at Willow's wake.'

'Have you spoken to her on the phone since then?'

I have to think about this one. There have been the with-held calls, the silent messages, the sigh, but no, I haven't spoken with Chloe. 'No, no . . . I've spoken with David obviously.'

'I understand he told you a bit about Chloe's problems.'

'The post-natal depression, yes.'

'Did he tell you anything else about their relationship?'

'Only that he was worried about her.' Any minute now, I think, she is going to flip open a notebook. But she doesn't write anything down. She just asks me questions in that plain, direct voice, looking at me with that plain, direct gaze.

Rees charges into the kitchen and jumps up at me. I catch hold of him, lift him, and he kicks his legs with glee. Toni turns to go, then turns back. 'Harry, the baby,' she says to me, 'how old is he?'

She must know the answer to this. 'Eight months?' I suggest, 'Thereabouts.'

She nods, and turns to leave.

Chloe's disappearance relegates the news of Ahmetaj's down-graded charges to page three of the local paper. It is Chloe who is the front-page story. The photo they run of her is not flattering – her delicate features do not reproduce well, making her appear pinched. Her hair is drawn back in the photograph. Although she is in a party dress and it is clear the photograph was taken at a social occasion, she is not smiling. There is a quote from David, about his distress. There is another quote, from the police, saying they are keeping an open mind, but the fact that her handbag was left in the car is naturally a cause for concern and, reading the piece as if I know nothing about it, I know what conclusion I would draw.

On page three of the paper, there is a long column about Ahmetaj and the fact that a large group of the clifftop-site residents have moved on. Immigration officials have expressed concern that some of the group have moved on to avoid detention. Ahmetaj had not yet been informed that he was about to be charged with failing to stop at the scene of an accident. Now the charge has been issued and he has gone, there is a warrant out for his arrest.

I know they won't find him. I saw it in his eyes, the night he came to my house, that here was a man who knew how not to be found.

Rees and I attempt to re-establish some sort of routine. It is so good to have him back, and now I do, I miss him far more than I did when he wasn't here. I take him to nursery with the greatest of reluctance and only because I think it's important for him to stick to the routine. When he is home, I can hardly bear to be in a different room from him and follow him if he runs off to his bedroom. I realise that I have got through the time without him by blanking him out, using my grief and anger as a smokescreen – but in the face of the compact, joyful reality of my boy, the smoke clears at last. Here is my son, my beautiful, living son. I have so much to make up for to him.

When he is back from nursery, in the afternoons, I am more attentive than I have been at any time since we lost Betty. We go on walks together – the weather is improving enough to make that an enticing prospect. We go shopping, go to cafés. He begins to talk to me about Betty in a way that is different from before. He hasn't used the past tense yet, but it is apparent he has absorbed that his big sister will not be returning, that he has lost his unknowingness. Once or twice, I catch him with a distracted air, staring at nothing, and I think how this is one of the many beauties of children his age, the way their thoughts flit across their features, how you can almost hear the cogs turning. I wonder at what point we learn to withhold ourselves – gradually, over a period of time, I suppose – the capacity to manipulate must come to us in pieces, before we even understand what that capacity is and just how much it can achieve.

One afternoon, as Rees and I are having an early supper together in the Captain's Fish Table, I raise the subject of Chloe. Rees has had chicken nuggets from the children's menu and

I have ordered haddock and chips even though I know that after a few bites, my stomach will turn. I have lost the capacity to digest grease. I have just peeled the batter off my haddock and placed pieces of fish on Rees's plate, quietly, while we talk. There is a chance he will eat it by mistake. I look at the fish on his plate surreptitiously, the tiny black veins in the white flesh. *My mouth corrupts me.* I pick up a chip with my fingers and try to dunk it in the small bowl of ketchup between us but it is already cold and when I push it into the sauce, it buckles.

'Did you like living with Daddy and Chloe?' I ask, with my mouth full in order to make the question sound casual.

Rees looks at me suspiciously. 'Chloe cried a lot but she let us have Cheerios. Every morning.'

'Us?'

'Me and Daddy.'

'I didn't know Daddy likes Cheerios.'

Rees nods solemnly, pleased to have superior knowledge of his father's breakfast habits.

'Why did Chloe cry?'

Rees shrugs. Why do grown-ups do anything?

'Did they talk about Betty at all?'

'Not really,' he says. 'They talked about how when Harry did a poo once it came out of the sides on to his sleepy-suit.'

After this, Rees talks about Harry for the rest of the meal. He put a Smartie in Harry's mouth and Chloe started shouting and Daddy said No, Rees, no, and it wasn't his fault, he didn't know babies weren't allowed Smarties. When Daddy put his finger in and pulled the Smartie out then Harry started crying so he must have liked it and he thinks they were being mean not to let him have it. Harry sits up, and can clap, but you still have to put a cushion behind him in case he falls backwards. He likes watching TV. He claps a lot then. He likes Rees best of all. Rees can make him laugh even when Daddy and Chloe can't.

Rees is clearly besotted. 'When can we see Harry?' he asks no less than three times during the meal.

'Do you miss Chloe, now she's gone away?' I ask casually, after we have finished our first course and are waiting for his ice cream and my coffee.

He frowns, shrugs. 'She's quite nice. She's good at drawing. Her spaghetti has bits in. It's too spicy. She gave it to me once. I could taste spice.'

David is off work and could, in theory, be accompanying Rees and me on some of these outings, bringing Harry along, but I don't push it. I know he will be absorbed in the hunt for Chloe, in talking to her friends and family, helping Toni, so I wait for him to contact me. The poster appeals round town, the police enquiries – so far, nothing has yielded results. The follow-up reports in subsequent editions of the local paper hint at Chloe's personal difficulties. David rings me most days, ostensibly to talk to Rees and to update me on what is happening but I know he needs me and eventually pluck up the courage to say, 'Why don't we take the boys out together tomorrow?'

Gradually, over the next couple of weeks, we begin to spend more time together. We take the boys for walks on the beach. We avoid the cliffs. We discover that eight miles away, in a village called South Ketton, there is a new playground with climbing frames made of old wooden planks and tyres on ropes.

One day, I go with David to the police station. Toni has asked David to drop in so that she can update him about the search for Chloe and for some reason she has asked me along. It is an awkward, unproductive conversation. We sit either side of a table in a small interview room. To the right of the table is a television on a stand. Rees and Harry are with us and Rees keeps looking at the television and nudging me, wanting me to ask Toni if he can watch something. I keep shushing him, shaking my head – under other circumstances, I would make a joke about it but the situation is too serious. Chloe had other bank and credit cards apart from the ones in her purse that day but no money has been withdrawn from any of her accounts. Nothing has turned up in the coastguard reports. The weather was very bad – fog out at sea, and icy rain – there have been no reports of anyone seeing her leave the car park or walk along the cliffs. David keeps his face very still as Toni tells us this. Sitting next to Toni is a male police officer in plain clothes who says nothing but when I glance at him I have an odd, uncomfortable feeling, as if he is watching me but has looked away in the second before I look at him.

I find Toni's formality with us disconcerting, considering how close she got to us in the wake of us our losing Betty. I wonder if she thinks it is inappropriate for me to be with David so much immediately after Chloe's disappearance but she was the one encouraging us to spend more time together, after all. I realise, with a flush of disappointment, that although she knows I am still bereaved, in her head she has moved on, to the next, more pressing thing. In that sense, she is just like everyone else. Everyone else has moved on in their heads, in one way or another. Only David and I are still stuck on Betty, only we understand how we always will be. David and I have not spoken of this.

It is only as we all rise from our chairs that the solemnity of the interview breaks down, a little. Rees hops from my lap and goes over to the television. David has been holding Harry on his shoulder but as he stands up, he passes him to me. He is a plump lump, Harry, soft and heavy and sweet-smelling, an easy baby, he seems to me. He smiles a lot. Automatically, I do that thing that all parents do when they are handed an infant, start to sway gently from side to side, even though Harry is quiet and not in need of pacifying.

David takes a step towards the television, where Rees is making faces in its blank grey screen. 'Do you know why they have a television in here?' he asks Rees.

Rees glances at Toni, who smiles at him. 'Is it so that they can watch programmes when they are bored of people talking?'

David shakes his head. 'It's so that they can show people CCTV films, you know, those cameras that they have in shops so that if people steal something they are on the film.'

'We waved at one!' Rees shouts, thinking of a shop he and I visited the previous day, delighted to think that Toni and the other policeman might have seen him on television.

'Yes, young man,' says the male policeman, who has a northern accent, 'and what some thieves don't realise is that when they come in here and we ask them if they stole something, it's no good them saying they didn't because we've got it right here and can show them how we know.'

Rees is very impressed. Toni and the other officer smile at each other, pleased to have impressed him.

'How did you know that?' I ask David as I move Harry to the other shoulder so I can pick up my handbag from the table. 'No, it's okay.'

David has reached out his hands to take Harry but drops them when I shake my head. 'Toni told me when I was in here before,' he says, 'after Betty, when we were talking about how to deal with the press. They were everywhere in town for a bit.'

The male officer has opened the door and Rees has charged off down the corridor. David follows him swiftly.

As Toni holds the door open for me, I say to her, 'I didn't realise David had been here before.'

'He did a lot,' she says, without looking at me. 'He protected you, you know.'

I give her a look.

She throws the look back at me. 'You know what the newspapers are like. One of them, unbelievable, he actually said to me, okay, we'll lay off the mum if you can give us the dad.'

We follow the others out into the corridor. I shift Harry on my shoulder again and he gives a little grizzle. David, Rees and the other officer have disappeared around a corner but as I go to follow them, Toni puts a hand on my arm, lightly. 'You know,' she says casually, 'I'm still your liaison officer too. If there was anything troubling you, about Betty I mean, you can still ask, I mean, if you were concerned about whether or not we'll find him. I'm sure we will.' She is looking at me.

'You mean Ahmetaj?'

She nods, and as she does, Rees sticks his head round the corner, 'Mum-*ee!*'

'I'm coming,' I call.

Toni is watching me in a way I cannot fathom.

David has parked his car on the street, directly outside the station. I buckle Harry into his seat – that's one thing I haven't forgotten how to do. As my fingers slip and click the metal into place, I think how comforting that small sound is, the sound that tells you your children are strapped in tight, safe. Rees is wriggling on his booster seat and I lean over Harry to pull his seatbelt across. As I do so, Harry arches his back, as much as he can do against the strap, grizzles more.

'Is he hungry?' I ask David as I sit down in the passenger seat.

'No, tired,' he says. 'He woke up early. It would be good if he stayed awake until we got home though, so I can take him out in the buggy. If he falls asleep in the car then one of us will have to sit with him for an hour.'

I turn in my seat. 'Rees, see if you can make Harry laugh.'

It is only a ten-minute drive to David's bungalow and thanks to Rees making noises and me turning to tickle Harry's feet, we keep him awake. David lifts him and takes him inside. Rees and I follow.

'Daddy, play battleship with me!' Rees shouts, jumping up and down, before he even has his shoes off.

'In a minute,' says David. 'I've just got to take Harry for a walk to get him asleep in his buggy.'

Rees is crestfallen. He kicks the radiator.

'I'll take Harry out,' I say.

'No, it's okay.' David's voice is exhausted. He hasn't said anything about what Toni and the other officer told us – or, rather, how little they had to tell us – but I can tell from the way he speaks that he is only holding it together by going through the motions. I wonder how much he thinks of Chloe, if he has decided, inside his head, what has happened. I have been careful not to ask.

'No, let me do it,' I say. 'Come on, it's okay, you haven't had Rees to yourself much, I don't mind, honestly.'

David looks at me and says, 'You'll freeze.'

It makes me smile. He always used to do that in the early days, notice what I was wearing, worry about me being cold – his gallantry, it outlived his love. He's right, though. I am wearing a denim jacket. There was a glimmer of sun when I left the house that morning and I was overly optimistic.

'Here,' says David. He turns and lifts a coat from the row of hooks on the wall. It is one of Chloe's. It is a waterproof but a very smart, stylish one, not at all sporty, made of a deep blue fabric with a shimmer to it. It is lined with fleece and has a high collar with a fake fur trim. I feel as much as see how expensive it must have been, as soon as I put it on. I am a little taller than Chloe but we are the same build. It fits just fine. It's very snug.

Harry is howling openly now, thrashing in his buggy. David tucks a blanket round him and says, 'He'll be out cold by the time you get to the path.' He has not taken a proper look at me wearing Chloe's coat.

'I'll walk around a bit to make sure.'

*

Pushing the buggy, I take a tour of the estate. It is blank and neat and empty, and I think again of how strange these new places are, as if they house new people, with no secrets, no lives. The road slopes away, downhill, from David and Chloe's place. No cars pass by and there are few cars on the dark tarmac forecourts. Everyone is at work, or school, it is the middle of the day. Harry's howls quickly diminish to snuffles and sighs. As David predicted, he is out quickly. I wonder if we should have changed his nappy first.

I walk around for about fifteen minutes, then head back up the rise to the bungalow. I am a few feet away from the door when it happens. Behind me, a car door slams hard but there is nothing unusual in that and I don't turn. As I lift my hand to ring the doorbell, there is the sound of footsteps skittering up the path behind me but I have no more than a second or two to register the unusual haste of them when there is a heavy thump upon my shoulder. I bend, letting out a shocked cry, but whatever sound I make is drowned by a high-pitched shriek. I turn with my arm raised to protect myself and see a woman in her sixties, shorter than I am and with tight, curly hair and glasses. I only get a glimpse of her face, mouth open, contorted with rage, before I have to turn sideways again to protect myself. She is raining blows on my arm and shoulder and letting out shrieks of inarticulate fury. Her fists are clenched – a blow strikes the side of my head and I stagger back against the door, momentarily afraid I will fall. Between her inarticulate cries she begins to say, 'You ... you ... *you!*'

The front door opens and David is upon us. He gets between me and the woman and uses an arm to lever her backwards, away from me. Her fists are still flailing and she is still shouting inarticulately. Baby Harry is sleeping through it all.

'Edith!' David is shouting. 'Edith, stop it!' Then, firmly, with depth, the kind of shout that warns of physical reprisal: 'Stop it *now!*'

She stops and falls back a step or two, her breath heaving inside her small frame. As I straighten, I see that her glasses are crooked. My hair is awry across my face and I clear it back with one hand, tuck it behind my ear, and stare at the woman who is still beside herself, spitting with fury. 'How dare you!' she shouts, looking me up and down. '*You*, of all people.'

I glance behind me to make sure that Rees has not come outside and is safely indoors, out of earshot. 'Who the fuck are you?' I say, with a clear note of aggression in my tone. I don't take kindly to being attacked. David may have come to my rescue, but I want this madwoman to know that without the element of surprise she wouldn't have got the better of me.

'I'm Chloe's *mother*,' she spits. 'And don't you dare use language to me.' She turns to David, 'In my daughter's *coat*, with my daughter's *baby*!'

David draws himself up to his full height. 'Edith, I asked Laura to take Harry out in the buggy so he could fall asleep. I wanted some time alone with my other son. I asked her, all right? It was cold and she didn't have a coat so I gave her Chloe's. I wouldn't have done it if I'd known you were going to be coming round. I know it must have given you a shock but that's no excuse for attacking Laura.'

The woman's face is still twisted with bitterness. 'You're as bad as she is. Don't you care? Chloe said you were a hard bastard and look how you've shipped *her* in to take over. Where's my daughter? Why aren't you out looking for her? You know what the police are saying, don't you? They think she's killed herself!' And at this, the woman collapses. She puts a hand out, waves it a little and then manages to find the fence. Her other hand is on her stomach as she bends, trying to catch her breath, making a gasping sound, a kind of dry sob, 'Oh . . .' she says, 'Oh . . .'

The anger has drained from me now. In its place, there is something hollow. This woman has lost her daughter. I look at David but he is staring at his mother-in-law. I slip Chloe's coat from my shoulders. What was I thinking of, wearing her coat? I fold it over my arm. I can't wait to be rid of the thing. 'Do you want to come in, have a cup of tea?' I say feebly, the inadequacy and stupidity of the suggestion painfully apparent even as I am making it; the number of cups of tea I was offered after Betty.

The woman straightens herself and wipes roughly at her face with her sleeve, then takes off her glasses and folds them. She does not answer me, merely gives me a glare of contempt. Then she turns and walks unsteadily back down the path. Halfway back to her car, she stops, then turns back. She looks at David and says, 'I'll come back to see my grandson when he's awake.' She looks at me. 'And when *she's* gone.'

The car is parked at an angle, one wheel up on the grass. She must have skewed to a halt when she saw me walking along, wearing Chloe's coat, pushing Chloe's baby.

Back inside the house, I hang the coat, very gently, back on the hook. As David closes the door quietly behind him, I turn to him and say, 'I feel awful.'

'Don't,' he says shortly.

'She must have thought I was Chloe . . .'

Inside the sitting room, I can hear the sound of the television, some loud and violent cartoon.

David shakes his head. 'She isn't just deranged with grief, you know, she's always been deranged. Chloe ran to her every time we had an argument, particularly when it was about you, and she always made it worse. She's a bloody nightmare. A lot of Chloe's problems stemmed from her, believe me, a lot of them. Don't feel sorry for her. She's capable of anything. I hated it when she had Harry on her own. I'm serious. I didn't like that woman near my son. If Chloe hadn't been so weirdly dependent on her, I wouldn't even have let her in the house. She was round here the night Chloe disappeared. That's why I couldn't let you come round. I didn't want her to meet you, even know what you looked like.'

But there was something familiar about her, I thought. 'Did you and Chloe argue about me much?'

'Of course we did.' He turns towards the sitting room, speaking over his shoulder as he goes. 'That's what we argued about mostly, of course. The ghost at our table, she called you.'

She's been gone less than a month and already he is using the past tense.

It is only later, an hour later, when we are feeding the children, that it comes to me. I have met Chloe's mother before. She was the small, fierce woman at Willow's wake, the one who scraped her stiletto heel against my shin. I think of my purple coat, the one inexplicably ruined by bleach, which is still hanging in my wardrobe. I think of Chloe's expensive waterproof hanging in the hallway, shimmering and warm.

While Rees watches television, David and I make something to eat. My shoulder aches. Shaken by her mother's attack, it is hard to be in Chloe's kitchen. Once I have put a saucepan of water on to boil, I sit down at the table and watch David while he chops broccoli and carrots into tiny pieces, ready to add to the white rice we will cook for Rees. When he has finished, he puts a few tiny trees of broccoli and cubes of carrot in a bowl and silently places the bowl in front of me. To please him, I lift a few into my mouth, and chew . . . While I do this, he goes over to the kitchen window and stands looking out of it for some time at the neat square of their garden. His hands are resting on the edge of the kitchen counter top and his head is bowed.

Eventually, he turns, resting himself back against the counter top, and looks at me: David, all long legs and folded arms and serious expression and that deep gaze of his. I look back.

'I'm really sorry you got caught up in that,' he says, after a while. 'I always had a feeling something like that might happen, even though I couldn't imagine it would be like this. I could never have imagined this, everything that's happened.'

'It isn't your fault,' I say. *It's mine*, I think. Shall I tell him? How can I ever tell him?

He looks at me sharply, pours his gaze on me. 'Isn't it, Laura?' he says, plainly and softly, and I realise that I have been so wrapped up in my own guilt and grief that I have never thought of how he might hold himself responsible, how he might have been thinking it was his infidelity that let the demons into our lives. When I don't answer, he repeats, 'Isn't it?'

After we have finished eating with Rees – David and I pushing a few grains of rice around our plates – we wake Harry, who has been asleep for much longer than he should have been. I mash a banana for him while David takes him to the bedroom to change his nappy: how odd, how natural, our sharing of these tasks. Rees fetches a box of rattles and jangly things from the hallway and lays them out across the kitchen table, in readiness for some sort of show for Harry when he returns.

'Should Harry be distracted while we are trying to get him to eat his banana?' I ask.

'I always do it,' Rees replies confidently.

Then, several things happen at once. The doorbell rings. I rise from where I am sitting at the table, stirring Harry's mashed banana so it won't become discoloured, and as I rise I see, in the periphery of my vision, the view out of the kitchen window into the back garden. A dark shape registers; I turn. There is a uniformed police officer standing in the garden, looking at me. This seems so odd that I stare back at him with some aggression. The back garden is not gated or fenced, so anyone can walk into it from the front of the house and a perfectly logical thought occurs to me: he must be lost, maybe he needs help. In the hallway, I can hear David's voice raised and I think, he answered the door quickly because he feared the return of Edith. Pincered by these two events, both of which require my attention, I stand helplessly in the kitchen.

Then Toni is in the kitchen doorway. She is in plain clothes and she is with another plainclothes officer, a large, stocky man. David is behind them and his face is a mask of shock. Behind him, but shouldering his way past into the kitchen, is a young male officer in uniform. At the same time, the door from the kitchen to the back garden opens and the other uniformed officer steps in. I have just enough time to look at David and think, *he can't take much more* . . . before the stocky male officer says, 'Laura Needham, we are here to arrest you on suspicion of conspiracy to murder Chloe Edith Carter,' and the uniformed officer pushes past David and raises handcuffs in his hand.

My first thought is, Rees, how can they do this with Rees in the room? I look round but he isn't where he was sitting at the table. He is hiding under the table. They don't even know he is here.

The young male officer clicks the handcuffs on to my wrists and I stare at them in disbelief. I stare at them, there on my wrists, while the uniformed officer reads me the caution, ' . . . but it may harm your defence if you do not mention when questioned something you later rely on in court.' The formality of it only adds to the feeling of play-acting, pantomime.

Toni says, 'Where is your mobile phone?' I lift my hand-cuffed wrists and indicate my handbag, which is on the counter top. Toni picks the handbag up, opens it and glances inside, closes it again.

'Is this your only mobile phone, Laura?' she asks.

'Of course,' David replies for me sharply, and Toni looks at him. It is the first thing he has said since they all came into the kitchen. 'Where are you taking her?'

'The police station, sir,' says the stocky officer, politely, as if he is talking to someone rather stupid.

'Can I come?' pipes up a voice from beneath the table, and the police officers turn. David reaches beneath the table and Rees scrambles out into his arms. When he sees the handcuffs on my wrist, his face freezes.

'No, darling,' I say, gently, smiling and smiling – this is all a game after all, my smile says. *Don't worry, it's just a game.* 'You and Daddy and Harry will be able to come and get me later.'

'That's right,' says David, holding Rees in his arms. 'We'll go and get her later, won't we?' and even the police officers, who would have wrestled me to the ground in a headlock if necessary, smile broadly at Rees and nod their agreement, playing the game.

The stocky officer takes my arm and, with Toni heading the way, leads me out of the kitchen, through the hall, to the van that is parked outside.

18

Chloe's body has never been found.

We think of our lives as linear, with a clear beginning and middle and end. We desire an order of events, whole and explicable, from the moment we are old enough to understand what order is. We are born, we grow up, if we are lucky we have children. Children reinforce the linearity of our lives with the straight lines of their own. They just get older and taller. They are very good at it. We age; we reach our end. All this gratifies us, whatever small successes or failures we experience along the way. The line is inexorable: time itself. Betty's death stopped time. The line dissolved and life became a point, fixed on the day that Betty died. Everything else that happened to me before or afterwards swirled around that point. The flamenco class I thought about doing just before David walked into my consulting room that day, was the class I thought about just before I met the man who fathered the child of mine that died. The coffee I am drinking now, in a café called The Sunflower in a shopping centre in Aberystwyth, is the coffee I am drinking at the end of my story of how my child died. Everything that happened before Betty's death caused it and everything that happened afterwards was a consequence of it.

Chloe's body has never been found.

As Toni and the other officers walk me out of David's bungalow to where their van is parked on the kerb, I find myself looking around, half expecting to see Edith, Chloe's mother, hiding behind a hedge. I am calm, though, very calm, while David is ashen. I feel terrible for him. He is clutching Rees,

Rees who will save him, who in his turn stares at the whole procedure with round wide eyes, as if nothing would surprise him any more. As I am guided politely into the van, as we drive away, my anxiety focuses entirely on what David will say to Rees after they have watched the van disappear and gone back inside the house. How will all this be explained to my boy? I have gone into a kind of default-anxiety, a maternal one, scarcely considering my own situation.

The police officers are cold but courteous. Toni behaves exactly the same as the others and there is no acknowledgement of the intimacy of our previous relationship. At the police station, she pulls on a pair of thin purple gloves and empties my bag, stating the contents out loud while the Custody Officer taps everything into a computer. I am asked a series of polite questions. Do I have any allergies? Are there any sharp objects on my person? Everyone is calm. There is no aggression in their actions or their words. It is like registering at a new dental clinic, or applying for a mortgage.

The uniformed officers take me to a cell to await the arrival of the duty solicitor. Only as the door slams behind me with metallic resonance do I register the reality of incarceration. I sit down on the narrow mattress on the concrete block against the wall. It is navy blue and has a plastic waterproof covering. The cell is cold and stinks of urine. There is a camera in a high corner, the lens covered by a plastic half-globe. They have told me that if I use the toilet in the opposite corner, a black square on the monitor will protect my privacy. I put my head in my hands and think of David and Rees. Then I imagine the Custody Officer outside observing me on the monitor, sitting on the bed with my head in my hands. I sit up and lean back against the wall, sighing, my eyes closed. It is a great relief that there is nothing I can do.

After about forty minutes, the door to the cell is opened with a series of clunks and two young woman officers in uniform step into the cell. One is holding a transparent plastic bag with something white in it. 'Would you stand up, please?' she says.

I stand and look at them.

'Would you remove your clothes,' the other woman officer asks.

'All of them?' I say, surprised.

She is very young, and gives a half-embarrassed laugh, 'Yes, all of them, I'm afraid.' She shrugs. 'Bra straps, you know.' This remark is cryptic to me – I assume they want the clothes in order to do some sort of forensic examination, although that doesn't make sense. It comes to me that they might be searching my house right now, or David's bungalow.

'Do I get them back?' I ask, nodding at the items as I hand them over.

The first officer has extracted the white object, which is a giant paper suit, a ludicrous garment, like a babygro. She places it on the waterproof covering of the mattress, alongside a pair of white trainers that she has been holding in the other hand. 'You'll get them back, don't worry,' she replies shortly.

The first thing the duty solicitor says as she steps in my cell door is, 'Laura, I've already kicked up a huge fuss about the fact that they've taken your clothes. It's completely ridiculous, they are being over-officious and we're going to make a formal complaint.'

I look at her; plump, glasses, olive skin and very short, tight brown curls close to her head. She is wearing a beige suit with smart flared trousers over a cream-coloured polo-necked top. I have never met her before but within a sentence, she has become my new best friend.

'I'm cold,' I say. It's true, I have been shivering for an hour. My paper suit makes a silly rustling sound whenever I move. The ludicrousness of the garment may not be protecting me from the cold but it is certainly protecting me from the seriousness of my situation. *David*. I think. *Where are you? Why don't you come and get me?*

'Of course you are,' she says. 'We'll make sure they let you get dressed before the interview, which I'm hoping will be soon.'

'Why did they take my clothes?'

'Suicide risk,' she says briskly, sitting down next to me on the mattress and flipping open a notebook. 'Which I said was completely stupid but they did the whole lost-a-child, arrested-on-serious-charge number and they are only covering themselves of course but it's completely stupid.' She looks at me. 'There's going to be press, I'm afraid, even if we get you out of here straight away, there's nothing we can do about that.' She pushes her glasses back up her nose. 'Now, let's get down to it, shall we?'

The interview takes place in the same small room that David and I took Rees to. The solicitor has been successful and I am back in my own clothes. I sit in the same chair I sat in before. The same television sits on a stand to one side of the desk. The interviewing officers are the stocky male officer who arrested me, and a woman officer I have not met before, also in plain clothes. My solicitor sits to one side.

We begin gently. They ask me to tell them how old I was when I first met David. This is sure territory for me and it's a relief to talk about something so normal, so explicable. I describe, in some detail, my first three encounters with him, in the pub, at the party, and at last in my consulting room. The officers listen quietly and politely, making the occasional comment, although I know this can't be what they are interested in, what they really want to know. Their interest quickens – the man leans forward slightly – when I describe how David proposed to me on the cliffs. Afterwards, made emotional by the memory, I fall quiet. The stocky male officer sniffs deeply and says, thoughtfully, 'Bit of a whirlwind romance then, you might say?'

Tears slide silently down my cheeks. I nod. My solicitor touches my elbow. I turn my head and see she is offering me a tissue. I blow my nose.

The woman officer says, lightly, 'So it must have been a bit of a blow, then, when your husband started having an affair?'

I nod, still blowing my nose. 'You could say that,' I say, allowing a hint of sarcasm to creep into my voice. Next to me, my solicitor stiffens.

'You must have felt really angry about the whole thing, and confused,' the male officer continues, 'really hard to understand, I'd say, when you've got your whole lives and the house and everything and the kiddie to think of. Why do you think he did it?'

I shake my head and open my mouth to answer but my solicitor jumps in with, 'You can't ask my client that. How is she supposed to know how someone else thinks or feels? You can't ask her that.'

The male police officer carries on looking at me but I catch the woman officer giving the solicitor a glance that says, *you're good*.

It is only much later on in the interview – I estimate we have been talking for around two hours by then – that the officers get a little rough with me. I must have hated Chloe, mustn't I? How did I feel when I found out she was pregnant? And then, when my daughter was killed, well, that was the last straw, wasn't it?

'Tell me about your history of mental illness . . .' says the male officer, flipping open a file in front of him. 'You were sectioned, weren't you?'

'It's hardly a history,' I reply. 'It was one night.'

'Well, no one's ever sectioned me,' he snorts back.

After he has verbally roughed me up a bit – the solicitor interjecting every now and then when he steps beyond the limits of what he is allowed to do – he leans back in his seat and folds his arms. The woman police officer takes over. They can do that, of course, work in relays. I am exhausted. You are supposed to be exhausted, I think to myself. *David.* I want David to come and take me home. I want to be on a sofa with him and Rees and Harry, watching rubbish television.

'Laura,' the woman officer says softly. She has a low voice and grey, expressive eyes. She is the one they bring in when you are tired. 'There's something I would like to show you, Laura,' she says. Next to the television on the stand, there is a shallow cardboard box of the type you might keep papers in. The stand is close enough for her to reach out and pick up the box without rising from her chair.

She puts the box on the table in front of us and opens the lid, then lifts out a transparent plastic bag. She places it on the table between us. The male officer says, for the benefit of the tape recorder, 'Officer Clarke is showing the suspect a stainless steel knife with a fifteen-centimetre blade.'

The knife wasn't meant for Chloe. It wasn't meant for anyone. It was a thing that I needed, a thing to hold on to, there was no intent behind it. I am so tired and so baffled. I've been here for hours. I want to go home. I am ready to say almost anything if only they will let me go home. *Rees.*

The soft-eyed, soft-voiced officer leans forward and says, very gently, 'Is the knife yours, Laura?'

I nod, tears welling up in my eyes. My solicitor tenses again and places a hand over mine. Sensing that she is about to interrupt, the male officer barks, 'Spend a lot of time up on the cliffs, do you? Would you like to tell us about it?'

The solicitor says firmly. 'Officers, it's nearly ten o'clock. My client is very tired. I think we should terminate this interview now, reconvene in the morning.'

'You're keeping me here?' I burst out.

'Your client doesn't seem to have any inkling of the seriousness of her situation, if you don't mind me saying so,' the male officer sniffs, sitting back in his seat and folding his arms. I hate him with a passion.

The woman officer puts a hand up, fingers splayed in a conciliatory gesture, and says, 'Yes, let's reconvene at nine o'clock in the morning.' She looks at me, leans forward. 'Laura, just before we finish, I just want to ask you one more question, is that okay?'

I nod, tearfully.

'Is there anything you would like to tell us about your relationship with Mr Aleksander Ahmetaj?'

'You don't have to answer that, Laura,' my solicitor jumps in. 'These officers have already agreed you are too tired to continue questioning.'

After we have been escorted back to my cell, the solicitor turns to the Duty Officer and says, 'I need a few minutes with my client.'

The Duty Officer is another of the bulky-type officers. He has meaty hands with short, embedded fingernails and very pale eyes, which, for some reason, I think of as psychotic-blue. He looks at me and says, 'You vegetarian?' I shake my head. 'Religious?' I shake it again. 'Right,' he says, and leaves the cell.

As soon as the door closes behind him, my solicitor looks at me and says, 'Who is Aleksander Ahmetaj?'

'They didn't tell you?' I ask, sitting down.

She shakes her head. 'They are insisting on staged disclosure. I believe I explained that before the interview.'

'He's the man who killed my daughter, in the accident.'

'Oh,' she says. 'Well, I had better do some homework on him when I get home, I suppose.' She pauses and looks at me. 'Anything I need to know?'

I look back at her. 'No,' I say.

After she has gone, the Duty Officer brings me a microwaved

meal. I think it is supposed to be some sort of meat product with mashed potato but it is hard to tell. I prod at the brown lumps of something with my plastic fork. They slither around in their slime of dark gravy. When the Duty Officer comes to collect the white plastic tray, he looks down at the uneaten meal and back at me with a look that says, not good enough for you, love? Without my asking, he has brought a very weak cup of tea, which I drink just to demonstrate I am not a snob.

Later, he brings in a thin blue blanket. The lighting in the cell will be dimmed, he says, but night-light will be left on all night. I lie down on the plastic mattress beneath the thin blanket and, incredibly, fall asleep for bit. I am woken by a drunk being brought into the cell next to mine in the middle of the night. He is swearing profusely. After that, I doze fitfully. I am very cold, still, but don't feel able to ask for another blanket. Every fifteen minutes, someone clangs back the small shutter in my cell door and peers in, checking I haven't died.

Breakfast is two slices of white toast smeared thickly with margarine, and more weak tea. I still haven't adjusted to the smell of the cells – the stink of urine is now combined with a disinfectant tone. The drunk in the cell next door is either gone or silent. I am stiff and shuddery with the cold so force myself to eat one of the slices of toast. When my solicitor arrives, the first thing she says, while she is still flipping open her notebook, is, 'Right, well I read up on the accident, and now I am a bit confused. Why are they asking you about your relationship with Ahmetaj when presumably you've never met him?'

I look at her. 'I've no idea.'

It begins high-octane, rough from the very start. The soft-eyed woman isn't there. The male officer from the previous day and another male officer fire questions at me relentlessly. Where was I on . . . ? They name several different dates, one after the other. Dates mean nothing to me. I get confused very rapidly. 'Taking my son to nursery,' I say in answer to one question and the officer snaps, 'What? On a Sunday?'

They begin to alternate.

'Your ex says you were so jealous you drove him crazy.'

'What do you do when you're jealous, Laura?'

'He says you can get quite violent. Chucked things at him.'

'Tell us about the time you broke a window? How many windows was it?'

They hardly let me answer. 'It wasn't,' I say.

'Wasn't what?'

'It wasn't a window. It was, it was . . .'

'It was what?'

'It was a door.'

'You broke a door?'

'No, a window,'

'I'm confused, which is it, a door or a window?'

'Break a lot of things, do you?' adds the second officer before I can answer.

'It was a window, a window in a door. A glass window, in a door.'

'Let's move on shall we, this knife.'

I feel as though I am on one of those fairground rides where you are spun round and the floor falls away beneath you but centrifugal force pins you upright to the wall. After two attempts, my solicitor succeeds in insisting we take a break.

After the break, the officers seem a bit more low-key, as if they are tired too. I feel relieved. The new one, who is not as bad as the one from the night before, leans forward in his chair and rests his forearms on the table, knitting his fingers. He looks at me with a weary air, as if he doesn't want to be here any more than I do.

'Laura,' he says. 'Look, we understand that you've been through a terrible trauma. We haven't really talked about that, have we? Well, me and Robert here, we're fathers too, you know. I've got three kiddies myself, any parent can understand, what you've been through, losing your little girl, well, it's just about the worst thing ever, isn't it?'

The cold, the sleeplessness, the worry about David and Rees – and now . . .

'Betty . . .' says the police officer, and the sound of her name in his mouth undoes me. 'Betty, was that short for Elizabeth?'

I shake my head. 'Betrys,' I manage to say, 'it was, it was short for Betrys, the Welsh form of Beatrice. Her father is . . .' my voice becomes a whisper, 'her father grew up in Wales, he, he . . .'

'Fantastic singers, the Welsh,' comments the other officer.

The first one leans even further forward. I am breathing deeply. 'Laura,' he says, and I suddenly want him to hold me, not in a sexual way, but to comfort me. I feel he is a decent man, not like the other one. I want him to embrace me and make everything okay. 'Why was Aleksander Ahmetaj seen standing on the doorstep of your house?'

There is a brief intake of breath from the solicitor then she says in a low voice, 'Don't say anything.' She looks at the officers and speaks firmly, 'I would like to stop the interview now, to confer with my client.'

'Request denied,' says the other officer.

'What happened when he came to your house, Laura?'

What happened? I went *down* on him. I fucked the man who killed my daughter on the bed I had only ever shared with her father. The impossibility of explaining this overwhelms me and I dissolve into helpless, racking sobs.

During the lunch break, the solicitor reminds me that the police can only hold me without charge for twenty-four hours, unless they apply to a superintendent for a twelve-hour extension, but he or she will only grant that if there is a good reason.

'Why didn't you tell me that Aleksander Ahmetaj had been to your house?' She is cool but polite.

I shake my head.

'Well, that explains why they wouldn't disclose the name of your alleged co-conspirator when I asked,' she says, matter-of-factly. 'They wanted to spring that one on you.'

After a further two hours of questioning, I am released on police bail. My conditions are that I must report to the police station in one month's time and that in the meantime, I must have no contact with Aleksander Leotrim Ahmetaj. A conspiracy charge requires more than one suspect. You cannot conspire with yourself, not in legal terms anyway. He is my co-conspirator, but the police have a problem – they can't find him. Later, I begin to understand that this was one of the reasons behind my arrest. A confession from me could have provided them with knowledge of Ahmetaj's whereabouts. The solicitor tells me over the phone the next day that the police wanted to add the bail condition that I had no contact with David but that she successfully argued that was unfair as he was the father of my son and they could not reasonably prevent me from seeing Rees – and David was not a suspect, after all. They would have checked him out very thoroughly. He would have been the first person they checked.

David and Rees and Harry all come to the police station to pick me up. David leaves the boys in the car, parked outside, while he comes into the reception area. I am standing waiting for him with my belongings and the paperwork from my arrest in a see-through plastic bag. The duty solicitor is standing next to me. As David pushes through the swing doors, our gazes meet and I break down with a gasping kind of sob and he crosses the room swiftly and pulls me into an embrace, clutching me fiercely, one arm around me and one hand on the back of my head. 'Get me out of here,' I whisper, and he bundles me outside. I don't even wish the solicitor goodbye.

Once we are in the car, he starts the engine immediately and drives back to my house as swiftly as he can within the law. Rees is beaming at me from the back. I reach my hand backwards so that I can touch his leg as David drives – Rees swings the leg happily, kicking the back of my seat. In the baby seat next to him, Harry is asleep, wearing a sleepy-suit with a folded blanket on top. When we pull up outside my house, I undo my seatbelt and open my door but then turn to see that David is not undoing his. For one sickening moment, I think that he is going to drop me off then leave, without even coming inside the house. I am aghast. What have the police said to him? 'David,' I say, and my voice is high and hollow, pleading, 'We have to talk.'

He stares at me. 'You didn't think I was going to leave you, did you?' He shakes his head. 'God, we have a lot of work to do.'

'Can you get my trucks, Mummy?' says Rees from the back.

I turn to him. Harry stirs in his sleep, letting out a strange whimpering cry, as if he is dreaming about being denied something.

'For the hotel,' Rees says.

I turn back to David. 'Pack a bag for a few days,' he says, 'as quickly as you can. Your solicitor is convinced the press are going to turn up any minute. We can't stay here and we can't stay in the bungalow. I've got stuff for the boys in the boot but Rees needs more socks.'

'My trucks! My trucks!' shouts Rees, bouncing in his seat.

'I'll get the trucks, Rees, don't worry,' I say. 'What about the police?' I ask David.

'I've told them,' he says. 'It's okay. As long as they know where you are, they are okay. Go on, quickly.'

I let myself in – already, the house no longer feels mine. I race upstairs. In my bedroom, I avert my gaze from the bed with its mushroom-coloured satin cushions as I pull an old sports bag down from the top of the wardrobe and begin to throw clothes into it.

I am on police bail for a month. The regional papers run with it, *Local Woman Arrested*, and David tells me that some of the nationals run it on the inside pages, although he keeps all the newspapers away from me and I don't feel the need to look. No one finds us in the hotel, an airy guesthouse twenty miles down the coast with a bay window in the breakfast room that looks out over a terraced garden. We stay for five days.

David never doubts me, not for a minute. He is convinced that Chloe threw herself off the cliff – and convinced he knows why she did it at that particular point. It was because that was where he had proposed to me, all those years ago. Chloe was always pathologically jealous of me – he says he told the police that when they interviewed him after her disappearance. She questioned him in great detail about our marriage and, in the early stages of their affair, he had told her about dragging me towards the overhang. He had done it in the way in which new lovers often confide in each other details of the spouses they are betraying, as a gesture, but later, he had cause to regret telling her that particular story. It became a huge issue for them, especially after he had said that he didn't want to remarry when our divorce became final. As their relationship disintegrated, Chloe threatened to jump from that very point on the cliff, told him he would force her into it one day. She said it more than once. Chloe had attempted suicide twice before, once with paracetamol, at the age of fifteen, and another time with painkillers, in her early twenties, after an affair with a married man ended badly. There is never any doubt in his mind as to what has happened. By the time he has finished telling me her troubled history, I am sorry for her in the way that any decent person would be, but I still cannot forgive her for falling for my husband or sending me the hate mail, and after a

294

while, I feel I can manage these emotions, my scorn, my pity, my confusion, all at once. I can manage them because David's confusions are even worse than mine. He is desperately sorry and guilty for Chloe's suicide and desperately angry with her for dying, he believes, out of a desire to compete in his head with me and, worse, his daughter. It would take a more specific professional than me to unpick this one, and I don't try.

On our last evening in the hotel, he and I sneak down to the bar once the boys are asleep – the receptionist operates one of those old-fashioned systems where she lets us leave the phone in the room off the hook so she can listen in and come and get us if one of the boys wakes. David and I walk into the deeply carpeted bar with its oil paintings in gilt frames on the wall and wooden surfaces polished to a deep shine. We perch on high stools at the bar, smiling at each other as we hitch ourselves on to them, acknowledging that this is the kind of thing young drinkers do, people out on a date, not people with our extensive histories.

'Fancy a whisky?' David says, studying the bottles behind the bar.

'No, no thanks,' I say quickly. 'I'll stick to wine.'

He orders me a red wine and himself a large whisky, no ice, and we have peanuts as well even though we ate earlier with the boys, and a comfortable silence falls because we both know that this is our last night in this anonymous hotel-land and tomorrow we have to return to our home town and try and work out a way to live. We have all been sleeping in the same hotel room – Harry in a hotel cot and Rees on a put-you-up, David and I in twin beds next to each other. I have woken most nights, as I always do, but instead of rising have lain still, listening to the breathing of the others in the room, surrounded by it. Tomorrow, we must leave our cocoon.

'I think we should go back to the bungalow,' David says. 'I don't want you and Rees alone in the house.'

'Okay,' I say.

'Where do you think she is?' David asks, turning his glass between his hands. The question is not maudlin or self-pitying. It isn't even sad.

'I think she's just asleep, nowhere,' I say softly. There is no confusion about whom we are discussing.

'I know,' he says. 'I've tried not to think that, although I know it's what you think. Asleep I can deal with, but not nowhere. How can she be nowhere?'

'Think of it as everywhere instead,' I say, and he smiles, a little.

'Yes,' he says, 'that's better.'

We are the only people in the bar. The man behind it is lifting down the wine glasses that hang upside down in the rack above him and holding them up to the light, then polishing them one by one with a cloth, holding them up again afterwards to appreciate the difference, let them gleam.

Chloe's body is never found and Ahmetaj is never found either, although there is still an outstanding warrant for his arrest. My own arrest occurred because of the discovery of the knife on the clifftop. It was shown to Toni, who identified it as similar to the knives she had seen in the knife block on the kitchen counter top, near the sink in my house. In addition, there was CCTV footage of my car entering the car park near to the camp. Once that was discovered, Toni or someone went and had a chat with a few of the neighbours and somebody said they saw a man answering Ahmetaj's description standing on my doorstep that evening – he would have been briefly visible as the security light in my porch came on.

That is the sum total of the evidence against me. I was arrested on a fishing expedition, my solicitor says, in the wake of Aleksander Ahmetaj's disappearance. They would have had arguments about whether or not to try it, she said, me being a grieving mother, and as such having access to a potentially sympathetic press. They would have been aware they might have to justify the arrest at a later date but also aware that they might have to justify not doing it. These things are always carefully weighed. It was apparent to me during the interview that the police did not believe my story about the knife. I said that I was nervous about my physical safety when I went for walks on the cliffs, that I always took a knife with me, wrapped in a tea-towel. When pressed, I said I did not answer the door to Ahmetaj, that I never answer my door after dark. I am a poor liar and this might have contradicted the neighbour witness. The police didn't believe me about a lot of things, but in the absence of any other evidence – and, crucially, in the absence of Ahmetaj – they have no way of contradicting me.

I might get a phone call or a letter, the solicitor says, but in the end I have to wait until my month is up and my return visit to the station. It is the male officer who interviewed me who tells me, formally, that I am being released from my bail and that no further action will be taken against me, although I may be re-arrested in the future if any new evidence comes to light. My guess is that they were hanging on in the hope Ahmetaj might be picked up in some other part of the country but as he hasn't been they have no choice but to drop all charges.

There are new occupants in the caravan park on the cliffs. They are Romanians. Already, there has been an altercation between one of them and two young local men, a fight in the supermarket car park, over a girl, so local rumour has it. The Romanians are more outgoing than the previous group and have been going to pubs and nightclubs. They are good-looking and cheerful and destined to be decorators and plumbers rather than hiding on the industrial estates. I can imagine the local girls falling for them in droves. The Upton Centre is planning a cultural evening.

David is broken. After our few days in the hotel, we return to the bungalow and for a while we keep the curtains closed at the front of the house and look over our shoulders as we walk out to the car but nobody bothers us. Even so, I know that the bungalow can only be a temporary arrangement.

He is broken into lots of little pieces. It is as if he managed to hold it together all through the horror of losing Betty, then Chloe's disappearance, then my arrest – but then, finally, when I am released from my police bail, it is as if all those things come rushing in together, a tidal wave. We are living together but sometimes it feels more like being alongside David than with him. It is like being with an old man who shuffles from room to room. Despite a mild argument on the subject, I insist on sleeping in a sleeping bag on the sofa in the sitting room. He and I need to be together, and not together. I know I have to let him grieve for Chloe in his own way. His anger towards her is gone now and there is simple despair in its place.

Rees is getting confused about where he actually lives, and the amount of time we are all spending together. He has started throwing tantrums over small things in a way he didn't before, and although he has been demanding sometimes amidst all this, this is the first time he has shown real signs of trauma. It is as if, like David, he has finally worked out it is safe to do so, that I will be there to look after him if he does. He makes a fuss about getting dressed in the morning, refuses nursery some-times, says he wants to be a baby like Harry, and be back inside my tummy. Sooner rather than later, we will have to clarify the situation for him.

One morning, a few days after I have been released from my bail, I wake early and wriggle out of the sleeping bag, then use the loo and go into the kitchen. David has been up feeding Harry already and then gone back to bed. He has left the door on the microwave oven open and I go over and close it gently. It gives a neat click. I put the tub of formula powder back in the cupboard and wipe the surface where he has left powder scattered over it on the granite. I make myself a cup of tea and take it back into the sitting room. Sometimes, I get back into the sleeping bag and watch early-morning television with the sound turned down low.

I am halfway across the light-filled hallway, thinking of television, when my eye catches at something in the periphery of my vision. I turn my head, looking around. I have the same uncomfortable feeling I get when I am asleep and one of the children cries out, a dim sense of something, a small sly knowledge that, if I concentrate for a moment, I will discover what it is that is not right. I stop where I am in the hallway, and there it is. I reach out and put down the full mug of tea, resting it on top of a pile of newspapers that is on a small table by the sitting-room door. I bend and pick up the envelope, then glance behind me, down the short corridor that leads to the two bedrooms. All is quiet. I take my tea and the envelope into the sitting room and close the door behind me, turning the handle slowly so as not to make a noise.

I put the tea on the coffee table, get into the sleeping bag and sit upright in it. Just like the others, the later others, the envelope has no name on the front. I slip it open with one finger. It is hand-written, on a page of A4 copy paper, neatly folded.

Dear Laura,

I suppose you must think you have won now, don't you? I suppose you think you've got everything and that you've got everybody fooled even the police and even that husband of yours who was too much of a fool to ever see through you. But don't you never ever forget that even though my daughter is gone I am still around. I am too clever for you and to imply you will get what is coming to you as I know what I can and can't say. Don't forget though.

Yours,

E.

I am innocent of Chloe's death: I am guilty as charged. I did not kill her, nor did Ahmetaj, but I discussed it with him, how much I wish she had never existed. He told me his story; I told him mine. In that sense, the police are right, I am guilty of conspiracy to murder but I am not guilty of Chloe's death. She killed herself. She must have done. For weeks I have gone over and over it in my head but it is this letter that convinces me I am innocent. Edith has accused me of many things but not of murdering her daughter. The fact that even she believes Chloe committed suicide convinces me, once and for all, that my conspiring with Ahmetaj had nothing to do with Chloe's death. I am guilty but I am innocent. Chloe is gone. It wasn't my fault.

I think of Jenny Ozu as I sit there, holding the letter. I think of how I had to hurt someone because of all the things that were hurting me and how I would never have seen it that way at that time. I think how there is always a way we can justify ourselves to ourselves, make ourselves moral, heroic even – even Edith probably believes herself to be an honest, decent person. There is no end to it, I think.

I fold the letter and place it back in the envelope, then hide it in the side pocket of the bag I packed before we went to the hotel. I decide to say nothing to David. We simply have to get far away, as far and as quickly as we can.

Rees and I look after Harry together. We enjoy it. It gives David a break and provides a way for Rees and I to collaborate.

'He's our baby, isn't he?' Rees says to me later that day, as we change his nappy on the living-room carpet, the foldable nappy mat tucked beneath him. 'Yes, darling,' I say, indicating that I want him to pass me the wipes, 'he is.'

Later, Rees and I take Harry and drive over to Eastley and go to Willetts. Harry sits on my lap and Rees plays with the leaflets in a stand by the door as I make an appointment for an estate agent to come and value the bungalow and my house. Afterwards, we drive round to Aunt Lorraine's. David's sister Ceri is there and the three of us take Rees out into the garden so that Rees can play football while the rest of us watch in the cold.

'When am I going to see my nephew then?' Lorraine asks me softly, as I kick the ball in Rees's direction. He is on a team with Ceri. Lorraine's tone is a little pleading, as if it is within my gift. I don't know what to say to her. David doesn't want to see a soul but me, not even his parents.

'It's going to take a while . . .' I say.

'Oh, David . . .' says Lorraine, with a tearful sigh.

Rees has got the ball and is dribbling ineffectually towards Ceri, trying to get past her, even though she is supposed to be on his team. She is pretending to tackle him.

'We are going to go back to Wales, I think,' I hear myself saying to Lorraine, and it feels surprisingly natural to be sharing this thought aloud, even though I have only just thought it, not even discussed it with David.

Lorraine looks at me.

'Me and David, and the boys,' I say. 'We can't stay here.' I don't know how much Lorraine knows about Chloe's mother – but that is only part of it, of course. We cannot live in our old house, we cannot live in the bungalow, we cannot live apart – what else can David and I do, now?

Lorraine looks weary and sad but gives a nod of assent. 'We still have lots of family in Aberystwyth,' she says. 'I've often thought of going back myself but I don't think Richard would have it.'

Rees scores a goal against Ceri and runs round the garden in delight, arms waving, yelling in victory.

That night, I am awoken by sounds of stumbling around the kitchen. David is often awake at night, even if Harry's erratic feeding patterns have not disturbed him. Sometimes I stay in my sleeping bag on the sofa and listen – cupboards opening, muffled sobs. This time, I rise. The bungalow is cold. I pick up the jumper I left lying on the armchair that evening and pull it on over my pyjamas, lifting my hair clear of the heavy collar. I look around but can't find my slippers, so pad barefoot through to the kitchen.

David is sitting at the table, his grey hair fluffy, cheeks stubbled, skin sagging a little – he has lost weight. How much older we both are. Before him, on the table, I see there is a large photo album, lying open. I recognise it as one from the early days of our marriage, when Betty was a baby. I didn't know he had that one, I think. I thought I had kept most of them.

He does not look up as I enter the room. I go over to the kettle, silently, fill it at the sink, re-plug it, switch it on. While I wait for it to boil, I lean against the counter top and put one foot on top of the other, rubbing. The bungalow kitchen has a slate floor as well as a granite worktop. It is cold and hard. I dropped a mug on it the other day and it shattered into a hundred pieces.

David is turning the pages of the photo album and crying, softly, silently. I glimpse the pictures as he turns them – Betty on a swing, in a garden, not ours. Betty dressed up in every scarf and hat she could find in the house. Betty, Betty, Betty ... how does he square his grief for Chloe with his grief for her? It baffles me, and I thought I was the expert.

'It feels as though I'm being punished,' he says, without looking up. 'For what I did to you and the children. That's what it feels like.'

This is not the first time he has said this. I go to him. I put an arm around his shoulders and pull him close. He turns into me. I bend and kiss the top of his head. 'You're not,' I say. He puts his arms around my waist and pulls me in, tightly. His grasp is so familiar, still, after everything. My body has not forgotten the feel of his. We stay like that for a long time, the kettle forgotten, the photo album on the table.

After a while, I lean back and disengage his arms. From the small bedroom beyond the hallway, there comes a child's whimper. 'Did you hear?' I ask.

He shakes his head.

'I'll just go and check on the boys.' I move towards the door.

'Laura,' he says. It is still strange and beautiful to hear him use my name.

In the doorway, I turn. He is looking at me.

When I return from checking on the boys, I stand in the kitchen doorway and lean against the frame. David is still sitting at the kitchen table with his back to me – either he has not heard my approach, or he is so deep in thought that the sound did not register. He does not turn. His shoulders are sunken. His head is in his hands. From where I stand, leaning casually, arms folded, he looks like what he is, a beaten man. He looks like a man in a painting, I think, an oil painting by someone famous. There are painters who can do that light – the way it falls in a yellow oval from the low-hanging light over the kitchen table, the way that oval casts the rest of the kitchen into a shapely darkness, as if the cupboards and the cooker and the sink are envious creatures crowding round the light. David is as motionless as stone.

What I felt for David in those early days shouldn't have matured into marriage and children – it was the sort of love adulterers have, fierce and full of wanting. It should have burnt itself out, like those things do, but instead something else was built upon it, real love, deep and cosy and mutual, and two children grew of that love. Maybe that's all it is, I think, as I stand watching this man with his head bowed at his kitchen table, this whole construct, love or whatever we want to call it – a raw need, as rough as tree bark, a fear of death so strong we can't stop ourselves from fucking in the cold and the dark. But if that is so, I think, staring at the back of David's head, then what is it I feel for him now, when we are both so beaten and low that sex seems like a long-distant dream or something we have only read about in books? What is this that we feel for each other now if not love? Love built on pain – the kind that lasts: whatever we love can be taken away from us at any moment but the loss of what we love belongs to us forever.

I go to him, pushing myself away from the kitchen door-frame as if I need momentum. I cross the kitchen and lay both hands on his shoulders and he raises his head and leans back against me, as if he knew I was there all the time and was just waiting for me to come to him. My arms slide round him. He clutches at them and turns his head into my stomach, and I hold him like that, against me, awkwardly, him sitting and me standing, for a long time.

Epilogue

Betty stands in front of the mirror, brushing her long fair hair. 'Mum, do you think the sleeves are a bit long?'

'A bit,' I say, pulling on my boots. Rees is in the kitchen. '*Rees!*' I shout at him, 'Come *on!*' I have resolved to use the car less often in the mornings – there is really no excuse for it, we just have to get ourselves out of the house a bit earlier, that's all. The problem is that Rees is too big for the buggy but too small to walk as swiftly as Betty and I – but if we leave in the next two minutes, we'll be fine.

Betty is looking at herself in her new jacket in the mirror, turning her head to and fro, with all the innocent vanity at her disposal. I rise from where I am sitting at the bottom of the stairs and go and hug her briefly. 'It's fine,' I say, even though I don't think the jacket is fine. I think it is thin and cheap-looking and I don't understand why she was so keen on it.

We bundle out of the house and hurry down our road, waving at Julie who is leaving her house at the same time with Alfie. 'Are you sure about later?' she shouts. I have told her I will pick Rees up myself from nursery because of collecting Rebecca as well and taking them both around to the Methodist Church Hall. My head is full of the day's complicated arrangements, the Venn diagram of different children and mothers it involves. This is the fabric of my life, the interwoven times and places and people, the diary in my head.

The school bell is ringing as we push into the playground, forging our way upstream through the throng of parents who are attempting to leave through the narrow gateway. We are late for school, they are late for work – or in a rush to be elsewhere for other reasons – and there is never any consensus over who has right of way in this situation, let alone the moral high ground. Once we have battled our way through, Rees rushes over to the wooden pig in the corner of the playground and I have a moment of Betty to myself, to bid her goodbye.

She is impatient. She has seen Willow heading into school. She gives me a brief hug and turns.

'Hey,' I shout after her. She turns back to me. I lift her dance kit bag up by its strap. It is heavier than usual because today, for once, I have remembered to put in her tap shoes and a drink and snack for her to have before Capoeira club. I am inwardly congratulating myself on this. She smiles and runs back to me. She grabs the bag from me, then, in a swift, embarrassed gesture, darts forward and gives me a peck on the cheek. 'Love you,' she says quietly, so none of her friends will hear, almost so she doesn't hear herself.

Normally, I would say *love you* back, but today my mind is on our new arrangement for that afternoon. 'So, remember, won't you?'

She rolls her eyes. '*Yes*, Mum,'

'How are you getting there?'

'We can go the short way or the long way. If we go the short way, we're to be extra careful when we cross the road.'

'Good girl,' I say, but before the words are spoken she has turned and run after her friends who have seen her and are waiting. I watch her catch up with them at the door. She and Willow are chatting to each other as they go in. Betty is smiling. I wait to see if she will turn and wave to me before they disappear inside. She doesn't.

Acknowledgements

I would like to gratefully acknowledge the help of an award from the Arts Council England, which came at a vital stage in the writing and research of this book. During that period, I was lucky enough to undertake a residency at the Banff Centre in Alberta, Canada, still the perfect place to write a novel. I would like to thank Inspector Andy Nelson and Superintendent Raj Kohli of the Metropolitan Police for their help with research, along with Georgina Field and Dr Brigid Sheppard for advice on all things medical. Sarah Savitt, Antony Harwood, Jacqui Lofthouse, Laurence Chester, Dorothy Crossan and Jane Hodges were kind enough to read the manuscript and offer suggestions. Any mistakes are entirely my responsibility.

L. D.